Sept 15 18

GUNSHOT ROAD

GUNSHOT ROAD

Adrian Hyland

Published by

Soho Press, Inc.

853 Broadway

New York, NY 10003

Library of Congress Cataloging-in-Publication Data

Hyland, Adrian.

Gunshot Road / Adrian Hyland.

p. cm.

ISBN 978-1-56947-636-9

1. Aboriginal Australians—Fiction. 2. Police—Australia—Northern
Territory—Fiction. 3. Geologists—Crimes against—Fiction.
4. Central Australia—Fiction. I. Title.

PR9619.4.H95G86 2010

823'.92—dc22

2009044016

10 9 8 7 6 5 4 3 2 1

For Sally

Author's note

Readers familiar with the Northern Territory of Australia will recognise that I've taken liberties with many factual matters, notably geography and language. My portrayal of the Indigenous characters is based upon insights gained during my years of working with a number of Central Australian communities; but the people, the language, the dreamings and places described are inventions.

GUNSHOT ROAD

Initiations

I CLOSED MY EYES, felt the ragged harmonies flowing through my head.

Pitch dark, but the dawn couldn't be far off. Hazel on the ground beside me, singing softly. Painted sisters dancing all around us, dust swirling up from bare feet. Cocky feathers catching firelight. Coloured skirts, circles and curves.

It was Young Man's Time in Bluebush. Boys were being made into men. Here in the women's camp, we were singing them goodbye.

The men were a couple of hundred yards to the west: a column of ghostly figures weaving in and out of a row of rattling branches. Clapsticks and boomerangs pounded the big bass rolling rhythm of the earth.

Gypsy Watson, our boss, the kirta, struck up another verse of the fire song: 'Warlu wiraji, warluku…'

The rest of us tagged along behind.

My breasts, cross-hatched with ochre, moved gently as I turned and took a look around.

You couldn't help but smile. The town mob: fractured and deracinated they might have been, torn apart by idleness and violence, by Hollywood and booze. But moments like these, when people came together, when they tried to recover the core, they gave you hope.

It was the songs that did it: the women didn't so much sing them as pick them up like radio receivers. You could imagine those great song cycles rolling across country, taking their shape from what they encountered: scraps of language, minerals and dreams, a hawk's flight, a feather's fall, the flash of a meteorite.

The resonance of that music is everywhere, even here, on the outskirts of the whitefeller town, out among the rubbish dumps and truck yards. It sings along the wires, it rings off bitumen and steel.

A disturbance—a slurred, drunken scream—somewhere to my right.

Maybe I spoke too soon.

Two women were yelling at each other. One was sitting down, obscured by the crowd. The other was all too visible: Rosie Brambles, looking like she'd just wandered out of the Drunks' Camp.

Rambling Rosie, her dress a hectic red, her headscarf smeared with sweat and grease: she was built like a buffalo, with broad shoulders and spindly legs. She was drunk and angry. Nothing unusual in that; Rosie was mostly drunk and often angry, but this wasn't the place for it.

Her antagonist was Cindy Mellow—mellow by name, far from it by nature—a manky-haired little spitfire from Curlew Creek. Sounded like their argument was about a bloke. Still nothing unusual. Rambling Rosie's life was a succession of layabout lovers, black, white and every shade between. Cindy was being held back by her aunties, but they couldn't hold her mouth: she cut loose with a string of insults, one of which was about a baby.

Rag to a bull, that. Years ago, one of Rosie's babies had been found—alive, by chance—abandoned in a rubbish bin.

Rosie erupted: 'Ah, you fuckin little bitch!' She ran to a fire, grabbed a branch of burning lancewood, came back swinging.

Old ladies scattered, little kids screamed.

I jumped to my feet.

'Rosie...'

She held the branch like a baseball bat, oblivious.

I moved closer, one arm extended.

'Rosie!' I raised my voice. 'Settle down...'

She looked around. Gunpowder glare. No recognition. Then she rushed at me with a savage swing of the brand. I curved back and it swept past my head, sent a shower of sparks and a blast of heat into my face. I smelled my own hair, smoking.

I'd thought I was ready for her, a part of me was. But another part was mesmerised, staring with dazzled fascination at the river of light the torch left in its wake. In that shimmering arc I saw galaxies and golden fish, splinters and wings, crystal chips. I saw the song we'd just been singing.

'Emily!' Hazel's warning scream.

I rolled out of the way as the fire swept past my head.

Enough was enough.

I snatched up a crowbar one of the old ladies had left behind. When Rosie came at me a third time I planted the crowie in the ground. The brand crashed into it with another explosion of sparks as I pivoted on the bar, slammed a thudding double-kick into her chest. She staggered backwards, hit the dirt. Suddenly still. Looked up, confused, winded, heaving.

Christ, Rosie. Don't have a heart attack on me. My first day on the job and they'll have me up on a murder charge.

3

Hazel came stomping over. 'What you doing, Rosie? Running round fighting, putting the wind up these old ladies and little girls!'

Rosie raised herself onto an elbow, stared at the ground, shamefaced. Finished, the fight knocked out of her. The women began to make their way back to their places. But I glanced at Gypsy Watson, saw that she was troubled.

I knelt beside her, put a hand on her knee. 'Don't worry, Napurulla. It's over now...'

She looked out over the dancing ground, her mouth at a downward angle. I followed her gaze. Rosie lurching off into the shadows. One of the teenage girls swaying under a set of headphones, travelling to the beat of a different drum. Cans of Coke, crucifixes and wristwatches, corrugated iron, powdered milk. In the distance the whitefeller lights of Bluebush cast an ugly orange pallor into the sky.

Gypsy was a Kantulyu woman, grown to adulthood in the desert out west. Hadn't seen a whitefeller until she was in her twenties. Last year, one of her grandsons hanged himself in the town jail. A couple of months ago her brother Ted Jupurulla, one of the main men round here, died of cancer—a long, horrible death. She'd been in mourning ever since.

She was watching her world fall apart.

'Over?' she intoned wearily, shaking her head. 'Yuwayi,' she crackled, 'but what over? They killin us with their machine dreams and poison. Kandiyi karlujana...'

The song is broken.

Which song? The one we'd just been singing, or the whole bloody opera? I gave her a hug, stood up, moved to the back of the crowd. The ceremony slowly resumed, other women took up the chant. But something was missing.

Somewhere among the hovels a rooster crowed. Didn't necessarily mean the approach of dawn—that bird's timing had been out of whack since it broke into Reggie Tapungati's dope stash—but it was a reminder. Time to be on my way. McGillivray had said he wanted me there at first light.

I threw a scrap of turkey, a lump of roo-tail and an orange into my little saddlebag and headed for the track to town.

Scorcher

I'D ONLY GONE A few yards when I became aware of bare feet padding up behind me.

Hazel, her upper body adorned with ochre, feathers in her hair, a friendly frown.

'Sneakin off, Tempest?'

'Didn't want to disturb you.'

She grinned. 'Disturb us? Heh! Even a tempest'd be peaceful after Rosie. You gotta go so early?'

'Tom told me to be there first thing. Don't want to give him or his mates the satisfaction of seeing me late for my first day at work. Especially the mates—'

She studied the distant town, a troubled expression on her face.

Somewhere out on Barker's Boulevard a muscle car pitched and screamed: one of the apprentices from the mine. Apprentice idiot, from the sound of him. A drunken voice from the whitefeller houses bayed at the moon. A choir of dogs howled the response.

'You sure you know what you're doin? This...job?' Her lips curled round the word like it had the pox.

'Dunno that I ever know what I'm doing, Haze. I've said I'll give it a go.'

She smiled, sympathetic. She knew my doubts better than I knew them myself; she'd been watching them play themselves out for long enough—since we were both kids on the Moonlight Downs cattle station, a couple of hundred k's to the north-west. I'd flown the coop early, gone to uni, seen the world. Hazel had never left.

The little community there had hung on over the years, through the usual stresses endured by these marginal properties on the edge of the desert. It had held together, like some sort of ragged-arse dysfunctional family, thanks in large part to the influence of Hazel's dad Lincoln Flinders and the efforts of Hazel herself.

Lincoln was dead now, savagely murdered not long ago. Just around the time I'd returned myself, come back from my restless travels and fruitless travails. Come home, hoping to find something, not knowing what.

I had a better idea now, though.

We'd taken the first tentative steps to independence: built a few rough houses, put in a water supply, planted an orchard. Our mate Bindi Watkins had started a cattle project, and was managing, in the main, to keep the staff from eating the capital. There was talk of a school, a store, a clinic.

The one thing we lacked was paid employment. So when Tom McGillivray, superintendent of the Bluebush Police and an old friend of the Tempest clan, came up with the offer of an Aboriginal Community Police Officer's position we were happy to accept.

The only complication was the person he insisted on filling the position.

'Join the cops, Emily!' Hazel was still shocked.

'Not real cops, Haze. ACPOs can only arrest people. I won't be shooting anyone.'

'Yeah but workin with them coppers…Old Tom, 'e's okay—we know im long time. Trust im. But them other kurlupartu…'

I'd been wondering myself how McGillivray's hairy-backed offsiders would react to a black woman in their midst.

'Bugger em,' I said with a bravado I wished I felt. 'It'll be an education.'

'Yuwayi, but who for?'

'It's only a few weeks, Haze.'

That was the deal: a month in town, working alongside Bluebush's finest, then I'd be based at Moonlight. I'd just come back from a short training course in Darwin in time to catch the tail end of the initiation rites.

The clincher in the deal—and this wasn't just the cherry on top, it was the whole damn cake and most of the icing—was a big fat four-wheel-drive. Government owned, fuelled and maintained. The community was tonguing at the prospect; the goannas of Moonlight Downs wouldn't know what hit em.

We paused at the perimeter of the town camp, looked back at the fire-laced ceremony. A chubby toddler broke free from the women, wobbled off in the direction of the men, his little backside bobbing. He hesitated, lost his nerve and rushed back into the comforting female huddle.

They all laughed. So did we, the sombre mood evaporating.

Say what you like about me and my mob, there's one thing you can't deny: we're survivors. You can kick us and kill us and drown us in bible and booze, but you better get used to us because we're not going away.

'So you're out bush, first day?'

'Tom got the call last night. Some old whitefeller killed at the Green Swamp Well Roadhouse.'

'What happen?'

'Dunno. Probably bashed to death with a cricket bat—deadly serious about their sport out there.'

Green Swamp Well's main claim to fame—apart from the world's biggest collection of beer coasters and mooning photos, its tough steaks and tougher coffee—was the annual Snowy Truscott Memorial Cricket Match.

Hazel glanced at the eastern sky. 'Gonna be a scorcher.'

She was right: the drop of rain we'd had yesterday would only add to the humidity, and the radio predicted a brutal 45 degrees. Performing any sort of outdoor activity today would be like doing laps in a pressure cooker.

We were in the middle of the build-up. That time of year temperate Australia thinks of as spring: after the winter dry and not yet properly into the wet, when temperatures, tempers and the odd bullet go through the roof and the rain is always somewhere else. You'd be out of your mind if you didn't go a little bit crazy.

'Look after yourself,' said Hazel. She kissed me on the cheek, returned to the dancing ground.

Waiting for the man

I THREADED MY WAY down the sand tracks and reached the outskirts of town. I stopped at Jockey Johnson's house, washed the ochre from my body with his garden hose, feeling a trace of regret: Hazel had painted me herself, and such was the deftness of her touch, even a painted body became a work of art.

I slipped into the khaki cop shirt they'd given me, folded up the bloke-length sleeves and unrolled the pants. Kept unrolling. I held them up: my predecessor must have been Serena Williams. The belt was going to buckle over my sternum. And wide? I could have stashed a bullock in there.

I decided to stick with the denim dress for now; it was short and cool, practical. Tom would understand. I was only a Clayton's cop, and since he'd been promoted to superintendent he had enough uniform for both of us.

I walked through the still-dark streets, gave a couple of dogs the evil eye. Sprung Hooch Miller pissing off his front porch.

'Bit of decorum, please, Hooch!' I called.

He paused, midstream, peered into the dark. 'Who's 'at?'

'Emily.'

'Tempest?'

'Yep.'

'That's orright then,' he said, getting back to the business in hand.

I cut across the lawn of the police station, hesitated, then ran my fingers across the bark of the ancient ghost gum there. Felt its smooth white strength. Wondered if that would be enough to get me through the day.

The Bluebush cop-shop. As a kid I'd been terrified of this place: to me and my mob it was the locus of all fear, the dark tower in a mediaeval legend, the place where little children—and grown men—went in and never came out. Now I was enlisting as one of its foot soldiers.

I knocked on the door, called out. Nobody answered.

Beaten the bastards, I thought with some satisfaction. Where was McGillivray's much-vaunted twenty-four seven community protection? I sat under the tree and waited.

Generators hummed, crickets called. A truck rattled into the loading bay of the supermarket over the road; a fat bloke in singlet and shorts—a member of the lumpy proletariat—emerged from the cabin, whistling magnificently, began hurling trays about.

A red F-250 truck drew into the car park. Two men climbed out, leaned against the tray, folded their arms, waited.

Cops: the body language was eloquent, even if the words were few. Neither of them noticed me.

One was stocky, double-chinned, wore his belly like a weapon; he had an A-frame mustache and a head like a wild pig. The other was stringy, with red hair, blistered lips and an Adam's apple I could spot at twenty feet: a long, thin face, like a blacksmith had laid it on an anvil and taken to it with a hammer.

'He's late,' grumbled A-frame. A surly timbre, even with his mate.

I held back.

From the car, the rhythm of a radio. 'Mother and Child Reunion'. The riff shivered my soul. I thought, fleetingly, of my own mother, a Wanyi woman from the Gulf country, dead for more than twenty years. My father mourned her still, had never remarried.

Another copper—muffin-shaped body, shaved head—came shambling down the road. This one was all too familiar: Constable Rex Griffiths, a neighbour of mine when I lived in town. I climbed to my feet. Hesitated.

'Where's the super?' I heard Griffo enquire.

'Fucked if we know. Said he'd be here by five-thirty.'

'Breakfast.' Griffo tossed a couple of greasy packages at them. I recognised the smell: hamburgers from the BP all-nighter. 'With the lot.'

'Beetroot?' asked Adam's Apple.

'Course. Nothin beats a root.'

'Speakin of which, doesn't our little black bint start today?'

'That'll be interesting.'

A dig in the ribs. 'Come on, Griffo, I heard you fancied her.'

'Gimme a break!'

'But those tits?'

'Yeah, and that mouth! And the look when you piss her off—like a fuckin blowtorch!'

I gave a little cough, stepped out from under the trees, thumbs in my pockets.

'Morning boys.' Silence: a row of open mouths, slithering eyes. 'Slack bastard, that McGillivray.'

I filled the awkward interval that followed by getting out the papers and rolling a smoke. Griffo was busy choking on his burger, but he did manage a round of beetroot-splattered introductions: the pig-man was Senior Constable Darren Harley, the redhead was Bunter Goodwin.

They all looked enormously relieved when McGillivray's Cruiser came rolling down the road. But it wasn't the superintendent at the wheel. The tinted window descended and the driver, a senior sergeant I didn't recognise, leaned over and told us to get in. 'Not you, Griffiths. McGillivray wants you to man the station.'

My new colleagues hopped to it—without, I noticed, the banter that would have accompanied an order from McGillivray himself. I rated the briefest of acknowledgments as I settled into the back seat.

'You'll be the new ACPO, then?' Observant. 'Emily, is it?'

'Yep.'

'Bruce Cockburn. No smoking in the car, thanks.'

'Sorry.' I killed it.

'Government vehicle,' he expanded.

'Right.'

He frowned, popped a stick of spearmint into his mouth with a vigour that made me suspect he was a recovering smoker himself. He had a deep-tanned face, blond hair, pepper-flecked, crisp cut. Smooth, regular features you might have called handsome if it weren't for the hint of a sneer curdling his upper lip. His forehead gleamed in the streetlight, as if he worked saddle cream into it before going to bed.

He examined me with harsh blue eyes. 'Thought they gave you a uniform?'

I gestured at the shoulder tabs of my flash new shirt.

'Where are the pants?'

'They came up to my neck.'

He looked at my neck, didn't seem to like what he saw.

'Where's the super?' asked Griffo, still malingering on the footpath.

'Up in Emergency.'

'What happened?'

'One of our'—the flicker of a glance in my direction—'indigenous brothers gave him a smack in the face.'

I read the glance. Shrugged to myself. Not my brother's keeper.

'What's the damage?'

'Broken nose. Maybe a skull fracture.'

'Shit.'

'Waiting for the X-rays when I left.'

He pulled away, left Griffo gawping on the pavement. He slowed down when we reached the hospital.

'We paying a visit?' I asked. 'I would have bought flowers.'

'Not we,' said Cockburn. 'You.'

'Oh?'

'Superintendent said he wants a word before we go down to Green Swamp.'

The man with the ice-cream face

I WALKED INTO EMERGENCY. Nobody home. A woman somewhere behind a curtain sounded pissed off with the service: 'But Doc, I got a lump on me arse the size of a tennis ball!'

'I have told you—it is a cyst.' A sharp, slightly accented voice. 'It will go away of its own accord.'

The Bluebush Hospital bragged about its open-door policy, so I thought I'd give it a work-out. I pushed in through the swinging doors.

A doctor—harried, hard-nosed, wearing her coat like a kevlar vest—sprang out of a cubicle and snapped at me, 'Who are you? What do you want?'

'Tom McGillivray.'

'No you're not.'

'He's what I want. Emily Tempest's who I am. He's my boss.' Somewhat belatedly, she noticed the uniform. Fair enough; it wasn't much of a uniform. I wouldn't have noticed it myself if I hadn't been wearing it. She nodded at a cubicle. 'He's in there.'

I drew back the curtain.

McGillivray was stretched out on a hospital trolley, and a more miserable sight I'd never laid eyes on. He was draped in a blood-stained hospital gown, knobbly knees spread left and right. A glimpse of something more horribly knobbly in between. His eyes were shut, his mouth would have looked better if it was too. There seemed to be fewer teeth than I remembered. His head was partially eclipsed by a massive bandage through which his fat nose protruded: the general effect was of a man who'd had an ice-cream cone rammed into his face.

On his chest, folded open, face down, was a book. I walked over, looked at the title. *Bury My Heart at Wounded Knee.*

'Where you want us to bury the rest of you?'

The bruised eyes crept open. Slowly, painfully, he tilted his head in my direction, groaned. 'Town tip'd do nicely.'

'Hate to tell you this Tom, but your donger's on display.'

He glanced down, delicately rearranged the covers.

I examined his face. 'What's the damage?'

'Nose in two places. Cheekbone in three.'

'Pride?'

'Multiple.'

'So who was it? The Sandhill Gang?'

A painful silence.

'Come on, Tom. I'm here to avenge you. The Westside Boys? Dick Pennyfeather?'

'It was dark.'

'Tom...'

He sighed, dropped his head back down onto the pillow. Mumbled, 'Aaangsaf...'

'Sorry?'

A deep breath. 'Googangzaf...'

16

'Not the Crankshafts?'

The ghost of a nod.

'You poor bastard.' The Crankshafts were the most ferocious family in the district, and had been carrying on a running battle with the cops since the day of the horse and saddle. 'Which one? Spider?'

No response.

'Bernie?'

Nothing.

'Godsake Tom—not all of them?' En masse, they were a sight to make the blood run cold and the feet run hot.

He mumbled into the bandages. 'Goo-gee.'

'Sorry, almost sounded like you said "Cookie".'

'I did.'

I tried and failed to keep a straight face.

Cookie Crankshaft, the grandfather of the clan, was one of my favourite countrymen, if for no other reason than that he was about the only one I could stand up and look straight in the eye. Neither Cookie nor I, in the unimaginable event of our wanting to, would have come up to Tom's nipples.

And then there was the minor matter of a walking frame.

'Come across him staggering round the bottom of Stealer's Wheel, marinated as per usual. The crowd's coming out of the Speedway any tick, so I try to get him off the road.' He touched his face, gingerly, flinched. 'Pitch black, didn't see a thing, but I think he smacked me with the frame. Either that or he had a star picket in his pants. When I woke up my head felt like it had gone ten rounds with Mike Tyson's teeth.'

'Serves you right for hassling defenceless old drunks.'

He rolled his eyes, an action that appeared to give him grief. 'About this job. When you agreed to take it on...'

'You mean when I gave in to your blackmail?'

'I figured I'd be around to keep an eye on you.'

17

'Well I'll be in Sergeant Cockburn's capable hands now.'

'Ugh...Cockburn...' He flopped back into the pillows.

'Come on Tom, spit it out.'

'Hear he's a top squash player.'

'Ah.' That was a worry.

'Only been over here a couple of months. Transfer from Queensland. You and him...'

'Yes?'

'He seems like a competent operator—plays it by the book. It's just...'

I helped him out. 'Nobody's told him the book hasn't been written yet?'

He gave a weary half-smile. 'Take a fuckin Shakespeare on speed to write the book for Bluebush.' He tried to get comfortable. Failed. 'Look, I dunno who shoved a burr up his arse, but—don't you rub it the wrong way.'

'I see.' The horrible image of me rubbing anything at all in the vicinity of Cockburn's arse defied elaboration.

I jumped to my feet. No point in hanging round. 'Don't you worry about me, Tom. Me and him, maybe we'll write the book between us.'

That wasn't the answer he wanted to hear. Either that or the painkillers were wearing off.

Hit the road running

IT HADN'T TAKEN ME long to make McGillivray's day; the sky was just starting to lighten. The police Toyota was loitering in the ambulance bay, motor running, lights low. I climbed aboard. My fellow passengers said nothing. Cockburn reversed, gunned her out onto the highway: the Toyota was on cruise control, and so was he.

The streetlights and houses thinned out, then fell away, their places taken by the saltbush and spinifex which dominate the Bluebush environs. Termite mounds loomed in the gathering light like an army of terracotta warriors.

Harley and Bunter struck up a desultory conversation about dog obedience training. Evidently Harley's bouncy young mongrel had been playing it fast and loose with the chickens; Bunter was dubious about the tactical response.

'Mate, I could understand you bashing its head in with a hammer, but did you have to do it in front of the *kids*?'

Harley shrugged. 'They're the ones wanted a dog.'

'At a *barbeque*?'

'What's it matter where? They gotta learn.'

Jesus wept. I turned for relief to the scenery, the objects rushing by: white plastic posts, red echoing reflectors, livid pinks and blues rippling in the east.

I gazed at the horizon and there, just for a moment, felt a shivering intimation of something loping along beyond it. Something quicksilver bright, ominous. Pulsating with animal heat.

What was that?

I was unaccountably shaken. The reflection of my own discomfort at the job I was doing? A premonition of the threatened heatwave?

I thought of Gypsy. Kandiyi karlujana. The song is broken.

A violent orange blob wobbled onto the horizon. Golden rays came levelling in through skeletal branches, flooded the inside of the cabin, copper-plating the coppers and gilding chrome. Cockburn's ears glowed like radioactive apricots.

As we climbed into the hills south of town, we pulled past an abandoned wreck on the side of the road. A green HQ Holden— battered about, not much in the way of window glass but four tyres. More paint than rust. A blackfeller car.

Abandoned?

There was something familiar about it. I scrolled through the database of community vehicles I kept inside my head. Maybe Magpie Jangala, a Kantulyu man from Stonehouse Creek.

I took a closer look. Something was out of place. There was a slight turbulence in the air. Ribbons of red dust—more dust than Magpie's old wagon should have stirred—trembled on shafts of light.

'Mind pulling over for a moment, sarge?' I said quietly.

'What?' said Cockburn.

'Something I want to check out.'

The shoulder blades went into defensive mode. 'We only just left town.'

'The blackfeller car,' said Bunter, who must have followed my gaze.

'For Christ's sake!' Cockburn spat. 'This isn't a breakdown service. We're on our way to a homicide.'

'Just for a second? There's...'

'No.'

'Stop the bloody car!' I heard myself yell, and Cockburn seemed as surprised as I was to find it slamming to a halt.

I was out the door before the wheels stopped rolling. As I sprinted I began to take in other signs of disturbance: scorched bitumen, slewing skid marks in the gravel. Flattened bushes, partially concealed by the Holden.

I broke through the scrub, and there was the chaos I'd expected.

A Range Rover on its back, down in the gully. A bloke lying alongside it, a trio of Aboriginal people around him.

'Ambulance!' I bellowed at my partners, then dashed down the slope.

Motors and wheels

IT WAS MAGPIE ALL right, standing alongside his wife, Meg Brambles. She was crouching, holding a rag to the injured man's face.

With them was a teenage boy: Danny. Their grandson—and Rambling Rosie's son. My second encounter with the Brambles, and the sun no more than a finger's breadth above the horizon.

The grandparents appeared anxious, but Danny looked positively traumatised. He was staring at the wreck, his elbows clenched, his face an echo of the mess of shattered metal and debris among which he stood.

A mob of dogs—Magpie's no doubt, he was always a big one for the dogs—skulked around, looking for a chance to score.

Magpie spotted me, seemed relieved. He was a nuggetty fellow, sprightly and spry, wearing patched pants and a pencil-thin mustache that made him look like a short black Errol Flynn.

He shook my hand, muttered a greeting.

Before I could respond we were bustled out of the way by Cockburn, cruising in to take control. He was on his home turf now, assessing damage, issuing orders, despatching lackeys. Competent, I had to admit. More puzzling was the flash of irritation when he glanced at me.

What now? I wondered. Would you rather we'd just driven past? Whoever was dead out on the Gunshot wasn't going to be needing us in a hurry. I was beginning to see what Tom meant about the burr up this guy's arse.

Harley came bustling in with a first-aid kit. Meg, no longer needed, came and stood with us.

'How's the whitefeller?' I asked.

'Reckon this one'll be okay; bit of a bump on the head. Wanted to get up, but I made im stay down. Stop the blood.'

Meg spent much of her life patching people up. Out at Stonehouse she was the health worker. And the teacher, come to think of it. And foster mother to half the dropouts and delinquents in the district. She'd done a bit of patching in her time.

The crash victim drew himself up onto an elbow, took us in, nodded his appreciation. He was red haired, with a soft, white face, hooded eyes, a blue denim shirt. He turned away when Harley offered him a swig of water, drank gratefully.

'Nother feller bin finish, parnparr,' she added.

'What other feller?'

A sudden oath, followed closely by a pistol shot, rang out from the far side of the vehicle.

I darted around. A dog lay on its side, splattered. As was the poor bastard who'd been driving the Range Rover. His upper body, half out the window, crushed by a ton of flying metal. His head a mess of ruddy gore and crushed bone.

'Bloody mongrel.' Cockburn was holstering his pistol. 'Licking this bloke's brains.'

'They normally go away if you say "Go away!"'

Just for a moment he looked as if he'd like to give me the same treatment he'd given the dog.

'Bunter!' He turned and barked at the red-haired copper. 'Cover him up.'

I went back to Danny and Meg. Magpie was moving around the crash site, gathering up debris and laying it alongside the path. Trying to be of some use, now that the professionals had taken over.

'You don't have to do that,' I told him. 'Ambulance'll be here soon. Tow trucks. More cops. Their job.'

'That feller bin lose 'is mate,' he said by way of explanation. 'I give im a hand.' He picked up a waterbottle, some scattered tools, a leather satchel and a tyre iron, laid them alongside the track.

'You did well, the three of you. Might have saved this bloke's life. Could have laid out here for days if you hadn't spotted him. Heading for town, were you?'

'Yuwayi. Comin in from Stonehouse.'

I turned to Danny. His eyes were hopping about like startled finches.

When I first came back to Bluebush a couple of years ago, Danny had struck me as the sweetest and freest of the town's teen spirits. He hardly ever went to school; few of his peer group did. But he cruised around town as though it was his own little play-ground, a quick smile and a cheeky word for everyone. He'd clip you on the arse and laugh as he sprinted by; flog a chip from your carton.

He must be fifteen now, a slender boy with a glorious jungle of flashing dreadlocks tightly coiled. A broad mouth, slightly random teeth, a wisp of bumfluff on his chin. His feet were dust covered, bare, ready to run. Lately, I'd heard, the running had turned to riding in hot cars and the chip habit to drink and drugs. Fun for a while, but the long-term prospects were poor. Non-existent, really.

'So Danny—you staying out there too? Stonehouse?'

He settled, ever so slightly. He'd always seemed somehow comforted by my presence. God knows why: I had the opposite effect on everybody else.

'Yuwayi.' A low voice. 'Quiet place.'

'It is.'

'No machines.'

'Machines?'

'All em Bluebush motors and wheels. Generator wind, clockin time. Sometimes you gotta get away.'

I paused. There was an edgy timbre to Danny's voice, and the words didn't make a huge amount of sense. I hadn't seen him for months. Maybe the drugs I'd heard about were catching up with him. With Rambling Rosie for a mother it was a miracle they'd given him any start at all.

Meg touched his elbow. 'Good boy, this one. Just worry too much for nothin.'

Typical Meg. She was one of the strong women of our community, the ones who took up the slack, who cared for the wasted and the wounded. That was why she and Magpie had set up Stonehouse Creek: as an antidote to the town. At any given moment, you'd find them out there: the petrol sniffers and meth-heads, broken-down cowboys and motherless children, drinkers and dreamers. She and Magpie would pick them up, take them out bush, give them a bit of breathing space. Show them their country.

All three of them looked nervous: the police, I assumed, or the accident, or both. 'Come on,' I said, 'no need for you to see this.'

I began to lead them back up to the road, but we'd only taken a couple of steps when a stern voice stopped us in our tracks.

'Emily!'

Cockburn.

We halted. Danny looked around, anxiously. Having a cop within striking distance—particularly one of the Cockburn stamp—obviously rattled him. Nothing surprising there: in his world, when there was a cop within striking distance, generally you got struck.

'Where do you think you're going?'

'Back to the car.'

'I need you to get a statement from these people.'

'Magpie and Meg.'

He hesitated. 'What?'

'That's their names. Magpie Jangala and Meg Brambles. And their grandson, Danny. He's not much of a talker—won't give you a word if you hassle him.'

We carried on up to the road. I could feel Cockburn's eyes burning into my back.

Their stories, when I did eventually get them down, confirmed what I'd surmised: they'd been travelling north; like me, they'd seen signs of an accident, gone to help. The passenger had been thrown clear. The driver had had his last rites delivered by a camp—now dead—dog. Both men, like most other whitefellers in the district, worked for Copperhead Mines.

The paramedics arrived, took away the passenger, name of Craig Flint, on a stretcher and Alan Feik, the driver, in a bag.

A tow truck rocked up. A cheery young bloke jumped down from the cab, took a look at the dead dog and the bloody mess a few feet from it.

'All that from the dog?'

'The driver.'

'Erk.'

A back-up van arrived from town, Griffo at the wheel. The senior sergeant gathered us together. Bunter and Griffo would wrap up here, Cockburn, Harley and I would head on down to the Gunshot Road.

The Gunshot Road. He made it sound like a punishment detail.

As we climbed into the car, I realised how sticky with sweat I was. The heat was working itself deep into the contours of my body, down between the follicles. I checked my watch. Still only seven-thirty. That heatwave was coming in fast, a simmering, vicious bastard of a thing.

I ran a finger beneath the collar of my shirt. At least we'd have air-conditioning.

Five minutes later it broke down.

Green Swamp Well

I PEELED MY SWEATY thighs off the vinyl and climbed out of the Tojo, grateful for the change of scenery. The main scenery to date had been the back of Harley's head. His neck a sweaty sausage, his scalp raw with a fine display of dandruff. He had twenty-two freckles and sunspots, numerous flakes of something white, possibly dried soap, teeth marks on his right ear and a skin cancer I would have warned him about if he'd been nicer to his dogs.

Cockburn must have had internal air-conditioning: still razor-creased and groomed, his healthy sheen not a degree ruddier. He looked like he was stepping out for a night at the casino.

Green Swamp Well was a collection of ramshackle white-wash buildings scattered around your typical outback pub. Wide verandas, shaded windows, gangrenous roofs buckling under the relentless Territory sun; denizens ditto.

'Population density greater than I expected,' remarked Cockburn.

He had a point: the car park was chockers. Everything from the ubiquitous bush utes to a motor bike, from a Transit van to a mini-bus—the latter full of Asian tourists, judging by the agglomeration of skinny legs and spectacles visible under the kurrajong tree. One beige Toyota was charmingly adorned with a stuffed pig's head lashed to the bull-bar. Most of the other vehicles were indistinguishable under a topcoat of red dust and amateur panel-beating, except for a stretch campervan labelled *Aboriginal Evangelical Fellowship* and a hearse. Behind that, a cop car.

'That'll be Jerker,' said Harley.

'Jerker?' Cockburn raised a brow.

'Brad Jenkins, from the Break. This is his crime of the century—he won't want to stuff it up.'

The copper in question came marching out to greet us. Jerker was a large, goofy-looking guy with shire-horse feet and blood-hound jowls. So this was the poor bastard in charge of the cop shop at Breaking Point, eighty k's down the highway. I wondered who he'd pissed off to get banished to the Break, but as the introductions approached I began to suspect it was an occupational health and safety issue for the boys in town. From five paces his breath smelled like refried sump oil.

Whatever energy Jerker saved on flossing, he put into his enthusiasm for the job. As Harley had suggested, he'd refused to let anybody leave the roadhouse until the investigating team arrived.

Not that there was going to be much of an investigation. By Jenkins' account, two of the old drunks who hung around the pub had had a booze-fuelled brawl in the shack across the road; one of them had woken up dead.

Cockburn didn't sound impressed; an eyebrow flickered, a lip twitched. 'You kept this crowd here for that?' he asked, nodding at the veranda, where a motley mob of travellers looked keen to be on their way.

Jenkins flushed. 'Knew you'd want statements from everyone here.'

'You had it figured for a yakuza hit?' The senior sergeant glanced at the Asians under the kurrajong.

'No sarge.' He looked puzzled. 'Figured it was the other feller in the shack.'

Cockburn sighed. 'We'll get to that. Victim's name?'

Jerker had to consult the notebook. 'Albert Ozolins...'

A tall fellow in a clean white shirt wandered out of the pub. Another redhead, mostly freckles and spaghetti legs.

'Thought you bastards'd never get here,' he grinned.

Cockburn wasn't joining in the conviviality. 'Who are you?'

'Undertakers.'

'We were held up,' Cockburn responded sharply.

'We heard. Rush hour on the road to Bluebush. Stiffs everywhere. Appreciate it if you could get this one out of the way as quick as possible. Longer we hang around...' He waved an arm; the heat, perhaps, or the flies; maybe it was tai chi.

'Forensics up from Alice yet?'

'Been and gone,' said Jerker. 'Didn't hang around—another customer at Saddler's Well, reckoned this one was a picnic by comparison. Said the report'll be in your office before you are.'

'Right,' said Cockburn, also waving. Definitely a fly. The sticky little insects were something chronic. We were swinging and swishing for all we were worth but they still ended up in every orifice imaginable.

He turned away, began leading us in the direction of the shack. 'Nobody's touched him?'

'Just forensics,' said Jenkins. 'Oh—and the priest.'

Cockburn stopped. 'Priest?'

Jenkins tugged at an ear lobe, sensed danger. 'Missionary

feller. Wanted to give the last rites. Or whatever.'

I glanced back at the campervan. Aboriginal Evangelical Fellowship. Not exactly a priest, but Jenkins didn't strike me as an expert on matters ecclesiastical.

Cockburn gave him the granite stare.

'Nobody goes near a crime scene until I give the all-clear. Is that understood?'

Jenkins studied the ground. 'Sorry boss.'

'This one sounds clear cut, but even so…'

The constable led us out in the direction of a hovel at the foot of a craggy red bluff, a couple of hundred yards south of the pub.

The shack was constructed, appropriately enough, of blood-wood beams and rusty corrugated iron, its starkness a sharp contrast to the firebright cliffs behind. Alongside the building was a carport made of steel rails. Scrap metal, perhaps, from the old Gunshot Mine. In the carport was a battered blue jeep.

The cabin seemed to be vibrating. A disturbing hum rattled my eardrums. As we drew closer I realised it was an effect generated by the cloud of flies cutting through the air. They crashed into the screens, ripped in and out of the open door. I spluttered and spat one from my mouth. Wondered where it had been.

I went up the steps, then paused, a peculiar chill stealing over my heart. I remembered my ominous feeling on the way down, the sense of something dangerous beyond the horizon.

Cockburn noticed my discomfort, showed a glint of cold pleasure. 'Better get used to it, Emily. Won't be the last body you have to look at.'

'Won't be the first, either.' I pushed my way past. This bloke was getting on my goat.

In and out of the shack

A MOUND IN THE centre of the room: a grey tarpaulin, big enough to cover the body but not the crusted black pool on the floor. An eruption of flies beat up from the sludge as Cockburn drew back the tarp.

I flinched, squinted and looked down. A bearded old man stared up at me with startled eyes, as if death had taken him by surprise. Not that there's anything unusual in that, I reflected. It doesn't usually send you an sms saying *Pick u up 2moz 7.30*.

His skin was desiccated leather, his hands filthy, his nails encrusted with crimson dirt. The face looked like somebody had jumped on it: a deflated football fringed with snow. Not a face I recognised, but there was a prickling familiarity about it.

'What was his name again?' I asked Jerker.

'Ozolins.'

However Mr Ozolins had looked in his prime, his distinguishing feature right now was the geological hammer embedded in the base of his throat.

The flies were drawn to it as well.

Cockburn studied the body, his face impassive. He put his bag on the floor, pulled out a video camera. Began sweeping the room.

'Bloke who did him was flaked out on the bed over there,' said Jenkins, nodding at a wire bunk.

Shit, I thought, staring at the bloody mess on the floor. He did *that*, then went and had a lie down? Made himself a nice cup of tea as well, did he?

'Feller from the pub come in and found em.'

While Cockburn did his thing, I did mine: poked my nose in, took a look around the old man's shack. It was better than looking at his corpse.

I made a mental note of the late Mr Ozolins' worldly possessions: broken furniture, scattered bottles, a blue kero lamp. A frypan on the stove, a chop marooned in a pool of congealed fat. His fridge a Coolgardie safe. A filing cabinet, its drawers half open.

Nothing out of the ordinary there, but the bookshelves—planks on bricks—held some surprising stuff.

'Well read old bloke,' I commented, casting an eye across the spines: *The Geology of Central Australia, The Proterozoic Bluebush Province,* Twidale's *Geomorphology*. Most of the books were of a geological age themselves. A stack of yellowing maps and cross-sections sprawled out onto the floor. There was, as well, the odd battered volume from other branches of science: physics, engineering. Newton's *Principia* nestled between Poincaré and *The Origin of Species*.

Cockburn glanced up from his camera, his face expressionless. 'We come all this way for some overdue library books?'

I glanced at the floor directly in front of the bookshelf.

'More dust on the floor than on the books themselves.'

'So?'

'Looks like somebody flicked through em.'

'Killer probably wanted something to read in bed.'

I examined the filing cabinet. Again, mostly geology: old army surplus notebooks stored in blue folders. I pulled one of them out. Sketches and diagrams, notes, maps, cross-sections.

On top of the cabinet, a Geiger counter, some bottles of acid, a Freiberg compass. In the corner of the room was a pile of ancient wine boxes. I opened a couple, found dust-covered rocks and minerals, most of the labels faded, fallen and spread across the floor.

I was struck by the lack of any signs of a personal life: no photographs, no mementos, no keepsakes, no items of any obvious sentimental value.

Only…there, on a dirty dresser beside the bed, next to the tube of Deep Heat: a bare patch.

Sure enough, fallen between the dresser and the bed, a small framed photograph. I dug it out: two little girls, mop haired, blonde, impish grins. Another older one, dark haired, sombre. A surprisingly recent shot. The old man might have lived here on his own, but he had somebody somewhere.

Cockburn put away the gear, joined Jenkins, who was on crowd control—he was the crowd—out on the veranda.

'So you're holding this other feller over at the pub?'

'Nowhere else to put him, sarge.'

'Who's keeping an eye on him?'

'Couple of Transport and Works blokes. Don't worry, he's going nowhere.'

'What was his name again?'

'Petherbridge.'

'And he's admitted that he did it?'

'Well…'

Exasperation rippled across Cockburn's face. 'Well what?'

'He hasn't said he didn't do it.'

'*I* haven't said I didn't do it either.'

'They had a brawl at the pub—a dozen witnesses saw em havin a go at each other. Ozolins came back here, Petherbridge followed. Admits they went another round. Says he passed out on the bed. Woke up when the publican come in.'

'Yeah, right.' Cockburn lifted his eyes to the heavens. 'Tell the undertaker he can get it out of here.'

As we walked over to the roadhouse, I glanced back at the shack and its surrounds. Rusting car parts, blue coiled fencing wire, shredded tyres. A broken wheelbarrow, shovels and picks. A rubbish dump, mostly bottles and bones, tins.

And to the west of the shack, up against the hills, a rock formation that didn't look right.

A slippage from the cliffs?

'What's with the rocks?' I asked Jenkins.

'Old bloke was crazy. Used to be a prospector. Spent his days out there, rearranging his bloody rock garden.'

'He built all that himself?'

'Suppose so. Been at it for weeks. Months. See him out here sometimes, muttering away, shifting things around.'

'Must have been a fit old bloke,' I commented.

Cockburn gave the rock pile a moment's consideration. 'Or a determined one. Crazy determined. Had a feller once, over Queensland. Same thing. Spend all morning digging a hole, afternoon filling it in again. Same hole. One day he decided it was finished. Jumped in, blew his brains out. Son-in-law said it was an accident. Told him, yeah; life's an accident.'

I glanced at him, mildly surprised.

We made our way to a crusty dwelling behind the pub.

A concrete blackfeller beside the garden path raised a spear at us. I gave him a sisterly wave as we filed past.

A weird little dog, a cross between a shitzu and a toilet brush with pop eyes and jutting lower teeth, confronted us at the door, tail erect. Confronted *me*, more to the point, clearly unimpressed by the colour of my hide. The animal had a growl like an electric toothbrush and gave it to me, full throttle.

A woman came to the door: body and dress featureless, her face thinner than strained tea. She called the dog away, distracted. Ran her fingers through her hair.

'Mrs Redman sarge,' said Jenkins.

'June,' she said; the vowel squeezed past her sinuses and came out as flat as the dog's face. 'Me and me husband own the place.'

June led us through to the kitchen, where two monstrous Works blokes towered over a stocky old man who sat contemplating a mug of what might have been wormwood.

'We'll be off then mate,' mumbled the lesser of the monsters, climbing to his feet.

'Good luck, Wireless,' said the other.

Wireless? The name Petherbridge hadn't meant anything to me, but Wireless sure as hell did.

Wireless and the Paradox

THE OLD MAN LOOKED up at us and I recognised him at once. I'd known him when I was a kid. Nowadays my father ran his own gold mine out at Burnt Shirt Gorge, but back then he was a prospector-cum-station worker, and Wireless was one of the eccentrics on the periphery of his circle. The nickname came from the fact that once you got him going he never stopped talking.

He'd shut up now, though. And shrivelled, it seemed. An impression enhanced by the after-image of the Works titans.

Truth be told, Wireless had never been the most pleasant of my father's acquaintances. He was one of your more theoretical bush bullshit artists, as likely to strut his stuff on half-arsed philosophy or layman's particle physics as he was on some putative nugget or lost reef. And cranky with it, old Wireless. He was always trying to best you in an argument. If he didn't manage it he'd flare up with a readiness that suggested an underlying insecurity, a suspicion that somewhere along the road he'd fucked up—taken a wrong fork. Or impaled himself on it.

From the look of him now, the fuck-ups had coalesced, big time. Arguing with your fellow no-hopers was one thing, slamming geo-picks into their throats was another. He was tapping on the table, chewing the rim of his cup, staring at the tablecloth with red rubber eyes. He was as bald as a bullet, with a blunt nose, a drooping jaw and a serious shortfall in the dental department. He looked like a snapping turtle that had lost its snap.

Cockburn sat opposite, pulled out a notebook. 'Just for the record, your name is John Vincent Petherbridge?'

'Wireless,' I interposed.

The senior sergeant looked up at me, his blue eyes querulous. 'What?'

'That's what his mates call him. Don't we, Wireless?'

The prospector's death mask was replaced by a quizzical flicker.

Cockburn's disdain was snowballing—about the only thing that was, given the weather. 'Acquainted with all the local quality, are we, Emily?'

'Grew up round here, mate.' He arched an eyebrow. 'We did tend to know each other.' I put a hand out in the old man's direction. 'Emily Tempest, Wireless. Jack's daughter.'

Recognition worked its way through his crumbled features. He shook my hand, his palm like gravel. 'Jeez Emily, sorry I didn't recognise you. Heard you was back, o course. What are you doin out here?'

'What are *you* doin, more to the point?'

The gravity of the situation came back at him, the spark went out of his eyes. He stared at his hands in horror. I couldn't blame him. The right one was crusted in blood and there was nothing to indicate that it was his own.

Cockburn did a drum roll on the table. 'Sorry to interrupt the reunion, but would you mind giving us your side of the story, Mr Petherbridge?'

Wireless averted his gaze. 'Not sure I know what my side of the story is. We might have had a drink or two. During the afternoon.'

'Folks at the pub tell us you were doing more than just drinking.'

'Well, drinkin and havin a yarn, o course. A discourse, you might say.'

'They could hear your...discourse a hundred yards away.'

'We get a bit heated when we get goin, must admit, Doc and me.'

I jumped to my feet. 'Christ! Wireless...!'

He looked up at me, fearful.

'That was *Doc* over there?'

My hand flew to the little fossil I always kept with me. A trilobite, given to me more than twenty years ago by the man now lying dead on the cabin floor. Doc.

I'd never heard a surname, and for all I knew the title might have been genuine. He was a geologist. He'd worked for the Geo Survey Office until he was fired for his increasingly oddball behaviour and heavy drinking, then he'd worked for the mines; when they fired him he'd gone prospecting.

The first time I met him was at Moonlight. There was an unusual stream of air emerging from a fissure in the west slope of Mirrinyu—Lizard Hill—not far from the homestead. The elders said it was a goanna breathing. Doc came through with the Geo Survey team and heard the story. When the rest of the crew moved on he stayed behind, camped next to the fissure. Took hourly barometric readings for five days straight. Dad got me to ride out and bring him food; Doc was so absorbed in his work, he'd forget to eat. Before he left he told me that the hill inhaled or exhaled according to the prevailing barometric pressure.

He and Wireless were old sparring partners. When they were in camp together they'd put an alarm clock on the ground between them and hit each other with twenty-minute monologues.

He bored the crap out of most people, but was kind to a curious little black kid. Forever pulling things out of a pocket: a ghost crystal or a double-rimming thunder-egg.

Or a trilobite. I'd carried it with me for a long time, and somewhere along the road I'd had it mounted on a chain. Still wore it for good luck.

It had been years; but even so, I felt bad for not recognising the bloke lying on the cabin floor. Although to be fair I'd been distracted by the object stuck in his neck.

'What were you arguing about?' Cockburn was saying.

Wireless blinked. 'Eh?'

'Your argument. What was it about?'

He tugged at the folds of skin around his throat. 'Xeno's Paradox. Far as I can remember.'

The coppers glanced at each other, bewildered.

'Xenos Paradox?'

'The Greek.'

'He one of the miners in the bar?' asked Jerker, flipping through his notebook.

'It's a famous philosophical conundrum, sarge,' I put in. 'The one about the rabbit and the turtle. Xeno was the feller who propounded it. Ancient Greek.'

For the first time since I'd met him, Cockburn looked nonplussed, like he'd wandered into a world that was beyond his comprehension. His jaw sagged ever so slightly.

'You were arguing over a dead...*philosopher*?'

Wireless shook his head. 'Maybe we did raise our voices a little, but can you blame me? He was ravin. Been ravin for months. Reckons he's solved the Paradox. Bullshit, I told him, you can't solve a paradox; there is no solution. That's why it's a paradox.

40

Been that way for months...'

'The Paradox?'

'Doc. You couldn't reason with him anymore, the old fool. Maybe he poked me a coupla times—he liked to throw his arms around when he got excited. Maybe I poked him back, I dunno. Somewhere in there I flaked out. Next thing I know Noel's shaking me and Doc's lying on the floor with that...his throat...'

He lapsed back into bewildered despondency; picked up his tin cup, stared into it as if he hoped it held some answers.

Cockburn checked his notebook. 'Who's Noel?'

'Noel Redman,' Jenkins responded. 'Owner of the pub.'

'Oh Wireless,' I murmured. 'What have you done?'

Cockburn clearly thought my acquaintance with both suspect and victim was cramping his style. 'Emily, why don't you shoot round to the bar? Tell Mr Redman we'd like a word with him.'

June cleared her throat. 'He was in the meat shed last I saw.'

Meat shed man

I STEPPED OUT INTO the dazzling glare. It felt like being zapped by a battery of lasers. I followed June's directions and came across a concentric building with fly-wire walls and a wet hessian door.

The little dog was on guard. It bristled when it saw me coming, unleashed a racket of yaps and flapping. The man inside—broad of back, jobby-jowled—was hacking into a strung-up side of beef with a cleaver. His face was a picture of twisted concentration, tongue slipping through tobacco-stained teeth, eyes only for the job at hand. Clearly a man who enjoyed his work. His right arm was thicker than his left, a mass of muscle and twisted vein. Sparks of blood and bone flew through the air.

'Mr Redman?'

He paused, turned round with a look that explained, perhaps, the harried wife. 'Depends who's askin.' His mouth barely moved.

'I'm with the cops.'

The dog seemed to know the word, let fly with a renewed flurry of vituperation.

'Stiffy!' snapped the boss; the dog changed down to a malevolent snarl, but the tail stayed at attention. Maybe that explained the name; I sure as hell hoped so.

'Senior sergeant wants a word.'

He put the cleaver down, shook his head. 'Fuckin ol Doc, eh? Pain in the arse to the very end. Be chargin a bloke for the funeral next.'

'I'm sure he wouldn't have got himself stabbed if he knew it was going to be such a nuisance.'

He frowned—a rock thrown into a pond of sweat and flesh. Wondered if I was taking the piss, but followed me outside. He walked with a slight limp, a hesitation in his gait.

'Bloody hot,' I commented.

The grunt may have been a reply. Redman was one of those Aussie males who find it easier to crack a ball-bearing than a smile. But he told his story readily enough and it confirmed what we'd already heard. The day had been hellish hot, the pub awash with booze of every denomination. Doc was meant to pay his rent by doing odd jobs around the place; lately, I gathered from the proprietor's tone, the jobs had been getting odder.

'Doc had a bit of a turn, a few months ago,' put in June. 'I tried to get him to go into hospital in Bluebush, but he wouldn't have a bar of it. Reckoned they'd never let him out.'

'And he wasn't wrong,' added her husband. 'Out of his tree, the old goat.'

'Weird kind of goat,' I couldn't help but point out.

'What?'

'In a tree.'

He and Cockburn gave me the twin stare. Redman pushed on, warming to his theme. 'Full of bullshit about, oh Christ,

43

what was it last week? Time running backwards, wasn't that it? Underground rivers! And what was that crap about Einstein?'

Wireless waved his arms in frustration. 'Reckoned he'd solved Einstein's last dilemma—the attempt to unify relativity and quantum mechanics. Solve it my arse! I told him, but he was beside himself, silly old bastard. And yet other times, black as a dog's guts. Paranoid. Said they were out to get him.'

I was puzzled. 'Who was out to get him?'

'You name it: Martians, devils. The CIA. Missionaries!'

The last was no surprise; Doc had always been the most proselytising of atheists; when he was up and running he made Christopher Hitchens look like an altar boy. Maybe in his demented state he thought the god botherers were getting one back at him.

I wondered if he'd been beyond irony when an evangelical preacher delivered his last rites.

'How did he get on with the missionary himself?' I asked.

'The which?'

'Whoever's driving the Evangelical Fellowship van out the front.'

'Ah—Pastor Bodycombe.' Wireless gave a fleeting smile. 'That was the only time I thought he was getting back to normal— loved revving up the Rev, did our Doc.'

'I bet he did.'

'But still, he was a troubled man. If anything, that was why I tried to get him going about the Paradox, Plato's Cave, that sort of stuff...'

Jenkins scratched his chin. 'Plato?'

'Please,' I muttered to myself, 'don't ask.'

Wireless pushed on. 'They were the things we'd talked and argued about for years; thought it'd settle him down. But it was no use; even there, he was off the planet.'

Cockburn raised an arm, trying to bring the conversation back to earth. 'Right, so he went a little whacky. Frustrating, I'm sure. The two of you had an argument. Things got out of hand, and you grabbed the hammer and belted him?'

Wireless stared miserably into the distance. Swallowed. 'Maybe...'

The Redmans backed up the sequence of events: Doc and Wireless had kicked off in the back bar, carried on all the way over to the shack. When Noel went to rustle the old boy up, he found him lying in a pool of blood. Wireless was passed out on the camp bed.

'How long you reckon he'd been dead?' asked Cockburn.

'June heard em still carrying on—what was it, love? Hour or so before I went over there.'

'I'd say so,' she drawled warily. 'About the time the tour group arrived. The Japanese.'

'And nobody else went near the shack?'

'Veranda was choc-a-bloc,' interjected Jenkins. 'Must have been a dozen people had a clear view of the place. They've all said the same thing: nobody in or out or anywhere near.'

Cockburn put a hand on the old man's shoulder. 'Sorry mate, looks like you're for it. Bit of luck, you'll get off with manslaughter.'

Jenkins rose to his feet. 'We gonna take statements?'

The senior sergeant checked his watch. 'Okay, but let's not bugger about.' He turned to the publican. 'What do you recommend from the menu?'

Redman flashed the boys-only smile. 'We're in beef country.'

'Emily, nip into the bar. Steaks all round.'

The proprietor waved an expansive arm in the direction of the kitchen. 'Tell Sandy it's on the house.'

Cockburn shook his head. 'Can't accept that Noel. Thanks for the offer. Tell em we'll be ready in forty minutes, max. And don't forget Wireless.'

45

The old man looked up, a pathetic gratitude in his eyes. 'Thanks sarge.'

'No worries. Might be the last you'll be having for a while.'

I stepped out once more into the blasting heat. Christ almighty what a day: I felt like a pig on a spit. If a heat-seeking missile were to arrive on the scene it wouldn't have known where to start.

I walked around the side of the pub, past the toilets, the delightful melody of 150-proof piss crashing into a urinal.

I stepped in the front door. Polished wood, whirling fans. Shafts of green-gold light streamed among bottles and mirrors.

The bloke behind the bar—Sandy, I assumed—wasn't quite as polished. Still youngish, but with an air of general disintegration. He had a DIY haircut and the fiery complexion of your everyday outback alcoholic.

He spotted me, and his eyes flicked at the dog-box window by the bar. A lot of these places still kept one for the blacks. His mouth started to move.

'Don't even think about it,' I warned him.

He suspended his instincts for long enough to look at me properly, changed tack.

'What would you like?'

'Some respect. And while you're working on that, five steaks. I'm with the police.'

He went to the kitchen window and said something to a steamy man in a once-white singlet whose appearance brought to mind my father's advice regarding roadhouse cuisine: always check for body parts.

The Rabble

I TOOK A LOOK around the room. There were maybe twenty people in there. A woman leaned over the pool table, generous buttocks sausaged into stretch pants. One of the old timers in the back bar—red-grey beard, flickering tongue, more sunspots on his skull than hairs—was slurping up the dregs of his lunch. He raised the plate and tipped the last of the gravy into a glass of rum. Drew a flask from a pocket and added a shot of slithery goo, sprinkled in something grey—not gunpowder surely?—and sank the results in one horrible hit.

He shuddered, shook his head into the bar and gasped: 'Ahhh…Bloody snake juice!' He issued a volley of subterranean noises—snorts and hoiks, rumbles and rough sighs, a general shakedown of the orifices that culminated in the expulsion of a mucus wad. It shot past his lonely front tooth and hit the trough at his feet with a wet slap.

'Talk about gob-smacked, eh Geordie?'

Geordie Formwood lowered the glass, studied me, ragged eyebrows arcing down, red eyes swirling suspiciously.

'Emily Tempest,' I clarified.

The eyebrows shot back up. 'Well I'll be fooked!'

'Not by me, you ugly old prick.'

He smiled broadly, rustled up more phlegm. 'Aye, that's the Emily I remember.'

Geordie had lived in Australia for fifty years, but he still hadn't shaken off the Aberdonian burr. He raised his glass and voice to his mates along the bar. 'Boys, boys, come and say hello to Motor Jack's daughter. Hear she's got a quicker lip than he has.'

It took about a minute flat to get the introductions out of the way: a half a dozen sun-dried miners from the nearby Gunshot Goldfields, an oyster-faced shot-blaster, a shovel-nosed truckie, a bikie with oxyacetylene eyes and a sweaty Texan well-sinker who could have kept himself in business drilling his own armpits.

Collectively—and when the Annual Green Swamp versus the World Cricket Match came round, they were indeed a collective, the dirtiest cricket team outside the sub-continent—they were known as the Rabble. They were the pack of reprobates for whom the Green Swamp Roadhouse was, god help them, their local.

Half of them had worked for my father over the years; the others had been tormented by his spin bowling, especially by the ball known locally as the 'dustcutter', which he slipped in every couple of overs and which could land anywhere but tended to collect your middle stump.

They gathered round, and somebody shoved a beer into my fist as they attempted to pump me for the inside story on the dustcutter. The argument was clearly a long-standing one: the consensus was that the delivery owed its fearful reputation to a triple differential between the torque of the ball, the angular momentum of his wrist and what the bikie, Jan, described as

48

the 'black hole effect' attributable to the missing tip of Jack's middle finger.

Doc and Wireless weren't the only philosophers in this neck of the scrub.

I was sharing with them my own theory—that there was no such thing as the dustcutter, and that Jack's success was due to his intuitive knowledge of human nature, which meant that it took him about three deliveries to suss anybody out and work out what they'd do next—when I felt a chill run down my back.

I turned around.

The senior sergeant was standing in the doorway.

The Rabble looked at him awkwardly, then at the floor. They did a lot of throat clearing and chin scratching. Like most dwellers out here on the fringes of civilisation, their relationship with the law could be described as 'complicated' at best.

Cockburn lowered his shades, took in the rough-cut assembly. Barely bothered to conceal his disdain.

'Nice to see you getting into the swing of things, Emily.'

'Gathering intelligence, boss.'

'Find much?' The skeletal remains of a smile.

'Takes time.'

'Which we haven't got. Let's take our statements and get out of here.'

Harley and Jenkins joined us, and we began the interviews. Raced through them, in fact, like a mob of horses heading for the home paddock.

The Japanese were the first to be sent packing. Harley started the interview, but Cockburn had to take over after the senior constable copped a withering tirade from a woman in black who wanted to know why he was interviewing her cleavage.

A few minutes with the tour leader—an eager fellow in yellow shorts, name of Lobert—was enough to convince him that they had nothing to add, and they were on the bus before they could say sayonara. Not that they were likely to be saying that in a hurry, since they turned out to be Taiwanese.

The rest of us were assigned a corner of the pub each. I copped the Rabble, while Harley and Jenkins worked their way through the dozen other travellers who'd found themselves caught up in the investigation.

My old miners didn't have much to offer, and I kept an ear on the other conversations. Harley seemed to be hitting it off with a sabre-toothed anthropologist, a snarling, spinifex-haired German woman keen to pin it on 'zie Fascists, always zie Fascists...' but with nothing to tell us who the fascists were, other than an intimation that Harley was of their number.

Among the others were a couple of public servants from the Land of the Long White Sock, a Copperhead mining engineer, a pair of Bluebush plumbers, a sprinkling of grey nomads and a strange little mustachioed spiv in chiselled pants who reeked of Brylcreem and gave his occupation as 'ex-army'.

Bunter tackled the Christian Evangelical Fellow, Pastor Bodycombe if I recalled correctly, a spindly creature in a green Hawaiian shirt with crosses on the collar, much given to wringing his hands and smiling the satisfied smile of the saved. He was weak chinned and clean shaven. Very weak chinned and very clean shaven: the effect was of a fish in spectacles.

Bodycombe seemed to be of the opinion that the deceased was better off in the arms of the Lord.

'Know him personally, did you then?' I heard Bunter ask.

'For my sins, yes,' replied the pastor, the tone of his voice telling you that getting the last word on Doc would have been his highlight of the week.

'Gave you a run for your money, I bet,' I threw into the interview.

Bodycombe peered at me, puzzled.

'Doc. Argumentative old cuss, wasn't he?'

'He wasn't the most docile member of my flock.'

'Hardly a member of your flock at all, I'd have thought—and yet you were keen to get over and give him a send-off.'

The tendons in the trout-like neck clenched.

'It would have been derelict of me not to.'

'Reckon Doc would have said so?'

The pastor raised his eyes to the ceiling; beyond the ceiling, up into the realms of the choir invisible. 'Who can tell what his state of mind was at the end? My duty is to offer grace—whether the individual has the will to accept...'

Bunter closed his notebook; Bodycombe picked up a nifty sports bag and slunk off in the direction of the veranda.

Geordie Formwood, sitting next to me, leaned over and growled, 'Dickweed. Just wanted to rub his nose in it.'

'Which dickweed wanted to rub whose nose in what?'

'Sky bloody pilot. Doc used to bore it up him every time they met.'

'How often did they meet?'

He shrugged. 'Whenever.'

'Yesterday?'

'Oh, aye. They been having this ongoing, em...debate. About evolution. Doc would show up with a piece of actual evidence— a fossil from the Precambrian, or some such—and the pastor'd shimmy that cat's-arse smile and say it was all part of a Greater Plan.'

'Well, maybe it was.'

Geordie's reply was a long snort and a longer pull of his malodorous brew.

'Just as a matter of interest,' I asked, 'where was Bodycombe when Doc and Wireless were having their little contretemps?'

'Pretty sure he was out on the veranda, sipping his lemonade.'

'Not all the time, but,' Jan chipped in. 'He had a kip in his van for a while; frazzled from all the atheism flying round.'

The pastor departed soon afterwards, and I watched carefully as he checked his van, topped up the water and oil and headed off down the Gunshot Road.

We interviewed everybody there, but it was a waste of time, the whole exercise. Despite the fact that there'd been a half a dozen people on the veranda at any time during the afternoon, nobody had seen anyone other than Wireless go near the shack. Even the Rabble, despite their best efforts, couldn't come up with anything that would put a dent in the case against him. 'Tripped and fell on his pick' was the best they could do.

As we finished with them the witnesses went their respective ways. We were hoeing into our steaks within the hour, my colleagues with gusto, Wireless less so. His mind was presumably on other things.

By the time we rose to leave, our prisoner was visibly disintegrating. His hands trembled, his mouth was working, his eyes flicker-drifted across the row of bottles behind the bar.

'Bloke couldn't have one for the road, sarge?'

'You're in custody, mate. Better learn to get along without it.'

Wireless grimaced.

'We won't worry about the cuffs, though.'

'Nice,' I commented, and copped a dose of the Cockburn glower for my troubles.

A woman on the edge

AS WE STEPPED OUT onto the veranda, the senior sergeant glanced across the road.

'Strewth, Jenkins. You planning on giving it away for Christmas?' The shack was still wrapped in red and white crime-scene tape. 'Better go and clean it up.'

We drove the couple of hundred yards to the shack. As we climbed out of the car, Harley glanced up at the surrounding hills and muttered an oath.

'What is it?'

'One of the Chinks is still here.'

I followed his gaze. There was a woman on the lower ledge of the cliff overlooking the shack.

'Bloody idiots must have left her behind.'

'Maybe she wasn't with them,' I suggested. 'Transit van's still in the car park.'

'Not a jumper, is she?' frowned Jerker.

Cockburn clicked his tongue. 'Whatever she is, she shouldn't be there.' He made a megaphone of his hands. 'Oi!'

The woman ignored him.

He bellowed again, with similar results.

'Bloody hell.' He turned to me. 'Emily, make yourself useful. Shinny up there and tell her to shove off. And not literally—we've already had our quota of casualties for the day.'

I kept my grumbles to myself. I hadn't spotted 'gofer' in the job description, but that was clearly how the senior sergeant saw me.

I studied the rock face. The crevasse down the middle of the cliff offered the quickest access, but it was also the trickiest. Getting up there looked like hard, hot work, and I didn't fancy breaking my neck first day on the job.

The west side was a better prospect: lightly canopied with shrubs, a little shade, a kinder slope.

I began the climb, and even that gentle effort took its toll, the red dirt on my forearms rapidly inscribed with sweat. I kept an eye on the woman, but as I drew closer I sensed that she wasn't in any danger. She was perched atop a skull-shaped boulder a metre or two from the summit. She had about her an air of tranquility and balance, as if precipitous terrain was second nature to her.

She was busily working away at a sketchbook, her face closed in on itself, focused.

I was just below her when I called out.

She glanced at me: it was the woman who'd given Harley a spray. She was close cropped with a smooth, tawny complexion, punishing eyes. She might have been attractive were it not for the stern cut of both jib and hair. She was wearing a black cotton dress, woven sandals, a turquoise armband.

'You interrupt the view,' she said brusquely. Just a little trouble with the *r* sound. She returned to her sketch.

'Bloody hot up here.' No response. 'Your friends leave you behind?'

She raised her head. 'Flen...friends?'

'The tour group.'

'The Taiwanese.' She scowled. 'I have met them for the first time last night.'

I needed to know what she was up to, and I was getting a sense that the hard-arsed approach wouldn't cut it. I sat beside her, leaned back against the rocks. She'd chosen a shady spot, but the granite radiated stored heat.

'Planning on staying here long?'

'I plan nothing but this drawing in my hand.'

Right. Maybe softly-softly wasn't going to work either.

'Where you from?' I asked.

'Sydney.'

'You don't sound like you were born there.'

'Nor you.'

'You were talking Chinese—is that where you're from?'

She leaned forward, spat succinctly over the edge.

Was that an answer? If it was, then maybe she was from one of the ethnic minorities. In another life, I'd spent a year or so scratching around the north-western fringes of the Empire, out on the Silk Road. I recognised the attitude: Uyghur? Kazakh? Tibetan? If so, her mob occupied a space in her nation's consciousness I found familiar.

'My boss down there is worried you shouldn't oughter be here.'

'Your boss?' She peered down the hill, deigned to notice them for the first time. Disdain sparkled in her eyes. 'You are policeman?'

'Dunno bout the man. Don't suppose I can argue with the rest.'

'I intended to ask you about this stone—what do you

say?—shape? forming?' She nodded at the pile of rocks at Doc's door.

'Formation.'

'Formation. But if you are not sure which side you are on...'

'What are you talking about?'

'This man who died—he lived in that little house?'

'He did, yeah.'

'Do you know why was he building a map in his backyard?'

'What?'

'Or...' She searched for the word. 'Ah—labyrinth. In the end, each becomes the other.'

'What the hell are you talking about?' I snapped. This woman—this foreigner—was trying to tell me my business. I may not know much, but I know rocks. I grew up with a prospector, spent my earliest days rambling with Dad over rough country looking at rocks. Did a year or two of earth sciences at Melbourne Uni. Hollows and blocks, buckled plates, pillars and cones. Rocks: they're a puzzle I want to read. Have read for as long as I can remember.

And as a black woman I tread near them with a very gentle step. I see their mythic dimension, their lunar beauty. I know them as stories and songs, as ancestors and sisters, as objects of affection and respect, sometimes fear.

So I was even more pissed off when I took a closer look at Doc's rock pile and saw she was right.

It wasn't just a madman's garden down there, a representation of its builder's addled brain. This tired old man had somehow managed to collect several tons of rock—mostly ironstone and gneiss—and from it created a structure with a definite pattern.

I leaned forward. The formation was a rough rectangle, cross-cut by a series of creek-like incisions. On its western side, what might have been a row of fan-shaped deltas below a range of hills. Like the woman had said, studying them from the air was like peering into a 3-D map, or a geological model.

But a model of what? Did the construction ring a bell? Possibly: the faintest tinkling. Nothing I could pin down.

I turned back to the woman. 'Who the hell are you?'

'He was murdered, this man?'

'Not for me to say.'

'Is it known who killed him?'

'You think I'm going to tell you that?'

'No. It seems not,' she turned away. Took up a pencil, slashed a few strokes onto the paper. 'If I want to understand what happens here,' the pencil sliced air, '...I would begin, perhaps, with these l...rocks.'

A bellow from below. '*Oi!*' Cockburn and the boys had gathered up the tape. Were getting impatient.

'If you're quite finished your APEC bloody summit up there...'

'Yeah, yeah,' I muttered. 'We're on our way!'

'We?' the woman put in. 'I think not.'

'Look honey, personally I don't care whether...'

I paused, distracted, my attention caught by a wagtail stuttering about in a ruby saltbush on the ledge above.

'Whether what?'

The bird disappeared. I frowned, put a foot on a jutting rock, dragged myself up to the summit. Slid into what might have been a natural—or manmade?—hollow among the scrappy saltbushes and rat's tail on the edge.

I touched a thorn and picked off the scrap of fresh green material I'd spotted from below. Took note of the woman's clothing. Black, head to toe.

I studied the rough ground. Scuff marks, recent. Somebody had been lying there, since the rain. In the past twenty-four hours.

'You been up here?'

'No.'

I examined the layout of the land between the hill and the shack,

57

threw a few possibilities around my brain. The direct route was fully exposed to the crowded pub veranda, but the western route, the one I'd taken? Somebody could well have climbed up under the cover of the scrub, made a fleeting descent to the cabin. Moving down the crevasse in the late afternoon glare, they could have gone unnoticed, returned the same way. Maybe even hidden behind the shack, blended with the crowd when the body was found.

I stood up. Again, I sensed it: a shiver of menace, a shudder of anxiety.

I shielded my eyes, gazed out over the aeolian landscape. The sun's rays blasted my skin. Splinters and wheels of light shot in from the white plains, spun about my brain. The country felt poised; primed, like a finger on a trigger.

I blinked, and the feeling disappeared.

Paranoia, surely? Maybe Doc's was rubbing off.

Over at the pub, a couple of flash four-wheel-drives had pulled in. Tourists. Paint-jobs sparkling, high-tech toys hanging off and welded on. Outer suburban plumbers or Pommy computer programmers on the Great Outback Adventure.

I spotted Noel Redman coming in from the meat shed, his fat arms laden, Stiffy strutting at his heels. Directly below, my colleagues were shuffling, restless. Cockburn was nowhere to be seen. Then the Cruiser's horn blared.

I called to the woman. 'I gotta go. You coming?'

'No.' She smiled. Her frown was friendlier. 'Be seeing you.'

'What's your name?'

She spat a quickfire response.

'Pardon?'

'In this country, where you are so poor with language, they seem to call me Jet.'

'Jet?' I muttered as I made my way back down the slope. 'That'd be right.'

A fissure in the ziggurat

I REACHED THE CLIFF base, came round to the front of the shack. Harley wiped some sweat and checked his watch. 'Took your time. Where's your Chink?'

'Still up there.'

'Is she?' Cockburn joined us, nodded at the rock formation behind the shack. Jet was perched alongside it, sketchbook out, pencil flying.

'She must have taken the shortcut. Which is what I wanted to talk to you about.'

'Eh?'

'We need to make a more detailed examination of the cliff top. Somebody's been up there.'

'What are you talking about?'

'A scrap of material on the bushes.'

'The woman,' suggested Harley.

'She's all in black—the material was green. Plus there are scuff marks…'

'Dingo. Wallaby. Hills are full of wildlife. Any footprints?'

'Not that I could see, but it's rocky up there.'

'Even if there were,' said Cockburn, 'this is a roadhouse. Tourists, miners, hippies wanting to commune with Mother Nature—any manner of idiot could go traipsing about.'

'Maybe, but these marks are recent. Why would you struggle up there on a day like this?'

'Your friend there did.'

'She's some sort of artist—weirdness is in the job description.'

Cockburn sighed, his patience wearing thin. He folded his arms, drummed a tattoo on his left elbow. 'Matter of balance—available resources against likely outcomes. I mean, we could call in the dogs and choppers, set up a bloody emu parade every time a couple of blokes thump each other in a bar. But it's just not feasible. Forensic's gone back to Alice. We haven't got the manpower, the time.'

I couldn't believe what I was hearing: this was a man's life we were talking about. 'I'm not asking for the bloody SAS—all I want is for you to get up there and…'

The beginnings of a fissure—the tiniest crack, really—appeared in the Cockburn ziggurat. 'What you're doing is scratching about looking for anything that's going to muddy the waters and make it less likely we'll convict your mate.' He leaned in at me. 'It's not going to happen. What we've got here is as straightforward a case as I've ever seen.'

'Maybe that's the problem. Everything looks straightforward to you.'

'*Jes*us!' The anger welled up, briefly, then his retentive instincts reasserted themselves. He dispersed a few flies, squared his legs. 'I've put up with enough of this crap. We're going back to Bluebush. I'm ordering you to come with us. If you choose to disobey, you can go poking around the hills until you're bloody well blue in the face. But don't think you'll have a job to come back to.'

I studied them. Cockburn, so self-controlled, controlling. Harley and Jenkins up on their hind legs like meerkats, our little argument the most entertaining thing they'd seen all day.

Support? Not likely.

I looked at Wireless, slumped against the column of the car, gazing listlessly into space. Talk of support, he was going to need all he could get.

'Give me a minute,' I said.

'That's sixty seconds and counting.'

I dashed out to where I'd last seen the Chinese woman. She'd disappeared. Then I spotted her black-clad rear. She was half-way up the rock pile, nose down, carrying out a close examination of god knows what.

'Hey, Jet!'

She turned around.

'Those sketches. Can I have one?'

She had a way of staring that stopped you in your tracks. 'Why?'

'Souvenir.'

She looked into my eyes, must have seen something. She jumped down, moving over the rocks with the casual agility of a rock wallaby. She flipped through the pad, pulled out one of the more detailed depictions of the formation.

'Use it wisely,' she said. Not quite a smile, but a flash of interest. Her eyes were like ripe mulberries. 'Might be worth fortune one day.'

Kite hawks

I PULLED UP ON the outskirts of Bluebush's dismal little cemetery, checked my watch. Nearly twelve. The church service had started at eleven, so they should be along any tick. I'd come to make my farewells to Doc and—and what? I wasn't sure. Lay some of the dust the old man's death had stirred up in my brain.

There were things about it that unsettled me.

There were things about most deaths that unsettled me, but this one I found particularly disturbing. Why, I couldn't say. My sympathy for the alleged killer? Maybe the tracks on the cliff top, or that bizarre rock formation in Doc's yard.

More than anything, it was that feeling of unease. It had been quietly biting, like a threatening fever, since that morning nearly a week ago now when we were heading for the Gunshot Road.

I hadn't made it to the church: organised religion and I

have had a rocky relationship since I was forced to fight off a hot-blooded Mormon—name of Randy, appropriately enough—when I was fourteen.

A lot of our mob have gone Christian these days. All those years of missionaries, misery and boredom, I suppose. With a sceptical father and a mob of fiercely traditional elders around me in my formative years, I was never a likely candidate.

But I reckoned I could put up with a bit of whitefeller God out here. The bush and the big blue sky were a bracing antidote.

I felt at my throat for the fossil Doc had dug out of the rocks on Moonlight Downs. Ran a thumb across the trilobite's ruffled spine. He'd told me it was six hundred million years old, put a rocket under my interest in things geological. The least I could do was go to the poor bastard's funeral.

A few minutes later the oddest cortege you were ever likely to see came grinding down the road. There was a boot-black hearse in the lead, but it was all downhill from there, a conga of zombie vehicles risen from the dead to claim another for their ranks: there were clapped out Inters and Blitzes, red F-Trucks with missing screens and one-eyed dogs, clanking battlewagons and utes that had been so patched up and cannibalised there was nothing left of the original.

The hearse slipped in through the gate, everybody else fought for the scraps of shade provided by the ghost gums. I waited until the last possible moment—I'd already grabbed the shadiest spot, and I wasn't exposing myself to that withering sun until I had to.

The Rabble—the ageing miners from the Gunshot Road—emerged from their vehicles slowly, reluctantly, as if they were being dragged out into the light by the hand of a monstrous God. They dribbed and drabbed their way to where the hearse had pulled up, hats in hands, shirts adrift, rum flasks buried in their back pockets.

Tiger Lyons pulled in close to me; his old Holden had a savage list to starboard, and so did he. He struggled out of the cab, all hobbles, wobbles and crusty bends, started out over the gravel like a dilapidated crab. He'd only taken a few steps when he stopped and looked up into the trees around the open grave. Flinched.

'Jesus fuck!' he spluttered. I couldn't exactly say the colour drained from his face, but the workaday alcoholic scarlet may have faded to a rough rosé.

As I turned to follow his gaze, there was an almighty thump on the roof of my vehicle.

'Good god! You really are a cop.' My father's head appeared at the window, the rest of him not far behind. He looked me up and down—mainly down: he was a solid six three to my wiry five four. 'Thought they were having me on.'

'I think they're having me on as well, Jack. All I've done so far is arrest Cookie Crankshaft.'

'What for?'

'Beating up Tom McGillivray.'

He blinked. 'Say again?'

'You heard.'

He checked out the uniform again. Scowled. 'Not putting yourself into any danger?'

'Yes—I may die of boredom. So far I've been hanging round the station reading files. The boss says I'm learning the ropes, but the main strand is how they take their tea.'

'Who is this boss?'

'Senior Sergeant Bruce Cockburn.'

He cracked his knuckles, narrowed his eyes. 'What's he like?'

'Keen. Likes to give motivational talks to the troops, then follow up with post-it notes. When I came in this morning there was one on my desk saying *Tidy desk, tidy mind.*'

He nodded. 'You always did have a dirty desk.'

He straightened up, stepped back from the car, cast an eye across the miserable scene before us. Father Dal Santo, the Filipino priest, was eyeing his watch.

'Nice of you to come and pay your last respects to Doc,' said Jack.

'I liked him. He was the one who got me interested in geology.'

'Thought I did that.'

'No Dad, you just taught me how to smash rocks. Doc had a little more finesse.'

'Finesse?'

'Knowledge.'

'Right.'

'Possibly even a degree.'

'Okay, I get the idea.'

We watched Tiger inching his awkward way back to the car.

'Tiger not a one for funerals?'

'Guess not,' said Jack, raising a puzzled eyebrow as the old miner reached into the cabin. The eyebrows went haywire when he emerged with a shotgun and began waving it in the general direction of the graveside.

'Christ!' came a cry. 'Tiger's goin on a rampage!'

Everybody hit the turf, a row of bony arses sticking up from behind the pathetic rose bushes and broken headstones. Only Father Dal Santo—steely of hair and character, said to be a feisty bugger at the best of times—stood his ground; maybe such things were part of the ritual at Filipino funerals.

Jack vanished, then reappeared, Jeeves-like, beside Tiger.

'Mate, mate...' He gently relieved him of the weapon. 'What are you doing?'

The old bloke looked bewildered.

'This is a funeral Tiger, not a wedding. No need for the shottie.'

'Fuckin vampires. Take a few of the bastards with me.'

I followed his outstretched finger. A squadron of hooded kite hawks brooding hypnotically in the lower branches of a ghost gum near the grave.

Jack nodded, passed the gun across to me. 'Better give this to Emily for safe keeping, eh? Wouldn't wanner give anybody the wrong idea.'

'Blood-suckin black fuckin...'

'They're just hawks, mate. Kite hawks. See em every day of the week. They don't suck your blood. Might nibble your nuts if you were road-kill, but we haven't come to that yet. Come on, Tiger—Doc's waitin to say goodbye.'

He took the old man's elbow, led him grumbling and stumbling out over the gravel.

As I locked the weapon away, I spotted a thin, boyish figure on the other side of the road.

Danny Brambles. I hadn't seen him since the crash out on the highway. He had his thumbs in his pockets and his eyes raised to where the kite hawks perched. He didn't look any keener on the birds than Tiger was.

I walked over to him. 'Danny.'

'Em'ly.'

'Where you headin?'

'Into town.' He shook his head, stared at me. 'Hey Em'ly, need to ask a favour.'

'Yes?' I noticed, for the first time, the slight sway, the blurred expression in his eyes. I spotted Willy and Dixon Crankshaft lurking in the distance. Guessed what was coming next.

'Couldn't fix us up for a coupla bucks, could you?'

'What's a couple?'

'Mebbe fifty?'

'Fifty! Cents, if you're lucky. Thought you were staying out at Stonehouse Creek.'

'Had to come in.'

'What for?'

He studied the ground, didn't answer the question, didn't have to: we both knew drink and drugs were the magnet that drew a lot of young people in from the bush.

He figured a change of topic was about due. 'Who they buryin?'

'You ever meet ol Doc?'

'That kartiya from Green Swamp? Seen him. He used to come out to Stonehouse. Lookin at the rocks.' He frowned. 'What appen?'

'You wouldn't wanner know.'

'Somebody finish im? Who?'

'Another miner, looks like.'

He nodded darkly. 'This country, dangerous for kartiya...'

'Dangerous for everybody—especially this time of the year.'

Danny's gaze sharpened, seemed to take in for the first time the uniform I was wearing. They still hadn't found a pair of pants that fit, but they had given me a badge. Emily Tempest: ACPO.

'I seen you at the car crash. You're a kurlupartu?' A cop.

'Nah, not really. I'm an undercover blackfeller.'

'But you got the outfit?'

'Just the top half, Danny.' I ran a hand down my skirt, grinned. 'Like to catch a glimpse of me skinny black legs from time to time, remind myself who I am.'

But he was uneasy, I could tell. When he was in town Danny ran with a pretty wild crowd and nothing in uniform had ever done him any favours.

I spotted my father among the mourners. He beckoned with his chin: festivities were about to get underway. 'I gotta show me face in there. Feller was a friend of Jack's.'

Danny nodded a farewell, set off to join his disreputable mates with an eagerness I didn't like the look of.

'Hey Danny!'

He paused.

'When you goin back out bush?'

'Soon.'

'You look after yourself in town—wouldn't wanner lock you up.'

He smiled, a flash of the cheeky-boy grin he'd had before the grog got him. 'Have to catch me first.'

Fun for all

I WENT INTO THE cemetery, nodded at a few individuals. Most of them were too busy staring at the ground to notice.

The atmosphere was...funereal. Grave. A pathetic little affair, shot through with the mourners' despair. Whether for the deceased or for themselves was difficult to tell. Maybe it was the resonant frequency of their collective DTs. Twenty or thirty people, mainly men of course, most of them looking mildly surprised that they weren't the guests of honour. Yet. For a lot of them it couldn't be far off.

Doc's wasn't the only ghost floating over the assembly. The other was Wireless. The bastards hadn't even given him bail, shipping him off to the remand centre in Alice Springs after the most perfunctory of hearings.

We seemed to be waiting for something. I stood at the back of the crowd, let my mind wander. Found myself contemplating the scenic wonders of the Rabble from the rear. Aside from your everyday sweat and diesel stains, there were the acid splashes and gelignite flashes of their trade, starbursts of crushed quartz and red ochre, smatters of ash and axle grease, goat shit and goulash from the roadhouse kitchen.

Staring at the play of light on their patched and baggy clothes was like staring into lino on the toilet floor. Images emerged; among them a wobbly map of Antarctica, a galloping dog and, across Pissy Wilson's broad arse, a Pieta. I was pondering what you'd get for that on eBay—apart from an intervention order—when I noticed that June Redman, the publican's wife from Green Swamp, had put in an appearance. Her charming other two-thirds was nowhere in evidence. From what I'd seen of him Noel Redman would probably be billing Doc's estate for her lost wages. She spotted me, nodded a greeting.

She was wearing heavy sunglasses, but the corners of her mouth suggested strain. Couldn't blame her: I'd be strained if I was married to that.

Father Dal Santo was holding an umbrella over his head in a hopeless attempt to ward off the sun. He was looking particularly shrivelled today. God save us, I thought, even the imports are getting on. He must have been round here for twenty years. I wondered idly if there were more where he came from. Perhaps young Filipinos were beginning to see the dark.

Two cars arrived a little after the others, pulled in behind my own. The first was a rugged white Holden Rodeo, from which two young men emerged.

Probably eighteen, twenty years old, both lean, physically poised, slightly ill-at-ease at finding themselves in this geriatric assembly. They were fitted out in the ubiquitous moleskins and riding boots of their caste. The main distinction between them was that one RM Williams shirt was a slightly darker blue than the other.

The second vehicle was a green Range Rover, the driver a solidly built older man in a suit, of all things. A black suit, the only one in sight. Even the undertakers hadn't gone that far.

He climbed out, stretched his back, walked across to join the boys—obviously his sons. He was clean shaven and dark eyed. Big hands, hairy knuckles; a gait somehow suggestive of a man accustomed to keeping a level head on rough terrain.

The other occupants of the Rover effected a more chaotic exit. A languid woman in a dark blue dress wafted from the passenger seat, opened the back door in a manner that bespoke a need to conserve energy. The reason for that shortly became obvious: two flashes of blue and gold burst forth, tumbled over and picked themselves up. Honey-haired girls of seven or eight, twins.

They darted around the other side of the car and scrambled back in; emerged moments later, vaguely pursued by a long-suffering older girl with a thin, pale face, dark hair and a sombre dress. The twins completed a circumnavigation of the car, stuttered to a halt when they ran into their mother, doubled back and disappeared into the rear door.

The father, anticipating their next move, went round to the driver's side and swept them into his arms as they leapt out. His family fell into an easy formation around him, and they headed in for the service together.

They'd all done this before.

'Mate, it's a bloody fun for all,' muttered Jack, wryly amused by the performance. As they joined the crowd I got a closer look at the little girls. The nearest craned her neck, grinned and slipped me a wink.

It was the wink that slotted them for me. The photo on Doc's bedside dresser.

I touched Jack's sleeve. 'Who are they?'

'Wishy and his clan. Doc's brother. Think her name's Loreena.'

'Shit. That's Doc's brother?'

'Younger.'

'Seems to have suffered the slings and arrows better than his brother.'

He stared at the coffin ruefully. 'Being sober helps. Used to be a surveyor round here, Wishy; mapped half the tracks out in the Terra Del Fuego.'

'Can't say I've seen him round.'

'Been away for years—WA, Top End. Heard he was back here with the Transport and Works mob.'

The funeral kicked off. Father Dal Santo raised his arms, appeared exhausted by the effort. He droned a couple of wafer-thin prayers, asked if anybody had anything to add. He was obviously hoping nobody had; the weather wasn't getting any cooler.

But the brother stepped forward. He cleared his throat, joined his hands. 'I didn't say much at the church. Mainly because Albie—most of you knew him as Doc, but to me he was always Albie—my brother was never much of a man for churches. Hated em, truth be told. Raging atheist if ever there was one. Sorry mate,' he added for the benefit of the puzzled priest.

I smiled. I could relate to that. And I could understand the family's dilemma: your Bluebush burying options were limited, to say the least. It was the Filipino priest, the lezzie ladies from the Outback Mission or the town tip.

Wishy Ozolins paused, took in the crowd, nodded at the coffin. 'Albie...Don't know where he's going, can't even say I know every-where he's been, especially the last few years. But I know where he came from because I was there, tagging along behind.'

He hesitated, wondering whether he was holding his audi-ence. He was sure as hell holding me. There was something about this fellow's voice that drew you in.

'Some of you—those who knew us from the early days—you

know the story; you got the same one. Family come out from Latvia after the war, things in their memories nobody oughta have and moved to the Gunshot Goldfields. Our mother died soon after, the old man went into his shell. From the time I was a little nipper he spent most of his life swingin a pick or settin charges underground. And it was my big brother who stepped into the breach.'

He drew a finger across his chin, scratched idly, like he was trying to rustle up a memory. He ran his eyes across the crowd, seemed to take us in, every last one of us. He was a commanding figure, this brother of Doc's.

'Like to share a story, if I may. There's this one time, Albie's following a lead—limonite, it was—trying to see how far it went. No reason, nothing to be gained, he just wanted to know. We're in the gully behind Black Patch Hill. Getting nowhere fast, digging into solid rock, so Albie flogs a few sticks of leaking gelignite off old Cranky Baker. Flogs a few too many sticks I presume, because the explosion turned the Patch into Dog Bite Ditch and blew the shithouse there to kingdom come.'

'That was Doc?' interrupted Tiger, his vampires momentarily forgotten. 'I remember that! Pickin turds out of our tea for days, we were! Always wondered who...'

Ozolins smiled, shaggy eyebrows arcing.

'Yeah, we weren't ownin up to that one in a hurry. But that was Albie. He always had a wild mind. Wild? Inspired, curious, full of questions, forever pulling things apart or blowing em up. Even then, he was a man of ideas.'

He screwed his face against the glare, gazed at the coffin.

'Sure, maybe those ideas got a bit too much for him in the end. Went a little haywire. Maybe he didn't find his Grand Unified Theory...'

'His GUT!' giggled one of the little girls, and the mother sighed, drew her closer.

'Maybe nardoo root was never gonna be the crop that'd feed the world. Maybe that—what was it again? Snowman Theory...'

'Snowball!' piped the girl from her mother's arms.

'Snowball, Snowman, whatever. Doesn't look like it's gonna revolutionise outback geology. I'm a practical bloke and I don't know about those things. But I do know that he was a brother to me when I needed one, and the world's a poorer place for his passing.'

He paused for a moment, glanced at his family. 'Tiffany?'

The little girl with the big mouth frowned, then stepped forward and placed an obsidian crystal on his coffin. It sat there, a mess of intersecting lights and dark flash.

'So long, brother.' The surveyor's face was like stone as he watched the coffin sink into the ground. The rest of the crowd formed a jagged line, shuffled forward. Fistfuls of hot red earth rained down into the hole.

Half an hour later I was rolling down the road, Wishy Ozolins' oration ringing round my brain. He'd painted a portrait of the Doc I remembered: a decent man. Full of enthusiasms and surprises.

Maybe he'd been overwhelmed in the end, but we're all overwhelmed sooner or later. Most of us by things a lot worse than our own zeal.

I felt I owed him something. We all did. If nothing else, we owed him more than the poor excuse for an investigation into his death carried out by my colleagues.

Had Wireless really killed him in some drunken argument about Greek philosophy, or had Doc been getting on somebody else's goat? Who'd rifled through his books and papers? Who'd been up on the cliff top, spying on his shack? And why could I not shake the image of that man-made rock formation from my head?

His head was full of questions. That was what his brother had said. They were the centre and the circumference of his world.

Had he asked one too many?

I'd been like a caged tiger ever since we got back from Green Swamp, rattling round the office, doing the filing, making tea. Reading Cockburn's stupid little post-it notes. Maybe it was time I started asking a few questions myself.

Doc's brother seemed like a good place to start.

A bird on the ground

THE TRANSPORT AND WORKS depot was on the outskirts of town. The front entrance was neat and green. Urban, urbane, with a number one cut and a battery of sprinklers tossing out loops of water.

The compound out back was a more honest manifestation of your whitefeller approach to the bush: huge and brutal, an armada of yellow earth-moving plant and equipment encased in barbed wire. The air was thick with diesel fumes and testosterone, the yard hummed with the hiss of pumps and guns, the rattle of running motors and men.

When I asked for Wishy Ozolins, a jaunty receptionist directed me through to the Regional Manager's office. There sat Ozolins himself, as out of place in an office as a camel at a cat show. He was an outdoors man if ever I saw one. That was where he'd been the first time I'd seen him: striding across the gravel with the sun on his face and his loved ones around him.

His office window looked out onto the yard, and from the angle of his desk and the grimace on his face as he contemplated the pile of paperwork in front of him, I suspected Ozolins spent a lot of time looking at it as well.

The cadaverous fellow standing alongside him had the rarefied air of someone who'd consecrated his life to the absolute mastery of something very, very small. He was peering down as Ozolins waded through a sea of numbers, nibbled pencil in hand.

'You still haven't updated and reconciled your accrual and usages over the last quarter,' grumbled the cadaver.

'Sorry?'

'The accruals! The usages!' The fellow sniffed through nostrils that must have given him hell on windy mornings. 'And you haven't applied the tax entry depreciation percentage rates to the assets register.'

'Was I supposed to?'

'The Audit Act says you're supposed to. I imagine the auditors will too.'

Ozolins flinched and twisted in his seat.

'Excuse me,' I said. 'Mr Ozolins?'

He raised his eyes. 'Jesus Christ!' he exclaimed, then leapt to his feet, came running at me. Ran right past and threw open the window. 'Stop right there!'

There must have been twenty men moving about the yard in a variety of occupations—loading trucks, flinging forty-fours, stripping equipment—but such was the level of command in the voice that every one of them—even the driver of a ten-tonne crane truck manoeuvring in the yard—stopped what he was doing.

Maybe not *every* one of them.

'Thornie!' he growled.

There was a bloke with a face like a dried waterhole in a lean-to near the office; the lean-to was rickety, its occupant ricketier.

He appeared to be grappling with a post-modern sculpture—a thing of plastic slats, aluminium tubing and garish green bolts. He pushed on with his task, oblivious to the imposing voice from above; if anything, he seemed to speed up, although on closer inspection it was only the shakes that accelerated—he was still getting nowhere, but getting there faster.

'Thornie!'

The bloke in the lean-to raised his head reluctantly, flush-faced, like a man trying to hide from a hangover.

'Wishy?'

'Told you to put a safety rail around that nest.'

I saw what Ozolins was referring to now. Out in the middle of the compound, on the ground in front of the truck: a plover's nest, the bird itself gazing out with nonchalant eyes. Hell of a place to start a family.

'Sorry, Wishy.' Thornie waved a jittery hand at whatever he was working on. 'It's this chair...'

'That's a chair?' He studied it. 'What for? An amoeba?'

'Mardi asked me to put it together...'

Ozolins rolled his eyes.

'...but it's got me fucked.'

Ozolins jumped out the window. He grabbed a sledge-hammer, an armful of star-pickets and a roll of orange netting, marched out and threw a protective barrier around the bird. When he was finished, he flashed a minatory gaze about the yard, waved the truck on. Everybody got back to work.

As he returned to the office he paused, looked down at Thornie and his bizarre construction. Most of the parts were still spread across a canvas tarp; those that were assembled didn't make a lot of sense: a mass of vicious triangles and other odd shapes. More like something you'd torture somebody with than offer them a seat in.

'Chair, you say?'

''s what she said.'

Ozolins picked up an aluminium tube, studied it, grabbed another piece, lined it up with the first, nodded to himself. You could almost see things click inside his head. He pulled Thornie's monstrosity apart and threw it together again with a speed so casual it was almost indecent.

Definitely an outdoors man, I decided, somebody who could think on his feet, come up with practical solutions.

When he finished, he stood with his hands on his hips, examined the chair.

'Ergonomic,' he explained to Thornie, and tried it out, cautiously at first, then with obvious pleasure. 'Hmmm. Not bad.' He put his hands behind his head and leaned back. 'If you like your ankles up your arse and your goolies in the gravel. Bigger model'd do the trick. Warren!'

The pallid fellow next to me stepped forward, poked a crabby nose out the window.

'Can we afford another one of these?'

'You don't sign off on those estimates, we'll have to hock the ones we've got.'

Ozolins took a last, reluctant look around the yard, came back in through the window, dolefully contemplated the paper glacier flowing across his desk.

He raised his head and seemed to realise, for the first time, that I was there.

'Who're you?'

He had a deep, gravelly voice, rough around the edges, but strangely reassuring when it homed in on you. You knew where you stood with a voice like that.

A woman lugging an armful of files and an arse like a wheelie bin poked her head into the room.

'Front office buzzed her through,' she snapped. 'If you'd listen to your...'

'Mardi! How do you get a chair like that out of stores?'

'Occupational health and safety. If you had a back like mine...'

Ozolins looked as though a dozen rejoinders were competing to be first out of his mouth, but he caught sight of the glaciating gaze and wisely restrained himself.

'Phew!' He turned back to me. 'Worried you were one of the auditors. They're due any tick.'

'Maybe I am.'

'Don't think so.'

I shook his hand. 'Emily Tempest.'

He seemed interested. Or at least relieved at the prospect of another distraction from the paperwork. He stared at the ceiling. 'You'd be one of the Tempests from Moonlight Downs then?'

'One of the two, yeah.'

'I know your old man. Saved my bacon once, west of Moonlight.'

'Oh?'

'I'm stuck in the mother of all bogs and ready to start hoofin it, when he appears out of nowhere and pulls me out. Him and an old blackfeller.'

'Remember the old feller's name?'

'Strewth, it was years ago. Washington, maybe?'

'Lincoln.'

He snapped his fingers. 'That's it. Right job, wrong man.'

'Surprised you didn't say Obama.'

'Clever bugger, whatever he was called. They're looking for me, knew I was out there. But they couldn't have seen my tracks: they were coming from the opposite direction. Asked the old feller how he knew I was in trouble and he just smiled.'

'Yeah, that was Lincoln. Had that enigmatic smile down pat.' A shadow passed over the conversation as I thought about the man I'd loved like a favourite uncle.

'What can I do for you, Emily?'

'Wanted to talk about your brother.'

He slapped the desk. 'Knew I'd seen you before! You were at the cemetery.'

'Wasn't all I was at.'

'What do you mean?'

'I was at Green Swamp just after he died. With the cops. I'm an ACPO.'

'That a skin disease?'

'Aboriginal Community Police.'

He glanced at my uniform.

'The other half's in the mail. What did they tell you about his death?'

'Same as they told everybody else, I gather. They got old Wireless locked up...'

'Stitched up, more like it.'

'What?'

'That's probably unfair. Let's just say there were a few...'

'Excuse me, Mr Ozolins.'

A teenage boy covered in sweat and a set of bedraggled overalls wandered into the room. Stood there chewing his lip and hopping from one foot to the other.

'Spit it out, Jason.'

'I'm loading the gear for the Kruger Bore crew, like you told me, but now the Cants Creek foreman reckons he's top priority. Says he's got a hot mix ready to pour. What am I supposed to do first?'

Ozolins went across to the window, made a megaphone of his hands: 'Oi! Bernie!'

A beefy bloke manhandling forty-fours onto a Hino truck stopped in his tracks. Paused, twisted his head in our direction, smiled like a man not used to smiling.

'Who's doing the south road?'

'Christy Wilson.'

'Let him go first. And when you do the pour, try to get some of it on the road.'

He grabbed a battered hat from the top of a filing cabinet, a bag from under the desk. 'Place is a madhouse. Time I wasn't here anyway.'

'But Wishy!' spluttered the bookkeeper. 'The auditor's due in this afternoon.'

'Same feller as last time? Weedy little pissant, dyes his mustache?'

'Possibly.'

'Fusses about his car?'

'Can't say I noticed.'

'Well I did, and I just arranged it so he won't be here until tomorrow.'

'What?'

'Roadworks on the southern approach.' A sardonic smile. 'Fresh pour. Unfortunate, but nothin we can do about it. I'll be in early—we'll sort it out then.' He turned back to me. 'Now, Emily Tempest. I dunno what you're on about, but I don't like the sound of it. Can I invite you round my place for a feed?'

'I'd be delighted.'

Corrugation Road

FIFTEEN MINUTES LATER I found myself following him into a large bush block at the southern end of Corrugation Road.

Wishy's house was one of the Bluebush originals. It was made out of blue-painted iron, a material that could be brutal in the heat, but this one was built with a clever eye to the weather. Shady location, wide verandas, apertures designed to catch the tiniest sliver of wind, numerous ponds and pools.

'That the child care centre?' I nodded at a giant ghost gum on the border of the property.

A rough-hewn tree-house sat in the upper branches, with a flying fox and a slide that would have given a school safety inspector nightmares. There was an archery target bristling with arrows, a tyre swing on a lower branch.

'Ya gotta watch em, but. They tend to put each other in the swing and use it as a target.'

Loreena was on her knees in the garden, fork in hand, a profusion of bougainvillea, gardenia and desert rose blooming around her. She was wearing a hat that could have been picked from one of the bushes. She introduced herself, led us inside. She'd been warned I was on the way, had prepared nibblies and drinks.

'Where's the horde?' Wishy asked warily.

'Out on the rampage.'

Wishy ushered me onto a sofa in his office, dropped a chilled brown bottle into my lap. We'd not got past first base when he paused, puzzled.

'Something wrong?' I asked.

'Quiet round here.'

'Thought that's what we wanted.'

'Not this quiet.'

His gaze swept the room, came to rest on the floor beneath his feet. Narrowed. 'Tiffany.'

No response.

He dropped an octave: 'Tiffany!'

The voice seemed to me to assume the tone of command I'd heard in the Works yard, but here it had no effect.

He sighed, resigned himself to something. 'Tiger Lily?'

A voice piped up from behind the couch.

'Yes, Daddy?'

'Would you like to come and say hello to the lady?'

A wiry little girl with a mop of golden hair squeezed out from the narrow gap between the couch and the wall.

'Emily, meet Tiffany...' She shot him a look that would have cut through reinforced concrete. '...who's decided that from here on she's going to be known as Tiger Lily.'

The girl beamed. 'I hit a six through the workshop window.'

'I'm not surprised.'

'Can you play cricket?'

84

'Sure.'

'Bowl?'

'A bit.'

'Come outside and I'll belt you through the window too.'

'Maybe not just now. Me and your dad need to talk.'

'After?'

'No worries. Looks like I'm here for dinner.'

Her father gave her a slap on the backside, shuffled her off in the direction of the door. 'Go tell your mother she wants you. And Tiger...' He thrust a long arm under the couch, emerged with the other half of the duo, wriggling and giggling. 'Take the Time Bomb with you.'

When the twins hesitated in the doorway, he rushed at them and clapped his hands. They stampeded from the room, but as we resumed our conversation I spotted a golden mop peeking over the window ledge and a tiny hand proffering a hopeful ball.

'Half an hour!' I whispered.

'And an extra ten minutes every time you pester us,' growled her father.

He rested his elbows on his knees, pinched the bridge of his nose, concentrating. 'So, Emily, what were you getting at back at the depot? About Albie.'

'You know how he died?'

'Some sort of drunken argument. Can't say I was surprised, truth be told. Albie'd been disintegrating at a rate of knots in recent years.'

'So everybody tells me...'

'Is there some doubt?'

'Probably not. But there are a few...anomalies.'

'Anomalies!' His face grew animated. 'Albie was an anomaly from go to whoa! A wandering Latvian eccentric who thought time was going backwards and nardoo root was going to save the world from famine.'

'Way the world's warming he may be right. Nardoo grows well in the dry.'

'He tried to tell me life evolved out of a snowball, for god's sake.'

'Well actually...'

He leaned forward, frowned. 'Yes?'

'He's not Robinson Crusoe there either.'

'Oh come on...'

'There is a geological theory that the Earth was covered in ice 600 million years ago, and the first complex life forms—which eventually became us—evolved out of the meltdown that followed. It's called Snowball Earth.'

He eyed me. 'Any chance you're as batty as he was?'

'Possibly.' I shrugged. 'But I did do a couple of years of earth science at Melbourne Uni. Like to keep my hand in.'

'Albie also reckoned he'd been hearing from our father. Reckoned he was still down the old Gunshot Mine, tapping messages in morse code, saying he'd be home for tea and could we heat up the stew? Anything about that at uni?'

'Must have skipped that class.'

He blinked. He'd just realised something. 'You haven't seen the autopsy report, have you?'

'Autopsy?'

'But you're a cop; I'd have thought that'd be the first thing you'd want to look at.'

'I'm an *ACPO*—only the real cops get told things.'

'Yeah, I've met your boss. He didn't strike me as the type to spread the love around.' Wishy frowned; picked at the label of his stubbie. 'Albie had a brain tumour.'

I took a moment to absorb that.

'Size of a golf ball. Must have been growing for months—years. Sure, he had a few inches of geo-pick in his throat, but he wouldn't have lasted long anyway.'

That explained a lot of things: the haywire behaviour, the delusions, the fights, the frustration.

But not everything.

Wishy read my mind. I detected, for the first time, a glint of steel behind that genial exterior. 'Still not satisfied, are you?'

'Just because you're paranoid doesn't mean they're not out to get you.'

He let his gaze drift up to the ceiling. An overhead fan sliced air, turned it into waves.

'What is it, then?'

'Look Wishy, I've only been in this job for a few days, so I'm not exactly an expert, but I knew your brother—liked him. And I've got an idea of how things work round here, which is more than I can say for most of my colleagues.'

'What do you mean?'

'I just thought they were a little slapdash, way they went about investigating his death. Almost as if they knew what they were going to find and couldn't be fucked looking for anything else.' I paused, caught his eye. 'We owe Doc more than that.'

'What do you think they missed?'

Better to keep my cards close; for all I knew, the man I was talking to was the person who'd been up on the ridge. That didn't seem likely, but I'd seen enough violent deaths to know the prime suspect usually came from somewhere in the family circle.

'Hard to put a finger on it.'

He wasn't impressed. 'You're not just doing this for old Wireless, are you? I've got as much sympathy for him as the next bloke, but there comes a point when you gotta take responsibility. Can't blame the grog forever. Besides, your sergeant—what was his name? Little Mister Efficient?'

'Cockburn.'

'With a "ck"?' He grinned. 'He told me Wireless was the only one there when it happened.'

'Maybe, but the weather that day was something chronic. The Green Swamp crowd were lolling around in an alcoholic stupor and staring into the sun. Most of em couldn't have told their arses from their armpits.'

He didn't seem convinced.

'Anyway,' I continued, 'I'd just like to know more about Doc. What made him tick...'

'Tick! Dunno if tick's the word. Detonate, maybe. Worse the last year or so—the tumour, I presume: mind on the rampage, body trying to keep up.'

'Any enemies you know of? He and Wireless might have had the odd philosophical argument, but they were mates. Was there anybody he really pissed off?'

Wishy swept his hands through the air in a gesture of futility.

'Was there anybody he *didn't* piss off? He worked for just about every employer in the Territory: most of the major mining companies, the Geo Survey, Copperhead. Sooner or later, they all decided he was a liability. How long since you'd seen him?'

I shrugged. 'Fifteen years, at least.'

'And how do you remember him?'

'A little eccentric.'

'Exactly. Take that, add twenty years of confusion, booze and brutal weather, bung in a brain tumour and Albie's what you got.'

'Completely loopy,' I nodded.

'Bull*shit*!' The disembodied word came shooting through the window. Tiger Lily appeared, her eyes damp and full of glare. 'He was the smartest man in the world, my Uncle Albie.'

Wishy rose from his chair, went across and knelt by the window, took her little hand in his big one.

'Course he was, honey. Emily knows that. He was just unwell. Like I told you. He had this...thing, growing in his brain, made him get a little mixed up.'

She backed off, but her lower lip was wobbling.

I came over. 'I'm sorry, Tiger Lily. It's just my big mouth. I met your uncle when I was about your age, and I thought he was wonderful—full of surprises—showing me things that made my hair stand on end.'

'Really?'

'Sure.'

'What?' She clenched her jaw, suspicious, braced herself for adult condescension.

'Like—er...' I remembered the trilobite, pulled the chain over my head and held it out to her. 'Like this.'

A spark of interest. 'What is it?'

'Something very special. It used to be a tiny animal, crawling across the ocean floor.'

She gave me the fuckwit look.

'I meant what *period* is it from? Most of them round here are Cambrian, but there are Silurians as well.'

I took a step back. 'Oh. I see. Precambrian, I think. Who taught you about fossils?'

Again, the withering glare. 'Who do you think?'

'Your Uncle Albie?'

'Yes, and that wasn't all...I've got a hundred and twenty-seven specimens in my collection, spread over three hundred million years. Did you know that...'

'Not now Tiger,' interrupted her father. 'Emily and I need to talk.'

She kept her gaze on the fossil.

'You know Tiger,' I said, 'Doc gave this to me, and I bet nothing would have made him happier than to know that I'd passed it on to you.' I pressed it into her hand, folded her fingers over it. 'Why don't you go out and start the game? When I've finished I'll come and show you how it's done.'

'Pig's arse you will.'

Her father and I watched her go, the little fossil tucked into her shirt.

'Well-spoken child, that,' I commented.

'Hung around too many bloody Works camps.' But he was smiling as he said it.

As she walked out onto the lawn, a cluster of kids accreted to her. Tiger Lily obviously had her father's natural leadership. The crowd was growing. In a matter of seconds, it seemed, she was doing cartwheels in front of an appreciative audience. The Time Bomb began shooting rubber-tipped arrows through her flying limbs. I took a closer look: couldn't see rubber tips.

I turned to Wishy. 'You seem to have come out of a background similar to your brother's in pretty good nick.'

'Yeah. Well maybe that's because he went on ahead and bore the brunt. That and the pure luck of meeting a good woman.'

'Where'd you and Loreena hook up?'

'On the Roper Bar. I was putting in a road. She was the bush nurse.'

I changed tack. 'Don't suppose your brother owned anything of value?'

'Value! Albie? He wouldn't have a pot to piss in. Had that prick from the pub asking me the same question the other day.'

'Noel Redman?'

'Reckoned Albie owed him two years back rent. Told the bastard he could shove it. Asks me what he's gonna do with his stuff. What stuff? I asked. Couple of broken chairs? Firewood! Geordie Formwood wanted the jeep for spare parts; said he was welcome to it. I took a run out there the other day, gathered up what I could, carted most of it off to the tip. Gave Redman his bloody money.'

'You paid Doc's rent?'

'Was always going to—just thought he could have waited until after the funeral to ask.'

I drained my stubbie, took a handful of chips. Munched them thoughtfully.

'I noticed Doc had a filing cabinet. What happened to that?'

He studied me. 'You are a hard case, aren't you?'

'Don't like leaving things half done.'

He went quiet for a moment. Rose to his feet. 'Comes to some bastard killing my brother and trying to shift the blame onto an old man, neither do I.'

Weirder by the year

HE LED ME INTO an adjoining office. There in a corner sat the battered filing cabinet I'd seen in Doc's room at Green Swamp Well.

'Been wondering what to do with this lot. You look like you'll make more sense out of it than I'm likely to.' He glanced at my glass. 'Top-up?'

'Maybe a cup of tea? Strong and black.'

'On the way. Might check up on the little monsters while I'm at it.'

He left the room, and I opened the middle drawer. Silverfish and sand came scuttling and trickling out, closely followed by the musty odour of moth-eaten paper. The junk that most lives come down to in the end.

And junk this lot certainly was: postcards from a journey that had grown weirder by the year. I spent a fascinating ten minutes ploughing through it: field notes, photographs, sketches and maps, the odd crumbling geological sample, magnetic images he'd brought with him from his time at the Geological Survey.

A little eccentric Doc might have been, but his filing system was accurate and comprehensive, a mass of papers and canvas-covered notebooks, all neatly stored in thick blue folders and ordered according to topic.

I quickly saw what his goal had been: to carry out a comprehensive survey of the Fuego Desert. He'd traversed it from east to west, recorded rock types, geological ages, erosion and landforms. He'd mapped glaciers, ranges, ridges and water fields.

But over the past year, his imagination had gone off at all sorts of tangents. I skimmed through his observations on nardoo root and its potential to solve the world food crisis, sketches and samples of wild grasses that he thought could be domesticated; blueprints for an array of eccentric devices: a whistle-detonated explosive, a hat with solar-powered air-conditioning and a saucepan that stirred itself.

By the end, it appeared, things were totally out of whack and he'd decided that time was going backwards. He scribbled timelines in which the geological ages of the Earth were reversed, drew sketches of mountains sinking back into the earth, continents drifting together, lava flowing uphill. He proposed a solution to the problem of Grand Unified Theory, made sketches for a time machine—powered by tektites.

Madness. Fascinating, although more from a literary than a scientific perspective. King Lear meets Edward Lear, with a dash of Heath Robinson. But there was something missing.

'Snowballs,' I said to Wishy when he came back in with laden arms. 'You said he was obsessed with the Snowball Earth Theory, but I can't find anything about it.'

'You sure?' He lowered the tray, poured me a cup of tea. 'He wouldn't shut up about it.'

'Positive. Look at *S*—nothing in there at all. Hang on...' I took a closer look.

'Yes?'

'Feel the file.'

He ran a finger along the divider, felt the bend in the metal frame, the bulge of the sides of the folder. Observed, as I had done, the wear and tear, the pattern in the dust. Came to the same conclusion I had.

'There *was* something there.'

'Question is, did Albie take it out—or did somebody else?'

'Wasn't in the shack, I can tell you that—I cleaned the place inside out. All of his papers were in the cabinet.'

'So where is it?'

He shrugged.

I made to replace the empty file. Caught a glimpse of something—a glossy triangle of paper on the floor of the drawer. Fished it out. It was a photograph, very old, yellowing: a rocky outcrop, somewhere in the desert. A stand of she-oaks, a drift of sand.

'Recognise this place?'

He studied it. 'Pile of rocks on a plain,' he said flatly. 'Seen a few of them in my time. Nothing to distinguish it from all the others, though.' He raised his eyebrows. 'Unless...'

He went across to his desk. Took out a magnifying glass, peered at the photo. Pulled a 250 survey map from a drawer, examined it, humming and mumbling to it in a way that made it clear he thought of maps as living things.

A lot of elders I've known think the same about another sort of map, the ones they sing.

'In the background there.' He ran a finger across the horizon. 'Pretty sure it's the southern end of the Ricketswood Ranges—from the west. Did a bit of scouting around for a quarry out there one time. If I'm right, then I'd say this photo was taken somewhere in the south-western stretches of the Fuego.'

'That narrows it down—a bit.'

Not a lot, though. Still thousands of square kilometres of spinifex to choose from.

Wishy obviously knew the roads, but who knew the off-roads? Who'd be able to distinguish this outcrop from hundreds of others spread across the desert?

The Kantulyu, of course. The desert people. The mob from Stonehouse Creek, Magpie and Meg. Danny Brambles' grandparents, the couple I'd met out on the road that first day on the job.

I turned the photo over. A scribbled note: *ice rocks/ the cap carbonates/ the question of age.*

I read the words a second time: they were the only remaining trace in the entire cabinet of the theory that had supposedly obsessed Doc. Ice rocks were boulders that had fallen from a frozen overlay of ice above; whether or not they supported the Snowball Theory depended on their age, and the strata in which they were found.

'What did Albie tell you about this snowball business?'

'What didn't he tell me about it! He was like a burst water main. Impossible to distinguish from all the other bullshit, of course. Last time I saw him...'

'When was that?'

Did Wishy look a little uncomfortable, or was it my imagination? 'Day before he died.'

'What?'

'I did mention it to your boss. I was coming back from Alice, popped out to the shack. I'd do that every so often, see how he was getting on.'

'And how was he getting on?'

'Shithouse. Crankier than ever. Confused. Used to try to persuade him to come in and stay with us, but I'd given up by then: would have had to drag him in by the scruff. Rough bloody set-up he had there, but it was what he was used to. And he had his rocks out back, of course.'

'Ah yes, the rock pile in the yard—I was going to ask you about that. Do you know what he was up to there?

'I asked him about it, sure—he was wearing himself out throwing a lot of rocks and mud together. I presumed it was part of his ongoing obsession with the Fuego—trying to solve some geological riddle or other. When he was with the Geo Survey, he was always making models. Do it with computers nowadays, of course, but Albie said you had to feel the geology with your hands. I must admit he was pretty bloody hush-hush about this one, though. He'd get this furtive glimmer in his eyes...'

'Furtive?'

'Paranoid, almost.' The second time I'd heard that said about Doc. 'What he was afraid of, god knows. Then he'd start rabbiting on about nardoo root or Greek philosophy or whatever was—*ooohhff*!' Wishy picked up the tennis ball that had just landed in his crotch, and traced its flight path back through the window.

I stood up; the crowd outside was growing thicker by the minute.

'Looks like they're trying to tell us something.'

'I'm surprised it was just a tennis ball—and that the window was open.'

I made my way to the door. 'Better give em a bit of a knock before dinner.'

Hit for six

WHILE WISHY AND I had been talking, the twins had organised the cream of the neighbourhood—among them a possum-eyed charmer in a crimson dress, a tall boy on a short horse and a hotwired kelpie—into a cricket team.

The younger of Wishy's sons was pushing a roller up and down an ant-bed pitch, the other was organising fielding practice.

'Where's Simone?' asked Wishy.

'Where do you reckon?' moaned Tiger Lily. 'Simmie!'

Everybody's eyes turned skyward, and the pallid face of the older daughter emerged from the tree-house.

'Can't a person ever get a bit of peace and quiet around this madhouse?'

'Come on, Sim,' said her father. 'Can't spend your life with your nose in a book.'

Spend her life with her nose in a book seemed to be exactly

what Simone wanted to do, but she was eventually persuaded to join in the game. More or less. She took up a fielding position on the fence and lowered her book only when the ball was in her immediate vicinity. She was wearing a long blue dress that failed to conceal her spindly legs.

As guest of honour I was invited to bowl the first ball. Tiger Lily took strike, eyed me hungrily. I lobbed a gentle lollipop at her—she was, after all, not much more than a toddler—and she let fly with full-blooded slog that sent the ball rocketing past my ear.

'Six!' she yelled. A grin, a contemptuous, told-you-so gleam in her eyes.

The kelpie dashed off after the ball, dropped it, slobber-coated, in my hand then bounced around trying to snatch it back.

My father, the mystery spinner from Green Swamp, might not have given me much, but he had taught me how to bowl. I upped the ante with my next delivery, a googly that would have taken her off-stump if she hadn't jumped down the pitch, met it on the up and lofted it into the coolibah.

'Nother six!'

Again, the dog. Again, the slobber and bounce.

I opted for a change of pace, and sent down a quicker ball—which was dispatched with a rattling cover drive. The ball shot across the outfield, ran up the veranda steps and startled another dog, a yellow one dozing by the door.

'How old did you say this kid was?' I grumbled to Wishy as I walked back to bowl the next delivery.

'Seven, last time I looked. Shit!' The ball had come fizzing back down the pitch, clunked into his ankle, and ricocheted into the outer. 'Maybe eight...'

'What did you raise her on?'

'Raised herself—Coco Pops, mainly.' He ceased hopping, rested his hands on his knees. 'Getting a bit old for this bloody game.'

I decided I was too; figured it'd be safer fielding to the little monster than bowling at her. Soon afterwards I found myself diving for a ball that bounced off the pony boy, cut back at me and crash-landed in a pile of boxes and rocks by the garage door. I took a moment to collect myself. As I climbed onto my knees, I glanced at the rocks, wondering why they looked familiar.

'Albie's rock collection,' said Loreena, who was weeding the garden nearby.

'Wishy brought em in?'

'Been at him to move the wretched things—breeding place for snakes, if nothing else.'

'Be happy to move em if you could tell me where to put em,' said Wishy, coming up behind us. 'No room in the house. Couldn't just dump em in the corner like Albie did.'

As I retrieved the ball, I shifted one of the rocks aside, then paused, my attention caught by a dull green seam running through it.

'Interesting,' I commented, picking the specimen up for a closer look.

'Oh?' asked Wishy.

'Native copper, I think. Dad's got a few pieces.'

'Worth anything?'

'Don't think so, but you oughta get somebody to look at the collection. Might be something useful in there.'

Wishy's eyebrows curved. 'Been hoarding this stuff all his life, Albie. Didn't give a rat's arse for what it was worth—just interested in the geology.'

'Maybe, but you never know...Dad sells the odd thing to a dealer in Melbourne. Feller by the name of Dale Cockayne.'

'Cocaine?—just what is it he deals in?'

'Anything mineralogical. Don't have a number, but if you googled him...'

'Watch it!'

The ball was coming in at head height, hard and fast. I threw up a hand. Managed to deflect it back towards Wishy, who, with a reflex remarkable for a man of his age, rolled to his left and caught it a whisker from the ground.

Tiger Lily departed with a glare and a grudging admission that the catch wasn't bad. The Time Bomb swaggered to the crease, and she was worse. Just as aggressive, but more cunning, bristling with sneaky little cuts and pull shots that had us scurrying about like hamsters, until her stumps were finally rattled by one of the boys.

Simone was gradually persuaded to take a more active part in the game, although she was nowhere near as athletic as her siblings. They all seemed to make subtle allowances: when she gathered up the ball, the intensity of the game ebbed a little, when she had the bat, the bowling slowed. There was even a gentle lob from one of the brothers that fell sweetly into her hands.

I thought, as I had at the funeral, what a finely tuned unit this family was—how intimately they knew each other's strengths and weaknesses, how much accommodation they made for one another.

So when Simone swooped at a ball, then stumbled and lay on the ground for a moment, gasping, I wasn't surprised that they decided it was time to up stumps. Simone disappeared inside the house. The neighbourhood kids dispersed, the twins beguiled me into a game of canasta that ended up in a rugby scrum. The boys fired up a barbie under the ghost gum while Wishy and Loreena prepared dinner at the kitchen bench.

I watched them together. Unsurprised to see how well they worked: one would hand the other a knife or piece of food without looking and let go, confident that the other was there. The space between them was familiar, intuitive territory.

The meal was good—heavy, old fashioned, heaps of spuds and onions, not a scrap of bok choy or rocket in sight—the company better. Simone had gone missing but various members of the family disappeared from time to time bearing plates of food, most of which seemed to come straight back.

When it was time to leave, I went inside to grab my hat. As I walked out over the veranda, I came across the older daughter resting on a couch—positioned, I noticed, in a manner that gave her a clear view of the family gathering.

I thought she was asleep, but as I slipped past, I saw that her eyes were open and focused on me.

'See ya later, Simone.'

'Bye.'

'Feeling better now?'

'Much better, thank you. You'll have to excuse me. I'm feeling a little tired. All this heat...'

There was a lantern at her head, a mosquito coil at her feet and, in her hands, a book—which she self-consciously flipped over as I drew near. A natural reaction for these parts. Books tend to be regarded as enemy despatches, readers as fair game.

'What are you reading?'

She hesitated, cautiously turned the book over.

'Emily Dickinson,' I read, surprised. A battered, moth-eaten paperback edition, one that had done a lot of miles.

'Do you know her?' Wary.

'*Because I would not stop for death...*'

I broke off. They were the first words that had sprung into my head, but there was something about the scene—the girl's pale, hollow cheeks, the intensity with which she clutched those cut-glass meditations on mortality—that sent a chill through me.

'You read a lot of poetry?' I asked.

'Mainly this.'

'Guess that's enough; they don't come any better. Where'd you get it?'

The ghost of a smile. 'I found it—years ago—in a roadhouse

in Longreach. In the toilet, actually. I felt guilty, taking it. I wondered if somebody hadn't left it there to inspire travellers. You know, as they set off on the journey.'

I grinned. 'Nah, you did the right thing. Longreach? They would have wiped their arses with it.'

She studied me. Didn't quite manage to suppress a small bubble of laughter. 'You seem to be an unusual person...'

'Mostly unusual persons, aren't we? When you get up close.'

'Maybe. But...I was watching, the way you look around, like you're hungry, taking everything in. Even a simple game of cricket.'

'Nothing simple about cricket when your sisters are playing it.'

'Of course there is—all that clash and batter. But not you.'

'Thought you were looking at your book.'

She ignored that. 'If I had to speculate, I'd say you were look-ing for something. I wonder what?'

I heard a throat clear behind me, turned around. Wishy was standing in the doorway, his face a rocky escarpment even Doc would have had trouble reading.

'I'll be on my way then.' I was suddenly uncomfortable.

As I stepped off the veranda, I paused, turned back to the girl on the couch.

'Hey Simmie...'

'Emily?'

'*I started early, took my dog,*
and visited the sea.'

The gloominess of the first lines I'd thrown at her seemed an unfortunate note to leave on.

Her face became radiant. 'You'd have to start awfully early to get to the sea from Bluebush, dog or no dog.'

'Wait long enough, the sea'll come to you. Your Uncle Albie knew that.'

'Good bye, Emily Tempest.'

'Be seeing you, Simone.'

Wishy walked me to my car; I almost had the feeling he was marching me to it.

'She's a nice girl, that.'

'She is.'

'You've got a lovely family.'

He nodded. 'I'm blessed.'

And yet, I thought to myself as I drove away. There's something there I can't quite put my finger on.

Office politics

I PULLED INTO THE police station car park, parked the Hilux next to a beautiful new police Landcruiser. It could only have been Cockburn's; any car like that coming into the region always went straight to the top.

I wasn't the vehicle's only admirer. Jukut and Nyayi, a couple of patch-and-baggy-pants boys from the Sandhill Camp, stood marvelling at it, the dazzle of its paintwork, the breadth of its technology. Even from the outside, you could tell the car had every accessory known to automotive engineering: spotties and PTO winch, snorkel, alloy wheels and bull-bar. Inside, god knew: Cockburn probably had a squash court in there.

Jukut made the mistake of pressing his nose against the glass. The moment he did so, a window in the station flew open and the senior sergeant's head appeared.

'Oi! You! Get your filthy hands off that vehicle!'

The kids disappeared; some primordial guilt made me want to join them. Seconds later Cockburn himself came out, moving like a man lunging at a well-placed drop shot.

He made a careful inspection of the window, then gazed up and down the street, searching for the dirty little bastards who'd violated his space. He pulled a shammy from his pants and began polishing.

He paused; his gaze fell on my pickup. He realised I was in it.

He flushed, thrust the rag back into a pocket, strode inside.

I gave him a few minutes. He was at the front desk, animatedly chatting to Harley and Bunter. Trail and Flam, two other constables, wandered in from the cells, where they'd been depositing a couple of smack-in-the-mouth drunks.

'New car, sarge?'

'Acting superintendent now, Emily. Paperwork came through this morning.'

'Congratulations.'

'So it's "sir" now thanks. And yes, the car came with the position. Managed to pull a few strings in Darwin. Just telling the lads: it's got the latest twin turbocharged V8 diesels. Ought to be the fastest thing on the road.'

He sounded so enthusiastic I couldn't bring myself to remind him how much of our work was off-road.

'Nice. Reckon I'll ever be allowed to drive it?'

'When you get to acting super.'

I smiled. 'Shouldn't take long then. What's the latest on McGillivray?'

'Couple of months. At least.'

'He's gone across to Queensland,' put in Griffo. 'Brother's place at Nambour.'

'Well, that ought to get him back on his feet—all that saltwater and sunshine.' I turned to Cockburn. 'Gotta moment, boss?'

'Sir.'

'Right. Sir. Wanted to talk about something.'

'Always got a moment for you, Emily.' He glanced at the boys, shared something that wasn't quite a smile. Suddenly I felt small and outnumbered among these burly white males. 'Maybe in your office...?'

He waved an arm at the room. 'Open door policy—key to a successful team.'

'I'll remember that for the post-its. When I get to acting super.'

His eyes narrowed.

'It's about this Green Swamp death...'

He tensed, ever so slightly, leaned back against the desk, crossed his arms. 'Yes, Emily?'

'I know the evidence against Wireless looks bad...'

'Bad? Irrefutable from where I stand. But it's out of our hands now: prosecutor'll take it from here.'

I took a deep breath.

'I think we need to examine it more closely.'

'Christ, Emily, couple of miners fighting in an isolated shack, one ends up with a pick in his throat. How close do you want?'

'I'm not saying he isn't guilty, but there's...there's something wrong with the whole set-up. It just doesn't feel right.'

'*Feel* right!' The words weren't just dripping with sarcasm, they were pissing it out, like he'd punctured an artery in the spleen. 'Probably didn't feel too good for the poor bastard on the other end of the pick, either.'

'There's just too many unanswered questions.'

'Unanswered questions!' he snorted. 'I can't remember a case where there's been *less* unanswered questions. There was nobody else within a bull's roar.'

'You'd hear a bull roar from the hill behind the shack.'

'Ah yes. Your killer in green cotton. Or maybe it was a dingo in a matinee jacket now?' The rest of the office shared a smirk.

It was the smile that did me.

'Yep, the Territory police covered themselves in glory that time, didn't they. You want Wireless to go down like Lindy Chamberlain?' My voice kicked up a gear. 'Somebody was up there spying on him. Well, why? Don't you think we oughta find out before we start cooking up a death sentence for the poor old bugger?'

Harley snorted. 'Death! He'll be out in a couple of years, soft-cock courts we gotta work with.'

I turned on him. 'You saw Wireless when they shuffled him away. He'll be the next funeral we go to.'

'Fucked if I'll be going to it; still haven't forgiven the old bugger for putting us through that fuckin weather the other day.'

'*You* couldn't handle the heat—you reckon our so-called witnesses were any better?'

Cockburn twisted his watch—and what a watch it was, all galloping hands and golden wheels. 'All you're doing, Emily, is muddying the waters. Might even stir up enough mud to get him off, Legal Aid gets wind of it. But is it going to change the basic facts? I don't think so.'

'Fact's an elusive thing, this part of the world. Sir.'

He looked like something nasty had fallen out of a tree and landed in his lap. Sighed heavily, popped a stick of spearmint into his mouth, made to go. 'Unless you can come up with fresh evidence...'

'Maybe I can.'

Five sets of eyes homed in on me.

'What?' Cockburn growled.

'Doc was researching the geology of the del Fuego Desert.'

'He did have a lot of it piled up in his backyard.'

'That was part of his research: the rocks were a model.'

'Model of what?'

'Not quite sure, but I do know he was investigating one theory in particular—known as Snowball Earth.'

'Snowball?' His gaze flitted to the window, through which a glimpse of the desert beyond the town boundary could be seen. 'Sounds relevant.'

'His research centred on a rock formation out west.'

'Fascinating. And this proves...what, exactly?'

'Well, I don't suppose it proves anything, but I went through his files, and any reference to the site or the theory has been systematically removed. You can see there was a file that had...'

'What do you mean, you went through his files?' Cockburn peered at me suspiciously.

I took a deep breath, wondered if I was going to be in the shit. 'I went and spoke to his brother.'

Cockburn glared. 'You what!'

I was.

'He told me...'

Cockburn turned on his heels. 'My office. Now!'

I glanced back at the rest of the team, all suddenly engrossed in paperwork.

What happened to the open door policy, I wondered as he closed it behind me.

He turned to face me, his blue eyes blades of ice, his mouth taut. Motioned me to a chair.

'I'm right, thanks.' Fight or flight—both easier on my feet.

'Siddown!'

I sat.

'Let me get this straight. Despite clear instructions to the contrary, you've been pursuing this matter on your own?'

'Well, I...'

'Harassing members of the victim's family?'

'I wouldn't call it...'

'Mister Ozolins isn't some drunken cobber of your old man's:

he's the regional manager of a government department.'

'What does it matter what he...'

'Blundering about in a manner which may well compromise an ongoing investigation. All of this without informing your superiors or co-operating with your colleagues in any way.' He leaned in so close I copped a blast of spearmint. 'Do you have any idea at all what your role in this region is meant to be?'

'Something to do with upholding the law?'

'You're meant to provide liaison between us and the Aborigines. Liaison: fancy word, but I hear you got a degree.'

He'd heard wrong—started three, finished none, the story of my life—but right now the shortcomings of my CV were the least of his concerns.

'It means talking to people,' he continued. 'To *your* people. Explaining the law to them. Trying to persuade them not to stuff a dozen brothers into the back of the pickup truck when they're running home from the boozer. Getting the kids to go to school. Maybe even gathering a bit of dirt on which of them's responsible for the epidemic of drugs and break-ins that seems to underpin the economy of this town.' He was warming to his theme, his voice rising but tightly controlled, his face as hard and sharp as a chisel. 'What it *doesn't* mean is sticking your bib in every time some whitefeller breaks the law north of Alice.'

'But I...'

'Your actions could allow a killer to go free. There are protocols, procedures, points of law, none of which you know anything about.'

'Protocols? Procedures? Is that as far as you can see?' I found my mouth shooting into overdrive, something it does all too easily. 'Are you a cop or a bureaucrat? If it's the latter then you oughter stay behind the desk and leave the policing to somebody else. And if you think you're a cop, maybe you could take a leaf out of your predecessor's book.'

'My predecessor.' His nostrils stiffened. 'That would be the feller let his head get smashed in by a geriatric cripple?'

'He dropped his guard for a moment. But he knows the job and he knows the country. Knows when to act, when to watch and wait. There are things out here you have to grow into. You and your protocols and points of law—there are protocols and points of law out there more subtle than the eye can see. Whitefeller eye, any rate.'

'Look Emily, you're talking black law? No worries.' He shifted the gum inside his mouth. 'That's got nothing to do with...'

'But it does. Don't ask me how or why, it just does. That Law's evolved over Christ knows how many years—or Christ doesn't, actually, cos it's older than He is—it affects everything.'

'Oh don't give me...'

'That's what's been bugging me about this business ever since Green Swamp. That's why I've been sniffing round, why I went and spoke to the brother. Something's out of place. Something's wrong. I know it is. I can feel it.'

'I'd say everything's out of place from your perspective.'

We locked eyes. 'What's that supposed to mean?'

'I mean when you've got a chip the size of a dump truck on your shoulder, maybe it throws your sense of perspective out a little. You're complicating a perfectly straightforward homicide investigation.'

'Bunch of blokes flashing a video round a cabin? There hasn't *been* a homicide investigation.'

He rose from his seat, went over and stood by the window, put a hand on the frame. His neck pulse became visible. I could almost hear his teeth grinding. He glanced at the door, wondering how this was going down with our audience. 'Are you questioning my competence?'

'I'm sure as hell questioning something—reckon that'd be a reasonable place to start.'

He turned, took a couple of steps towards me. 'Don't think I didn't have you sussed out first time I laid eyes on you.' His voice grew hard and sharp. 'All this earth-my-mother bullshit.'

I heard myself yelling, saw his face loom large, my fist slam into the desk: never use the word 'mother' to taunt somebody who hasn't got one. 'First time you laid eyes on me? Before you even knew I existed, you mean?'

This wasn't how I'd meant the discussion to go, but right now my genes or hormones or some other unstoppable bloody force of nature wasn't giving me much choice. 'Colour of my skin'd slot me into the fuckin box for you, you white prick! *Sir.*'

I stormed out of the office, past the studiously heads-down constables. I could sense the gawks and grins as I slammed the door.

I jumped into the pickup, hit the bitumen, charged out to the Watchtower, flat-chat. Not much chance of a speeding ticket today: every cop in the district was back there sniggering at my humiliation.

I sat in the cab glowering, fired up a smoke with trembling fingers. Scrawled Cockburn's face in the dashboard's dust, then smashed it with the palm of my hand. The smug, smarmy bastard. Deaf to anything but his protocols and points of law, his big fat car and his pissy little post-it notes, so stupidly sure that he had all the answers.

As if.

'Cockburn, Cockburn…' I muttered to the wind. 'You know fuck all.'

I'd been away, sure, but I knew this country: I knew its people, crazy and sane, I knew its cracked landscape. I understood the way the two intertwined.

Something was amiss. Out of place. I could feel it in my bones. I'd first suspected it that morning on the road to Green Swamp: I remembered that strange, stomach-churning sense I'd had of something moving beyond the horizon. And it was still there, buzzing away in some dim-lit corner of my brain, driving me out onto the edge.

My blood was just off the boil an hour later when I headed back to town. As I cut through the back streets, I passed the government housing area. Couldn't help but notice the new police Cruiser squatting in the driveway of the most anal house in the street: viciously manicured lawn, pesticide splatter-marks, pot plants lined up like a police academy parade. Even the driveway had been blasted with a fire hose.

Cockburn, for sure. He'd been washing the car, even though it was brand new. Venting his spleen on an automobile. That'd be right. I allowed myself a brief smile: maybe I was getting to him as much as he was getting to me.

The blinds were drawn, the air-conditioner roared from the roof.

Cockburn at ease: the prospect beggared the imagination. I knew nothing about his personal life, but could imagine the officious prick sitting in there getting his rocks off on pornos. Or sixties musicals. Working out on the home gym, polishing the trophies, stringing the racquets.

Fuck him, I wasn't finished yet. If I was going down, it might as well be in flames.

I hit the brakes, dropped a U-ie, pulled into the curb, went up and thumped on the door.

Coontown

A TEENAGE BOY ANSWERED. Maybe fifteen years old. He had a basketball in his hands, a surly expression on his face, a neat, athletic build. Shoulder-length, ice-blond hair.

Kids. Shit. I hadn't thought of that. Cockburn had a family.

The boy looked as surprised—and as pleased—to see me as I was to see him.

'What do you want?'

'My name's Emily Tempest. I work with your old man. Is he in?'

He gazed at me blankly, then turned away without a word. Obviously a graduate of his father's charm school.

I heard him calling from somewhere round the back of the house: 'Dad!' Then a string of furious whispers, among which I thought I heard the word 'coon'.

A woman came to the door. Thin faced, bottle blonde, pretty

in an anaemic way. Lippy and liner, lycra top, running shoes. Was everyone in the family a bloody jock?

'I'm sorry. You must be Emily.' She ran a nervous hand down a taut thigh, glanced back over her shoulder. 'I'm Kerry Cockburn. Bruce won't be a moment.'

We stood there awkwardly as the conversation out back grew more intense. I found my eagerness for a fight evaporating fast.

'Don't want to disturb you.'

'It's no trouble, really—he knows you're here.'

'Maybe I could come back later...'

'No, please, come in.' She ushered me into a spotless living room. 'Can I get you something to drink?'

'Thanks. Glass of cold water'd be lovely. Bloody hot out there...'

Bloody hot in here too, if the argument between the Cockburn males was anything to go by. When Kerry disappeared into the kitchen, I pulled back a blind, glanced out into the backyard.

Cockburn was standing on the patio, legs squared, veins popping, anger twisting his mouth. He was wearing crisp shorts and a fluorescent green singlet, blue thongs. He had a spray can in one hand. Looked like the altercation had interrupted his daily slaughter of the weeds.

His son stood in front of him, and the pair were having words. More than words: fingers were being pointed, fists clenched. There were old battles being re-fought here. Despite his wife's assurances, it didn't look like the acting superintendent would be joining us straightaway.

I couldn't hear much of what they were saying over the air-conditioner, but suddenly the boy exploded: 'Family! What kind of family do you call this! You drag us here to some dirty coon town where the air's so hot you catch fuckin fire just walkin down the *street*...!'

'How dare you talk like that to your father?'

'Father!' The boy spat the word as if it were a curse. He spun round, began to walk away.

'Jarrod! You stop right there!'

He did pause, but only for long enough to fling the basket-ball at his father; Cockburn threw up an arm, deflected it into a window. Glass splintered and flew.

Cockburn looked up, caught my eye. I lowered the blind. I heard a screen door slam, and the boy stormed through the house. As he passed the open doorway he glanced at me, his features distorted with rage.

Not at me, I intuited: at his martinet father and the one-pub, two-horse shit-hole of a town he'd forced his family to live in.

Coon town? Maybe it did have something to do with me.

Jarrod burst out the front door, his long arms quivering at his sides, stomped off down the road.

I shifted nervously, wondering how the hell I was going to extricate myself from this mess. I'd come here looking for a fight, but not this one.

Moments later Cockburn was standing there, head scarfed with scowls. He gazed at the door, simmering, then turned to me.

Shit, was I going to cop it now?

'I'm sorry,' I was amazed to hear him murmur. 'Sorry you had to hear that.'

I groped around for a response. 'No need,' was the best I could come up with.

'You're a visitor to my home.'

'Uninvited.'

He thrummed his fingers on the wall, seemed not to know which way to turn. 'Teenagers…' He tried a diplomatic smile, but it was a pathetic effort.

'Tell me about it,' I commiserated. I couldn't help myself; the man was suffering. 'Doesn't seem that long ago I was having that kind of scene with my own old man.'

Cockburn seemed lost for words. I was seeing a side of him I hadn't seen before: the ill-at-ease, captain-losing-the-crew side.

'I guess Bluebush is a bit of a let-down after Queensland,' I added. 'All those beaches, all that blue water.'

'That other thing…you heard what he said…'

An excruciating silence, broken only by the rattle of the air-con.

'He's just a boy,' I said.

'He's never heard that word in this house. Not from his mother, not from me.' He paused, drew a hand across his cheeks. 'Whatever you might think.'

'Would have heard it in plenty of others; don't have to slit your wrists. Don't you want to go after him?'

'He usually comes back by himself.'

'He's done this before?' I thanked the Lord I wasn't a parent.

Cockburn walked over to the door, gazed out through the dark mesh. He stood there, hands on hips, jaw working at a piece of gum.

'Sort of—he's at that age—has to challenge everything.'

If you run your home anything like you run a police station, I thought, I'm not surprised. Did they communicate by post-it note?

Out loud I said, 'Yeah—I can identify with that,' and shrugged. 'Not happy with anything, and when things change not happy with that either.'

'He did have it pretty good over in Rockie. Even if he didn't know it…'

I looked out the window, out onto the sad, sunblasted streets of Bluebush. Not much to see. A dog struggled against the tide of heat, tongue lolling; it bunched up, dropped a jobbie on the pavement. A mad-looking fellow in lycra jogged past. Walked past, to be strictly truthful, but moving as if he meant it. Poncing down the road like he had a duck shoved up his arse. The other side of the drain offered a panoramic view of the Drunks' Camp.

I tried to imagine what it would be like for a fifteen-year-old boy, finding yourself in this pissant town after all that Queensland tropicana. Found myself thinking back to my own tearaway years, the monthly rage, the river of tears, the sublimated grief for my mother.

'You know,' I said, 'whenever I got the shits and took off… which was often enough…there was always a part of me wanted my old man to come and find me.'

Cockburn raised his head.

'It was like a test,' I elaborated.

'Test?' His teeth clenched. 'I'll give him a test. He's not coming back into this house until he apologises.'

'Your house, your rules—never big on apologies at our place. But looking at me and Dad from a distance, I reckon I was daring him. Trying to see how much he cared.'

Cockburn caught sight of his wife, hovering nervously around the kitchen.

'I'm only saying what it was like for me.'

He steepled his thumbs, rocked back and forth, distractedly.

'And did he?'

'Did he what?'

'Find you.'

'Eventually.' I smiled curtly. 'Didn't want to make it too easy for him.'

'How do you get on with him now?'

'Motor Jack? Quirky old bastard. Couldn't imagine the world without him.'

He rested an arm on a display cabinet—bristling, I couldn't help but notice, with squash trophies; at least I'd been right there.

'McGillivray told me a bit about your background. White bloke, isn't he, your father? Some station out on the plains?'

'Back then? Moonlight Downs, yeah.'

Kerry appeared in the doorway, water glasses in hand, gave one of them to me. 'Had its hairy moments, growing up out there, I'd imagine.'

'Mate, sometimes I thought it was gonna kill me. Trying to work out where I fitted in. Whether I was black or white. Whether I wanted to conquer the world, or cut and run. Dunno if I ever threw a basketball through the window, but I did the Moonlight equivalent—heaps. Plenty of fighting sticks flying round the camp when I was in it. Jack was usually there to pick up the pieces.'

Cockburn and his wife glanced at each other.

'Mind you,' I added, 'he had to know where to look.'

I took a sip of water; ice tinkled and clinked. Cockburn ran his tongue around his cheeks, like he was searching for the spearmint.

'Come on,' I said. 'Must be a lot easier in town than out bush—I had a horse! My poor old man had hundreds of square miles to cover.'

'The sports ground,' suggested Kerry. 'Spends half his life down there, Bruce, shooting hoops, running up and down. Him and Crimsy and the others.'

'Huh!' grumbled Cockburn. 'Crimsy!'

'At least he's a friend, Bruce. Not what you'd call a respectable family, but...'

'His father's a crook!'

Her voice shivered in response. 'His father's a boilermaker, Bruce, with an ancient conviction for receiving stolen goods. And frankly, where would Jarrod be without him? Him and the others. The boy needs friends.'

There was a protracted silence, broken only by the tapping of Cockburn's foot on the floor. He cracked his knuckles and sighed, then turned, slowly, began to walk towards the door. Picked up a red baseball cap and pair of shades from a table. As he went out he paused, tilted his head back at me.

'What was it you wanted, Emily?'

'Not sure if now's the time...'

'This about Green Swamp?'

'I just want a few days down there, pottering around. Maybe talk to the Stonehouse mob.'

'Stonehouse?'

'Community out west of the roadhouse. People we met at the accident the other day. I'd like to ask them about this place Doc was doing his research. They'd know, if anybody does.'

'All right.'

'Might speak to the miners as well, see if any of em can shed any...'

'I said all right.'

'All right what?'

He walked over to a key rack in the kitchen, picked out a bunch of keys. 'Get you out of my hair for a couple of days.' With the keys in hand, he was the boss again. 'Radio schedule every morning. Purchase order book in the glove box. Manual oughta tell you everything you want to know. Make sure you're watered and fuelled up. No hitch-hikers! Official business only.' He tossed the keys at me. 'And if there's a scratch on my Toyota, it's coming out of your wages.'

'I haven't seen any wages yet.'

He paused in the doorway. 'You haven't earned em yet.'

Oh Danny boy

I PULLED INTO THE supermarket, stocked up on a few essentials—tobacco, tea and tampons. As I stood at the check-out, I heard a kerfuffle going on outside: a door slamming, an angry shout, a burst of footsteps whipping round the corner.

I rushed outside, as did Merv Todd, owner of Bluebush Electronics next door.

'You little cunt!' the unhappy businessman roared in my direction.

Here we go, I thought. But it wasn't aimed at me. He came dashing past, or as close to a dash as the middle-aged gut would get him, then saw sense and gave up. Leaned over, hands on knees, gasping.

'Emily,' he panted when he saw me. 'Heard you were on the job. Thought you were supposed to control the thieving little bastards in this town.'

'Signed up with the cops Merv, not the Third Reich.'

'You recognise him?'

'All I saw was a pair of heels.'

'I'll have his hide if he ever puts a foot inside my store again.'

'Was that a mixed metaphor?'

'No, it was an iPod Touch and it was worth five hundred bucks.'

I took down the details, scouted round the usual haunts and suspects, found no trace of the stolen iPod or its stealer. Headed for home. Which, when I was in Bluebush, was my boyfriend Jojo's shack out on the Three Mile.

As I was driving out there I spotted a solitary figure beneath a bloodwood. A boy, I thought. He was leaning against the trunk and staring into the desert that gnawed at the town's edge. I drew closer, noticed a set of headphones on his ears, a silver iPod in his hands.

I pulled over, turned the motor off. So absorbed was he in his music or his thoughts, he didn't notice me.

To the west, the desert of emblems, a cycle of endless rivers and winds, of hot red hills and yellow plains.

To the east, behind him, was the town: a whitefeller whirl-wind of concrete hotboxes and shimmering bitumen racked by smelters and smokestacks, by toxic blue dams, the even more toxic bottle shops and pubs.

Between the two—framed, somehow, by these contrasting images—was Danny Brambles.

There were bits of leaf in his dreadlocks, beads of sweat on his brow. His fingers were working at the player.

I climbed down, tapped him on the shoulder.

'Danny.'

He jumped, looked at me—and at the police car I was driv-ing—nervously. Took out the phones, tried to bury the iPod in his hands.

'Em'ly.'

'Warm day.'

'Yep.'

'Merv have anything decent loaded on the iPod?'

He licked his lips. 'Er—this one mine.'

'Gotta receipt for it?'

'Receipt?'

'Come on, Danny, I know somebody just flogged it from Merv Todd. I assume that was you, but if we returned it straightaway, maybe arranged for you to do a bit of work out at the hobby farm, he might be willing to forget about it.'

'Aw, Emily...' He sighed, ran a thumb across its glistening surface. 'You know how much music they put in this little machine?'

'Some more work at the farm, you might be able to buy one for yourself.'

He scratched his head, looked like he was about to do a runner, thought better of it. Not that many places to run round here, especially from the likes of me. He gave it a last caress, handed it over.

'Where you want to go?' I asked.

He looked at the car warily, then shrugged.

'Still the same old Emily, I suppose. Maybe round me dad's place?'

Danny's father was Bandy Mabulu, a Queensland yeller-feller who'd come through years before as a guitarist with Rick and Thel's Travelling Country Band and never made it out of Bluebush. I'd been too young to know him back then but I could imagine: a glimmer in his eye, a swagger in his hips and a bedroll that had played host to half the eligible females in the district—and a good portion of the ineligible ones.

Somewhere along the way he drifted through a piecemeal relationship with Rosie Brambles, the original good-time girl.

The good times had long gone; the only thing left of their liaison was the boy in front of me.

Bandy had done most of the parenting since the day he came back to the Gutter Camp and found his four-year-old son screaming in the middle of a body-bruising drunken brawl. And despite everything, he'd turned out to be a pretty good father.

I opened the door. 'Come on, Danny.'

He climbed aboard, and five minutes later we pulled into Bandy's place—a concrete bomb-shelter in Bleaker Street. A huddle of deflated figures were stretched out in the shade of a candelabra wattle. Some of them stirred as we approached. A couple hauled themselves to their feet—alarmed, presumably, by the vehicle—and shuffled away.

Cowboy Coulter came lurching round from the back of the house wearing dirty blue jeans and an ugly smile; took umbrage at the presence of some poor sod in one of the bedrolls and began kicking the crap out of him.

The said sod looked like copping a terrible hiding, but got his act together sufficiently to climb out of the blanket and fight back. I recognised him: Jimmy Grimshaw, a featherweight whitefeller, notorious for his sneaky drop-kick and his merciless tackle-grab.

Jimmy, uncharacteristically, went straight for Cowboy's throat, and the pair of them disappeared in a cloud of flowers and dust. I was desperately trying not to remember that I was a cop of sorts, and presumably meant to do something about such disturbances.

Danny's father emerged from the house. He spotted us, dragged the combatants to their feet and sent them on their respective ways with a couple of well-aimed kicks. Came over and shook his son's hand.

'Danny boy. Emily.'

'Bandy.'

He was wearing khaki shorts and a shark-tooth necklace; his powerful arms were a jungle of tattoos, blue and green. People said he had Pacific Islander blood in him. He sure as hell had something: he brought to mind the razor-eyed Tongans who haunt the doors of your nastier Melbourne nightclubs. Somewhere in his late forties, he was still a brutally handsome man.

'What was that all about?' I nodded at the departing revellers.

'Cowboy'n Jimmy? Pah! Nothing. Bit of an early morning workout.'

'It's dinner time.'

'Is it? Must be putting in some overtime.' An evil leer. 'So Em, heard you become a *const*-able...'

'Want to watch your language round the forces of the law, mate.'

'But you really are a cop?'

'An ACPO. And I oughter hand the badge over to you, way you sorted Cowboy.'

'Cowboy? He's a poddy-boy, handle him the right way.'

'I'll remember that if I ever have to drag him out of a punch-up at the Black Dog.'

He extended an arm at the open door, spoke with an odd formality. 'Could I ask you in for a cup of tea?'

'Sure. We need to talk about Danny.'

Bandy massaged his brow with his knuckles, an expression of utter weariness stealing across his face.

'You're here on business?'

'Sort of.'

'Now what's he done?'

I felt a surge of pity for the poor bastard. Years of trying to keep the mother on the straight and narrow, now the son was turning out the same way.

'Not that bad, Bandy. Nothing that can't be sorted,' I did my best to reassure him. 'Did a bit of shopping up town, didn't hang round to pay the bill.'

'Oh Danny, Danny,' he moaned, rounding on the boy. 'How many times do I gotta…?'

'It's all right,' I intervened. 'I'll be able to sort it. It's Merv Todd. I know he needs some fencing out the Happy Farm.'

'Fuckit boy!' His face grew darker. 'You been stealing from Merv? That's where I buy me amps, all me gear.'

'Had a gig last night, did you Bandy?' I glanced at the sleepers under the tree. Bandy looked like he needed some distracting, and there was nothing as distracting for him as music. 'Place seems a little hectic.'

'Ay, feller gets a few bob in his pocket and the buzzards are back.'

Bandy still did the occasional gig round town. His voice was tobacco-cracked and raspy, the fingers had slowed down—he used to do 'White Rabbit' at the speed of light, nowadays it was at the speed of rabbit. But he still had the music in him. The trouble was that he had a lot of other things in him as well, none of them likely to make him a poster-boy for the Aboriginal Health Service.

'Where'd you play, the Dog or the Dog?'

There were two pubs in Bluebush, the White Dog and its disreputable relative, the Black.

'Black.'

'Ah jeez Bandy, not the house band again?'

Random Andy Bytheway had recently come into an inheritance—word was it came by way of a midnight flight from Asia—and had taken over the Black Dog. He was trying to improve its image, to 'attract the cream de la cream' as he put it in the press release. Saturday dances, poker nights, a bit of spit and polish—polish, mainly. There was already plenty of spit. But no amount of prawn cocktails or greasy-voiced MCs could counter the vibe of fifty years' blood and vomit in the woodwork.

'They needed a lead guitar.'

'But the ethics!'

'Andy pays good money. *Real* money—unlike certain other bastards round this town.'

I pondered that. 'They make you play Bee Gees?'

He grimaced. 'Worse...'

'Surely not?'

He nodded guiltily. 'Air Supply.'

'Fuck.'

He slunk into the house; we followed. Bandy made the tea, a strong man cradling cups and pots as if they were something precious; he pulled a packet of Teddy Bear biscuits from the cupboard, blew away the weevils delicately.

A television roared in the background; a baby began to scream from one of the bedrooms. A svelte, hippy-looking white chick I didn't recognise drifted in, slipped a nipple into its mouth, lay down and fell asleep. Bandy's latest conquest, I assumed.

Danny sat on the edge of his seat, his eyes flickering uncomfortably. He nibbled his Teddy Bear, sipped his tea, drummed a rattling tattoo on the table.

'How's the Cowboys coming on, Ban?'

Bandy had been struggling for years to hold the Coral Cowboys—the world's only country-blues-Hawaiian-reggae outfit—together. The personnel changed according to who was in or out of hospital, prison or favour.

'Lookin good. Got Lefty Lovett on drums now.'

'A one-armed drummer.'

'Yeah, but what an arm—and he's still got his feet. Ricochet Geer on bass.' He caught my expression. 'You gotta problem with Ricochet too?'

'No, no.' But the Coral Cowboys might have, if he didn't get off the burglary and assault charges I knew he had coming up.

'Doin a gig down the Memo Club next Sat'dy week, Em. Why don't you come along?'

'Sounds good. Should be back by then.'

'Back from where?'

'I'm out bush tomorrow, down to Stonehouse Creek.'

'Say hello to them old people for me.' Despite his troubles with Rosie, Bandy had always enjoyed a warm relationship with her parents.

'Will do—and I should be back in time for the show. I'll put on me dancing shoes.'

'Need running shoes, keep up with Lefty when he gets going.'

I finished my tea, checked my watch. If I was going to catch Merv before he shut up shop, it was time to go. Danny followed me to the front gate.

'I'll go and give this back to Mister Todd.' I tapped the iPod. 'See if I can do a deal.'

'Yuwayi,' he murmured, then gasped and jumped as a jack-hammer roared into life a couple of houses down. A truckload of Works blokes were digging up the footpath: one on the jack, four supervising.

'Meanwhile, you stay out of trouble, okay?'

He muttered an answer, but I didn't like the restless look that flickered across his face as I drove away.

Jesus, I wondered. What is that boy on?

Three Mile

I CAUGHT MERV TODD as he was locking up, handed over the iPod, managed to persuade him to give Danny a few days' work, said we'd sort it when I got back to town. Ten minutes later I was rattling down the red dirt road that led to Jojo's shack.

Jojo's shack. The phrase said more about our relationship than I wanted it to. My park ranger boyfriend was as sweet as cherry pie, in or out of the bedroll, but we both had other things in our lives. Two serial non-committers. I still thought of it as his place, not ours. I spent most of my time at Moonlight Downs, he spent most of his out in the desert; at present he was working on the establishment of a bilby sanctuary somewhere in the del Fuego.

I turned into the drive, caught a glimpse of a figure on the veranda. My heart leapt: Jojo? I came closer. Saw a woman in a turquoise dress, and my heart settled and warmed. Hazel Flinders.

A warm embrace, a whisper. 'Em.'

'Haze.'

'You said I was welcome anytime.'

'Any and every.'

We linked arms, walked inside, chatted as I made tea.

'How long you stopping?'

'Just tonight—back out to Moonlight in the morning.'

'What brings you in?'

'Deliver some paintings. That gallery you told me bout, in Sydney...'

'Ubinger's?'

'That lady come all the way out ere to see me; she want more of my work.'

'Said she would, Haze. They know quality when they see it.' It had taken a lot of persuading. She was intensely shy about her art, but a few weeks ago we'd bundled up a few of her paintings, sent them off to a dealer I'd met down south.

'Talking about a solo exhibition.'

'Not surprised.' Hazel's paintings were extraordinary: they didn't just talk about country, they manifested it.

'She want me to come down the big smoke.'

'When?'

'Sometime.' A note of uncertainty. 'Anytime, she said. Pick a date, they'll arrange a show. Reckon I oughta go?'

Hazel: so strong and self-assured in her own world, so ill-at-ease in the whitefeller one. 'Nest of snakes down there, Haze. Tell em you need a police escort.' I nodded at the car.

She smiled, frowned. 'That's the other reason I come in. See how you're getting on in this kurlupartu job.'

'It's about to get interesting.'

'Don't like the sound of that.'

'Heading out bush tomorrow.'

Her eyes lit up. 'Comin out Moonlight way?'

'Opposite direction. Back down the Gunshot.'

'Oh?' She turned her head to the west. 'Maybe you'll catch up with that feller of yours.'

'Doubt it. Jojo's fallen in with a bunch of bilbies. Those little marsupial fuckers are seeing a lot more of him than I am.'

We parked ourselves on the veranda, cup in hand, back to back. I heard a car come rumbling down the track, and Bandy Mabulu's purple panel van pulled up in front of us. It was getting on for dark, but I could make out a figure I took to be Danny huddled in the passenger seat.

I got up and leaned against a pole. 'Bandy.'

'Em.'

He climbed out of the car, looked back down the track, a tense glance: making sure he wasn't being followed.

'You know Hazel Flinders, Bandy?'

'Sure. Moonlight girl. How are ya, Hazel?'

She grunted a reply.

'Everything okay, Ban?'

'We got a problem.'

'We?'

'Me and the boy.'

Hazel rose to her feet. 'Better leave you to it.' She went inside, clearly not wanting to get involved with police work.

'What's wrong?' I asked Bandy. 'Go back and get a plasma TV off Merv this time?'

'Worse—his car.' Bandy squirmed, watching my expression. 'It's them bloody Crankshaft boys—Danny just come along for the ride. Cops caught up with em out on Brumby Road—they made a break for the bush, but somebody must have spotted Danny. They come sniffin round half an hour ago. Didn't know nothing for sure, but thirty seconds with Danny and they'd know. Boy couldn't lie to save himself.'

'Which cops?'

'Fat one was doin all the talkin.'

Harley.

I lowered my voice. 'Bandy, I really don't know if you're doing him any favours, hiding him away like this. What if I take him back down the station straightaway, explain…'

'They'd lock him away for years! I know them buggers. He's already on a good behaviour bond.'

He strode past me, almost pulled me towards the end of the veranda. Dragging me out of earshot from the boy. I caught his ragged eyes in the window's light. 'He wouldn't survive, Em. I can *feel* it.'

'We're not talking Devil's Island here, Bandy. I don't know what else he's got on his sheet, but the worst that'll happen is a spell in the Juvie Detention Centre; half the boys in town have been there.'

'But he's not strong, Danny. Place like that, break him in half. He's been so strange lately—yellin in the night, runnin away—Christ knows what he's been takin…'

I crossed my arms. 'Had some pretty good role models, hasn't he?'

'Orright, I know. I haven't been the perfect father. And as for his mother…' He shrugged, helpless. 'But that's why I'm desperate to see he doesn't go the same way.'

I was moved by the sight of him standing there, feet squared, hat scrunched up in his hand. 'Sorry Bandy, that was unfair. You've done a great job—it's just hard for a young boy—this bloody town…'

'Like a glob of sump oil in yer throat,' Bandy nodded. 'That's why I wanner get him out bush.' He gazed at me with pleading eyes. 'Only one place I'd feel safe about him being right now, and you're heading there in the morning.'

I heard a noise behind us: Danny was standing at the foot of the stairs. How much he'd heard I wasn't sure, but one glimpse of that haunted face—you could almost see the blue lights spinning in his irises, hear the silent siren in his ears—and I was gone.

What were Cockburn's parting words?

No hitch hikers.

I wondered how he'd feel about a fugitive from the law.

'It make me nervous'

BANDY LEFT WITH A gruff hug and a warning to Danny: stay out of trouble and town. Drove back down the track in his rumbling van. When he'd gone, we stood there in an awkward silence.

'Be leaving at first light,' I said.

No answer.

'Want something to eat?'

He might have mumbled something, but food was the last thing on his mind.

We went inside, joined Hazel. Danny looked rattled and restless, shamefaced. He moved around the room, laying hands on the thick wooden beams like he hoped to absorb their equanimity.

After a while his natural curiosity kicked in and he began picking up objects from the mantelpiece—a chime I'd brought back from China, an azurite crystal, a wooden elephant—turning them over in his thin fingers. Still nervous, though; he looked like the elephant was about to trample him.

Hazel was sitting with her back against the hearth, watching. 'There's a story behind that statue,' she said.

'What's that?' he asked suspiciously.

'You tell him, Em.'

'Few years ago, I was in Thailand...'

'You been Thailand?'

'She been everywhere, boy,' said Hazel. 'Shut up and listen.'

'You seen a real elephant?'

'Seen one? I *rode* one.'

His eyebrows arced. 'How was that?'

'Wouldn't recommend it—bloody thing bolted on me.'

His jaw dropped. 'What happened?'

'Some idiot took a photo and spooked it. Jockey abandoned ship, so I did too. Jumped off plenty of horses in my time, but this was a damn sight bigger than a horse and I landed on me arse. Couldn't walk straight for a week, shuffling around Thailand like a hobbled mare.'

He laughed, the kind of spontaneous campfire outburst he might have let out in his better days.

'Come on, Danny.' I tapped him on the shoulder. 'Don't tell me you're not famishing.'

'He's a boy,' said Hazel. 'Always famishin.'

'Might have something,' the boy conceded.

Hazel and I knocked up a feed of scrambled eggs, sausages and fried tomatoes. While we were working I heard the ring of steel strings floating in through the open door.

I went onto the veranda. He'd found the old guitar I left there.

My guitar: what a joke that was. I'd rescued it from the hard rubbish collection a few weeks before, figured I'd see if I could make anything out of the old-time country songs that were forever rolling through my head. All I'd made to date was a mess of my fingertips and a couple of buzzy chords.

'Can you tune that thing?' I asked.

'Might try.'

He ran a thumb across the strings, fiddled with the heads, had it beautifully tuned before that first accidental chord faded away. Then he sat on the couch and picked away at a rolling melody in such a casual way that his fingers seemed to float over the strings.

Hazel came and stood in the doorway, listened. 'Boy, why you runnin round stealin cars when you got it in you to make a sound like that?'

We shouldn't have been surprised, given his genes.

He played some more, sent silver chains of melody spooling off into the night. When he laid the instrument aside, he seemed more settled: music did things for him. I dished up and he ate hungrily, asked for more. When we'd finished we all sat out on the steps, Danny with the guitar in his hands, idly strumming. He paused and cracked his knuckles. Stretched his linked hands overhead, dreadlocks dangling over the instrument.

Hazel went in to make more tea, came out with a sheet of paper in her hands, a puzzled expression on her brow.

'What's this?'

I looked up.

'Remember I went to Green Swamp last week? Old white bloke who died? Had a pile of rocks in his yard. That's a sketch of it.'

She tilted it, held it up to the light. 'More than a pile of rocks. Who drew it?'

'Chinese woman; some sort of artist.'

'She got a sharp eye.'

'Mean anything to you?'

She ran a finger across its rough surface, shuddered. 'I don't like it.'

'Made me feel uncomfortable too. Buggered if I know why.'

'People shouldn't oughter touch country. Stir things up. Devil things. Dangerous.'

'Maybe he had a reason. He wasn't a bad man, Doc.'

'Maybe.' She didn't look convinced, and the sense of wellbeing we'd been circling had somehow evaporated. Danny leaned over, took a long look at the picture. Seemed even more troubled than Hazel, and with good reason. The rocks were on his country, not hers. If there was a price to be paid, it would be him and his mob who did the paying.

Somewhere down by the creek a kurlunkurru called. Danny looked at me and shuddered; round here the peaceful dove carries a warning of imminent death.

He stared off into the distance, frowned.

'What that noise?'

'The bird?'

'No—out past that one—more like machine. That whistling pitch and drill...'

I listened intently, but could hear nothing out of the ordinary. He sat with one foot in the dirt, chewed a lip, studied the shivering dark like he feared it was about to swallow him whole.

We went inside. I made up a bed for him on the lounge room floor. As he crawled into it, I saw him cast an apprehensive eye around the room, the nervousness coming in like a chilling mist.

Hazel drifted off into the pure, untroubled sleep of the just. What was holding me back? The boy's anxiety. I could feel it through the wall: the sharp, shallow breaths, the stiff limbs. The silence. It was a hot night, but there was more to his discomfort than weather.

I went and stood in the doorway. He'd left the light on, and was lying on top of the bedroll; his legs were splayed, his hands over his ears.

'You okay there, Danny?'

No response.

'Danny?'

He took away his hands. 'Em'ly?'

'Yep?'

'I might move my bed outside. That okay?'

'Sure. What's the problem?'

There was a long silence.

'Danny, talking might help.'

A further delay, then he whispered, 'That clock.'

'The clock?'

'Make me nervous.'

I followed his gaze; Jojo's old green alarm clock was clunking away on the mantelpiece.

'I can shut it up.'

'Don't want to be a trouble to you.'

'No trouble.' I picked up the ancient timepiece, turned it over in my hands. How to turn the bastard off? It was a chunky monster, covered in buttons and knobs, flashes of rust. Barnacles, probably. It had been round since the Flood.

I made a frustrating exploration of the clock's gadgetry, then gave up and threw it out the window, heard it land with a clang and a tinkle on something hard. 'Fuck Jojo and his clock — it's as unreliable as he is. Anything else you want me to throw out while I'm at it?'

'Isn't he gonna be cranky?'

'Nah. I'll sort him out, the stingy bastard. Think you'll sleep now?'

'Might try.'

I went back into my room. All was quiet, then a whisper came from Hazel's side of the bed: 'That's a troubled boy.'

'Think he'll be okay now.'

I rolled and snuggled up against her, drifted off to sleep. Woke in the depths of the night knowing something was wrong. Knew, before I got up and looked, that Danny's bedroll was empty.

Jesus, what now?

I remembered the boy's comment on the road the other day, how he'd gone to Stonehouse to get away from the 'motors and wheels' of Bluebush; I thought about his 'whistling pitch and drill' tonight. Persistent mechanical noises: they got under his skin. Weird. And worrying: in his drug-and-booze-addled condition, Danny was developing an allergy to the twenty-first century.

What had set him off this time? Were there any other noises in the shack that could be bugging him?

The fridge started up: a jagged, intermittent buzz.

Shit a brick. Big ask to throw that out the window. Wasn't too keen on turning it off, either: a sausage wouldn't last five minutes without refrigeration this time of the year; milk, meat, cheese. Cold beer.

I scouted around, checked the main room, the veranda. The boy was nowhere to be seen. Had he run away? Was he out stealing more cars with the Crankshafts?

Then I heard the soft strains of the guitar: metallic sparkle-notes drifted in through the screen door. I followed the music, spotted him sitting under a coral tree on the edge of the clearing, approached slowly.

His voice came drifting in, a young boy's delicate lilt, every note spot on.

We been out in the desert, four or five days
In the wind and the weather, the midsummer haze
Worn out and torn out, battered and blown
So we turned the Toyota and headed for home

He stopped singing, picked out the melody, a sweet thing, full of curves and unexpected turns.

'Danny?'

He spun around, his big eyes flashing in the moonlight.

'Sorry Em'ly.'

I shook my head. 'Nothing to be sorry for.'

He fidgeted, random little riffs and runs on the neck of the instrument. 'Got a bit rattled. Singin helps me settle down. Didn't mean to wake you.'

'If I was woken up like that every night, I wouldn't be complaining. Lovely song. You write it?'

'S'pose so.'

'What's it about?'

'You got me thinking when you showed me that picture. Wrote that one about a trip I made with that old uncle of mine, the Jupurulla bin finish now. He used to go out bush with Doc.'

'Well it's beautiful.' I watched him for a moment. 'Think you can go to sleep now?'

'Maybe,' he replied, but his hands were shaking. By the time I made it back to bed the music had started up again.

Hazel put a hand on mine. 'You doin the right thing, Em, takin that boy back to his people.'

Stonehouse Creek

DANNY AND I SET out early, left Hazel standing in the doorway. When we crossed the town boundary, I lit up a smoke, threw some Pigrum Brothers onto the stereo and gave the massive turbos their head. The car leapt down the highway like a beast uncaged.

We reached the Gunshot Road in a couple of hours, turned west. Drove past the roadhouse without stopping.

The country grew drier, harder, the vegetation more sparse. We drove past perished cattle, puffed, primed, ready to explode. Dead trees, lonely fenceposts ringbarked by time's fire. Hot again; it was going to be hot for months.

Eventually we came to the rusty bones of an ancient Bedford truck with an arrow and the words *Stonehouse Creek* painted onto its remaining door. We followed the arrow, turned south. Spent the next three hours slogging across a slew of corrugations, bulldust and sump-crunching termite mounds.

Proper bush work for Cockburn's car. It seemed to be coping.

I was feeling anxious as we drove into the camp: somebody else's country, somebody else's dreams. Rocking up in a police car, I had to be careful not to stir up old ghosts. The last police punitive expedition swept through Kantulyu country within living memory. Those men, intent upon revenge for the spearing of a white prospector who couldn't keep his penis in his pants, rampaged through the countryside for weeks on end, killing whoever they came into contact with. Hundreds of Kantulyu died. The survivors fled in terror and ended up on the missions and settlements.

Now a handful of people wandered out to greet us. Suspicious at first—the car, I assumed—then enthusiastic, as Danny emerged. He drifted off to join the other boys, and I found myself standing awkwardly in the middle of the community.

The most prominent object in sight was an old club lounge, the stuffing knocked out of it but the fabric a faded, evanescent blue against the white sand.

For the rest, Stonehouse Creek was the usual remote community cluster of hairy hovels and rundown shacks, with a hand pump for water and a shovel for a shithouse. But beautiful, in its own way, nestled at the foot of a sail-shaped crimson pillar and fringed by ghost gums and a dry creek.

The camp's gross domestic product consisted mainly of dogs, and an unusually gross collection they were. Flea-bitten, fly-blown, covered in scabs and scars, sick-pink, skinny bald, they raised their weary heads. Decided I wasn't worth the bother, went back to sleep.

An unholy trinity of donkeys wandered about the place: reformed ferals with wall eyes and sneaky teeth, they were furiously devouring any plant foolish enough to raise its head above the sand.

One old man—skinny, with a cowboy hat and a set of bullet-proof spectacles—rose from a card game, shot a wad of tobacco into the dust and marched in my direction, his legs wondering where the horse had gone.

'Why hello there, sergeant!' he shouted.

Excellent; a promotion already.

We shook hands, or at least palms. I only just managed to conceal my discomfort at the touch of leprous stumps where there should have been fingers.

He immediately launched into a story—as far as I could tell, which wasn't far since his English was poor, my Kantulyu worse and the twain didn't look like meeting. The narrative hopped about like a flea on a hot dog. Something about a copper, a camel and a mischievous spirit, a little hairy man much given to toying with sleepers' dreams and nose hairs who may or may not have been my interlocutor in another incarnation.

The tale could well have been the funniest ever told—certainly its raconteur seemed to think so—but after a confusing four or five minutes I began searching for an escape route.

I was rescued by Meg Brambles, who came over, limping and grinning. 'Shut up you old fool,' she laughed—a sentiment with which he expressed hearty agreement.

'It's that outfit you wearin,' she explained. 'Mister Watson used to be a police tracker—got you mixed up with some other police-man he met along the way.'

She showed me the remnants of the stone house for which the community had been named. Not much more than a tumble-down chimney now, but seventy years ago it was the residence of a Spanish missionary who'd started out on canticles and altar wine, ended up a roaring drunk and father to half a dozen little yellerfellers.

Meg drew me into the circle of women sitting under a mulga tree, and I spent the next hour or two in their company—scratching away at a scrawny garden of watermelon and grapes, lugging water from the pump, helping decipher a Wordfind book somebody had scavenged from the Bluebush tip.

I met one woman about my own age: Kitty O'Keelly, tall and slim, with deep-set eyes and generous hair, beautiful when her mouth was shut—which it hardly ever was. After listening to her round up—and on—the kids, I prayed to god she never got stuck into me.

There was one old man I sensed to be the centre of something. He was nestled under a wirewood tree, eyes half shut against the glare, legs crossed. People cast tentative glances in his direction, as if they were waiting for him to give the all-clear.

He was fiddling with a tinny cassette player from which the unctuous tones of Garth Brooks fluttered and wowed. Eventually, he climbed to his feet and hobbled over with the aid of two sticks, stooped so low you'd have thought he carried his father on his back. Danny went out and helped him in; they were close, it was clear.

When they drew near I realised the problem wasn't that the old feller's eyes were half-shut against the glare, it was that they were fully shut against the world. The poor bastard was blind. Sandy Blight they call it out here: trachoma, a disease that affects a lot of our old people.

His name was Eli Japanangka Windmill. He was wearing baggy pants and a baggier beard, a stockman's hat and a pigeon-coloured singlet. His handshake was soft, but there was a reflex energy about it that suggested he must have been powerfully built before age and affliction laid him low.

'You welcome, Missus. Where your mob from?'

'Grew up at Moonlight Downs but my mum, she come from the Gulf.'

'Saltwater country.' He nodded thoughtfully.

'Yuwayi.'

'You be stoppin 'ere tonight?'

'If that's okay?'

'Yuwayi, you welcome. Kurlupartu, innit?' he enquired.

143

'Copper? Yeah, sort of.'

He seemed to find this amusing, then said, 'Blackfeller missus one all right—bringin back this boy bilonga we.'

Giving Danny a lift had been a smarter move than I realised.

'Yeah, he wanted a bit of peace and quiet; too much trouble in town.'

'Yuwayi.' He turned his sightless eyes to the north, shook his head. 'Drink—make a man mad.'

He didn't say much more; indeed, I suspected he knew everything about me before he'd opened his mouth. But when Danny led him back to his nook, I felt like I'd been given an imprimatur.

Bodycombe

STONEHOUSE HADN'T STRUCK ME as the kind of place where visitors would be dropping in on a regular basis, so I was surprised when we heard an engine revving in the distance.

'Who's this?' I asked Meg. We were sitting picking nits out of the kids' hair.

She put a hand to her ear. 'Preacher feller—man of God.'

Sure enough a vehicle which, like the great white shark, came with its own ambience, rolled into camp. It was a massive four-wheel-drive campervan, clearly fitted with all the comforts of home. On its door, a logo lifted from a fast-food franchise and the words *Aboriginal Evangelical Fellowship*.

The Aboriginal Evangelical Fellow himself—Pastor Bodycombe, I recalled from our meeting at the roadhouse—stepped down from the cab, headed for Magpie. Gave him an enthusiastic crunch of the metacarpals and a slap of the shoulders, and proceeded to press any other flesh that couldn't get out of the way fast enough. He did the rounds Canberra-style, rabbiting on in pidgin, making a show of tasting bush tucker. Licking his lips at a witchetty grub and grinning: 'Mmmm—proper juicy one!' I wouldn't have been surprised if he whipped out the dentures and tried to stun the natives with his whitefeller tooth magic.

Even without the patronising bullshit, the very existence of the fellow, the underlying arrogance of the missionary endeavour, annoyed the hell out of me. But I held back. This wasn't my country, and giving in to the familiar stirring of my hackles would only get me into trouble.

In any case, nobody else seemed to mind. They listened politely when he gave them a reading from the Bible, lined up when he dished out the bread and red cordial. They partook of the feeble food and feebler prayers, offered each other signs of peace, mumbled their agreement when he exhorted them to thank the Lord for His gifts.

I suffered it all in silence—until the very end. As the pastor was packing away the tools of his trade, he spotted the demolition donkeys in the distance.

'Ah—God's ponies!'

'What that?' asked Meg.

'The donkeys.' He favoured us with a knowing smile. 'That animal Jesus bin ride.'

That was too much. I tilted my hat back, took a swig of tea, raised the cup at him. 'I wouldn't get too excited, padre. So did Bruno.'

'Sorry?' The pastor turned around, trying to settle on the source of this puzzling intervention. Sussed me out.

'Bruno Giordano. Figured out the earth revolved around the sun. Your mob put him on a donkey and paraded him through the streets of Rome, then burned him alive.'

He blinked. 'My mob?'

'Friars of St John the Beheaded.'

He jerked his head back. 'Hardly my mob.'

'Oh, sorry—thought you were a Christian.'

He would have scratched his chin if there'd been one to scratch. 'And you would be...?'

'Emily Tempest.'

'Have we met before?'

'Green Swamp, the day Doc died.'

A cattle prod smile. 'Ah yes, I remember.'

'I was with the cops.'

'Quite.'

The smile didn't budge, looked like it had been whittled into his face. But when he climbed back into his truck soon afterwards, he glanced back at me, and the eyes boiled with malevolence. Somebody had stolen his pissy little thunder and he wasn't happy.

Ground work

WHEN THE MAN OF God had gone, I went and sat on the ground next to Magpie and Meg. The former was using a screwdriver to tackle the encrustation of grass seeds that was stuffing up the radiator of his HQ Holden, the latter was issuing orders.

'Ah, you oughta use that brush thing!'

Magpie leaned over, extracted a wire brush from a briefcase.

'You look like a stockbroker,' I informed him, nodding at the case.

'Well I'm broke all right,' he answered ruefully. He had an appealing habit of raising a brow when something struck him as amusing. Since just about everything did, his default expression was one of happy astonishment.

I checked out his tool bag, which was actually an old map case with leather loops and a brass buckle on the strap. It was half open: I spotted a water bottle, a blue folder, a Stanley knife, a compass with the cover missing and a cloven bone. He could only have come across a bag like that at the op-shop. Or the town tip, another popular outfitting source. Magpie by name, magpie by nature.

Time to raise the real reason for my visit. 'You mob knew that old kartiya from the roadhouse—the one who passed away the other day?'

They looked serious. The old man put down the brush, poured us all a cup of tea.

'Yuwayi—we bin meet him,' said Meg. 'Doc, innit?'

'That's him. Danny told me he used to go out bush with that Jupurulla, the one who's finished up now.'

'Yuwayi—they bin make a lotta trips together.'

I was tempted to ask more, but we were treading on dangerous ground. Death brings up a battery of taboos round here.

I showed them Doc's photo.

'You wouldn't know this place, would you?'

Magpie studied it with an intense curiosity—not that that told me much: Magpie would have studied his morning cuppa with intense curiosity. Finally he stroked his little mustache and said, 'More better we show to old Windmill.'

This'll be interesting, I thought, wondering what a blind man would make of a photograph.

We took the photo over to Eli, sitting in his shelter nursing a pannikin of tea.

The two men rattled away in Kantulyu, Magpie—from what I could understand—describing the scattered rocks in the foreground, the fluted slopes, the rugged summit.

Eli scratched the ground, produced what might have been a map.

'Irinipatta,' he announced.

'Irinipatta? That's its name?'

'Yuwayi. Fire dreamin place,' said Eli. 'North-west from 'ere.'

He tilted his chin and pointed with his lips in that direction. 'Whitefeller call it...what that one?'

'Dingo Springs,' said Magpie.

'Yuwayi. That Dingo. Little bit long way.'

Suddenly I understood. Magpie knew perfectly well what the photo showed. But Irinipatta—Dingo Springs—was Eli's dreaming. Only he had the right to speak on its behalf.

'You been there, Japanangka?' I asked him.

'Foot walkin days.' He launched into a few bars of a song, tugged his beard, laughed. 'Since when I got no whiskers!'

Magpie's gaze drifted across to the Cockburn Toyota and a hungry look stole into his eyes. 'Maybe we might take you out there ourselves?' he beamed hopefully.

I sussed him out straightaway. Rediscovering traditional country was always a struggle. The environment was degraded by thirty years' neglect. Overrun with feral pests and plants, the wells grown over, many of the animals vanished. These people were mostly old, their knowledge and their bodies fading. Motor cars were as crucial a resource as spearthrowers and water carriers had ever been. The police Cruiser, with its long-range tanks, its winch and water, a radio in the dash and a sister at the wheel, was a mouth-watering opportunity.

My first reaction was, hell yes. But did I have enough fuel? I regretted not taking the opportunity to fill up at Green Swamp.

Cockburn's new toy: I shivered, examined the Cruiser nervously. A bush bash through the toughest terrain in the world was perhaps not what he'd had in mind when he gave me the keys.

Bugger it. It was still a police vehicle, and what I was doing was police business. Sort of maybe. I'd just make sure I took good care of it.

My confidence vanished when I woke up the next morning and discovered that the kids had scratched their names into the paintwork on the back door.

'Jesus,' I muttered, running a hand across the scrawl.

'Jesus' indeed—He was right there, His name hacked in among the Rufuses and Wesleys. Pastor Bodycombe had more influence in this place than I'd realised.

Swallowing my fear, I switched on the radio.

'Bluebush 350 to base. Do you read me? Over.'

'Base to Bluebush 350.' Shit. Cockburn himself. 'Morning, Emily. What's your location? Over.'

'Still out at Stonehouse Creek, sir. Over.'

'You looking after that vehicle? Over.'

I managed to skirt the issue of the paintwork enhancement, but he wasn't impressed when I told him we were heading to Dingo Springs.

'You're heading where? Over.'

'Dingo Springs. Over.'

'Where the hell's that? Over.'

'Somewhere to the west. Over.'

'Somewhere!' His irritation crackled through the static. 'What's that supposed to mean? Perth? Who are you travelling with? Over.'

I took a look at the waiting crowd: rampaging kids, old men with miscellaneous bones hanging out of their pockets. A dog with a head like a wet wedding cake wandered by, a plume of flies unreeling behind it. Good god, it had a turd-filled sock hanging out of its anus.

No hitchhikers.

'Sorry sir, you're breaking up. Poor reception area. Over.'

'You be careful with…'

'I'll try again in the morning. Over.'

'Listen to…'

I switched the radio off. The receiver shuddered, and so did I.

Nor'-nor'-west of nowhere

ANOTHER VEHICLE, A YELLOW Toyota, had come back during the night with a bleary-eyed Nipper Crankshaft at the wheel. Nipper was called that not because he was small; he wasn't. It was because when the going got rough—and it was rarely smooth—he liked a little nip of the hot stuff.

He'd picked up a couple of hitch-hikers: his nephews, Benny and Bernie Crankshaft, both nursing monster hangovers. The car was in worse shape than its occupants; the tail pipe was hanging off, the petrol cap was a pair of undies.

Bernie came to, took a while to work out where he was. He was a town man these days, a tall, powerful fellow with a shock of black hair—a walking conkerberry bush. When he found out we were about to embark on a bush trip he immediately took charge in the inimitable Crankshaft manner.

He found his rifle among the rubbish, fired off a couple of test shots, scavenged a water bottle and a clasp knife, announced that he was ready to lead the expedition.

I noticed the flicker of a smile on Eli Windmill's lips.

We set out soon afterwards, a convoy of three vehicles, maybe twenty people all up. Eli and Magpie ended up in the seat alongside me, although the hyperactive Magpie spent more time out of the car than in it.

You don't often manage highway speeds when you're grinding through rough scrub. Between the low-gear crawl and the numerous puncture stops, he had plenty of time to dart off and run down a goanna, light a fire, leap up and navigate from the bull-bar. At one stage, as we wound our way through a patch of swamp grass, he dashed on ahead, my only sight of him a broad-brimmed hat bobbing on a sea of tussocks.

Maybe it was the heat; worried about fuel, I kept the air-con off and the windows down as we growled along in low gear. Maybe it was the intensity of the Kantulyu's emotions at opening up a parcel of lost country. Maybe it was the power of the dreaming paths we were following.

Whatever the reason, the day passed in a kind of delirium, a feverish dream in which time, geography and our little band of travellers coalesced.

Eli was curled up next to me. Most of the time he seemed to be asleep. It wasn't until we'd been on the go for an hour that I realised it was he—old, blind, crippled, gasping for breath—who was running the show.

Every so often he'd stir himself to ask a question: 'Coupla big rocks up there, innit? West side?'

He was usually right.

'Go under their shadow. See that hill up ahead? Sharp point, like a needle?'

Once again, there was.

'Pawalyu. Go round about it. Up along the creek.'

Then he'd go back to sleep. We'd make subtle changes in response to his suggestions, and the other vehicles would swing in behind us.

One time we dropped down into a shallow gully and he told me, 'Turn little bit west when you see them big rock. Boulder. Jawangu n'other side that hill.'

'Which hill?'

'Southside. Where the clouds are comin up.'

He was right: there were clouds coming up over a hill to the south, but how the hell had he known that?

Danny spent most of the day beside him, his expression illuminated and loose, joyful almost, drinking it all in.

We drove all day, made camp in the middle of a radium sunset. My companions were excited and happy: one bearded old lady struck up a song, plainsang lovingly, a single tooth exquisite in her tin smile. The others pitched in, illiterate poets hammering ancient melodies: they sang canticles and star charts, hunting songs, invocations of invisible rivers. They were celebrating the return to country they'd last visited on foot.

Danny sat close to Eli, his legs crossed, his face alight. He was a town boy and young, but fascinated. Keen to learn. From time to time the blind man would tap him on the knee, offer a whispered explanation.

While they were singing, I sat by the fire, scribbling into a notebook. Determined to catch the essence of the trip while it was still fresh in my mind.

Where do we go?

Over rolling termite plains, through cracked ranges, crooked gullies, stretches of vicious scrub that scrapes our flanks and tears at our tyres.

To the edge of a lake of snow; we walk out onto it, salt crystal crunching underfoot, the noonday glare like lightning.

To the rim of a crater the size of a football field: 'made by snake, that one...' says Eli.

Up fierce red cliffs, along the ridges of vast, crescent-shaped hills.

What do we see?

A hawk falling from the sky, smoke pluming behind it.

The bones of a horse that went too far, was caught by the dry: scraps of leather and rusted metal, grinning teeth.

What do we feel?

Mostly—hot. This is a fire dreaming we're following, and that's what it feels like. The heat clings and parches, rises inside you like yeast.

What do I learn?

That the Kantulyu word for compass—warlujinta—is the same as circle, that the word for watch—warlukari—is the same as the word for sun. Both circular, both living.

And that fire—warlu—is at the heart of both.

Dingo Springs

LATE ON THE SECOND day we struggled round the south side of a range, and there it was, three or four kilometres away: the rocky outcrop from Doc's photo.

'Irinipatta,' chanted Eli. Dingo Springs.

I drove towards it slowly. The outcrop was an island of jumbled rock that glowed in the hovering sun like the fires of its dreaming. It was crystalline in the main, a mass of rhomboidal joint blocks with the odd slab of speckled ironstone on the higher reaches. The vegetation was sparse: a few figs and a bush olive, tenacious little caustic vines that clung to the grooved slopes.

We climbed out of the vehicles, walked towards the site. A pair of dingoes broke cover and dashed across the sand, vanished into some invisible declivity.

The women tore off branches, formed a line and moved around the base of the outcrop, sweeping the rocks as they approached, making their peace with whatever spirits lingered there.

A wallaby came out of the rocks, took a few awkward bounds, stood looking at us.

'Quiet one,' murmured Meg, puzzled.

Eli tilted his head in the animal's direction, his jaw stiff. 'Maybe sick?'

'Maybe.'

Perhaps because of its tameness, the distant look in its eyes, nobody seemed inclined to kill it.

The granite walls were worn mirror-smooth at wallaby height, polished; there must have been a lot of them here at some time.

I took a close look at a cutaway rock face on the eastern approach, saw at once why the place had intrigued Doc. From a geological perspective, the outcrop was extraordinarily diverse. Some of the rocks were clearly volcanic: rhyolite flows, perhaps. Yet directly abutting them were dropstones. Ice rocks, if I remembered my theory correctly, fallen from the frozen sheet that had covered the globe six hundred million years ago.

There were other seams embedded there I couldn't recognise: banded dolomites? Doc's cap carbonates, perhaps. Rocks that could only have been formed by a rapid change of atmospheric conditions to extreme heat.

Even with my limited knowledge such a diverse stratification—rocks from the ages of ice and fire in a single outcrop—seemed unusual.

But what did it have to do with the murder I'd come to investigate? Why would anybody want to expunge any reference to this place from a geriatric geologist's records? The outcrop may have pointed towards some sort of geological discovery, but who the hell would have killed him over that? Another geologist? Crazy. I'd heard of geos going hammer and tongs over competing theories, but the hammers didn't usually end up in their throats.

Was there something else here? Had Doc stumbled across a metalliferous lode, gold, platinum or the like? It didn't look like it, but I'd need more equipment than I had with me now to be certain.

I was struck by the variety of fossil evidence, much of it from the Ediacaran period. Geordie Formwood had told me about Doc waving fossils under the Reverend Bodycombe's nose when they were arguing about evolution. Was this where Doc had found them? But there were fossils all over the desert. Surely the Rev wouldn't have murdered him over evo-bloody-lution?

Another idea drifted in from left field. Could Doc have been killed for some interference in blackfeller law? God knows, it was possible. I'd made a similar mistake myself once; paid a heavy price for it. And this place was obviously an important dreaming site...

The thought disappeared as quickly as it came: no kudaichi I'd ever heard of would even be able to read Doc's notes, much less steal them. I'd come here with a group of traditional owners: they, more than anyone, would have known if a law had been broken, and yet they'd been keen to make the trip.

Magpie and Meg joined me, and together we began the climb to the summit, maybe sixty feet above ground. Half way up was a spring, a trickle of water flowing from a fissure, which created the illusion that the rocks were weeping.

I cupped my hands, was about to take a drink, when we were distracted by a call from below.

'Em'ly!'

Danny.

Eli was crawling towards us on his hands and knees, his face peeling and panicked, racked with grimaces and wrinkles. He seemed to have aged ten years—and he hadn't looked like he had ten years in him to begin with. Danny moved alongside, struggling to support him.

'What you doin, old man?' implored Meg as we helped him to his feet. 'Shouldn't oughter come up all this way on your own.'

'Somethin wrong...'

His ancient goanna claw clutched the air, frustrated, helpless. We stood there, mystified.

'Nothin wrong, Japanangka.'

He gazed into his own darkness, shook his head. 'All buggered up...Not workin...'

Magpie frowned. 'What not workin...?'

'Fire song. I don't understand.'

Meg put a hand on his shoulders. 'Please, Japanangka, take it easy.' Her voice was as soft as the desert after light rain. 'We getting old, all of us, jumpin at shadows, runnin round in circles. But we back on our own country now—right way. Young people around us, the land comin back to life...'

'But aiee...' He sighed, felt his way towards a rock, flopped against it. Tears, or beads of sweat, glistened through the stipple on his cheeks. 'Maybe just me, me and these useless bloody eyes...'

But it wasn't just Japanangka: I noticed Danny studying him, a dark cloud moving across his face. Whatever Japanangka's finely tuned radar was picking up, Danny was getting by osmosis. I worried for him. His outer layer was a delicate membrane, letting through too much of the world.

Danny led the old man back down and did his best to make him comfortable. They made an odd couple, the slight young man, the heavy-set elder. An instinct for country the link between them. And a shared sense of jeopardy and loss.

Magpie stretched his back, studied the land below. 'Track down there: motor car bin 'ere, little while back.'

It took me a moment to discern them: twin red ribbons of dirt cutting through yellow porcupine grass.

'Heading directly back east,' I said. 'What's over that direction?'

'Keep goin straight, take you allaway back to Gunshot Road. Roadhouse.'

'Maybe the way Doc and Jupurulla come out here?'

'We might have a look.'

We scrambled down the far side of the outcrop, walked over to examine the tracks.

'What were they driving?'

'That old blue Jeep bilonga Doc.' These tracks were wide, wider than Doc's Jeep would have made.

'So somebody else has been out here?'

'Look like.'

He studied the wheel marks, picked up a handful of sand, let it drift through his dirty fingers.

'How old?' I asked.

'Fresh.'

An idle thought strayed across my mind. 'Wouldn't be from that campervan the pastor drives?'

He gave the idea a moment's consideration, then scratched his chin. 'Maybe not's wide as that.'

He turned his eyes to the east, emitted a soft worried whistle, his tongue up against the stumps of his teeth.

We headed back to the cars, an uncomfortable sensation stealing over me—and, I couldn't help feeling, my companion.

What did Dingo Springs have to do with Doc's murder? And why was it affecting us all in a way that seemed so out of proportion to the deaths of two old men?

We piled the fires high that evening, but the atmosphere in camp was a far cry from the cut-glass beauty of the night before. The sky seemed darker, the stars on fire. The Kantulyu were rattled and restless. A choir of dingoes yelped from the hills, pissed off that we'd driven them from their home.

Eli sat on his bedroll, chanting softly but purposefully, pausing to sip at his pannikin of tea. Danny was looking edgy: once or twice he got up, stood staring into the darkness, nostrils aquiver. Meg said a prayer—to Jesus, praying for Him to watch over us in the night. The notion of praying to an alien god while on a journey into her own traditions didn't seem to strike anyone but me as strange.

I drifted off early, but it was a fitful sleep. I'd only just closed my eyes, it seemed, when I was awoken by a terrified scream.

Bad dreams

DANNY WAS HALF OUT of his bedroll, his thin body shivering in the moonlight, his hands clutching his temples.

Meg was already at his side, soothing with soft old hands and murmurs. Eventually the boy was calmed enough to lie back down.

'Bad dreams...' he moaned.

Meg looked down at him, her face fraught with anxiety.

'What's happenin to this boy, Em'ly?'

'Think the world's happening to him, Meg.'

'He bin smoke that Mary Jane in town?' she asked shrewdly. 'Make him little bit crazy?'

I shouldn't have been surprised; she'd have seen her own daughter, Danny's mother Rosie, ripped mindless on every imaginable substance. Meg had spent years dragging her out of drunk tanks, hospital wards and morning-after ditches. She probably knew more about intoxicants than any rehab worker.

'You name it, he's tried it. Comin off any of that stuff drills a borehole into your brain. But with you mob looking after him,' I tried for a reassuring smile, 'he'll settle down, I'm sure.'

I looked at Danny lying there, a sheen of sweat across his brow, mouth moving silently, felt a surge of affection for him. Torn by dreams and delusions he might have been, but he was trying. He'd come out bush, spent time with his elders, tried to learn their vanishing words and ways.

For a boy who'd grown up running wild on the broken-bottle and tin-can fringes of Bluebush, he was doing all right. There was something almost heroic about his efforts.

Meg had made up a concoction of milkweed and bark from an umbrella bush, worked it into Danny's brow. She placed some aromatic herbs on the fire, made him a pillow of lemongrass. Something in the herbal cocktail must have worked: he began to breathe more easily.

'We gotta look out for these young ones,' she said. 'They all we got.'

I rolled onto my back, gazed up into the deranged planetarium that was the night sky, brooded on the traps and snares that lay in wait for a child of Danny's generation. God knows, I'd been snagged on a few of them myself. It was returning to the Centre that had saved me. The way I saw it, in coming out here, the boy was searching for a centre of his own.

I realised an underlay of distant noise cushioned my thoughts. It almost sounded like a vehicle revving, but that was unlikely, out here in the middle of nowhere. Had some animal—one of the dingoes, a wild horse—started a little landslide? Difficult to tell: sounds played tricks in the desert at night, carried for miles on the stock-still air.

'You hear something just then, Meg?'

She peered out into the darkness, shook her head. 'Nothing.'

That was hardly conclusive; a lot of our old ones have damaged hearing. The prospect of another vehicle sneaking round made me strangely uncomfortable. I picked up my torch, pulled on my boots.

'Might have a quick scout round before I turn in.'

The idea made her nervous. 'More better you stay here, Nangali. Out there in the dark, little bit danger. Might be cheeky devil-devil, might be something worse.'

'I'll be right.'

But her warning resonated as I scratched around the bottom of the outcrop, then climbed to its summit. I stood on a boulder and scrutinised the dark blue plains.

Nothing: if it was a vehicle out there, it'd stopped, or was crawling along without headlights. I listened carefully, heard nothing.

I made my way down the far slope and onto the flats, the torch beam sweeping before me. Apart from the usual scuttling creatures of the night—a bat swooped, a ningaui dashed at a barking spider—all was quiet.

I turned to go, but was shaken out of my meditations when a huge mulga snake suddenly twisted underfoot, clattered off into the undergrowth.

Shit a brick!

I tripped, heart pounding, found myself tumbling into a gully. My arms went windmilling and my legs flew out. I fell into something face first. Something soft, slimy, like rotten fruit, but webbed with cutting edges and sharp points. A deeply disgusting odour crunched my nose.

I flashed the torch, gasped in horror: I'd landed in the rotting corpse of a maggot-eyed wallaby. I swivelled the beam: there were more of them in the gully, maybe a dozen, covered in a layer of dirt and white powder. Lime? I wasn't hanging round to figure it out.

I scrambled to my feet, set out running and didn't stop until I reached the camp and found the water tank. I scrubbed my hands, scoured my arms and face, rinsed my mouth, gagging, trying not to spew. More or less failing.

Magpie rolled over in his bedroll. 'You right there, Nangali?'

I spat a mouthful of gunk, avoided a direct reply. I felt reluctant to tell him about the dead wallabies; this mob had enough on their plates without worrying about some maniac cruising around slaughtering wildlife, which was what appeared to have happened. A few months ago, at Moonlight, we'd come across a gang of Bluebush meatworkers whose idea of recreation was to hunt roos from the back of a trail bike—with machetes.

'Snake, out there,' I replied. 'Bloody big one. Gave me a fright.'

He nestled back into the hat he was using for a pillow. 'You watch that one now. Might be snake, might be dream.'

He seemed pretty cool about it, but he wasn't so cool in the morning when he discovered another snake—smaller but just as lethal, a death adder—lurking under his own bedroll. He stared at the reptile, aghast, mumbled something doom-laden, then raised his voice.

'Orright, you mob, time to get on the road.'

I wouldn't have thought it possible for him to accelerate—figured he was already moving at top speed—but accelerate he did, breaking camp at the speed of light and wind at the speed of sound. Hurling our gear together and getting us out of there quick fast.

Everybody joined in. We were going home.

It was almost as if they sensed the slaughtered animals. That, or something else—maybe Eli's forebodings—had thrown a wet blanket over the journey. The high spirits of the previous day, the sense of rediscovery and return to country, had evaporated but nobody seemed to know why.

Or if they did, they weren't telling me.

Homeward bound

BEFORE WE LEFT I put in a quick radio call to base. Cockburn was otherwise engaged, thank god, and Harley was his usual taciturn self. I told him I'd be back in a day or two and signed off.

We took the short cut back to the Gunshot Road—I needed fuel, and none of us wanted to hang around. Although the fresh wheel tracks made for a smooth ride compared to our labyrinthine, puncture-packed wanderings on the way out, the mood of the party never managed to shake itself from the depths.

Danny seemed more downcast than anyone. He sat in the back of my vehicle, close to Windmill, spent the day mumbling to himself and staring out the window. His cheeks were blue, his lips cracked, his long eyelashes intertwined with goo.

The snakes, in keeping with the mood, were thick on the ground for the whole of the trip in. We spotted at least half a dozen of them, one a monster that insinuated itself into the track with a brutal nonchalance and wasn't changing course for anyone. When I drove at the reptile, trying to hurry it along, it curved into the air then lashed at our bull-bar with a viciousness that had the kids in the back diving for the blankets.

I drove round the snake, my chest pounding. Caught a flash of light from an ironstone spur to the south, saw something up there move. A head, I was sure. Who would be spying on us?

I took another look, but saw nothing. A trick of the light? Maybe, but how to account for the sudden shiver down my spine?

'Anybody else out here?' I asked Magpie.

'Eh?'

'Thought I saw somebody…'

'Where?' He twisted about.

'On that black hill.'

Magpie studied the rise, his eyes narrowing suspiciously. 'Maybe kangaroo. Emu.'

'It was a person, I'm sure. Why don't we go back and have a look?'

But they all seemed horrified at that suggestion, and I wasn't too keen on it myself. Meg sat there looking thoughtful. A few minutes later, she suggested: 'Back on that hill maybe that was Andulka you seen.'

'Andulka?'

'Jangala from Majumanu.'

'Oh, I know who he is. You reckon he's still alive?'

'He's out here somewhere.'

'I heard he had a mountain fall on top of him, Meg.'

'Might be. What's a mountain to a feller who can fly?'

I settled back into the seat, gave the matter some thought. Andulka Jangala: I'd been hearing about him for most of my life, but it was hard to tell where reality ended and myth began.

Certainly there'd been a young man of that name, and an

167

unusual feller he'd been. One of the last nomads to emerge from the desert, he was a famous nangkari who walked in with his family, twenty-five years ago. A Kantulyu man, he would have been a close relative of the Stonehouse mob.

I'd seen him myself one time when I was a kid. Never forgot him: sleek of limb and smooth of brow, he was a contemplative figure with the sky in his eyes and one foot in the other world. His dreaming was fire.

Andulka had settled into the Majumanu community, but he never overcame the suspicion of the whitefeller world that had kept him in the desert all those years. His forays into town were few and far between. He was deeply disturbed by the mining activity in the region, worried all that digging and drilling was unsettling the spirits underground. He began to spend more and more time out bush, wandering around on his own, digging out soaks, burning off rubbish grass, singing the songs that kept the country whole.

Three or four years ago, when Copperhead was reworking the old Green Saturn mine, an earthquake rocked the region. Andulka said it was a warning: he showed up at the site and made a pest of himself, poking around the diggings, tinkering with machines, arguing with the workers. They told him to bugger off, but it seemed he couldn't hear them.

Finally, one dazzling afternoon—it was before I came back to the Centre, but I heard the story from my father—the Green Saturn shot-fire crew spotted him on the crest of a hill just as they were setting off a massive chain blast. Andulka was smack in the middle of the pattern. They roared a warning, but the charge had already gone and the hill vanished.

Police rescue mob searched for days but they had no chance of finding a body with half a mountain on top of it.

'Andulka!' I shook my head, studied Meg. 'Surely we'd have heard something if he was still alive?'

'But we have,' she replied.

'Where?'

'In dream.'

'Oh yeah.'

Magpie detected the cynicism in my voice. 'N'other feller seen him too.'

'Which other feller?'

'Them Majumanu mob.'

'What have they seen?'

'Smoke. Tracks.'

'Right.' I'd heard the stories, of course. From time to time, some traveller out that way would wake to feel an unaccountable presence out past the campfire's glow, would feel he was being watched. Some wanderer picking his way down a remote gorge would hear the mysterious echo of a song that flowed like fire and whisper 'Andulka!' Some hunter would spot a smoke plume that looked man-made where no men were.

The rumours intensified, the legend grew. People said they'd seen him at the Isa Rodeo, or on the train to Adelaide. They said he could appear in two places at once, turn into a bat and fly by night, conjure fireballs and whirlwinds from thin air.

I didn't believe a word of it, but what the hell: our mob have lost so many myths along the way, I couldn't see any harm in inventing a few new ones.

Magpie gave up in the face of my relentless scepticism, nodded back at the hill, threw another hat into the ring.

'Might be that ranger feller up there...'

'Ranger?' My heart skipped.

'Wildlife.'

'Which one?'

'Oh, forget his name, but you know im, that feller from Bluebush, got the little red hat, all-a-time laughin...'

Sounded like Jojo, the prick. Running around the bush having

169

fun while I was playing with myself in a lonely bed or getting caught up in the bush bash from hell.

Magpie ran his fingers through his whiskers. 'He come through a coupla weeks ago, lookin for them bilyaju.'

Bilbies. That'd be my wandering boyfriend all right.

But there was no way that would have been him up on the hill spying on us; Jojo was a congenial character who'd pull over to say hello and end up sharing a meal and hanging on to your life story, honestly believing it was the most fascinating thing he'd ever heard.

'Wouldn't know where he was now, would you?' I asked hopefully.

Magpie gave the desert the benefit of his long, thoughtful gaze: 'Might be somewhere...'

Might be some-fucking-where! Fat lot of use that was to me; a hundred and fifty thousand square k's of dirt out there, and he could be in any one of them. And oh, I wanted him now, wanted to kiss that stupid, sleepy, reassuring grin, feel those rough hands slipping into my pants.

The gloom that had been running beneath the surface since Dingo Springs kicked in with a vengeance. Everybody felt it; even the little kids stared at the ground, po-faced, as if they couldn't wait to get back to the dirty beds and lolly water of Stonehouse Creek.

As we drew closer to the Gunshot Road, the wheel marks turned into an honest track. By afternoon we were flying along. The mood of our party, however, was far from flying, and it was a relief to us all when the track turned into a road. We drove past the old Gunshot Minefield, and soon afterwards the Green Swamp Roadhouse appeared in the distance.

Nipper went in to hassle for more credit, everybody else scattered for toilet or bar, depending on the relative condition of bladder and tongue. I refuelled the car, and was about to refuel myself when I noticed an old blue Nissan over by the well. The vehicle looked familiar. Jacob Jangala, perhaps, from Dixon's Creek?

I wandered over, had a peek at the tray. They'd be partying at Dixon's Creek tonight: there was a turkey covered in branches, a couple of kangaroos, a porcupine, a drum full of bush oranges and—I took another look—a bilby!

'Eh! What's this?' A booming voice behind me. 'Fuckin kurlupartu stealin a poor blackfeller's tucker now?'

I spun round. There was a burly stockman in a big blue denim shirt standing there. He had a Crankshaft at either side, and they all seemed mightily amused at having caught me unawares.

'Jacob!' I said, a little sheepishly. 'I was just having a look.'

He grinned. 'Nah, you're right, Em. Benny told me you been out west.'

'What's with the bilby? You're not supposed to hunt them, you know. Whitefeller law lookin after that one.'

'Mmmm—good eatin but.'

'Where'd you get it?'

'Out the Wild Tucker Sanctuary.'

'The *what*?'

'Ranger feller makin it out on Galena Creek. Markin it out with a fencepost.'

'Ranger? Which ranger?'

'Jojo.' He scrutinised the expression on my face. 'You know him?'

'Yeah, I know him—and it's not a tucker sanctuary, Jacob—they don't do take-aways. So Jojo's out there, is he?'

'Yuwayi. I was talking to him just this morning. Been out there hunting these bilyaju.'

'He's hunting them with a camera and a notebook, Jacob. The idea is to protect them from hungry buggers like you.'

He broke into a laugh, a big, disjointed affair, like a road-train

171

changing gears; Benny and Bernie made up the chorus. 'Nah, I'm bullshittin, Em. Shot a fox, had that one in its mouth. Jojo'd be grateful—fuckin foxes are his main trouble, knockin off the bilbies.'

I could see how Jojo and this rambunctious character would get along.

I looked back down the road. 'Galena Creek, eh? Where is that exactly?'

'Hour or two back along the Gunshot, north side of the road.'

He drew a sketch map in the sand, and I copied it into my notebook.

'Jacob, couldn't do me a huge favour, could you?'

'What?'

'Take my passengers back to Stonehouse?'

He gave the request a split second's consideration. 'No worries.' Never one to dilly-dally was Jacob. 'Bout time I went down—see that old uncle mine.'

'Which uncle's that?'

'Mister Watson.'

'Ah, Mister Watson. Get him to tell you the one about the copper and the nose hair.'

'I heard that one.'

'Figure out what it was about?'

'Don't think he knows himself.'

Before we went our separate ways, I had a word with Danny, who was waiting under a tree with the men.

'This is where we say goodbye.'

I was moved—and slightly worried—by the wave of anxiety that broke across his face.

'You gotta go, Emily?'

I ruffled his hair. 'Supposed to be back days ago—they'll have the cops out looking for us, and we wouldn't want that.'

'Can I come too?'

'Not a good idea, Danny—still a bit hot for you in town.'

He craned his neck, took in the wide horizon, the roadhouse, Doc's cabin across the road. He took a closer look at the rocks piled up behind it.

'Them the rocks in your picture?' he asked warily.

'They are.'

'What for that ol man pile up all them rocks?'

'Buggered if I know.'

Suddenly he seemed so young, so vulnerable. I took his hand.

'Listen up, Danny: if ever you need me, I'll be there. You've only gotta get word through—plenty of ways to do that—radio, motor car—and I'll come running. That's a promise, okay?'

He looked at me, through me, the fear receding in his eyes.

'A promise?'

'Rolled gold. Stick around with this mob for now, we need you to help these old blokes.'

As if on cue, Eli came over, put his hand through the crook of Danny's arm: his vision might be gone, but his ears were sharp, his brain sharper.

'Young feller gotta be my eyes,' he said with a broad smile.

Danny nodded, seemed reconciled to the situation. I gave them both a farewell hug, was moved to see them standing there, arms linked, as I turned and drove to the west.

Jacob flagged me down.

'Bluebush is the other way.'

'Going via Galena Creek.'

He smiled conspiratorially. 'What you doin out there?'

I gave him a wink, my spirits already on the rise.

'Gotta see a man about a bilby.'

Mister Pig's Head

I CRUISED ALONG THE Gunshot Road, shading my eyes and peering into the afternoon glare, desperately searching for the Galena turn-off. I only had another hour's light, and didn't fancy my chances of finding Jojo in the dark. The map was crap and Jacob's directions crapper.

I wasn't paying a huge amount of attention to the road, I admit—a nasty habit I've acquired since coming back out bush. Sometimes I even read while I'm driving. Nothing heavy, mind you—crime, perhaps, maybe a magazine. I'm not the only culprit, I'm sure. Meeting another vehicle out here is an event of such magnitude you tend to get out and talk about it.

So it was partly my fault that I was damn near killed. But only partly: if the other bastard hadn't come fanging round the bend in the centre of the road, we wouldn't have come anywhere near as close to colliding as we did.

As it was, a split-second glimmer in the corner of my eye made me fling the wheel to the right and go thrashing off into the gravel. The beige Toyota seemed to be ninety percent bull-bar and rubber, but its rear bumper clipped mine and threw me into a fishtail.

Somewhere in the ensuing seconds, I experienced that gut-wrenching moment of weightlessness that rises inside when you're up on two wheels and about to flip. At what felt like the last possible moment, the gods of gravity and balance reasserted themselves, and the car came crashing back onto all fours.

I clutched the wheel desperately as we smashed through gravel and scrub and gradually decelerated to a velocity at which I could ease her down through the gears.

My vehicle drew to a halt—unlike the other bastard, I was pissed off to see, who hammered along the road as if nothing had happened, chains clattering, canvas canopy flapping in the wind.

I flopped onto the wheel, my heart kicking like a bull in a chute. Threw an angry glance at the disappearing Toyota. No chance of a licence plate in all that dust, but one bizarre image had imprinted itself on my mind's eye: had terror been playing tricks with me, or had I really spotted a pig's head mounted on the bull-bar?

A pig's head. Very Territory, but still not something you saw every day. And yet I had seen it before. Wasn't there something like that parked at Green Swamp on the day of Doc's death? I'd have words with that porcophile prick if I ever saw him again.

I checked out the damage: a terrible array of scratches and scars down the right side. Cockburn was going to love that. I walked around the back, dreading what I might see.

'Ah, the fuck!' I threw my hat onto the ground, kicked a rock.

The rear bumper was torn out of its socket, the support panel twisted. My larynx seemed to drop into my colon. I leaned into a tree for support, almost weeping. He was going to tear me limb from limb.

Maybe I could get a bit of panel-beating done before I handed the car back to Cockburn? Maybe the sensitive family man I'd glimpsed would understand that these things happen on the job, let me off lightly? Maybe the pig's head that had just run me off the road would reattach itself to its long-lost body and grow a set of wings.

Bloody hell, this trip was turning into a disaster. I climbed aboard and headed west, still looking for the Galena turn-off. I wanted to see Jojo, now more than ever.

As I drove, questions about the rampaging utility rose to the surface of my mind. Where had it come from? The car was a bit up-market for any of the Rabble. Some whistle-headed deadbeat from the town, no doubt.

Could the driver have been the nosey bastard who'd been spying on us? Or, for that matter, killing wallabies out at Dingo Spring? He sure as hell wasn't a rep for the World Wildlife Fund.

I was still seething when I spotted a set of fresh wheel marks cutting in from the south. I pulled over, examined them.

The Pig's Head, for sure. The dust hadn't settled yet.

I looked down to where the tracks disappeared into a patch of mulga scrub lining a rough creek bed. What had he been up to in there? Why had he been haring down the road? Was he running away from something, or did he always drive like that?

I stood on the steps to get a better look. Spotted something, a cloud of black smoke in the distance.

Curiosity told me to follow the tracks in the direction of the smoke haze, caution and the prospect of a little Jojo TLC told me to push on to the west.

I compromised: told myself I'd give it half an hour, turned south and followed the creek.

It was rough going, but the Tojo was up to it. I threw her into rock-crawling mode, and for ten minutes I gave the vehicle its head as we pitched and canted along rocky slopes and beetling creek beds.

Eventually the terrain levelled out and I came to the source of the smoke: a wildfire rolling through the spinifex. It had already burned a patch a kilometre or two square, but was running up against the barren slopes and unlikely to get much further.

Lightning strike? There hadn't been any. Runaway campfire? Perhaps. I poked around the eastern edge of the burn, found an abandoned campsite. Empty bottles and tinnies, wrappers and patches, a punctured jerry can. All recent. Lengths of black metal: used welding rods.

Mr Pig's Head? Probably.

What had he been welding?

I picked up a handful of hot stubble, blew it away. Fragments and floating ash drifted across my fingers.

Something stayed in the palm of my hand. Melted plastic. Poly pipe.

The beer and the jerry I could understand—everybody out here needed fuel—but the poly?

Irrigation.

What was he growing?

I walked out over the burn, scratched around. Nothing jumped out at me; whatever had been here was thoroughly destroyed.

I glanced at the westering sun, stored my suspicions away. They'd keep, as would Pig's Head Bloke. Time to be on my way.

Galena Creek

ANOTHER DRY CREEK—GALENA, this one. More signs of habitation. Welcoming, familiar signs: a twenty-foot canvas tarp hung from the trees, a bench of bush timber hammered together by an incompetent hand, a Mexican hammock, the weirdest chair imaginable—basically a bolt of canvas stretched across angled branches. A locked chest where I presumed he kept his tucker.

And, hanging from the centre pole, a picture of—me! All was forgiven.

But in the nude, the dirty bastard! There I was, emerging from a rock hole, hair whirling, water wheeling, taken by surprise.

When had he taken that, the randy git? Must have been that evening a couple of months ago when the weather was ratcheting into killer mode and water was the only solution; we'd thrown our bedrolls into the pickup truck, driven up to Purtulyu rockhole, spent a beautiful night under the stars and each other.

I took a look around the camp: everything was here except the feller I'd come to see.

Come on Jojo, where the hell are you?

I hadn't allowed for this, a three-hour detour only to find his camp empty. I didn't have time to hang around, and he could be gone for days. I knew the way his mind worked: something attracted him—something unusual—an albino wallaby, a flight of king and queen termites, an eagle spiralling in the wrong direction—and he wouldn't budge until he had it figured out and filed for future reference.

The sun was gone now, but the bush hummed with the scarlet afterburn, transfigured.

'Jojo,' I said out loud, 'please don't do this to me.'

And then I heard it, the answer to my prayers: the deep rumbling motor I knew so well.

Thirty seconds later I caught a glimpse of a Parks and Wildlife Toyota—Annie, by name—wending her way along the Galena creek bed.

I grinned. Too good an opportunity to miss. I whipped my boots off, shimmied up a tree, watched as the car came easing into camp. I judged the moment and dropped down onto the roof rack. Leaned forward and thrust my head in through the open window.

'You're under arrest!'

Then came very close to falling off.

Wrong man.

Stiff and sore

NO IT WASN'T: SOMEWHERE in among the prickle patch was a red beanie.

I hadn't recognised him: windswept and wild-haired, scraggily bearded, nearly as black as me; he'd been in the bush so long he'd started to decompose.

'Fuck!' he exclaimed, his jaw dropping.

'If you insist.'

I swung down through the rear window, feet first, popped up behind him and buried my face in the foliage that had enveloped his head; found something cartilaginous, hopefully an ear.

'Hello Jojo,' I said into it.

'Emily!' He laughed hard, pushed himself away, shaking his head. His hair rustled, it was so thickly encrusted with sweat and dirt. 'Scared the shit out of me. What the hell are you doing here?'

'I think it's called foreplay, but it's been so long they may have another name for it now.'

'But how'd you find me?'

I lifted my head up from where it had been busily trying to untangle a lobe from its encompassing curls. 'Everybody seems to know where you are except me.' I paused, gave him the hard stare. 'You gotta problem?'

'Course not—been planning on coming in.'

I reached over, laid a hand on his shorts. 'Well you can come in right now.'

He grinned and groaned. 'Dunno if I'm up to that.'

'I'll get you up to it,' I said, fossicking around.

'Don't you at least want to say hello?'

'I am saying hello.'

'Been perched up a tree all day. I'm all stiff and sore...'

'Well, we're half way there.'

'Yeah but...'

'No buts. Other than mine.'

'Just give me a minute to...'

'Deliver a lecture on the mating habits of the rufous wallaby? No thanks, honey—got mating habits of my own to accommodate.'

I ran my tongue round his throat, breathed deep, savoured the desert aromas: the oils and the burns, the bush tobacco, indigo and mint, red iron dirt.

'Come here you,' I whispered, slipping a hand down onto the lever and easing the seat back. I climbed over his shoulders and worked my way down through buttons and belts, shedding the odd article of clothing myself. Tackled his trousers head first.

'Why hello there.' I grinned up at him. 'Thought you said you weren't up to it?'

'Seems to have a life of his own.'

I licked my lips. So did he. I took him into my mouth.

'Ouch!' he yelped.

'Ouch?'

'No teeth, please.'

'Sorry—they must have grown.'

'Take it easy,' he groaned. 'Been a while for me too...'

'Well whose fault is that?'

'Don't speak with your mouth full. Might get more than you bargained for.'

'Good-oh.'

'Yeah, but Krakatoa...?'

'Let er rip.'

'You won't eat for a week. Ouch! Hey, how long since you cut your toenails?'

'Mind your own business.'

'It is my business. Think you just cut my ear off. Feel like Peter in the Garden.'

'It was him did the chopping, idiot. Where's the Lord, then?'

'Jesus!'

'Oh, there He is...'

'Thought I said no teeth!'

'...but it isn't over till the cock's crowed. Three times, if I recall.'

A minute or two flew by, then he emitted an ominously wobbly groan.

'Oi, hang on,' I said.

'What do you mean, hang on?' he gulped. 'We're talking irresistible forces and immovable objects here.'

'I wouldn't call your object immovable, but I'd like to...' I swivelled around, threw a leg over and thrust down onto him, arched my back and gripped the wheel, '...be there when it happens.'

'Hey, watch me mirror!'

'Oh shut the fuck up.'

'I love it when you...aaaaggh!'

He shuddered and grunted, threw his hips forward and his

arms out, wrapped me in a frantic embrace—then flopped back into the seat. He stared at the roof, gave me an idiot grin, then closed his eyes, the hopeless bastard.

'That's it?'

He was drifting off into Sleepy Hollow.

'Er—hello?'

No response.

'Oi! Jojo!'

He stirred himself for long enough to mumble, 'Aw come on, Em, I'm fucked.'

'Well I'm not—not properly, anyway.'

'Okay, okay. Just gimme five.'

A drawn-out silence ensued. Pleasant enough, if you like that sort of thing—a hawk moth waved at us from the other side of the windscreen, a nightjar drifted in to say hello—but my mind was on lower things. Crickets called, katydids didn't. Something rustled in the back of the car: not a snake, I hoped. Though if it was it was showing more life than certain other snakes in the vicinity.

I tapped Jojo on the forehead.

'Five what?' I enquired politely. 'Days? Weeks?'

Was something stirring down there?

'Minutes,' he mumbled.

Yes, it was.

'Starting when?'

A smile in his eyes. 'Oh—bout four and a half minutes ago.'

Breakfast at Jojo's

I WOKE AT FIRST light.

He was looking particularly ugly this morning: head on the pillow, pop-eyed, covered in knobbly spikes, staring me in the face. His tongue shot out and zapped a passing ant.

'Jojo!'

'Emily?' He turned around from where he was kick-starting the fire.

'There's a thorny devil on the bedroll.'

'Oh good. I was wondering where it got to.'

He came over, picked the lizard up and gave it a friendly nuzzle of the whiskers.

'You two know each other?' I asked.

'Been hanging round for a few days.'

'I mighta heard him in the car last night.'

'Probably.'

'He gotta name?'

'Roughhead. And he's a she.'

'Figures.' I sniffed, suddenly felt famished. 'What's for breakfast?'

'For her or you?'

'She's already had hers.'

He grinned, laid the lizard aside, held up a tin of beef stew.

'Bully beef! You're having me on?' I was mildly shocked.

'Keeps you regular.'

'In what? Dashes to the shithouse? I been eating *au naturel* for the past few days: porcupine, turkey...'

'Yeah, you and every other bugger. It's my job to look after those poor besieged critters. I'll see what I can do to spice her up.'

He rummaged around in the back of his car, came up with some bush potatoes, pigweed, mallee seeds and nuts. Threw them into oven or ash, as seemed appropriate.

As he was standing up, a wood swallow darted between us, almost brushed his leg. 'Do it again!' he smiled, but the bird was gone.

I nestled in his arms while we watched our breakfast simmer.

'So what's been going on, Em?'

'What's been coming off, more like it.'

'That's what's puzzling me—I couldn't help but notice—one of the things that came off last night looked suspiciously like a police uniform. And unless I'm wrong, that Toyota under the beefwood is a cop car.'

I rolled a smoke and gave him the story—cautiously. With good reason: Jojo was as enthusiastic about my new career as everybody else had been.

'And you're saying Tom McGillivray *encouraged* you to take this on?' He scratched his beard, bewildered.

'Sure he did.'

'Yeah. And you're out here checking out Doc's death? They let you run around on your own like that?'

'Well...'

'I can imagine. Didn't know what they were letting loose. Good god!' He stared into the fire for a minute. 'Came across him out here myself, you know.'

'God?'

'Him too. But I meant Doc. Bumped into him and old Ted Jupurulla once, out on Jingilyi Creek, west of the Gunshot.'

'I heard they did a bit of running round out there. Travelling to Dingo Springs, were they?'

He followed a trail of smoke as it unravelled into the air, nodded thoughtfully. 'Maybe—I never made it out that far, but they were heading in that direction. Another time I found him out here on his own, the silly old bugger.'

'When was that?'

'Not that long ago. Few months, maybe.'

'Didn't think he was up to solitary expeditions then.'

'He wasn't. Disoriented, perishing, flat tyre—smashing away at his wheel with a hammer, trying to get the nuts loose. Raving like a lunatic...'

'Don't suppose you remember what he was raving about?' Everybody I'd met so far had described Doc as ranting and raving; Jojo was the sort of man who might have paid attention to the gibberish. He was good at unpicking things.

'Sure. Most of it was rubbish: world burning up, bastards won't be happy till they've killed us all, that sort of thing.'

World burning up? That made sense in a weird, Doc sort of way. One of the tenets of the Snowball theory is that, after the great freeze, the climate swung the other way, and there was a period of intense global warming. Given the temporal distortions going on in his addled brain, maybe he thought it was happening now.

Come to think of it, he wasn't that far off the mark; the weather had been hell of late, an ominous portent of what we all knew was coming.

'One thing puzzled me,' added Jojo. 'He said he wanted it set in stone—no bastard'd believe him otherwise.'

The image of Doc's rock garden flashed into my mind.

'Wanted *what* set in stone? That the world's warming up?'

'Thought so at first—but then he said something really strange—said it was all his fault.'

'What—the warming?'

'Maybe—it was a rather disjointed conversation.' He narrowed his eyes, trying to dredge up the details. 'But I got the impression he was talking about old Ted.'

'Eh? Blamed himself for the old man's illness?'

'Sounded like it.'

'Odd.'

'I thought so too. I was curious enough to ask the bush nurse about it, and she set me straight: Ted was dying of cancer.'

'Yeah, but who could tell what was going on in Doc's head? He had a brain tumour himself.'

Jojo poured us both a tea, swivelled his round the cup. Frowned. 'Seems to be a lot of cancer running round this part of the world.'

'That's the twenty-first century for you, Jojo: carcinogenic. And hell, they were both getting on. Gotta go, you gotta go. So what did you do with Doc? Bring him back in?'

'Part of the way, but then we ran into some fellers from the mines.'

'The Rabble?'

'No, the new place, Green Saturn. They were pretty helpful; drove him home, went back later and picked up the car. Heard later they had it repaired and delivered back to him.'

'Decent of them. And that was the last time you saw him?'

He gave our breakfast a stir and the question a moment's consideration. 'Nope, come across him again, just before he died.'

'How long before he died?'

'Maybe a week.'

'Not on his own, surely?'

'No, doubt whether he could even handle a car by then. He was with his brother.'

I just about dropped my pannikin. 'He was with Wishy?'

'What's the problem? That's what brothers are for.'

'I'm surprised nobody told me—especially Wishy himself. I was just talking to him a few days ago.'

'Wouldn't read too much into it. The old feller was barely conscious—curled up in the corner of the cab, talking to his Geiger counter and eating a milk arrowroot.'

I flicked the remnants of my cigarette into the fire.

'Wishy mention what they were up to?'

'Said the old boy was sick—figured a bush-bash into his favourite part of the world might cheer him up.'

'I suppose that makes as much sense as anything else round here.'

A hiss and a trickle of liquid emerged from the oven in the ashes.

'Tucker sounds ready.'

I dished up, sampled the stew.

'Not bad,' I had to admit. The seeds and herbs gave it an unexpected pungency. Made it taste less like dog food.

The lines around his eyes crinkled in a smile. 'You expected anything less?'

'Never know what to expect when you're around, Jojo.'

'How long can you stay?'

'Should have been back yesterday. Boss breathing fire down my neck.'

'Tom McGillivray breathing fire? Not unless somebody put a match to it, surely?'

'Yeah, but it's not Tom. He's off sick.'

His bushy eyebrows curved. 'You didn't mention that. What happened?'

'Cookie Crankshaft.'

'Eh?'

'Smack in the face with a walking frame.'

He winced. 'The old Crankshaft fighting spirit! What's the new bloke like?'

'Cockburn? Neat.'

'So what does he make of you?'

'Not much. Plays a lot of squash. Chews a lot of gum. Likes to keep his uniform clean and his car cleaner.'

A worried expression rolled across his face. 'That wouldn't be his car you're driving now, would it? That battered old bomb?'

'Didn't look like that when I started out.'

'I see.' He scrutinised the car. 'And he's particularly attached to it?'

'Thinks the sun shines out of its tailpipe.'

'Might be a short career, this copper turnout.'

He walked over to the Tojo, surveyed its wounds.

'I'll see what I can do.'

We finished the meal, then Jojo dug out a toolbox, had a go at the car. After a brilliant bit of improvising he had it in a reasonable semblance of its former shape. He knocked out the more obvious dents, jemmied the bumper back into its bracket, gave it a polish with a concoction of bush oils. But no amount of ingenuity could make up for the lack of proper equipment.

When he'd finished, he stood back, crossed his arms, studied his handiwork. Shook his head.

'So how big a prick's this boss?'

'The full Ron Jeremy.'

Jojo ran a finger across the vehicle's bodywork. It had the lightly hammered surface of a Jamaican steel drum. 'If I were you I'd park it outside the cop shop after dark and run.'

I ran a finger across his own lightly hammered surface. 'So what are we going to do till then?'

'Well...'

He sat me on the bonnet, ran his knuckles down my spine and a cheek across my neck. His breath smelled like desert rose. 'We could see if there's anything left in the toolbox...'

Devil in the dark

I LEFT LATER THAT afternoon, reluctant to get back to the office while Cockburn was likely to be lurking. Jojo promised he'd be following in a few days.

It was getting on for dark when I reached the Green Swamp Roadhouse. I had no intention of stopping, but as I cruised past, I glanced at the mirror, caught a glimmer of light in the window of Doc's cabin.

I pulled over, my curiosity and suspicions piqued. Maybe murderers really do return to the scene of the crime. I backed up, took another look: the light had vanished.

I grabbed a fighting stick from the back of the vehicle, stole across the stretch of dirt, came up along the west side of the dwelling, peered in through a window.

The room was in darkness. I pressed against the wall, listening intently, watching in case the intruder made a break for it.

Five minutes crawled by. Nothing.

I crept around to the back, found the door unlocked. Stepped into the shack, flicked on the torch.

Fuck! I gasped in pain as something smashed into my hand. The attack seemed to come from nowhere—but I sensed another one on the way. I threw the fighting stick up, deflected the blow and launched myself in the direction it came from. Made contact with someone—someone who promptly grabbed an arm and flicked me westwards.

Fuck this, my stomach said to my brain as they sailed through the air and landed in a heap on the far side of the room.

I rolled over and swivelled the flashlight into the face of my assailant.

'My god!'

She was in a fighting stance, foot forward, poker in hand, ready to strike another blow. Wearing a ferocious glare and not much more. What was her name again?

'Jet?'

She blinked, eased off on the glare. 'The policeman?'

'Wish you'd stop calling me a man.'

'I apologise. Did I bl...break you?'

I climbed to my feet. 'Only slightly.'

She put the bar down, ran a hand through her hair, loosened up. 'It is the men.'

'It is. What men?'

'All of the men—in this country. They make me crazy,' she exclaimed, waving her arms around to demonstrate how crazy they made her.

'I see.'

'All the time, they never stop, these hairy desert monsters, slamming on the door, coming at all hours, sniffing around me like I am a woman dog in the...whatever...'

'Heat.'

'The heat, perhaps, yes. Or the dry. Or the alcohol. Or the no-women.' She scowled suspiciously. 'Have they murdered all the women? Where are they?'

'White women, there never were. Not many. Just my mob.'

'Yes, your...*mob*. I learn the expression. Your people from the Stone House Creek, I know them. They were here just yesterday.'

'The Stonehouse mob?'

'Yes, Magpie and Meg, Danny and the Crankshafts, the fat lady in running shoes—they come back from a long trip—into the desert.' She turned her head to the west as she spoke, made it sound like the outer reaches of hell.

'I know; I was with em. They called in here after I left?'

'Yes—Mister Nipper wished for money.' She moved around the room, lighting lanterns, throwing shadows in every direction. 'I have even been to their dirty little village.'

'You've been to Stonehouse Creek?'

'I went out with Kitty...'

'Ah, you've met Kitty too.'

'She is my friend—when she is not asking for money. Then I am her play.'

Kitty and Jet: a fascinating thought. I couldn't imagine either of them being anybody's prey. 'Jet?'

'Yes?'

'Mind telling me what you're doing here? I mean, I could have knocked your block off back there.'

'My block?' She looked around, puzzled.

'Head.'

A sardonic smile. 'Your block was, perhaps, in greater danger than my own.'

I rubbed my wrist, examined it: nothing broken, but it was going to be a dozen shades of blue by morning. 'Probably right.'

'I told you, did I not? I must spend some time here, try to

comprehend this puzzle of a place.'

'I suppose you did. Didn't realise you planned to do this much...comprehending.'

'And I have my job.'

'Your what?'

'Come with the house.'

'At the pub? You're working for Noel Redman?'

'Yes.'

It beggared the imagination, the thought of this slinky young thing working for the Great Ape over the road. At least she knew how to look after herself.

'A little cleaning,' she explained. 'The office work, sometimes I work the bar, pull the beer...'

I could imagine—beers and leers.

'So how're you enjoying it?'

'More, I would say, than the poor gentleman who occupied this house before me.'

'Ah, yes. Doc. He's the reason I'm here.'

She eyed me sharply, put a thumbnail in her mouth.

'Can I offer you a cup of tea?'

'What's that—compensation for the arm?'

She glanced at it curtly and said, 'It will repair.' Not a model of compassion.

She rummaged through a backpack by the bed, threw on a few scraps of clothing. Made her way to the fireplace, threw on a few scraps of wood.

Soon afterwards we were out on the veranda, cradling cups of yellow butter-laced tea and taking in the sights of Green Swamp— i.e. the pub across the road, where the lights were glowing and the volume rising. It was coming up to peak period, with ringers and Rabble furiously drinking themselves into an hour or two of respite from the oblivion of their lives.

Jet didn't beat about the bush. 'This man who died. Mister

Ozolins. Doc, they call him, I know. What are your questions?'

'You know he was a geologist?'

'I have seen his rocks. Used some of them in my work.'

'What is your work?'

'I make things.'

'Things?'

'Objects.' That was helpful. 'Art, when I am fortunate.'

'Out of rocks?'

She sliced the air with a dismissive hand. 'Out of whatever works.' Well, that answered that. 'But this...*quest* of yours. It has to do with his death?'

'Probably not, but I like to be sure.'

'I told you, did I not? You should look at the rock formation he was building. That is what I have been doing.'

I paused, studied her severe features in the moonlight. My curiosity was piqued.

'So what have you made of it?'

'As yet I have made—nothing. The beginnings of a beginning, no more.' She put her teacup down, did the hand-waving thing again. 'It is labyrinth, mandala. But where I come from, we spend our lives looking into mandala. After a time—perhaps a lifetime—you begin to see meaning.'

'I think that's what Doc was doing. He was investigating the geology of a site out west—place called Dingo Springs.'

She went quiet. 'Dingo Spring?'

'Yes.'

'The Dingo—it is the wild dog, no?'

'Yep.'

She took a noisy slurp of tea. 'My employer...'

'Noel?'

'He has the land out there.'

'I don't think so. It's crown land. Nobody owns it, not in the whitefeller way.'

'He has a government paper for the looking of gold.'

'A mineral exploration lease?'

She shrugged.

Not so unusual, I supposed. A lot of people on the fringes of the mining industry like to try their hand; there were MELs dotted all round the countryside. But then she added, 'He owned it in company with your Mister Ozolins, I believe. The Doc.'

'How the hell do you know that?'

'I have been doing a bookkeeping for Mr Ledman.' She frowned, pursed her lips. 'Red!'

'Doesn't matter—wasn't far off the mark. So you do Noel's books? You are multi-skilled.'

'I am not good. In truth, I am hopeless. But I am Chinese— they make the assumption, I bury the mistake. Sometimes I open the mail. The other day was letter from—the Department of the Mining, no?'

'More or less.'

'Inside was a renewing notice for a mineral exploring lease. The place was the same—this Dingo Springs. And the names were two together: Ozolins and Redman.'

I gave that a moment's consideration. If Redman had a lease out there, in partnership with Doc it complicated things enormously. With Doc out of the way, Redman would have first crack at anything of value.

No choice now: I had to question the publican, see what he had to say for himself.

There was a sudden ruckus from the pub. A jumbled figure flew out the door, picked itself up and dusted off, rejoined the party, skull first. A raucous chorus from within: pool balls, pinballs, cannonading laughter.

Happy hour at the Green Swamp. I sure as hell didn't fancy trying to tackle Redman in the middle of that. Cockburn was going to have to wait another day to get his Toyota back.

Somewhere inside, I was grateful for the delay.

I leaned back against a post, wondered about the sharp-eyed woman before me.

'Where are you from, Jet?'

'You said before: China.'

'I've met a few Chinese immigrants. They tend to be accountants.'

'I also: for Mister Redman.'

'Your conversation is full of mandalas and labyrinths. I don't think you're an accountant. Which part of China?'

'The north-west.'

'Gansu? Xinjiang?'

She scrutinised me suspiciously. 'You have been?'

'China? Few years ago now.'

'You know Qinghai?'

'Sure.'

'My people: the Tibetan. Minority.'

'I see.'

That explained a lot of things: her comfort with the vertiginous incline, her mandalas, her terrible greasy tea.

'How long have you been in Australia?'

'Five years now.'

'And you live in Sydney?'

'For now I live in this cabin.'

'What brought you to Central Australia?'

She tipped her head back. 'Aaiee—I see why you are police.'

'Just curious.'

'Curious!' she said dismissively, then seemed to resign herself to the fact that I was a nosey little bastard. 'I have colleague in Sydney. Countryman, many years in Australia. Also artist. When I am miss my country, crying for things I have left behind, he tells me to come to this out back. Says I may find here some of the things.'

'Like what?'

'My god, this Emily Tempest!' Her bevelled face shivered in the half-light. 'Things in common? Where to begin! Hawks and stars. Men on horseback. Ghosts and ropes of air. Gods who live in songs and make mountains. Pushy women! Dreams!' She rose to her feet. 'For which it is time, no?'

She threw the remnants of her noxious brew into the darkness, went inside. Presumably that was goodnight.

Pushy women? She could talk! The past was clearly a no-go area.

I unleashed the bedroll, climbed aboard, lay staring into the fiery sky and thinking about landscapes and the people they gave birth to.

Running with the wonder dog

I WENT OVER EARLY the next morning, came across June mopping a slop of god-knows-what off the lounge floor.

She raised a wet hand and a weary brow, drawled my name.

'Morning, June. Boy up and about?'

'Meat shed.' She flicked a thumb in its direction.

'What's that, his home away from home?'

She rolled her eyes: 'Got his little chores he likes to attend.'

I eyed the menu. 'What's a girl gotta do to get a feed round here?'

'Sandy's still recovering from last night, but I can knock you up some bacon and eggs.'

'The perfect antidote.'

'To what?'

I grimaced. 'Jet's rice gruel.'

'You had breakfast with Jet?'

'Got in late last night. You looked a little hectic—she was the closest thing to a B&B. B1 was okay, but the breakfast was crap.'

June smiled. 'Did you try the greasy tea?'

'The gruel's worse. Never was quite sure what the word gruel meant—now I know. It's a combination of glue and cruel.'

'Maybe we ought to put it on the menu, number of Asians we're getting through.'

'Just don't let it contaminate the food.'

I went off in search of her husband.

Stiffy the hyperactive hound was on guard at the meat shed door, and put on the usual hysterical display.

Redman was laying into a slab of something that had been mooching around a paddock not long before. This was obviously the high point of his day: he was a man who loved the heft of a weapon, the crackle and crunch of frozen bone. He turned round, seemed—if the energy he put into the next blow was any indication—as happy to see me as the dog was.

'Miss Tempest.'

He laid the cleaver aside, stretched his back, rearranged the contents of his Y-fronts. He was charmingly attired today in off-white slacks—a mile or two off—matching singlet and an overhanging roll of blubber. The combination of heat, cold and sweat was doing alarming things to the scribbly veins in his nose. He gave vent to the wheezy exhalation of the seriously out-of-condition man.

'What brings you out this way?' he enquired.

'Just come in from the Gunshot Road.'

'Goldfields?'

'Further west.'

'Chip off the old block, eh? Prospecting?'

'Maybe, but not for gold. I'm on duty—had a few questions I wanted to ask.'

A slight crimping at the temples. 'Fire away.'

'I understand you've got a mineral lease out west.'

He looked as cagey as a camp dog—and as itchy; either that or he was trying to invigorate a frost-bitten nostril. 'And if I have?'

'In partnership with Doc, is it?'

He gave me a malignant stare. Stiffy caught the mood, resumed yapping.

'Bugger me breathless,' said Redman, 'is this never going to end?'

'You could get a labrador.'

'I mean the trouble that old fool is causing me, even after he's kicked the bucket. First I have to put up with his lunatic ravings and his hopeless work ethic, and now I get some smartarse little midget copper coming in here looking like she thinks I shanked him.'

I nodded at the cleaver. 'Well you do seem to know your way around a sharp implement.'

The stare intensified.

'Look, all I want's a few straight answers, and I'll leave you and Stiffy in peace. Tell me about the lease.'

The flakes of ice on his brow rearranged themselves, like iron filings on a magnet. 'Lease? Which one?'

'The one out west.'

'Yeah, but which one out west?'

'You got more than one?'

'Had half a dozen of em over the years. Each time it's the same bullshit story: Doc worked out there years ago, prospecting for Copperhead. Reckoned he'd sussed out the mother of all lodes, the other half of Broken Hill, Lasseter's fuckin Reef, whatever— all he needed was a bit of help to find it. So I bankrolled him, paid for the leases and fitted him out, even fed the crazy bastard. And it wasn't until I actually went out there…'

'You went bush with Doc?'

'Mostly I just forked out the money and signed the leases. Didn't head out west with him till early this year. Wanted to see

201

what he was actually doing with my money.'

Looked like Doc had been conning every able-bodied man in the region into chauffeuring for him.

'Where'd you go?'

'Where didn't we go? All over the del Fuego, far as I could figure out: a great long scraggly expedition to hell and back, roughest country you could imagine, scorpions and snakes, broken axles, punctures. Took me a week of bloody misery to work it out.'

'To work what out?'

His mouth narrowed into a tight circle. 'That it was crap, the whole thing! Doc couldn't have cared less about gold—what he was trying to do was figure the geology. Measuring faults and fracture lines, testing the water. He'd only taken out the leases so no other bugger'd come along and rough it up before he'd had a proper look at it. Oh, he could spruik, all right—raving about rainforests, glaciers...'

'And snowballs?'

'Yeah, he told me about the snowballs. Ice across the desert sixty million years ago'—out by an order of ten, but never mind—'but gold? Minerals? Anything that's gonna put dinner on the table? Nada!'

'Breakfast, Emily!' June's voice came drizzling out of the dining room.

I turned back to her husband, was mildly alarmed to see him running a fat finger along the length of the cleaver. I instinctively backed off.

'Been back there since?'

'Flat out runnin this place.'

'But your name's still on the exploration licences...'

'Well I did pay for the bloody things.'

'And you'll reap whatever benefits there are.'

'Oh for Christ's sake!' He slammed the cleaver into the side of beef. 'This is harassment.'

'Noel?' June appeared in the doorway. She studied him anxiously, then turned to me.

'Maybe you better come and have breakfast, Emily. Noel's been under a lot of pressure lately.' She looked back at her husband, who was still shaking. 'Have you had your tablets, darl?'

'Tablets!' Anger chopping holes in his diction. 'Like to find her a fuckin tablet—made of marble.'

'Now Noel, that's not going to...'

'Little bitch barges in here, virtually saying I killed the old...'

'I'm sure that's not what she meant.'

Maybe it wasn't, I said to myself as I walked away. But I'm sure as hell thinking about it now.

I sat down to breakfast. I suppose it was bacon and eggs, but it could have been grilled gruel for all I noticed, so furiously was my mind swarming with questions.

How far could I believe Redman? He'd sounded convincing, I had to admit; if he could fake that amount of aggro he was up there with Robert De Niro. But I wasn't ready to dismiss the possibility Doc had stumbled across something of value and been killed for it.

Then again, what about Mr Pig's Head? He'd been growing something out there, and it wasn't cauliflowers. Could Doc have sprung him, threatened to turn him in? He'd been a cantankerous old bastard at the best of times.

And where did Wishy Ozolins fit into all of this? For some reason I couldn't shake the suspicion—the fear, almost, because I liked the man—that he did.

I paid my bill, drove back to the shack, parked in the shade of Doc's carport. Noticed, for the first time, a little row of faded flags on the side of the veranda.

Jet was on her knees, chisel in one hand, hammer in the other, ferociously laying into a slab of granite. The flare of her shoulder blades, the ripple down the spine: she was oblivious to everything but the job at hand.

I stood back, studied her creation.

The patch of dirt beside the shack was covered in a strangely magnetic web of rocks and wood. Quartz crystals were positioned about the installation in a way that sent their reflected light sheering like water down corridors of stone.

A series of sketches lay against the edge of the rocks. I saw they were interpretations of Doc's original formation, made from every conceivable perspective and covered in diagrams and dotted lines, circles and arrows, mathematical equations.

'This is how you…investigate, then?'

She turned around, her eyes mercurial. Downed tools, stood up, ran her hands across her face, her tongue across her lips. She was wearing blue shorts, a black singlet, dirty boots and a river of sweat.

'This creation of the Doc's—it fascinates. I try to—to copy? Yes. But more. To complete. To give that man the silence for which he would search.'

'When you find it, let me know what it looks like, will you?'

She flashed sharp little fox teeth. 'It begins, perhaps, with a cup of tea?'

'Maybe a quick one before I hit the road. But please—I'll be mother.'

I ignored her puzzled expression, went inside, scoured the cupboards, found some of Doc's old Bushells. Made two teas, one black, the other yellow, joined her on the veranda. She had her boots off, her beautifully shaped feet exposed to the morning sun.

I sat there, my gaze drawn irresistibly to her creation.

'Where'd you learn to do that sort of work, Jet?'

'In nunnery.'

I sprayed a mouthful of tea across my knees. 'You're a nun?'

'In Qinghai—many make nun. When young woman, I make the—how you say? Promise?'

'Vow?'

'Vow. Our work restoring the sculpture destroyed in Culture Revolution.'

'Lot of things destroyed in the Cultural Revolution, I know.'

She tossed her head, spat. 'Is karma. But I find the figures I make—the carving and the hammers—they overwhelm. Rise up inside, will not lie down. For me, I understand, it is the art that is my path. My fate.'

'So you threw away the beads and took up the hammer?'

A wry movement of the lips. 'Some of the beads. Sometimes the hammer.'

We sat there quietly, soaked up the serenity. Enjoy it while you can, I told myself—serenity will be a scarce commodity once Cockburn gets his hooks into you. You shouldn't be doing this, you should be getting back to town, facing the music. I closed my eyes, came close to drifting off. Jet lay a foot against mine.

Yap! Yap! Yap! I sprang up and spilled my tea.

There was a demented toilet brush dancing frantically at the foot of the stairs: Stiffy the Wonder Dog—the wonder being that no bastard had put him out of our misery yet—had tracked me down.

He bounced about, tail bristling, lower teeth taking up most of his face. I wondered whether he'd been trained to hate Asians as much as he hated blacks, whether he was an equal opportunity bigot.

I found a lump of wood, waved it at him. 'Gworn ya little mongrel, piss off!'

Stiffy went apeshit. Dogshit, in fact. He just about came in mid-air, such was his excitement. He had a go at my leg, so I kicked him into a spiralling backward somersault.

Fuck, that was an annoying animal. I rose to go inside.

'Desist,' snapped Jet.

I turned around.

205

Stiffy was gone.

'Shit—you learn that in the nunnery?'

'I surprise myself. The dog has perhaps found something more interesting.'

She walked to the edge of the veranda, stood with her hands on her hips. 'It ascends the slope.'

I glanced across at the pub. Speaking of interesting, the first customers had arrived.

One of them was a beige pickup with a pig's head on the bull-bar.

'You know that Toyota, Jet?'

She peered across at it. 'I see the people more than what they drive.'

'Bit hard to ignore that one: it's got a pig's head on it.'

'Ah yes—a man with a lead beard.'

'Lead?'

She frowned. 'Red.'

'He gotta name?'

'You do not talk to that one. He has wall around him—invisible bricks, no? But I have heard him called—Blent, perhaps?'

Blent. 'He a regular, this Blent?'

'Perhaps not. Sometimes on a weekend, a fly…Friday night.'

'Maybe the name's Brent.'

'That is what I said. I believe he is a man from Bluebush.'

I nodded, pleased to have saved myself a bit of running around. Like I'd guessed, the feller was a townie.

'Might have a word with him before I go.'

She was studying my face with interest. 'Do you ever take a moment to look around, meditate upon the silence?'

'Course I do. Sometimes.' I scratched my chin, wondering when the hell I ever did anything that could be remotely described as 'meditating upon silence'.

'Ah, I think not.' She stretched her legs, closed her eyes, let the morning sun wash over her face. 'For me, it is the silence that defines this country. The peace.'

The words were barely out of her mouth when the cliff overhanging the cabin fell on top of us.

Landslide

IT BEGAN INNOCUOUSLY ENOUGH: a muffled thump from above, a puff of dust, an echo recoiling out over the plains.

We jumped up in time to see the skull-shaped boulder—the one Jet had been sitting on the first time I laid eyes on her—come tumbling down the slope. It gathered momentum, took to the air in a ballistic trajectory, slammed into the back of the shack.

We stood there, stunned.

There was a faint shudder in the fault line that ran across the bottom of the overhang, then it suddenly seemed the crest of the hill was reconfiguring itself, mid-air.

Jet spat some words. From the tone, a rough translation might have been 'Holy fuck!'

I set off running.

She was a better judge of landslides than me: she was Tibetan, after all. I felt her grab my arm.

'No!' she screamed.

She began to run towards the approaching rock storm. A black boulder was leading the charge, advancing in mighty leaps and bounds. One of the leaps took it over our heads.

Had Jet taken leave of her senses?

Then I realised she was weaving her way to the only conceivable shelter we had time to reach: Doc's iron carport.

We dived inside, rolled into the lee of the Cruiser, clutched each other in terror as the full force of the barrage struck with a roar to wake the dead. It smashed into the roof, bombarded walls and beams, scythed out over the ground I'd have been caught cold on if she hadn't drawn me here.

The building shuddered and shook—and seemed to hold.

The roar died down almost as quickly as it had come.

I peered out through a blanket of blinding dust. 'Is it over?'

'Maybe.'

She lay beside me, her face aglitter with crushed mica, her sharp nose dusty.

Suddenly she leaned forward, kissed me.

I raised an eyebrow. 'Oh?'

She smiled. 'A celebration.'

'Of…?'

'Survival.'

We climbed out from under Cockburn's car. I was relieved to see that it hadn't sustained any further damage. I looked up at the groaning roof.

'Is that going to hold?'

She followed my gaze. 'Maybe…'

A trickle of dust fell into her face.

'Maybe not.' She dived out into the open air.

Just as I followed suit the centre post snapped and a mass of jumbled rocks and blocks fell through the roof and crushed the vehicle.

We picked ourselves out of the dirt, dusted off, gazed at the chaos, dismayed: cabin and carport were gone, reduced to rubble. We were pretty well reduced to rubble ourselves. Doc's rock formation had disappeared, Jet's sculpture along with it, buried under god knows how many tons of rock—as we would have been, if not for our solid steel carapace.

The mob from the pub—June, Sandy the barman, a few early customers—came running over to lend a hand. Noel Redman, not so big on the hand-lending thing, lagged suspiciously behind.

'Are you all right?' asked June.

'We're fine,' I replied. 'Bloody lucky,' I added, nodding at the obliterated buildings.

But we weren't all fine, and we hadn't all been lucky. The publican, poking about the wreckage, emerged with the body of his dog, whose yapping days were done. Stiff no more—well, maybe for a wee bit more; then it would be all wriggling worms for Stiffy.

Redman shot a hostile glare in my direction, went off to bury his little mate.

Don't blame me, I said to myself. I didn't squash the mongrel; and it would have been justifiable canicide if I had.

June took us over to the pub, administered heavy doses of hot tea and cold beer—the outback panacea—each of which I willingly accepted. Jet opted for the packet of tea she kept in the Transit van, brewed up, joined me on the veranda. She sat and stared at the carnage of the cabin, her gaze growing sharper by the second.

'Cunt-faced fucking dingoes,' she said at last.

I raised my eyebrows. 'Nice to see you picking up the vernacular. Who are you talking about?'

She hawked, spat viciously.

'They change their faces and colours from time to time, rearrange the disguise, but underneath, they are the same, no?'

'Maybe.'

'You heard it?'

'Ye-es,' I replied, reluctant to admit, even to myself, what I'd heard: the muffled explosion before the rock fall.

I sighed quietly.

Why was everything so complicated?

Landslides happen all the time in this steep, rocky country; they're a natural phenomenon.

This one wasn't.

I took a look at the car park: I hadn't noticed any red-bearded bastard who looked like he'd answer to the name 'Blent' among our rescuers, but the Pig's Head had disappeared.

'Sound like you're speaking from personal experience there, Jet.'

She took a noisy swig of tea, stared ahead, glowering.

'Met a few dingoes in your time?'

She said nothing.

'Jet?'

I gave up, rolled a smoke. She seemed mesmerised by the movement of my fingers, the tobacco twist, the crackling paper.

'Dirty custom,' she commented.

'This from a woman who works with mud?'

'My father habit as well.'

'Mud?'

'Smoke.'

'I see.'

'My father is quiet man, you understand? Peace.' The words came out of her slowly. 'Carpenter in a fox-fur hat.'

Was I about to get some blood out of the stone?

'Work with hands: the long saw, the strip of wood. Doesn't want nun for daughter—but accept. Artist less. But accept. After nunnery, I go home, work in family house—by lake near city. Lake of souls, you know?'

'Souls?'

'You should understand. Lake is...voice of deity.'

'Sort of a sacred site?'

'Perhaps. In my country, like yours, many such place. But also army, riding in hard cars and carrying guns. Bring their weapons and poisons: test bombs, radiation, rubbish. Chinese.' She leaned forward, hawked and spat again, across the railing. 'Invisible sickness and death spread through lake to fish, then to the hunters of fish; nuns protest. Governor—Mister Xing—answer with gun: many nuns beaten, or jail, or run away.'

An acid smile cut into the contours of her face.

'In city square statue of Chairman Mao Zedong; symbol of harmony between our great peoples. One night I ride into town, carry my tools. In morning, crowds gather and laugh so hard they split the sides: chairman's arse transform to face of Governor Xing.'

She stared into her teacup, savouring the memory. 'I watch from the hills, hiding, no find. But they recognise my hand, I am known. So my father they take to labour camp. In one month, is dead. Two months, mother as well. From the grief—perhaps from shame for troublesome daughter.'

I stared at her. Didn't know what to say.

'I take horse and *chupa*, ride off into the wind. Cross plains. Mountains. Travel in truck, bus, whatever; walk through snow to my breast. Move with deadness in my heart, with pictures and memories burning in my brain. Make way across Tibet, Nepal. With time—here.'

I looked out at the wreckage of the cabin. In its broken walls and beams I saw an echo of the story I'd just been told.

'I see.'

She nodded to herself, studied the western plains, sniffed suspiciously. 'There seems to be no army here...'

'We're not very big on armies.'

'Public security?'

'Just me.'

'Puh!' She wasn't impressed. 'Atomic bomb?'

'Not lately. Few back in the fifties.'

She swirled her tea, stared into it.

'You have something,' she growled. 'Something they want.'

'They?'

'The dingoes.' She threw away the dregs, rose to her feet. 'Beware.'

She stomped across to the wreckage. I trailed after.

She picked her way back into the shack, salvaged her boots and a set of chisels from the rubble. Fossicked around some more, dragged aside a pulverised table, came across a dust-covered folio. She brushed and blew away the debris, found a few of her sketches, lined them up against the rocks. Scrutinised them with a fierce eye.

Then she began picking up pieces of rubble, examining them, fitting them together, laying them out in front of the shack.

'What are you doing, Jet?'

She paused, a big rock in her little hands, the biceps in her skinny arms surprisingly curved: 'I finish what I begin.'

What Doc began too, I thought.

I worked alongside her for a couple of hours, gathering up rocks and rubble, laying them out in a rough approximation of Doc's original. Jet did the arranging, issued orders, worked quickly and efficiently.

Finally the heat drove us up onto the pub veranda. We were sitting there, feet on the railing, drinks in hand, when a police vehicle came rolling down the road, pulled up in front of us.

First Griffo emerged, then Cockburn sprang out of the driver's seat, hands on hips, gum in mouth, customary sniff hovering about the nose. His gaze zeroed in on me.

'Emily.'

'Sir.'

He lowered his shades at Jet but managed to keep his suspicions to himself. 'Got a report of a rock fall.'

'That's right.'

'Road still open?'

'Pretty much.'

'Any damage?'

'Er…some.'

'More specific?' His brow furrowed; he took a step back, scanned the parking lot. 'Where's my car?'

'Ah, yes—your car…'

He followed my gaze, lit on the remnants of Doc's dwelling, among which could be glimpsed a glimmer of mangled metal, a buckled bumper, a shattered blue light.

'Fuck me gently.'

The acting superintendent said not a word on the way back in; he didn't have to—his radioactive ears said it all. But as we walked into the station, he leaned back at me and snapped, 'Graveyard shift. Tomorrow. Tell her about it Griffo.'

He took a few more steps, then added, 'And get yourself a proper bloody uniform.'

Graveyard

GRIFFO PAUSED WHEN WE came to the Black Dog, checked his watch, licked his lips. 'Might just nip in for a bit of cool air.'

I caught the glance between him and Bunter. They'd be nipping more than air, but hell, I couldn't blame them. How could it be this hot at one o'clock in the morning? My body was closing in on me. I swept a length of sweaty hair from my face, dragged the daggy new uniform trousers out of my crack.

This was my third night on the graveyard shift—so called not because it was quiet but because, if you did it long enough, that was where you'd end up.

The shift itself wasn't a Cockburn initiative. His innovation was that you did it on foot. 'Keeping in step with the community' he called it, which probably sounded impressive in the press releases and memos to Darwin.

For the poor bastards who had to actually do it, it meant

wading through a sea of blood without a vehicle to retreat to.

I looked up and down the main street, wondering whether I should follow the boys in.

Megahead O'Loughlin, owner of Bluebush's leading laundromat, came staggering down the road with a box of chocolates in his hands. Despite the sobriquet, his most prominent feature was his belly: he had the silhouette of a camel on its hind legs. He stumbled, spilled the chocolates, watched in despair as they rolled across the footpath. I helped him to his feet, sent him on his way.

There was a crowd milling about the vacant lot across the road, a woman with a rusty-ball-bearing voice ripping into somebody, but there wasn't an actual riot going on. That would come later, when the pubs threw out the refuse.

In the gutter sat Benny Springer, rubber eyed and tearing at a rag of meat. He took a pull of his beer and vomited onto his own boots. That decided it for me. I followed my colleagues into the pub.

I glanced at a poster on the door. *Strip 'n Prawn Night*. So much for Random Andy's cream de la cream. The star turn was one Miss Lickety Split, who may or may not have been the woman on stage when I entered the crowded, cavernous bar.

I naively assumed, from the fact that she was stark naked, covered in white foam—maybe that was the cream?—and whipping her arse around like a blimp in a blizzard, that the show had reached its climax. But no, there was more to come: a buck-toothed meatworker, who couldn't believe his luck when she dragged him up onto the stage. She dropped his pants, whipped on a condom, threw him to the floor and straddled him on the spot.

The crowd went nuts.

'My god.' I elbowed Bunter. 'Is that legal?'

He shrugged and grinned. 'If it isn't, I'll let you be the one to break it to em.' He nodded at the baying mob. They were meatworkers in the main, and even those who weren't would be working the meat tonight. A gelled fellow in a purple shirt three sizes too small leapt onto the table, hooted and thrust his hips forward. The bouncers adjusted their knuckles and moved in.

Bunter and Griffo settled against the bar, enjoying the show.

I elbowed again. 'Think I'll take my chances outside.'

As I came out onto the footpath, I spotted a disturbance among the crowd in the vacant lot. There was an angry bellow, then came the unmistakable thud of a fist thumping into thick flesh, a female moan. Sounded like Ms Rusty Bearings was copping the comeback.

I called into my collar mic for back-up, hitched up the pants, ran across the road, came upon a burly feller kneeling on a woman and punching her into the gravel.

I kept going at full pelt, knocked him off balance, managed to get him cuffed before he knew what hit him. Which would have been a satisfactory conclusion to the incident had not the victim found her feet and turned out to be Cindy Mellow. A fighting stick materialised in her right hand.

The first blow hit my prisoner in the head and he went down. The second hit me in the head and I joined him. The third crashed across my back and I wondered how I was going to get out of this in one piece. The fourth was heading in my direction when Rosie Brambles, clearly intent on picking up where she'd left off last time I saw her, came out of nowhere and launched herself at Cindy.

The rest of the mob automatically aligned themselves according to their family or drinking affiliations. By the time the police vans arrived, there was a full-scale brawl raging, with one traumatised ACPO attached to 110 kilos of comatose blubber huddling under a bench in the middle of it.

When it was all over and the offenders were scattered or canned, I prodded my lumpy skin, found myself surprisingly intact. I hitched a ride back to the station in one of the vans.

'Town's fallin apart,' grumbled Flam, shaking his head and kissing a split knuckle.

Bunter grunted his concurrence. 'Was it ever together?'

'Was before you buggers arrived,' I threw in, a comment to which they reacted with surprisingly good grace.

'It's the economy.' Griffo went all big-picture on us. 'Town's dying in the arse; no jobs, no hope, nothing to do all day but sit around and suck piss.'

He had a point; Bluebush had never been so depressed. The cattle stations were being hit by the worst drought in living memory, things were looking lean out at the meatworks. Even Copperhead Mines, the bedrock on which the town was built, had been laying off workers.

There'd been high hopes and a lot of talk around the reopening of Green Saturn, the Copperhead offshoot down on the Gunshot Road, but it had turned out to be no more than that: talk, spin, bullshit. Probably designed to lever up the share price. The deep-shaft gold mine was apparently bringing in excellent dividends for somebody and pumping out press releases full of phrases like 'high-tech' and 'cutting-edge'. But for your battling Bluebush business that translated to a handful of contractors working on a fly-in, fly-out basis. Precious little of their cash found its way into local pockets.

These thoughts were interrupted by an emergency radio call: somebody was being assaulted down at the retirement village.

'See what I mean?' Bunter spun the wheel. 'Even the pensioners are getting into it.'

'Surprised they got the energy,' commented Griffo.

Somebody had the energy, if the blood-curdling moan we heard from Fanny Bolt's flat as we pulled into the drive was anything to go by. I prayed it wasn't Fanny. Widow of the last mayor but one, record-breaking president of the Country Women's Association, she'd been a livewire in her prime. Nowadays she weighed in at twenty-eight stone. I didn't fancy trying to arrest or resuscitate that.

Griffo burst from the car and led the way. I followed, moving quickly at first, then slowing as I hit the veranda and heard a tobacco-cracked basso profundo that could only be Fanny's growling through the screen door: 'Ah, why do you always wanta fuck like a dog!'

Because any other position would be fatal, I thought to myself as Griffo burst through the door. He flicked a switch and found himself gazing on the deeply disturbing image of the former First Lady kneeling on the bed, butt-naked and taking it in the rear from Jimmy Windschuttle.

I ducked for cover as Griffo backed out of the room, scraping and bowing and flinching in the face of the blizzard of abuse he was copping from Fanny.

He was still banging his head against the wheel when we got back to the station.

'Get over it,' grunted Harley when he heard the story in the staff kitchen. 'Attention-seeking behaviour, I call it.'

'You had to see it,' groaned Griffo. 'I might need counselling.'

'Like stubbing a cigarette in a blancmange,' I threw in.

Harley smirked. 'Wish I had seen it.'

'You sick bastard,' grinned Bunter as he and Griffo went off to do their paperwork.

I fossicked around the fridge, came up with some Weetbix and bananas. Harley nuked a pie, made a murky coffee, sat opposite.

'So, young Emily, how you enjoying the graveyard?'

'Not dull.'

'Shouldn't oughter go wrecking the super's Cruiser. By the way,' he buried his face in the pie, came up with a gob-full, gravy dribbling, 'that Toyota you were asking about…'

'The pig's head?'

I'd shared my theory that the driver of the pickup had an illicit crop out on the Gunshot Road, could have had a motive for killing Doc. Cockburn, still in mourning for his Tojo, paid scant attention. The others had shown even less interest, and I was surprised when Harley came up with a name.

'Brent Paisley.'

Jet's 'Blent'.

'You know him?' I asked.

'Not that many Toyotas cruising around with a boar on the bar. Yeah, we know him. Owns the welding workshop out on Hammer Avenue.'

'Terry Greenleaf's?'

'Paisley's now. And you're right about him being out west. Spoke to a mate at Crown Lands—he's got an exploration lease out on the Gunshot Road. Had a word with Jerker—gonna check it out.'

'I might just...'

'Reason I'm telling you this,' Harley interrupted, 'is cause Paisley's an animal. Plus, he hates cops. Couldn't help but notice you tend to lead with your chin: thought I better warn you to steer clear, case you spot him round town, get more than you bargained for.'

Not what I expected: was I becoming part of the team? God help me.

'Cockie might not know him'—the first time I'd heard the acting super called that; I bet they didn't say it to his face. 'The rest of us sure as hell do.'

'He got a record?'

'Long as yer arm. Longer,' he added, glancing at my arm.

'Been inside?'

'More in than out.'

'What for?'

He polished off the pie, pulled out a bag of iced donuts.

'Longest? Ten-year stretch in Long Bay—aggravated rape.'

'How do you aggravate a rape?'

'Bit off an ear.' He rummaged through the donut bag. Selected his victim, took a massive chunk out of it.

'Picked up for a hot car boost when he was thirteen, and it's all been downhill from there. Assault, armed rob, dealing…Working his way through the book.'

'Anything local?'

He waved a half-eaten donut at me. 'Not yet. Only been in the Territory for a couple of years. Worked underground at the Burning Angel, then he bought out Terry Greenleaf. Fuck knows where he got the brass for that, but you can bet it wasn't anything honest.'

'You're well informed.'

'This town, ya gotta be.' He popped the last of the donut into his gob. 'Save yer neck some day.'

I touched his elbow. 'Thanks for that, Darren.'

A flash of gold among the gums, mustache curling up through the popping pores and blackheads: surely not a Harley smile? 'No worries.' My god—it was. 'Long-term, we'll nail the bastard; short-term, you just stay out of his way.'

I really was grateful.

Not that I had any intention of staying out of anyone's way, but at least I knew now to tread warily. Long term?

Bugger that.

Bright spark

HAMMER AVENUE WAS ON the ragged edge of town, out where the bitumen disintegrates and the dogs are heavier than the machines they guard. I dropped round to the workshop later that afternoon.

The sign on the gate: *Bright Spark: Metal Fabrications.* Droll. I parked out the front, walked in.

The pickup, a Toyota HZ575, was squatting in the parking bay; it had a battery of spotlights, truck radials, more bars than Brunswick Street: roll-bar, tow-bar, bull-bar, nerf-bar.

The grisly head on the bull-bar was saying more in death than it ever had in life; if nothing else, it said that the bloke who put it there was a muppet. Whether he was a dangerous muppet remained to be seen.

From somewhere inside the building I heard the sound of an oxy welder. I walked up to the doorway: arcing sparks, bitter fumes. Rivulets of light flickered across a greasy concrete floor.

The head of the bloke inside, when it emerged from the mask, bore a distinct resemblance to the mascot on the vehicle: full of god-knows-what, ragged about the edges, with a drizzly beard, sunken eyes, dropped cheeks. A hot, red face, maybe in its late thirties.

He stood up, removed his leather gloves: the tip of a finger missing, most of the others scarred or burnt. Whatever crimes Paisley had committed, all those and more, he may have done, but he'd obviously put a lot of muscle and blood into his trade. My old man was a bush mechanic: I recognised the signs.

He proffered a businesslike greeting, but the bonhomie disappeared when I identified myself. You could feel the temperature drop. Suddenly we were in a war zone.

'I had a few questions about the Gunshot Road.'

'You can ask. Doesn't mean I'm gonna answer.'

'You've got a mineral exploration lease out there.'

He picked up a hammer, smashed the off-cuts from the steel frame. Jagged metal clattered onto concrete. 'Sounds like you already know what you wanner hear.'

'West of the roadhouse.'

'There a question comin?' The more we spoke, it seemed, the surlier he got. The tendons clenched in his neck. Volcanic forces were brewing beneath the surface of that monolithic personality.

'Go down there often?'

'When it suits me. When I get sick...' he delivered a brutal blow with the hammer, '...of fuckin jacks breathing down the back of my neck.'

'They haven't been breathing that hard. Must be, oh, weeks since your last conviction.'

'Years. Three.' Another blow. 'And they fuckin fitted me up for that. Cunt couldn't go straight if he tried.'

I took a look around the workshop. Dirty rainbows on the

floor, butchered buckets and slabs of metal, burnt slag. It was a building defined by sharp angles and edges: grinders and vices, benches and boxes of welding rods. Paisley and his head were the only blurred things there.

'The other day I was driving out on the Gunshot Road,' I said, 'some idiot ran me off it. Idiot with a pig's head on his bull-bar.'

'You oughter be more careful.'

'What were you doing out there?'

'Didn't say I was.'

'And if you were?'

'Then I would have been minding me own business.' He paused. Peered at me, puzzled, sniffed the air, sucked the sweat out of his mustache. His eyes swarmed with a cornered-animal suspicion. 'What'd you say your name was?'

'Emily Tempest.'

'What sort of a cop are you, anyway?'

'None of your business.'

Suddenly it dawned on him. 'You're not a proper pig at all, out here on your own, runnin round out bush. That joke of a uniform. You're just the fuckin black tracker.'

'I'm working my way up.'

'Bugger off and track some blacks.'

He fired up an oxy-acetylene torch, waved it in my face.

'Careful with that thing.' I took a step back, stumbled against a broken tailgate.

A rare sighting of what was left of the Paisley teeth. 'Worried you'll end up on the bull-bar?'

'Worried you'll end up in the back of the van.'

I was tempted to say more, but the look that shot across his face deterred me. Paisley was an over-heated furnace: flip the wrong switch and he'd explode.

The switch? Clearly, the threat of incarceration; he'd been inside, didn't want to go back.

And there was something weird about his eyes. Something hot-wired, wounded. This guy had done time for dealing, according to Harley. From the look on him now he'd been hoovering up the residuals.

'What are you?' he snarled. 'Some jumped-up little gin from the fringe camp, put on a pigskin jacket and thinks she can come kickin a white man's door down?'

He lowered the mask, leaned over, flashed a cleavage of Monrovian proportions. The interview was over.

I walked out, noticed another building in the yard, a khaki corrugated iron shed against the back fence. More of a bunker this one: oblong, with a heavily bolted door, a Gothic dog, a row of windows, dark and barred.

The Paisley residence? Not exactly an ivy-covered cottage, but he hadn't struck me as an ivy-covered kind of guy. I was lucky he hadn't struck me at all.

Curiosity—that terrible monkey that's been riding on my back forever—impelled me towards the shed.

I'd only taken a couple of steps when a door on the west side of the workshop crashed open. Paisley's rusty smudge of a head appeared.

'Shithouse sense of direction for a tracker.'

'I'm better out bush.'

'You're on private property.' Aside from a quiver of the nostrils, the face was rigid. 'Less you gotta warrant, the exit's over there.' He jerked his chin at the gate.

'Zulu!' he barked, and whistled.

The dog—a cross between a doberman, a Baskerville and a Mack truck—uncurled itself and flexed its teeth. It was chained, but only barely. The corroded links failed to inspire confidence.

I turned round, walked back out to my car. The inside of the workshop was shrouded in darkness, but I could feel Paisley in there, staring, trying to creep me out.

225

Pretty well succeeding.

I shuddered and got behind the wheel. Drove down to the White Dog for a soothing afternoon libation with the regulars, those who were still kicking. I used to pull beers at the White when I first came back to Bluebush, and I felt at home among those wobbly old gentlemen.

I spent a distracting hour laughing at stale jokes and listening to Roy Orbison sing high harmony to the smack of pool balls and the rattle of rheumatic bones. They even had Cold Chisel on the jukebox. Stan, the licensee, was catching up with the times: he'd got as far as the seventies.

It was getting on for sundown when I headed back up to Midnight Choir, the small peak that looked down over the western edge of town. I took my field glasses, grunted to the summit, nestled down in a spot that afforded me a comfortable view of Paisley's workshop.

If this prick had anything to do with Doc's death, I'd find out. If he had anything to do with anything, I'd find out. I didn't like being driven off the road. I didn't take to having welders waved in my face. And I sure as hell wasn't going to be called a jumped-up little gin and not do something about it.

B and E

I RAISED THE GLASSES, zeroed in on him. He was hammering away in the half light, metal ringing, sparks flying through the shadows. Over the next hour the odd customer dropped by. Some of them I recognised: Brian Johnston, the manager of Brindle Bore, picked up a pair of gates. Young Daisy Cutter and his overblown FX pickup truck roared off in a blaze of rubber and debt. Archie Skinner, grinning at the wheel of the two-tonner from Fiend's Creek, drove away with a set of iron grids.

Even the Reverend Bodycombe put in an appearance: the Great White Whale rumbled into the yard and Paisley inspected some sort of damage to the front end, scribbled a quote. Had the Rev been running over donkeys?

Sometime round six Paisley closed the workshop, drove away in the Pig's Head. I sat tight and waited. He came back half an hour later, climbed out of the cab with hot food and cold beer.

He tossed something at the dog, went inside, shoulders hunched, singlet hanging loose. Settling in for a long night of watching art-house movies, I assumed—*The Shawshank Redemption* at a guess, the favourite of criminals everywhere—and talking to the dog or pulling the pud, or whatever it was your Bluebush yob did to while away the summer evening.

I was wrong.

The gate stayed open, and the after-hours Paisley was even busier than the business-hours one. By ten o'clock half a dozen vehicles had cruised in and out the yard.

Most of them were anonymous in the dark, but I did spot Con Panopoulos, proprietor of Bluebush's greasiest mustache—this time of the year, he could have deep-fried his chips in it—ramshackle taxi operator and purveyor of fine food to the masses. Con snuck in a couple of times, his lights low, his profile lower, didn't hang around.

It was nearly two before Paisley finally bade the last of his visitors farewell, turned out the lights, locked the gates and drove away.

He didn't sleep there. Good. I gave it another half an hour, then made my way down the slope.

Tried the gate.

Shit! A monster came roaring out of the dark and lunged at the wire: ferocious teeth tearing at chain mesh, spittle dripping, eyes on fire.

Zulu. I staggered backwards, gasping. Clutched my pounding heart and thought: Emily Tempest, girl detective. Who the hell stages a B and E and forgets about the guard dog?

My options were limited. Shoot the mongrel? An elephant gun would have done the trick, but I didn't have one handy. Call up my father, who could charm the pants from man—or at least woman—and beast? No way: Jack took a dim view of my misadventures, and hadn't quite figured out that I was all growed up now; he'd have me out of there and grounded before I knew what hit me.

I studied the yard. In the dim glow of the floodlight over the workshop door, I could make out piles of steel, glimmering mesh, squat drums. I worked my way round the side of the compound. Zulu followed me every step of the way, balls bobbing, spiked collar bristling. The occasional hint that I was welcome to have another go rumbled from his barrel chest.

I was standing there, anxiously surveying the scene, when something rasped against my bare leg.

'Christ!' I would have hit the roof if there'd been a roof to hit.

The simpering mewl that came back at me revealed my attacker to be one of the rat-eaten cats that skulk about the seedier quarters of the Bluebush night. This one was on the scrounge. It purred, a crackling, asthmatic whine, scraped its ribs against my ankles, curved a mangy tail. It must have had me figured for one of the strange old ladies who ran around feeding the strays with milk and Kit-e-Kat.

'Gworn,' I snarled, but the creature persisted.

I kicked it away, at which the moggy got the message, arced up and languidly raked its claws across my calf.

Bastard! I cast an appraising eye across the yard, grabbed the cat by the tail, then whirled it over the wire and into the patch of alley between fence and shed.

The cat effected a wildly yodelling descent and hit the dirt howling, looked up to see Mount Vesuvius bearing down on it and took off. Zulu gave pursuit. During the ensuing cacophony, I ran at a fencepost, scurried up its length, dropped down into the yard and lit out for the set of iron gates I'd spotted leaning against the shed.

The dog twigged, did a lightning turn, came back at me.

I pulled at the gates and they weren't gates, they were heavy grids, and they weren't going anywhere. Shit! I jumped onto an adjoining forty-four and heaved as the dog came galloping over the gravel.

The doberman leapt and the grids came crashing down, trapped the beast in a makeshift enclosure between fence and wall.

Zulu wasn't happy, and let the world know it with a din to wake the dead. How long before somebody responded? His guess was as good as mine: we were out on the lonely edge of town, but even here, I supposed, the occasional security man trundled by, the odd long-haul driver pulled in for a knee-trembler with some drug-fucked prossie he'd picked up at the BP.

I pulled out my torch, examined the building. Heavy mesh welded onto the windows, a fat chain curled around the door.

I gave the chain a rueful shake. Amazing: it wasn't locked. Paisley must have had a lot of faith in the dog, and fair enough— it would have scared most people senseless. Would have scared me senseless if I'd had some sense to begin with.

I uncoiled the chain, crept into the building, swept it with the torch: grubby Formica table, Jim Beam bottles and greasy leftover chips. On the bench, an array of tools: spanners and hammers, safety glasses, a set of night goggles. On the wall, more tools. Most of them penetrating pouty-lipped women with trash tans and silicone tits.

There was a rack of heavy hunting bows: two recurve, one cross. Probably the source of the boar's head on the bull-bar, but nothing illegal. Nothing that couldn't be found in redneck retreats from Bourke to Broome.

Had I risked my neck, tackled dog and fence, broken god knows how many laws, for this?

There was a back room. Might as well be hung for a sheep...I found the door, opened it slowly. As I did so, a flicker of suspicion zapped across my brain.

The night goggles. What were they doing there?

As the suspicion hit me, so did the length of twenty gauge chain: it crashed into my upper body and slammed me into the wall.

I caught a flying glimpse of Paisley, foot forward, winding up for another blow. I flung up an arm to fend it off, ducked my head, kicked out. All futile. The terrible metal came ripping in once more and exploded into darkness.

A bloodshot moon

MY SKULL THUMPED AGAINST metal. Not bare metal. A touch of rough material in the mix. Canvas? The left side of my brain felt like there was a poultice nailed to it and cinched with barbed wire.

An engine roared.

I was in the back of a vehicle, bouncing over rough dirt roads. The tarp flapped: patches of starry sky, treetop shadows. No street-lights, no houses, nothing but the roaring empty outback night.

I found myself struggling for breath. What the...? My mouth was taped. So were my hands, strapped to the back of the tray: duct tape and rope. My legs were lashed together at the ankles. I was lying face down on a rough surface: scrappy tarp on a patterned metal floor.

I fought a wave of nausea, raised myself onto an elbow, craned my neck, managed to reach the window. I made out a dim figure in the ghostly echo of the dash lights' green. Paisley, eyes on the road, cigarette in his mouth, starlight in his beard.

Jesus fuck—what was going on here?

I struggled at the bonds. Couldn't budge them; he knew how to secure a load.

I worked at the tape. Got nowhere. Feather cuts in the wrists, torn lips. Trussed-up fly in a spider's web. The more you struggle…

The despair started in my groin and surged through my body. Fuck this! I muttered and spat into the gag. How do I get myself into these things?

What was the plan? Kill me and bury the body in the scrub? No. If that was what he had in mind he would have finished me off when he had me out cold.

We raced along, the white road smoking behind us. Then we slowed down, and the ride got rougher: up and over a windrow, onto churned earth, straddling ditches and gullies, scrub tearing at the drop-sides.

Off-road. My body jumped and thudded against the floor.

Twenty minutes of that, and the vehicle jerked to a halt. A door opened and shut. Panic speared my ribs, squeezed the breath out of my throat. I curled up, struggled at the bonds. Nothing.

Footsteps. The tarp drawn back. Paisley appeared, a blurred silhouette against a blue and silver background. Water and stars.

What was that terrible acrid smell?

The Retention Dams. Oh fuck, that made it worse, if such a thing was possible. He'd brought me to the most barren, blasted spot in the country, the chemical-encrusted wasteland west of the mines. Out where Copperhead had been dumping its waste for fifty years. Hissing blue cyanic ponds and mullock heaps, enough to send a chill through the heart of the hardest miner. Soon to be my final resting place.

Paisley had a rifle in his right hand—*must be the cautious type, I'm hardly going to make a run for it*—and his eyes were gleaming. No...the brute was wearing glasses. I hoped to hell they weren't reading specs, the sort of thing you'd put on for close work.

He flashed a torch, examined me. Everything presumably to his satisfaction: arms, mouth, ankles bound, eyes rolling in terror, heart punching like a rock drill.

A hungry look shot across his face, honed his mouth. Cleaved my heart.

He clambered into the canopy, rested the rifle against the well, rummaged though the gear at the back. Emerged *oh sweet Jesus* with a pick and shovel. He leaned them against the tailgate: careful with the tools of his trade, wouldn't want to give himself a splinter digging my grave.

He turned back to me, and I caught the gleam of a knife in his right hand. As he moved forward I swung with my legs to kick him in the balls. Failed miserably. He leaned forward, crouching over me in the cramped tray. Dropped an elbow into my back, crushed my head into the floor. I struggled, but he was an inexorable mass. The power of all that metal-born muscle crunched into my skinny little backbone.

He whispered into my ear, a gravelly exhalation. 'Not so quick with the lip now, eh?' He raised the knife to my head. To my throat.

Now, I thought. *I'm about to die.*

He sliced through the tape around my mouth, ripped it away, tearing hair and skin.

'Like to hear you—nobody else will.'

He reached down, hacking at the bonds around my feet. Ripped away the denim skirt and underwear, dragged my legs apart. Took a long look.

I felt a wild lurch in my gut. Oh Christ, that was why he'd kept me alive this long.

His strange, dead face loomed over me, eyes red rimmed behind the glasses, untouched by human feeling. Uneven teeth, two missing. A slobbering hop-head maniac. His massive spanner-hands pinned me to the floor.

The weight. There was nothing I could do to shift it; my feeble struggles seemed to amuse him. He sniggered as he reached down and rubbed something into me. Grease?

Was there any point yelling? No. I yelled anyway. I twisted my head, took a look around.

Something, anything I could use for a weapon.

Dream on. The truck was full of equipment, to be sure—spanners and files, hammers and rods. All useful if I had them in my hands, but my hands were bound.

There was a welder against the sides of the tray, a couple of gas bottles. I'd have blown us both to smithereens if that was the only option, but he wasn't about to sit back and let me do that.

I felt him tugging at his belt, loosening his trousers. He leaned into me, and I felt the momentary touch of his cock high on my leg before the ramming and tearing. *Ripping me apart.*

Waves of despair breaking through my body.

I pressed my face to the floor, tears stinging. Moonlight washed over the gear cluttered about me.

Moonlight.

Somewhere, through the pain, through the grunting, a dove called. A diamond dove: my dreaming, the *purrpurrpur* a song that wrapped itself like wings around my soul.

I opened my eyes.

Find yourself. Reach for your strength. This man is nothing. The country lives in you: your people have been here forever.

I twisted my neck, peered back down the tray, past his pumping flanks.

The gun. It was resting against the well, the barrel angling ten degrees above us. I inched my right leg over, touched the stock with a toe, found the trigger guard. Felt my way round it, made a guess at the angles. Was the safety on? Didn't feel like it.

Paisley panted and thrust, shuddered and shook and, at last, flopped down on top of me. His body hair like a layer of toxic ash, buttons and zips biting. He buried his rough head in my shoulder, dribbled. I felt broken teeth, a tongue.

You piece of filth, don't go to sleep on me.

He began to raise himself.

I seemed somehow to be gazing down on the scene, like a floating raptor. Or a hovering dove. I saw his arms unwind, his back arch. The airborne perspective sharpened my judgment and hurled me into the moment, into an epiphany of angles and trajectory.

I concentrated, clenched my eyes, twisted over and flicked the rifle with my toes. Felt the barrel graze my leg and land in the small of his back.

The blast smacked at my brain. Cordite suffused the cramped atmosphere, a hot, sharp smell. No idea where the bullet had gone, but maybe Paisley would be thrown for long enough...

He lurched and dropped back down. What was going on? I felt him shudder and twist, flop alongside me. His eyes locked onto mine, then disappeared. The glasses were gone, the mouth was working hard. Nothing came out. He struggled to rise, got as far as one elbow. Collapsed.

I felt a charge of hope run through my body. Knew there was a bullet in him somewhere.

'Oh the cunt, as if they didn't warn...' His voice trailed away, crumbled into a string of disjointed groans. We lay alongside each other, an obscene parody, a sculpture of two hell-bound lovers cast in brimstone.

I tried to wriggle as far away as possible, to the other side of the tarp; the other side of the world wouldn't have been far enough.

I groped around, feeling for something I could use to free

myself. Scrabbled around the floor with my chin. Came across a chunk of metal, the tip of a welding rod. Clenched it between my teeth, sawed into the tape around my hands. Dropped it. Tried again. Lost it. Twisted my neck, picked it up, my mouth full of dirt and bitter filings. I clenched it so tightly my cheeks bled. Worked away. Every thrust sent stabbing pains into my mouth.

'...the fuck you doing?'

Paisley, stirring, gurgling, breathing blood; sharp red eyes on fire. He raised an arm, threw it across my back. Dead weight: no power there. I shook him off, got back to work.

The beginnings of something giving in the tape.

Paisley's groans were growing weaker.

I thrust fiercely, back and forth, pulled for all I was worth. The rent grew longer. A final surge, and my hands came free.

I climbed to my knees. Scrambled to the back of the tray, desperate to be out from under that canopy of horrors. I drew the flaps back, jumped down.

A sudden snarl, a rush of paws and a fiery tearing in my right leg.

Zulu.

I rolled back into the tray and the dog came with me, its ferocious jaws latched onto my calf. I threw out a hand, landed on a spanner, bashed it across the skull. It ignored the blow, shook, emitted grinding, gravelly snarls. I touched the rifle, snatched it up, rammed it into the ribs and pulled the trigger. The dog flew back with the blast. Curled over and lay whining.

I put another one into its head. I ran from the truck, screaming and weeping. Crumpled against a tree. Retched.

Spewed my insides out, compulsive spasms tearing my stomach and throat. I wanted to bury myself in the sand, but there was no sand, there was only a vile green sludge that stung my feet and rippled with my vomit.

At last I shuddered to a halt. Breathed deep. I steeled myself, straightened up, took a look around: a bloodshot moon bled tears of light on ghost lagoons. A maggot-eaten bird was the only sign of life.

Dear god, what a place. Nobody ever came out here. The spirit of the country was long gone, eaten away by acid. I would have lain here forever, my bones corroding, my soul screaming into eternity.

I returned to the car, jumped into the driver's seat, rammed her into gear. Drove flat out, cutting across country, flying over ridges and rises, smashing termite mounds and branches. At one point I was up on two wheels, cutting a swathe through the poisonous pools that oozed from the cracks in the dam walls.

Dead country loomed up into the cones of light: crumbling samphire bushes caked with blue dust, the hollow ghosts of rats and snakes, frogs frozen in time.

I powered on, afraid to stop, hanging on to the motor's rise and fall, terrified that any fall might become a stall and leave me stranded among these monstrosities.

I splashed through foetid gutters and cuttings, grey slime whirling in my wake. Then diminishing. The earth became redder, the grass more yellow, the leaves more green. The country coming back to life.

I drove past a skull and crossbone sign on a sagging barbed wire fence: *DO NOT ENTER. By Order: W. Demsky, CEO, Copperhead Mines.*

I eased off on the throttle. Not long to go and this cursed place would be behind me. I sighed.

And a bloody hand burst through the window. Clenched my face, fingers in my eyes, my mouth.

Paisley: he'd climbed out of the tray, worked his way round. He was standing on the steps, one arm on the pillar.

I thumped him, bit hard on a thumb, lost control of the vehicle. We went into a fish-tail, quivered ominously.

A ghost gum loomed in the headlights. I threw the wheel to the right, crashed into its branches, side on. Saw a dead branch lance the bastard, catch him under the ribs. His face whipped away behind me, racked by shock and pain. I gunned the motor, risked a backward glance: Paisley wriggling on the tree, speared like a barramundi.

I crashed through sagging fences and fallen gates, rotting logs. Came to the creek and belted down its banks. Reached the town dam. Clean water glimmered in the moonlight.

I skittered down to the water's edge, slammed on the brakes, leapt out. Stripped off, dived in. Wanted to wash my soul, eradicate the memory of that hot red metal breath, those dead mechanical eyes, that alien vileness.

Then, a long while later, I lay on the banks and wept. Wept myself out. It's only a thing, I told myself. A man's body.

It cannot touch your diamond soul.

I punched the sand, hard. Felt, through the pain, the first sign of life—anger—seeping back into my bones. Fuck him, I spat through a twisted grimace. Fuck him a million times over. A curse on him and his kind forever. He will not do this to me. It's over. Over.

I stood up, saw the lights of Bluebush in the distance. Dragged the rags of my clothing together, drove into town, walked up the station steps.

Harley was at the desk. His mustache drooped. 'What the...?'

I caught a glimpse of myself in the window behind him: bedraggled and bleeding, wet hair falling on my shoulders, eyes wild.

'Paisley. You were right about him.'

'What?'

239

'Told me to watch out.'

The floorboards moving under foot, their colours swimming into one another.

'You had a run-in with him? Where is he now?'

'Up a ghost gum.'

'What's he doing there?'

'Becoming one himself.'

'Becoming…?' The senior constable looked lost.

'A ghost.'

My eyes fell on a clock. Four-thirty. It had been a long night.

I sat on the bench. Thought better of that and lay down. Harley was reaching for the phone.

All for nothing

I SPENT THE NEXT couple of days in a hospital bed, a foetal position and a dark blue funk. Curtains drawn and a plate of untouched food coming and going from the table. All I wanted to do was drink—water, gallons of the stuff. There was something inside me I couldn't wash away.

Sounds drifted in from outside. The Bluebush dawn chorus: the baying of the dogs, the screaming of the drunks. They were how I told night from day; apart from that, the world was a blurred fug of intersecting pains and punishing thoughts.

Physically, they assured me, there was nothing much wrong: battered and blue I might have been, covered in stitches and scars and sticking plaster, missing a tooth or two. But there were no bones broken, no vital organs damaged.

Emotionally, it was a different matter. Rage and shame, deaf to reason, swept through me in storms that tore away the flimsy tarps lashed above my soul.

The hard-nosed doctor, the one I'd met before, whose name turned out to be Marta Kokinos, proved to be surprisingly considerate. Patching up sexually assaulted black women was obviously an area in which you developed an expertise in Bluebush.

People tried to see me; I told Marta I didn't want visitors, and she was ferocious defending my privacy.

The first intruder to get through the stone curtain was the last person I wanted to see. Bruce Cockburn came strutting into the room late on the second afternoon, hair polished, hat in hand, uniform neatly pressed. Face the same but more so. I couldn't have cared less if I never saw the needle-brained bastard again.

But there were, it seemed, matters arising.

'Emily.'

I looked up at him through swollen, gooey eyes. 'Sir.'

That was as far as the conversation got before there was a crash of doors and a bearish figure came charging into the room in his wake. He had Cockburn up against the wall and gasping for breath before I knew what was happening: my father, looking for someone to kill.

Since I'd already killed the appropriate someone, he must have decided the acting super was the next best thing.

'You the fuckwit filling in for Tom McGillivray?'

Cockburn's response was a strangulated gurgle.

'What did you think you were doing, letting an innocent young girl loose among the scum-sucking lowlife sliming around this cesspit of a town?'

Cockburn, despite a twenty-year age advantage and what I suspected was a more than adequate ability, seemed strangely disinclined to defend himself. I did it for him.

'Keep your shirt on, Jack,' I croaked. 'Innocent? Give us all a break. He warned me not to go sniffing around—I went sniffing around. Poked me nose in. Wasn't his fault I got it bit off.'

He pressed the policeman deeper into the wall, actually lifted him off his feet.

'Jack!' I watched Cockburn turn purple, his precise little teeth wondering which way to turn. 'That's not gonna help!'

He ignored me. I grabbed a cup of water from the table and threw it at his broad back. He looked around, dropped his bundle. Came over and wrapped me in an ursine embrace.

'Jeez, honey, Emily darling, I just heard...I was out bush.'

Were those just my own tears I could feel running down my cheeks?

'It's okay, Dad.' I patted him on the back, rubbed what was left of his hair. 'It's over now.'

'It is.' I felt his whiskers scrape my cheek.

'I'll survive.'

'You will.'

'And I even managed to achieve something.'

He raised his head, lowered his brow. 'What was that?'

I peered over his shoulder, tried to catch Cockburn's eye. Found it surprisingly difficult to do so. The supercilious sneer was nowhere to be seen.

'Get Wireless off the hook.'

Cockburn looked up, then away, then down, cleared his throat.

'Come on,' I persisted. 'You can't possibly hold him now.'

'Emily...'

'We know Paisley was at the roadhouse that day. He's a convicted drug dealer, a homicidal maniac, a career criminal with a violent history. Surely it's obvious: Doc stumbled across his plantation, threatened to turn him in. Paisley was as cunning a jackal as ever walked the earth. There's no way a jury would convict Wireless now; I'll tell em if you won't.'

I caught Cockburn and Jack glancing at each other in a way I didn't like the look of.

'What?' I growled at the policeman. 'Have you idiots even figured out that Paisley's the front runner for Doc's demise? That's why I was checking him out.'

'We have,' he mumbled, finding his tongue at last. 'Be up to the Coroner to decide, but it's looking that way.'

'Looking! What's it gotta do—jump down your bloody throat? Go over the evidence, see if you can find anything to put him in the frame.'

'We have gone over the evidence.'

'Well?'

'You're right,' he sighed. 'Paisley was at the murder scene. Can't say when, but his prints have shown up among the ones we collected.'

'Have you looked around his workshop?'

'Commercial quantities of speed and ganja hidden in a gas bottle. Con Panopoulos has fessed up: Paisley had a plantation out on the Gunshot, Con was doing the deliveries. Jenkins has checked it out.'

I raised myself, shook a bandaged fist at him.

'Well what are you waiting for? Why isn't it Goodbye Hop-head and Welcome Home Wireless?'

After an arduous silence, Jack took my hand in one of his great paws. 'Wireless died a couple of days ago.'

I blinked, shook my head, sank back into the pillow. 'No.'

'Alice Springs. In the Big House.'

I turned away. Stared at the wall.

All for nothing. All that.

I'd been tortured and tormented, shattered and battered blacker than I already was, forced to put down a couple of mad dogs—all so that poor old Wireless could turn up his toes in the last place on earth he'd have wanted to.

Freedom and fresh air, a refusal to fit into the straitjacket of society, a hunger for time and space to spin the bullshit and grumble about the world: they were what had driven those old eccentrics out to Gunshot Road in the first place, those were the values that sustained them. They might not have seemed much to a straight-as-a-gun barrel autocrat like Cockburn, but they were all Wireless had. For him to die in some rat-stinking cell for something he hadn't done was more than I could bear.

Cockburn mangled his syntax and his hat. 'Stroke; massive. Probably going to happen no matter where...'

I glared at him. 'Oh, just get out of here.'

'We did nothing un...'

'You're damned right you did nothing.'

'We followed standard operating procedures...'

'Get out!' I spotted my police shirt poking out of a drawer, ripped it out and threw it at him. 'And you can take this and stick it up your standard operating procedures with a very long pole.'

Doctor Marta appeared, bustled them out of the room, held my hand, offered me a shot of something. Whatever it was it worked: I curled back into a ball, stared out a tear-stained window and fell asleep weeping.

Moving out there still

WHEN I CAME TO, it was night time. And I felt…

It was time to go.

Suddenly I'd had enough of this white-feller environment, its sterilised air, its marble sheets and stainless steel. Its coppers who cart you off and kill you with their standard operating procedures.

I wanted out, the sooner the better.

I climbed to my feet, came close to falling right back down, head dipping and heaving, stomach the same. Floors and windows flying in every direction. My mouth felt like it had a dead rat in it.

I sat on the edge of the bed, breathed deep, tried again. Fell over. Had somebody given me a transfusion of wet cement?

I had another go and made it upright this time.

I rummaged through the bedside chest. Found some Drum tobacco and papers; Dad must have put them there, bless the

cranky old bastard. I couldn't find much in the way of clothes, but.
I settled for the dainty blue dressing gown I found in the drawer.
Not that I needed it for warmth; it would still be hot outside, but
I wanted something to cover the bare bum I could feel bobbing
out the back of my hospital gown.

As I stepped out into the corridor, a sharp call cut through the
pharmaceutical air.

'You! Stop there.' Doctor Marta's voice.

Not aimed at me. Gunther Blitzen was creeping down the
other end of the corridor, one arm in a sling, the other attached to
a drip. He gestured at it.

'It's got wheels,' he complained. 'What else are they for?'

'To help you get up and go to the toilet so a nurse doesn't have
to come and wipe your big hairy bottom.'

'Just a quick snort—it's nearly closing time.'

Gunther had a rep round town, but he'd met his match in
Marta. 'Back to bed!'

I hobbled off in the opposite direction, wandered a maze of
corridors, went through a door and found myself out on the hospital lawn. Sat on a bench. Fired up a ciggie, sucked the guts out of
it and felt the warm night air lilting across my skin.

I devoured that first sweet smoke, hurried on to the next.
Thought long and hard about how I'd fucked up. Poor bloody
old Wireless. What a way to go. And what had I done to help
him? Stuff all.

Somewhere in the midst of that blistering self-assessment I
became aware that there were shadowy figures moving along the
pavement opposite. As they moved in and out of a streetlight's
arc, I recognised them: the Wilyaku crew, a trio of Crankshafts, a
couple of Whiskey sisters.

A few minutes later Elsie Waterman and Cynthia Winton
wandered by, Alf Tuckerberry hot on their heels. Alf had fought
his way round the country with Jimmy Sharman's Boxing Tent

but the closest he came to a box these days was the cardboard one he slept in.

They were moving with a surprisingly lively step. Either there was a free feed on somewhere or somebody had cracked a keg.

Without quite knowing why, I stood up, drew the gown around my shoulders and followed them. I took vague pleasure in the concrete under my feet, felt the pain recede, ever so slightly, the life come creeping back into my limbs as the blood flowed.

As we drew close to the centre of town, I realised there were more walkers behind me, too far back to recognise but chattering happily and tossing jokes around. Coils of laughter peeled off into the dark.

Gradually the crowd thickened: the old and the young, the hobbled and the halt, they came wandering in from alleyways and side streets, from creaking gates and fallen doors. I drifted along in the comforting anonymity of the night.

We were almost up to the main street when I realised where we were headed: the Bluebush Memorial Hall, whence the sound of music told me there was a party going on. I felt the bass before I heard it, a frenzied riff shivering air. As I drew closer, I recognised that unique blend of reggae/country/Pacific Islander blues that could mean only one thing: the Coral Cowboys were back in business.

I remembered Bandy Mabulu telling me he had a gig organised. This must be it.

I didn't fancy making an appearance in my present state, so I snuck around the back of the hall, tried to peek in through a window. I was about to tackle one of the scraggy bushes along the wall when a nearby door flew open—somebody wanting a smoke or a snog. A storm of light and sound came blowing out.

Bandy was on stage, his powerful voice belting out over the crowd. Ricochet was laying on the harmonies and Lefty was doing an amazing job on the skins, his one good arm covering more ground than a Japanese tennis player.

Everybody was up on the dance floor. There were no spectators at an event like this: pensioners bopping about on skinny lizard legs, snotty-nosed toddlers running rings around the room, shipwrecked cowboys in tattooed boots, rock and roll girls in spangled tops adorned with meaningless phrases like *Aerial Ways* and *Shot of Love*. And they were beautiful when they moved, a rainbow explosion of pure joy as the music formed and dissolved around them.

I sat with my back against a peppercorn tree, watching. Felt a tear slide down my face. I closed my eyes; was surprised, when I opened them again, to see that the dancers were still there. They seemed like more than I deserved.

Later on, some bloke from the crowd—shaggy britches, baggy belly, raggedy-ann hair—shambled up onto the stage. At just about any other venue in the world he would have been thrown out on his ear. Bandy put an arm around him and passed him a guitar.

'Listen up, you mob,' he called out to the crowd. 'We gotta special treat from a great man!'

As the newcomer approached the mic, I recognised him: Kenny Wednesday, a Kantulyu feller who lived at the Gutter Camp. These days Kenny and sobriety were at best nodding acquaintances, but when he was young he'd been the main man for Buffalo Express, the best of the early bands around here.

The audience hushed, expectant.

'Evenin folks,' Kenny grinned. Unleashed several megawatts of dormant rock-star charisma. 'Gonna send yez off to bed with a new song. Hot off the strings, eh?'

He struck a minor chord, broke it open into a rippling arpeggio. A floating, waltz-time ballad lilted out from the stage.

My brother move through time and light
Like a mirror through the hills
A star-black fire dreamin man
The one they couldn't kill
He took a spear, he took a swag
He singing up a storm
He light a fire, the rain come down
The country being born
He walkin round the waterholes
West of the wheeling mills
They say he's gone, but me I know
He's moving out there still

By the time the chorus came round, the rest of the band were playing along:

Beyond the broken bottle
Beyond the white man's will
They say he's gone, but me I know
He's moving out there still

Kenny's voice was a subterranean growl, but somewhere among its cracks and crevices lurked a sweet melody.

I had no idea what the song was about. Who was moving out where still? He'd said something in the opening line about a brother. As far as I could recall, Kenny didn't have a brother, but then 'brother' could mean all sorts of things round here. Anybody in the same skin group—one in eight males—was a brother. Any mate could be called 'brother'. Any other blackfeller was a bro. He could have been talking about anyone. Only…

Andulka, the mystery nomad. He was a Jungarayi. He and Kenny even shared the same dreaming: fire.

Once again it seemed Andulka, dead for years—blown up and buried under a mountain at Green Saturn—was acting as a lightning rod for his people's spirit.

The man himself was unimportant. A shiver in the wind, a spike in the sun's glare; it was what he stood for that mattered. Andulka loomed large in their collective imagination. They saw him crafting a solitary path out there, moving down dry waterways, over the cracking blacksoil plains. They felt the great song cycles surge through his bones. In him, the stories came to life, the past became present.

I thought about the dance-hall audience before me, the drunk and the disabled, the petrol sniffers and Thursday night fighters, the very old and the very young.

My people.

I seem to have spent most of my life on the road, running from what I never knew. But watching Kenny and the crowd, it struck me that we're all wanderers in one way or another, we're all looking for a home.

The women in the audience: god only knew how many of them had been raped or battered and abused in their lives. Probably most of them. And they'd survived.

For the first time I knew, deep in my body, what I'd been telling my brain for the last two days.

I would too.

Gutter Camp

THE CROWD DISPERSED SOON afterwards, and I drifted along in their company. People recognised me, laughed appreciatively at my skimpy little outfit, thought it was cool. When we came to the hospital, I couldn't bring myself to enter those cold glass white-feller doors. I kept going, found myself wandering alongside a big woman who gazed at me with bloodshot eyes.

'Em'ly Tempest!'

'Rosie.' Brambles.

'Where you goin, my little parnparr?' Her voice, smashed by years of abuse, was sympathetic, almost warm. I wondered if she remembered that every time we ran into one another it was in the middle of a brawl.

'Buggered if I know, Rosie.'

We were at the Gutter Camp now, a ring of ramshackle shelters in a sea of moonlit cans and broken bottles, a huddle of shabby figures crouching at fires and sipping at pannikins—of tea, I was surprised to observe. Not a drop of liquor to be smelled. The uplifting mood of the Memo Hall must have settled upon the entire town.

Rosie peered into my smashed-up face, seemed to recognise something. A kindred spirit? 'You lookin lost, Em. Got somewhere to sleep?'

'Been in hospital, Rosie.'

'Aw, you doan wanner go back there.'

'No, don't suppose I do.'

'You welcome to stay here.'

Kenny Wednesday was picking away at a two-string guitar. I made a mental note to give him my own instrument first chance I got: he'd make better use of it than I ever would. Cynthia Winton was feeding a baby. The Crankshafts were snoring in three-part disharmony.

'Appreciate that, Rosie.'

'Why you in hospital? Some feller give you a flogging, did he?'

'Sort of.'

'Ah, my poor Nangali. They mostly bastards—and the bitches are worse. You gotta watch that sneaky little piece, Cindy—she keeps a butterfly knife in her bra. I tried to give you a hand the other night.'

'Thanks for that—you saved my arse.'

She went quiet for a moment, then said, 'I hear you been runnin round out west with that little boy of mine.'

'Danny? Yeah, you should be proud of him. Turning into a real bush feller now. I love that boy: out there with them old people, learning lingo, singing the songs, fetchin his own food.'

Rosie cast a mournful eye about the tatterdemalion camp.

'Yuwayi—he better off out there,' she said, and I caught a glimpse of the woman she must have been before the booze got hold of her. The woman who'd landed Bandy, mothered Danny.

She threw a Crankshaft out of his bedroll, dragged it up close to hers, gave me tea and toast and golden syrup, watched over me.

Somewhere over near the men, I heard Kenny Wednesday humming to himself.

'Kenny!'

'Emmy?'

'That song you sang at the hall. That was a beautiful song.'

'Why thank you.'

The fire flared and cast an eerie wash across us all.

'It was about Andulka, wasn't it?'

'My paparti, yuwayi.'

'You really think he's still wandering round out west?'

'Oh, he's out there.'

'I heard he had a mountain fall on top of him.'

'Take more than a mountain, kill a feller like that.' He broke into a laugh of such extravagance that I couldn't help but join in. 'You ever meet that man?'

'Yeah, I met him one time.'

'Where that?'

I told him the story of my run-in with Andulka.

I was about ten or eleven at the time. My father had been doing a bit of prospecting out north-west of Majumanu, the community into which Andulka had wandered the year before.

Motor Jack's reputation preceded him, and he was prevailed upon to take a quick look at a new grader they were having trouble with. The quick look ended up as a week's work—the new grader was a second-hand snowplough palmed off onto the community by some enterprising salesman in Alice—and I was put into the school.

One sweltering afternoon Myrna, the teaching assistant, piled us into the back of a truck and drove out to the waterhole. I was first off the back, went galloping down the track.

I leapt over a log and came to a scrambling halt as the monstrous king brown basking there reared up and made to strike. Would have struck, if a boomerang hadn't come whirling out of nowhere and knocked it aside.

The boomerang was closely followed by a lithe young man who whipped the snake into the air and broke its back.

He regarded me, stern faced, dour eyed, uttered a sharp reproof. Glided down to the waterhole with an equipoise I've remembered to this day.

Behind me I heard a sharp intake of breath: Myrna, holding back a clutch of goggle-eyed kids.

'Who was that?' I asked.

'Andulka,' she whispered.

I swallowed hard; the man from the desert had a hell of a rep round here. He could kill you with a look.

'What he say?'

'He bin say you not from here. You move too fast: more better you slow down, take time for the country to know you.'

I frowned after him, as embarrassed by my own foolishness as I was annoyed at his arrogance.

My only other encounter with Andulka came the very next day as Jack and I were heading back out bush. We came across a mob of young fellers pushing a reluctant panel van down the road. From the sound the motor was making—none at all—they'd be pushing all the way to Bluebush.

Jack took a look under the bonnet. I watched as he worked his way through the systems: petrol, plugs, points.

'No spark,' he announced.

A trio of young men peered in from the opposite side of the engine. One of them was Andulka.

When Jack found a spare plug in his toolbox and installed it, Andulka gazed at the spark flying between the points, puzzled, suspicious. Jack threw the old one away and, as we walked off,

I saw Andulka pick it up. He studied it with such an intense curiosity that I couldn't help myself.

'Hey, Jungarayi!'

He looked up.

'Tricky thing, a machine. Better get a wriggle on if you want to understand it, old man like you.'

Andulka gazed at me, a ribbon of brown light turning in his eyes, then broke into a grin of such candour that I couldn't get it out of my head for days.

By the time I finished the story, the Gutter Camp had gone quiet. Either asleep or listening.

A voice cut into the silence from the direction of Kenny Wednesday's bedroll. 'You said it, just like that?'

'Think so.'

'Told him to get a wriggle on?'

'Far as I can recall, yep.'

'Andulka?'

'*Yes.*'

A further interlude, then another voice from the Crankshaft ensemble. 'Jeez, Em—you got bigger balls than me.'

Radio waves and green fire

I WAS AWAKE EARLY. Not as early as the flies, but. They were swarming overhead—and under chin, up nose, into the scabs and scars across my face. I pulled the blanket over, gazed out through a narrow slit.

A thin blue ribbon of smoke genied up from the fire. A scrap of meat glistered in a pan, yellow fat on charcoal bone. A play of colour ran through the ashes. Sand in the hair, grit in the eye. The shards of a thousand beer-bottle nights glinted in the dirt.

A little bus rolled up and two Indian nuns got out. One bun-shaped and sweet, the other a slice of crusty white, issuing orders. We all sprang to.

They gave me some first-class soup and a second-hand dress, seemed to know my name. Apparently there was an APB gone out. They offered me a lift back to hospital, but I told them I'd walk.

I knew I had to go back—there were people who'd be worrying for me. I didn't want to give them any more grief than I already had.

I gave Rosie a parting squeeze, headed off down the road.

The feeling on me was strange. Light-headed, invigorated. Like I was walking through a dream, the scuffed lawns and rutted nature strips of Bluebush soft-edged and fantastical.

The corrugated iron Catholic church loomed to the left of me, shimmering on the periphery of my altered state. I glanced into its cool, dark chambers. Turned, impelled by god knows what impulse, and walked in.

Stood on the threshold.

There was, I had to admit, a certain serenity about the place. The windows gleamed with blue-green light, the altar with bronze vessels, beautifully shaped. A candle glimmered on a stand. The interior as a whole radiated silence.

I walked down the aisle. I couldn't bring myself to kneel, but I sat in a pew, folded my hands, closed my eyes, took a series of deep, slow breaths.

If I'd intended anything, it was to sit there and soak up a minute or two's solitude before making my appearance at the hospital. But time slipped by, and it wasn't until I heard a noise behind me that I realised I was no longer alone. I glanced around: there was a man kneeling in one of the pews near the rear of the church.

Damn! My reputation was shot.

Or was it? He showed no sign of recognising, or even noticing, me: he was busily communicating with the Lord, his eyes were closed, his hands clenched, his lips moving. He was of medium height, an anonymous fellow with neat, thinning hair, gold-rimmed spectacles and a good shirt. Pink stripes.

Mister Suburbia; but that was his business. I just wished he wasn't there.

I was about to make a run for the exit when I heard more voices outside. Sunday morning: a service was about to begin. A blob of shadow pooled in the doorway, closely followed by the potato-sack figures of Graham Shuttlesmith and wife. Graham was the mayor of Bluebush, Lorraine the power behind the throne.

Trapped. I hunched into my pew, kept my back to them. More churchgoers arrived.

In five minutes the room was packed and Father Dal Santo was doing his thing up on the stage. God help me, the second Christian ceremony I'd been subjected to in a couple of weeks. Third, if you counted the funeral. Hoping it wasn't contagious was as close as I came to prayer.

I cast an oblique eye over the crowd, was surprised to see how many of the town's elite were there—as well as the Shuttlesmiths, I recognised George Gellie, MLA, Reg Smithers, DFC, the President of the RSL, Walter Demsky, the CEO of Copperhead Mines. I felt abashed at finding myself among such a distinguished alphabetical array: Emily Tempest, Sweet FA.

A lemon-faced old puss sat next to me, poked me with a skinny finger and proffered her hymnal, insisting I sing. A woman with a bird's nest on her head and legs like a relief map of the Blue Mountains pumped the only organ she'd ever pump. A mother and a mob of wriggling kids sat in front: the little one yawned, stretched, put a hand on my leg, ran her fingers up it, turned around and smiled delightedly.

I managed to lie low until the collection, when I suddenly found myself staring into the puzzled, ugly mug of our local member of parliament. He was horrified to see me: his bottom lip quivered, as did his bottom. Gellie by name...

Blacks were obviously a rarity round here.

He recovered well, though, waved the collection plate at me.

This is a turn-around, I thought: the MP asking the black woman for money. And I didn't have any to give him, a fact which gave me a perverse satisfaction.

Gellie strode back down the aisle, tipped the money into a bag, gave it a crisp shake: mission accomplished. I turned back to the altar, then heard an ominously familiar voice cut through the sombre atmosphere of the church.

'Scuse me, mister...'

I looked around.

Danny Brambles. Christ, where did he spring from? I thought he was still out bush.

He was standing in the doorway looking like something that had crawled out of the Retention Dams: grubby, drunk, desperate. He was wearing a torn Demons footy jumper, black shorts, bare feet.

Gellie took him in—the staggering stance, the dazed expression—raised an eyebrow, curled a lip, moved away.

Danny wasn't giving up on that much money without a struggle.

'Couldn't spare a couple of bucks, could ya mate?'

Gellie's sneer intensified, his pace quickened. His own face wasn't unblemished by the ravages of alcohol, but he had the wherewithal to do his drinking behind closed doors.

'Please, mister...' Danny made the mistake of touching him on the elbow.

The politician whipped his arm away, his nostrils growing darker by the nanosecond. 'Get your hands off me!'

Danny stopped, tilted his head to the left, blinked and ran his fingers through his hair. He cast an eye around the room and seemed for the first time to have an inkling of what he'd wandered into.

The congregation stared. The ladies rattled their beads and tutted, the menfolk glanced at each other and rolled their eyes, wondering how the hell you tackled a drunken coon at a Sunday morning service.

Father Dal Santo wasn't troubled by any such uncertainties. 'You! Boy!' he bristled from the pulpit. 'How dare you come here in such a condition?'

His stroppy little teeth reminded me of someone—or something: Stiffy, the not-so-dearly departed pest of Green Swamp.

Danny turned to him, ever so slowly, shot a look of bleary-eyed animosity in the priest's direction.

'Condition?' The dreadlocks flashed.

'This is the House of God!'

'Of God?' The words were mostly hisses and whispers in his mouth. 'Oh, the pastor tell us about your god. He's a hard god, that one. Hit us with sickness and…burn us. Dynamite Christ, that one.'

'Why you little devil!'

'Devil? Ah, your devil or god depend which way the light shine.'

Danny took a step to the left, then stumbled, leaned against a pew, sank slowly to the floor.

He sat with his back to the seat, screwed up his face, stared at the ceiling like he expected it to fall in on top of him.

An old head with young hair popped out of the sacristy 'I've called the police—they're on the way.'

'Ah, jeez.' I rose from my seat, my earlier nervousness forgotten. 'I wish you hadn't done that.'

I could imagine the mess the bloody cops would make of this. The bloke would have been better off calling the Indian nuns—at least they were nice: they gave you chicken soup and red dresses. All the cops gave you was grief.

'Danny…' I moved down the aisle.

He noticed me for the first time, startled. 'Em'ly Tempest? You for real?'

'Far as I can tell.'

'Heard you was in hospital.'

'Not now.'

'Where you come from?'

'Just passing by, Danny. Thought you might need a hand.'

His brow twisted. 'You still in the police?'

'Not any more.'

'Tha's good. More better you go back out to Moonlight. Safer there. Out west my country they kill you if you open your mouth.'

His eyes drifted, lit upon one of the Stations of the Cross: Christ and the Crown of Thorns. He stared at the scene, horrified. The drawn, tormented face, the drops of blood, the desperate eyes.

He turned back to me. His face was a contorted mirror of the one on the wall.

'Fire out there, Em, running underground, through the air, like knives flashin. Green fire, burns your blood, kills you slow and hard. You can hear it if you listen.'

He was almost weeping. I'd never seen him quite this disturbed before. He wasn't just drunk; it was much more than that. He was having some sort of psychotic episode—the DTs, I assumed, or the drugs or both. It was as if the blood had drained from his body, the energy from his muscles. His anxiety about noises had exploded into full-blown paranoia.

The nerves, I thought, those twisted, frayed circuits of the brain: they're a bloody minefield. And when you put a foot wrong, by god, they take a toll. He'd always been a delicate boy, but he'd gone from anxious to barking mad in the space of a few days.

When had I last laid eyes on him? When we said goodbye at the roadhouse, a couple of weeks ago. What the hell had happened between then and now? He was looking worse than me, and I'd been battered, raped and damn near totalled by a landslide.

I scanned the room, desperate to get him out of there before the cops arrived. I had visions of him belting somebody, being dragged off to jail, subjected to god knows what horrors.

As if in answer to my prayers, somebody from the congregation stepped forward.

'Can I help?'

It was the man who'd been in church before the service. Mr Pink-striped Suburbia. But I felt bad about the mockery: straight as a die the bloke might have been, but he was the only one there sensitive enough to realise that Danny was more in need of compassion than coppers.

'Sure as hell hope so.'

'Maybe we should take him home—if he's got one?'

'He has. You got a car?'

He looked like I was asking if he had a head. 'Of course.'

'That'd be wonderful. He really doesn't want to get tangled up with the law right now; he's in enough trouble already.'

He came up beside me, moving with a cautious gait and a diplomatic smile. 'He seemed to think you were the law.'

'Used to be an Aboriginal Police Officer. Not any more. Where you parked?'

'Just outside.'

I knelt next to the crumpled boy. 'Danny, listen to me...'

His eyelids fluttered. 'What's happening, Em?'

'We're taking you home, okay? Back to Bandy's.'

He gazed up at me, sloppy-eyed, his breath deep-fried in kerosene. But he let us help him to his feet.

Mr Suburbia and I took an elbow each. We guided the boy into a metal-blue Range Rover, and I joined him in the back seat.

As we were reversing out, I spotted the police van zipping down the road, the uber-simpatico Harley at the wheel. Danny noticed it as well, stirred restlessly.

'Settle down,' I told him. 'There's nobody going to hurt you.'

'But they do. All of us. I read it in the paper.'

'What did it say?'

'Oh Emily, you have to be careful—they kill you if you know, cut your fuckin throat.' I glanced at our driver: not the sort of language he would have expected to hear when he set out for church that morning, but he seemed to be taking it in his stride. 'They killin our country...'

'Who is?'

A glazed stare, a down-turned mouth. 'I don't know.'

'How are they killing it?'

'Radio waves,' he mumbled, almost inaudible.

'*Radio* waves?' Jesus, he was a mess.

'Something like that,' he rasped. 'They're everywhere.'

'Radio waves? Well they are, but they don't do much harm as far as I know. Who told you about them?'

'I read it in the paper.'

'Which paper?'

'Oh, I dunno—some whitefeller paper.' That narrowed it down. He seemed lost in the echo of his own reflection in the window. 'These whitefellers and their paper: they got so many—newspaper, dunny paper, money, maps an cigarettes.' He giggled; no humour in it. 'Light em up, curl around the edges and you burn.'

He caught sight of the crucifix mounted on the church roof, stared at it, puzzled. 'Em'ly?' he asked.

'Yes, Danny?'

'These kartiya—what for they gotta tear the shade apart? Them and their machine god?'

'Wish I knew.'

'The pastor tell us he come from the desert, this God.' His gaze turned to the west; he shuddered. 'I'm thinking he bring it along with him.'

I tapped the driver's seat. 'Let's go.'

Our good samaritan glanced back at us, concern and curiosity fighting for possession of his face. He was obviously a decent enough guy but, like a lot of whitefellers at the upper end of the food chain, it was a safe bet he spent his life virtually quarantined from the Aboriginal people he lived among.

I knew the type. You could go from the air-conditioned office to the exclusive club, then back to the cyclone-wired house and the big dog and barely notice a blackfeller all the while, except to step over the odd one in the gutter.

'Where to?'

'Bleaker Street.'

'Down past the government offices?'

'You got it.'

Cockroach capital

WE CRUISED THROUGH THE Sunday morning streets, reached Bandy's house in short order.

He was at home, thank god; he came out, automatically took charge.

'Danny, Danny,' he moaned when I told him what had happened. He helped him inside, but they'd only got as far as the gate when the boy slipped from his grasp and tumbled to the ground. I rushed to give him a hand, and the driver joined us; between the three of us, we got him up the path and into the house. Once we were inside, Bandy shepherded him towards a spare bed.

'Put the kettle on, Em?' he called back at me.

Mr Suburbia and I stood in the kitchen. While I made tea, he looked around the room, eyebrows raised. First time you've been inside a blackfeller house, I thought to myself. A couple of cockroaches copulated on the upper wall, a mouse popped its head out of a loaf of bread. A layer of dust coated everything. Welcome to the world.

'Want a cuppa?' I asked.

A glance at the crud-encrusted dishes in the sink. 'Maybe not right now.'

He cleared a space at the kitchen table, making a neat heap of the litter. Pizza boxes, a folder of chord charts. A scatter of picks, other guitarist's paraphernalia; an old leather bag, more folders spilling out, looked like it was where Bandy kept his music.

'Sorry,' the fellow said. 'I didn't catch your name.'

'Emily.'

'Emily. I'm Kevin.'

We shook hands. From a back room we heard a young boy's voice, a dark moan.

'Maybe we should have taken him up to the hospital?' suggested Kevin.

'Don't think so.' Bandy had a way of moving up on you, like a stalking bull. 'Them whitefeller bureaucracies get their claws into you, never know where it's gonna end. Had that copper come back again, Em.'

'Hurley?'

'Still sniffin round about the boy. Don't worry—I've been through this before. I'll keep an eye on him. Cup of tea'll settle him down.'

He shook the driver's hand. 'Bandy Mabulu, mate.'

'Kevin Brock.'

'Like to thank you for bringing me boy home.' He opened the sugar jar, pulled out a handful of money. 'Can I give you a few bucks for your trouble?'

Kevin waved him away. 'Please—it was nothing.'

'Cup of tea, then?'

He glanced at his watch. 'Thanks, some other time. The wife

will think I've been kidnapped.'

Bandy saw him to the door, came back, went and stood by his son. Danny was curled up on the bed, possibly asleep, but far from at ease. One arm flung across the pillow, one leg dangling over the side. Sweat everywhere.

'Let's hope he gets some rest,' I said. 'He's had a hell of a shock.'

Bandy shook his head, weary to the bone. 'Poor little bastard spends his life in a state of shock.'

'Never seen him quite this bad. And in church! Father Dal Santo didn't know whether to shit or sing a hymn. When did he come back to town?'

'Late last night.'

'Say why he came in?'

He ran his tongue along his upper lip, seemed uncomfortable. 'Wanted to speak to you.'

'Yeah?'

'Told him not to hassle you—he freaked out when he heard you were in hospital. Wandered off. Somewhere in there he must have hooked up with his drinking buddies. Next thing I know you're delivering him back here, zapped out of his brain.'

'Zapped all right. He was raving on about radio waves and fire or some bloody thing.'

'Radio waves? Fire?'

'When we were out west we were following a fire dreaming,' I grimaced. 'Powerful stuff, Bandy. Maybe too much for him.'

Bandy shuffled and cleared his throat. 'Look Em...I know you've been through a terrible time yourself.' As did the whole bloody town, apparently. 'I appreciate you taking an interest in the boy, but maybe it's time you took more of an interest in yourself. He's my son. Don't worry. Mighta been a bit distracted from time to time, but I'm still his old man. I'll look out for him.'

'Course you will, Bandy. I never doubted it.' I caught the

glimmer in his eyes, knew the boy was in safe hands. 'But he's not well.'

Danny rustled in the bed: he was breathing with a sharp, sucking motion, as if some internal fire was sucking the oxygen out of him.

'There's a doctor up the hospital—Kokinos—Marta; I trust her.'

Bandy gave that a moment's consideration. 'Must admit, be a relief to get help from a professional. You're sure she won't rat him out to the cops?'

'She'll guard his privacy like a tiger.'

'Maybe when he settles down I'll take him up there.'

'You do that.'

I drained my cup, rose to my feet. 'Time I was getting back.'

'Give you a lift, but I better not leave the boy.'

'Course not. I been loafing around in bed all week, walk'd do me good.'

Mister Suburbia

IT WAS A SCORCHER of a morning, though. I was pleasantly surprised when I came out the front gate and saw the blue Rover was still there. A tinted window slid down, Kevin's head appeared.

'Offer you a ride somewhere?'

'Thought the wife was waiting.'

'Didn't seem right to leave you wandering around in this heat.'

'You're a marvel, buddy. If you could run me back up to the hospital?'

'No problem.'

I made to enter, then hesitated when a jackhammer started up across the road. The Works blokes were on the job again. Or one of them, at least, a whip-thin fellow in a fluorescent jacket who was ripping into the footpath. On a Sunday now—did these bastards never rest? I went over and tapped him on the shoulder.

'Excuse me!'

He startled, didn't seem to appreciate the interruption: the lock of orange hair poking out from under the hard hat bristled.

'Wouldn't be able to tone it down a bit, would you?'

He shot me a look that said, quite sensibly, 'Mind telling me how to tone a jackhammer down?'

'Maybe you could start down the other end of the street?' I suggested. 'We've got a sick boy in here.'

The bloke assented with a stringy shrug and I climbed back into the Rover. A late model job, its air-con ice cool, its seats inviting the passenger—even trash like me—to snuggle up and make herself at home.

'Sorry,' said Kevin as we took off, 'what was your name again?'

'Emily—Tempest.'

'Tempest...? Tempest. Rings a bell.'

'Not an alarm, I hope.'

'Ah yes, the fellow from the Burnt Shirt Mine. Jack Tempest. A relative?'

'Distant. He's me father.'

'You should be proud of him. He's a minor legend around these parts; Burnt Shirt's the most successful small-scale operation in the region.' A wafer-thin smile. 'Smart move, then, my giving you a hand. You'll be worth a lot of money one day.'

'Money! From Jack? I'll be lucky to get the shirt! You obviously don't know him personally.'

'Can't say I do, no.'

'He's made and lost at least three fortunes that I know of in the past twenty years.'

He shrugged. 'Nature of the game, alas.'

A pause. 'You in the game yourself?' I enquired, racking my brain for conversation openers.

'Mining? Yes, more on the admin side, though.' That figured: he looked like an office johnny.

'Copperhead?'

'In a roundabout way.'

'Mate, everything's Copperhead if your roundabout's big enough.'

'King of the Mountain Holdings. We're strategic management consultants.'

Another pause. 'What's strategic management entail then?'

'Mostly sitting at a computer trying to anticipate mineral prices.' He shrugged, almost apologetic. 'A far cry from the world your old man moves in…'

'That explains it.'

'Explains what?'

'The soft hands, the clean fingernails, the flash car…'

He glanced ruefully at his hands on the wheel. 'They look after us. We give back, though.'

'Yeah?'

'Yes. I like to think we make a contribution. Not just to the company: to the community—to the nation. What we dig out of the ground is our biggest export earner. It doesn't just pay for the car I drive—ultimately, it pays for the way of life we all enjoy— even you.'

'Jeez mate, I come pretty cheap: tin of tobacco, tank of petrol, packet of sausages if I'm lucky.' He smiled. 'You're preaching to the converted, though—remember, my old man's a miner.'

'Then you'd understand: we work long and hard for the perks—even those of us behind desks—and we take risks.'

'Well, you took a risk this morning…'

'Oh?'

'Helping a troubled boy in front of that mob in church. And I'm grateful to you for it.'

He fiddled with his spectacles, uncomfortable with the praise. 'It was nothing. Should be your first port of call, really.'

'What should be?'

'The church. If we can't show some compassion to those of our parish who are in need, what's the point of the whole thing?'

'Pity everybody doesn't share the sentiment.'

I settled into the seat, enjoyed the chilled air rippling up my dress. Kevin eased the car out onto the main drag, drove slowly and carefully. 'We have been encouraging Copperhead to take a more pro-active role in relation to the Indigenous community,' he expanded. 'Apprenticeship schemes, land reclamation programs, that sort of thing. Hundreds of employees at the Copperhead: guess how many Aboriginals?'

'Not many.'

He thumped the wheel; this was something of a hobby-horse. 'Two! That's it! And neither of them locals. They've been incredibly backward in that regard—and short sighted. Finding staff is the hardest thing about running a remote operation, and yet they've got a ready-made workforce sitting on their doorstep. Your young friend back there—what was his name again? Danny?'

'Danny Brambles.'

'And he's from Bluebush?'

'His country's down south from here. Stonehouse Creek, out on the Gunshot Road.'

'Stonehouse? Don't believe I've heard of it.'

'You're not alone there.'

'Well, maybe I could find something for him. Landscaping, mechanics. Do you know what his interests are?'

'Right now? Drinking, smoking and playing guitar.'

'I see.' He gave the matter some thought. 'Obviously comes from a decent family, though. Can he read and write?'

'Had a very disrupted education...' I thought about the song he'd sung out at the shack. 'Don't know what his reading's like, but he's got a way with words. He's just a little unstable...'

'Yes, I got that impression.' He made the turn into Hospital Drive. 'Did you have any idea what he was talking about?'

'God knows. Radio waves? I'm pretty sure it's not them that's frying his brain.'

The driver concurred with a wry smile as we pulled into the hospital car park.

'Well, thanks for your help back there, Kevin.'

'A pleasure, Emily. Look, I meant what I said about the boy. I'll have a word with Personnel—see what we can find.'

He gave me a sympathetic toot as he drove away.

A job for Danny? I thought. Good luck.

Visiting hours

I WAS PLEASED TO see a familiar, dust-caked Toyota outside the building, the Parks and Wildlife logo on her door. I walked into reception, spotted my man engaged in an animated conversation with Doctor Marta.

I walked up behind them, spoke softly. 'Hey, Jo.'

He spun round, engulfed me in arms and stubble.

'Still haven't had that shave,' I mumbled from under his beard. 'Feels like a porcupine jumping on my head.'

'Emily, I've been so bloody worried about you.'

He looked me up and down, then crushed me again.

'Eh, slow down,' I grimaced. 'Like to come out of this with a few bones unbroken.'

'Where the hell have you been? I've been driving round half the night looking for you.'

'As have our security people,' frowned Marta.

'Sorry about that.'

'Emily Tempest apologising?' Jojo turned to the doctor. 'What have you got her on?' Marta looked a little taken aback herself.

I shrugged: 'Just wanted a bit of fresh air. Didn't mean to cause you any grief.'

'Somebody said they spotted you at the Memo dance. I searched the usual haunts. Lot of unusual ones.'

'Did you try the Gutter Camp?'

He scratched his beard. 'Not that unusual.'

'Or the Catholic church?'

'Jesus.'

'As it were.'

He held me at arm's length, regarded me suspiciously.

'Not on the road to Damascus, I hope?'

'Don't worry Jojo, take more than a psychopathic coke-head to turn me on to the Lord. Poor young Danny Brambles was in there...'

'Rosie's boy?'

'Yeah. Totally wired, he was. Trying to borrow money from the collection plate. God knows what he's on. Never seen anybody hit the skids so fast.'

He stared upwards, narrowed his eyes. 'Wasn't that long ago, he was the quickest thing on the Bluebush basketball court. Knew he'd been drinking, but I saw him out bush a while back...'

'Stonehouse?'

'Near there, yeah—out hunting with his grandparents. Thought he was looking good.'

'Well he's looking bloody awful now.' I shrugged. 'Not that I can talk—let's get out of here.'

'You want to discharge yourself?'

The doctor rattled a stethoscope. 'I wouldn't recommend that, Emily, not yet. You've had a terrible experience; we'd like to keep an eye on you for a few more days.'

276

'What is this, the Hotel California?' I put an arm around Jojo's waist, drew him in close. 'Thanks Marta, but I've had all the hospital I need right now. Jojo's spent long enough dragging bilbies back from the edge; bout time he did the same for me.'

'Her Master's voice,' said Jojo. 'Sorry doc, I think we're on our way. When Emily sets her mind to something...'

Marta frowned. 'On your concussed head let it be, then—and I'll note on your file that it's against my advice. You need rest. Jojo, bring her back if there's the slightest change in her condition. And I'll take those stitches out on Thursday.'

A hospital pass

AS WE WERE HEADING through the front door we bumped—
literally—into Wishy Ozolins lumbering in from the opposite direction, his mouth grim, his arms laden with flowers and chocolates.

'Emily,' he said awkwardly. 'I was just coming to visit you.'

'Made it by the skin of your fingers.'

'You going home already?'

'Time off for bad behaviour.'

'I—heard what…I mean, about your…' His voice caught.

I put him out of his misery. 'Shit happens, Wishy. Fortunately,
most of it happened to the shit.'

He gazed down at me, his expression almost paternal, his
blue eyes damp and swimming with emotions I found it hard to
decipher. Affection, which was welcome—I liked him too. And
pity—inevitable, perhaps, but from my perspective the less of it
the better.

But there was something else there, something as elusive and tricky as a speck of gold in a gravel wash. Sorrow? Not guilt, surely. What did he have to feel guilty about?

He stepped back, nodded at the waiting car. 'You'll want to be on your way then?'

'That's the general idea, but technically we're still on hospital grounds, so if those Ferrero Rochers have got my name on them...'

'Must be getting better,' said Jojo. 'Her mind's moving on to lower things.'

Wishy smiled, presented me with the chocolates, added the flowers with as much aplomb as most men of his ilk could muster in such a situation.

'Why thank you.' I buried my face in the bouquet, breathed a heady blend of bougainvillea and gardenia. 'From your own garden?'

'They are.'

'Say hello to those gorgeous girls of yours for me,' I threw back at him as we walked out the door. 'Tell em I've been polishing up my bowling—be back for the rematch before they know what hit em. And thank Loreena for the flowers.'

We left him looking lost in the foyer.

'He'll have to wait a while to do that,' Jojo commented as we walked towards the Tojo.

'Do what?'

'Thank Loreena.'

'Why's that?'

'She's in the States.'

I almost dropped the chocolates.

'As in United?'

'Yep.'

'What the hell's she doing there?' I was more than a little put out that Jojo, just back from a spell out bush, seemed to know more of what was going on round town than I did. That was Jojo, though; he had a way of gaining instant trust and stumbling onto information that your more spiky individual—me, for instance—had to work for.

'The oldest girl...'

'Simone.'

'She and her mother flew out yesterday. Gone to Seattle for an operation.'

My chest tightened. A sense of foreboding reared.

'What sort of operation?'

'A transplant.'

'A trans...what of?

'Her bone marrow.'

'What's that mean?'

'I suspect it means leukaemia.'

'Oh, that poor girl. I knew there was something wrong.'

We climbed aboard, but I was too stunned by the information I'd just received to do anything other than sit there and find what comfort I could in the familiar seat, shaped to my body, the eucalypt and bougainvillea smells that permeated the vehicle.

'How do you know all this?' I asked.

'Wishy's was one of the places I called on when I was running round looking for you this morning. Found myself being interrogated by a rather commanding little person called—Tiger Lily, was it?'

'It wasn't, but it is now.'

'She filled me in. Would have given me the full medical history if her father hadn't joined us. He wasn't saying much...'

'Never seems to...'

'...but he's flying out himself, tomorrow morning.'

That all made sense; it explained Simone's wasted appearance, her relentless personality, the trouble I'd sensed brewing beneath that solid family surface. I liked that girl a lot, but the news of her illness left me with a stronger sense of unease than it should have.

We sat there, corralled by silence. The first time we'd been alone since...

Jojo put an arm around my shoulder, his face up close to mine. 'Grim times,' he said.

'You can say that again. My god, what she must be going through.'

'I meant you.'

'Oh. That...'

'Can't say how sorry I am about this whole horrible business, Em.'

I felt the sadness, the shame, come biting at the borders. I didn't want to go there. Worried I'd never make it back.

'My fault,' I said curtly. 'I fucked up.'

'We all fuck up, time to time. Don't usually pay a price like that.'

I found some skin among the whiskers, gave it a kiss. 'It's okay, Jojo. Thanks, but I can handle it.'

He got the message, backed off and backed out. Headed for the Three Mile.

We pulled up at the shack, and I spotted a lick of smoke drifting in from the scrub alongside it.

'Visitor,' Jojo said.

I climbed down. Under a tree, a shimmering, bluesmoke fire. On the other side of it, a square-browed woman in a turquoise dress.

I walked towards her. She looked up through the haze, her eyes as luminous as a worn-out horse's flanks.

'Hey sister.'

'Hazel.'

I sat beside her. 'Where'd you spring from?'

'Jojo come out to Moonlight and got me.'

'Trust Jojo. Never stay still, that feller.'

'I was comin in anyway.'

'Why?'

She took my hand. 'Knew you was in trouble Emmy.'

'How?'

Her silence said more than most speech.

My head found its way to her lap, my tears onto her dress. She ran her fingers through my hair, her palms along my spine. The smoke stung, but it was a good, invigorating feeling. I looked at the base of the fire, saw melting spinifex rosin. A healing agent. Like the bush oils she worked into my temples, the songs she whispered in my ear.

'I'll get over it, Haze.'

'Dunno that you ever get over it, Em. Not all the way. Carry it round forever. But you get by. Jeez, we're all carryin something.'

Strings of thick black hair drifted across her forehead. Her arms felt like a blanket round my body, then they were a blanket. I looked up, saw Jojo kneeling alongside us. He'd covered us with an old Wagga rug. He stoked the fire, kissed my forehead.

It's not the smoke, I reflected as I floated away; it's not the rosin or the oil, or even the songs.

It's the love that bears them.

Fire dreams

SOMEWHERE IN THE HALF-LIGHT I felt my body being hoisted into the air. I opened my eyes: Jojo carrying me in through the back door. He laid me on the bed, pulled a sheet up over my shoulders.

I drifted off to sleep, but it was still a dark, troubled experience, shot through with red and blue nightmares. I knew I'd hit rock bottom when I found myself driving in panic across a vast, sun-racked plain, hotly pursued by...by a wildfire, of all things.

I was at the wheel of my little white Hilux. I sped away, then glanced back: a sudden shift in the wind, and the fire was in front of me, its red glare blasting through the windscreen, blinding my eyes, burning my lips.

I swung round to the west, but it was there as well. Only then did I realise that the fire wasn't spreading of its own accord: there was a man racing across its front. He held a flaming brand in one hand and was touching it to the spinifex, torching it as he ran.

Paisley? I thought for one gut-shuddering moment. But no, the runner was black, his bare body glistening with goanna grease and sorry scars.

Tiny animals—dunnarts and geckoes, bearded dragons—scuttled and fled before the inferno; birds of prey circled above, dived through the smoke and picked them off with a fearful screeching.

I wheeled around, fled to the east, but it was no use: I was surrounded. Choking black clouds blotted the sky, savage light splintered and flicked through the cab. Something—someone?—crashed onto the roof, began hammering wildly.

I woke up, gasping with fear and shuddering with a sudden insight: this business wasn't over.

It wasn't over. Oh Christ—what did that mean?

I recognised the fire man running through my dream: Andulka. And I saw what he stood for: a refusal to compromise, to accept anything less than the truth.

Emily Tempest, I told myself, you compromised. You settled for the slipshod, the second rate, the half-arsed.

I'd tried to tell myself I'd solved the mystery of Doc's murder, but that was bullshit, I knew. Truth was, I'd been hammered once, was scared to get up in case I was hammered again.

Not good enough.

A volley of unanswered questions ricocheted through my mind.

Had Doc really been murdered because he'd stumbled onto a hidden ganja plantation? If that was all there was to it, why had the Snowball files been removed? Would Paisley have hung around to go through Doc's cabinet on the off chance that somebody would make a connection between his little horticultural enterprise and an obscure geological site out west?

Paisley's final words came slithering in, past my mental blocks:

'As if they didn't warn...' What was that all about? As if who hadn't warned him?

Was there something about Dingo Springs I didn't know? Doc had inveigled Noel Redman into taking out a mineral exploration licence on the site: in his mind, doubtless it was to ensure unfettered access for his research, but what if he'd stumbled across something else, something somebody was willing to kill for?

That line of enquiry introduced a range of options. Redman himself, for one; he stood to gain if there was anything of value on the site. There were other incriminating factors: it was Redman who discovered the body, he'd had a gutful of the geriatric geologist, he'd jumped like a prodded bull when I asked about the leases.

Then there was the landslide. Stiffy had raced up the hill just before the explosion—had he been running to his boss? Or had he been running at someone else, doing his little watchdog number?

Even the Reverend Bodycombe wasn't above suspicion. There'd been ongoing antagonism between him and Doc. He'd disappeared into his van around the time of the murder. And he was a sneaky bastard if ever I saw one—an opinion which, I had to admit, may have been tainted by my general policy of never trusting anybody with crosses on the collar.

And there was one other person floating around the peripheries of my mind: Wishy.

Nothing I could put my finger on, but he'd been acting strangely. He hadn't told me he'd gone out west with his brother. He was Doc's heir; and, as he himself had admitted, Doc could be the most maddening man alive. And his daughter, Simone: was there a motive there? He wasn't exactly on Struggle Street, but sending her off into the money-grubbing clutches of the American health system would have racked up some serious bills.

And finally, running like a ground bass beneath these

speculations, there was the image of Doc's rock formation: I had no idea of how it fitted into the dark events of recent weeks, but I couldn't rid myself of the suspicion—the premonition, almost—that it did. I could almost sense Doc somewhere near, reaching out, trying to tell me something.

Those frenzied seconds of the landslide flashed through my mind. Had its purpose been to get rid of me—or of Jet and her sculpture? Had Doc's killer known it was the key to the mystery of his death?

A fire ceremony, a broken song, a dead geologist, a landslide, a teenager with a lethal illness, a sculpture of stone and wood. Disparate elements, like planets orbiting a star.

But what—or who—was the star?

How did they connect? Why couldn't I escape the suspicion that they did?

A further insight slipped in, uninvited, unannounced. Unwanted, really, because it chilled me. There was a single mind at work here, an invisible force, manipulating, keeping the plates spinning, setting traps, unleashing feints and diversions, staying a step ahead of me.

I groaned, worn out, overwhelmed by the sheer effort of thinking, exhausted by the last few days. I rolled back onto the pillow and buried my head in my arms, the explosive footsteps from the nightmare still ringing through my head.

I was wide awake now, but there it was again, that noise, echoing around the shack.

Somebody was hammering on the front door.

I checked my watch. After midnight. What was going on? Jojo had woken as well—the neighbours had probably woken, and they were miles away. He was on his feet—or one of them, stumbling into a pair of shorts and hopping to the door.

Water dreams

'HANG ON,' HE MUMBLED. 'Hang on.'

I raised my head, made out a female figure, heard a frantic voice riddled with gasps and sobs.

'Em'ly Tempest there? Trouble in town, too much trouble...'

'What the...' exclaimed Jojo. 'Meg?'

I climbed out of bed, winced: oi, that hurt! My bones were being attacked by termites. I grabbed a sarong, hobbled to the door.

Meg Brambles was standing on the threshold, almost pushing into the room; Magpie hovered in the background, hat in hand. The yellow Toyota was parked in the driveway, diesel motor pinging.

'Oh Nangali...' She almost cried with relief when she saw me.

'What's going on, Meg?'

'Em'ly, you still in the police?'

'Well, not...'

'You gotta come, gotta come now. We need you!' A slew of disjointed words poured forth. 'Terrible business in town. I worry they killin that boy.'

'Slow down, Meg. Who's killing who?'

'Bin a shocking fight, up town. One whitefeller finish. Kurlupartu lockem up that grandson bilonga we.'

'Danny?'

'Yuwayi.'

'What for?'

'Maybe for fighting, maybe drink—I don't understand. His daddy got took to hospital.'

Another drunken brawl at the house? Bandy badly injured? Possible, I knew: decent a feller as he was, Bandy inhabited a world in which violence was only ever a sniff or swig away.

Jojo was climbing into the boots he left by the door.

'Let me handle this, Em.'

'No way.' I pulled on a pair of cargo pants and a shirt, grabbed my bag.

He turned me towards him, regarded me with pleading eyes.

'Emily—haven't you had enough?'

I hesitated; but not for long. 'Promised that boy I'd be there for him.'

The back door opened: Hazel came in from her campsite under the tree, stopped short when she saw us standing there.

'What's going on?'

'The boy's in trouble again.'

'Danny?'

'Fraid so. I'll sort it out.' She peered at me suspiciously. 'Meg, where did all this happen?'

'The basketball court.'

'Come on—we can talk on the way.'

I drove my own car, Meg beside me, shaking in her seat, moaning softly. Jojo and Magpie followed. We left Hazel on the veranda, a blanket on her shoulders, a frown on her brow.

'You see any of this yourself?' I asked Meg.

'No, we bin sleepin down the South Camp.'

'How'd you hear about it?'

'Young Jimmy Crankshaft come down, tell us there been a big fight up town, said the kurlupartu lock up Danny, said his daddy bin hurt bad.'

'When did you mob come in to Bluebush?'

'Yesterday.'

'What brought you in?'

'Danny wanted to talk to you.'

'You know what was upsetting him?'

She sighed, stared out the window. 'He bin unhappy ever since we come back from that trip to Dingo Spring.'

'This morning he was raving about radio waves and god knows what. You don't know what set him off, do you?'

Her thin grey hair flickered in the wind; she pushed it out of her face, rested her chin on a hand. 'When we bin travelling back to Stonehouse the other day, we stop along Green Swamp Roadhouse. Danny got talking to that China girl.'

I groaned quietly. Jet. That'd be right—she'd drive anybody mad. People seem to think I can be a handful, but that runaway nun made me look like a muesli-munching pacifist.

'Danny ask her about that stone statue thing...'

'The sculpture?'

'Yuwayi, that one the China girl bin build. Before we leave, Danny walk old Windmill through it, ask him to feel it with his hands.'

I thought about Doc. Same tactile approach to his particular discipline.

'Did he make anything of it?'

'Yuwayi. He tell us it's a map.' She tapped on the dash, made a map of sorts herself. 'Like a painting, you know?'

'Yeah.' Maps and artworks have a close relationship round here; half the paintings in the galleries of Alice Springs are maps of one sort or another. Of minds, if not places. 'Map of what?'

'Dreamin out west.'

'Fire dreaming?' I wondered whether my own dream had been the premonition it felt like.

'Water.'

'What?'

'That water dreaming running down from Kirlipatu to Eagle Creek, you know?'

'Not really.' The country out west is interwoven with so many dreams it would take forever to unravel them. 'I'll take your word for it.'

As I drove, I struggled to fit these latest pieces into the puzzle: Doc had constructed—and Jet copied, and Windmill identified—a three-dimensional map of a water songline that ran across the country out west.

Which could mean anything or nothing at all. Might simply be the random intersection of two geriatric imaginations. But why had it rattled Danny so deeply? Something he knew that I didn't, or just his drug-fired imagination?

I'd have to follow up on this later; right now, I had more pressing things to attend to. We were on the edge of town and the basketball courts were looming.

Scattered around the rickety grandstand was that ominous assemblage of paddy wagons and ambulances, of tech officers and spectators I'd come to recognise as a crime scene.

Playing under lights

THEY'D SET UP A floodlight. Its yellow arc lit a bleak body lying in a pool of blood. Bunter was standing guard as a tech guy scraped something into an evidence bag. Harley stood back, leaning against a fence and dragging on a smoke.

I got out, glanced at the corpse. a whitefeller, burly and burnt. Face up. Not a face I knew. He had a marine haircut, black jeans, a glistening T-shirt.

I spotted Cockburn standing with a couple of uniforms talking to—talking at—a group of young men. He had them up against the mesh fence, back-up ready in case they bolted. I came up beside him.

'Sir?'

He was busily scribbling onto a pad, but I felt him tense the moment I opened my mouth. 'Kind of busy right now, Emily.'

'Where's Danny?'

'You oughter be in hospital.'

'Just want to know what the hell happened.'

I recognised some of the young men: town boys, one or two from the Westside camp, others from the Scorpions, some of them still in basketball gear. Their eyelids flickered and twitched, their fingers tugged and drummed. No sign of Danny.

'What's happened is that these...*youths*'—from the tone of voice, *little black shits* might have expressed his thoughts more frankly—'were doing what they do best: drinking, fighting and generally fucking up. Only this time it's got out of hand, and an innocent bystander—a white man—has wound up with a knife in the heart.'

I nodded at the buzzcut in the gravel.

'Who was he?'

'Still trying to work that out. Someone said he might be a relative of one of the boys in the fight.'

He caught my puzzled expression.

'There were some white boys involved as well,' he explained. 'Bit of unfinished business from an earlier basketball match. Most of them scattered before we got here.'

And you only managed to pinch the black ones?

'But I still don't understand. They told me you'd arrested Danny Brambles...'

'The boy?' He checked his notes, turned away with a casual click of the tongue. 'That's right: he's back at the jail now. He was the one who did the stabbing.'

I touched him on the elbow. 'That's not possible, sir.'

He cast an oblique eye at me: 'Saw it happen then, did you Emily?'

'You know I didn't, but I do know the boy. There's no way he could have...'

'We've got witnesses—one of them a police officer.'

'It just doesn't make sense. What happened to Bandy?'

'Who?'

'His father.'

'The older bloke? Lost a lot of blood, but they tell me he should survive.'

'Survive what?'

'A cut throat.'

'Shit!' I glanced at the dead man. 'He did that?'

'Looks like it.'

'Pretty enthusiastic innocent bloody bystander.'

'Well if he was, he's paid the price for it. Now if you don't mind...' He returned his attentions to the detainees.

As I made my way back to the car, I spotted a couple of white boys lurking in the shadow of the grandstand, leaning against the scaffolding and staring at the gravel. I took another look at the nearest of them: shoulder-length blond hair, slim build, athletic. Cockburn's son.

I went across to him.

'Jarrod.'

He was slow to recognise me. The light was poor, but there was more to it than that: the boy looked like he was in shock.

'Jarrod? You remember me? Emily. I work with your old man.'

His eyes drifted onto me fleetingly, then flickered across to his father. 'Course I remember you,' he mumbled. 'You're the one who...'

'Did you see what happened here tonight?'

He stared at the ground, his face disappearing in a hank of yellow hair. 'Not supposed to talk about it.'

'Who said that?'

'Dad.'

The other boy—hardscrabble skin, squat, with a peeling red nose—wasn't as reticent. 'Come on, man, she's with the cops too. Just tell her what you told me.'

'Dad said…'

'Jarrod seen it all,' he interrupted. 'He stabbed him.'

'Shut up, Crimsy.'

'Who's "he"?' I pressed.

'The skinny feller, the one they got locked up; used to play for the Scorps. Danny, is it? There's a bit of a fight going on over at the court, right?—us and the Scorps, nothing much—feller comes over to see what's goin on and Danny just stuck him in the guts…'

'Emily!' Cockburn's stentorian voice cut into the tale from across the court. I turned around. 'That's a witness in a homicide you're interfering with there. You want to end up in custody as well?'

I made to respond, then decided against it. I'd heard enough. Crimsy didn't seem all that bright, but nor did he seem a liar. I walked away, my head spinning. It all sounded unreal, horrible beyond words. What the fuck was happening to this town? Was the weather driving everybody out of their minds?

I made my way back to the car, shoulders slumped, eyes downcast. Magpie and Meg were waiting anxiously. A grim-faced Jojo came and joined us.

'Learn anything?' I asked him.

'More than I wanted to: looks bad for Danny. And for Bandy, but the paramedics reckon he'll survive.'

'That's about what I got, too. Cockburn says one of his men saw it happen.'

'Harley. There was a punch-up after the game; night patrol was trying to break it up. Sounds like the feller was stabbed over behind the grandstand.'

'None of this makes sense,' I said. 'Danny kill someone? He's a scrawny fifteen-year-old boy; he'd jump if a clock bonged.'

But I thought about him, the way he'd been in church this morning. The flare in his eyes, the anger and confusion, the deliria. What did I know? I'd been stuffing up everything else of late; no reason I shouldn't have got this wrong too.

I gazed out over the sporting complex: the police moved about, their silhouettes radiating diamond light, their shadows troll-like.

I remembered my promise to Danny: I'd look out for him.

Over by the crime-scene tape, Harley lit up a smoke; I read brutal indifference in the cup of his hands. Bunter scratched his balls and yawned. They did this every night of the week. Cockburn turned to another of the young men; I saw the contempt in his stiff shoulders and military bearing.

Could I entrust Danny's well-being to this lot?

Like hell I could.

Windringers

I SMACKED JOJO ON the back. 'Let's go.'

'Where to?'

'See Danny.'

But they wouldn't let us. The four of us fronted up at the cop shop, but Griffo was on the desk and he had strict instructions: no access to the public until he'd been interviewed.

'But I'm not the public,' I argued. 'I'm one of you, remember? One of us!'

'You were until you resigned.'

'Words spoken in haste.'

'Well, haste makes waste. And believe me, Emily, your career is wasted.'

I placed a hand on his desk. Chose my words carefully.

'I had just been raped.'

He flinched, looked away.

'There'll be a formal interview as soon as we can arrange it,' he muttered to the wall. 'His family'll be allowed access then.'

'His father's in hospital with a cut throat; his mother's Rosie Brambles.'

Griffo chewed a thumbnail.

'All I want is a few minutes—he's a mixed-up boy—you can't just throw him in that black bloody hole and forget about him. Anything happens, Griffo, it'll be on your head—I'll make damn sure of that.'

I saw he was wavering, pressed home my advantage. 'Anyway, nobody's accepted my resignation. I haven't signed anything official. Technically, I'm probably still a member of the force.'

He shuffled some papers, swallowed hard. When I saw him glance at the clock on the wall, I knew I'd won.

'Five minutes.' He held up his splayed fingers in case I didn't know what five was. 'And just you.'

He led me through gloomy corridors, took the key from the safe, showed me the cell.

I slid back the hatch. Danny was stretched out on a metal bunk with his back to us, barely visible in the bare bulb's pathetic glow. He was still in the Demons jumper he'd been wearing this morning. The red fabric bunched up around his ribs, seemed to trickle over his skin like a layer of sweat or...

'Christ, Griffo, he's covered in blood!'

'From the victim. No injury to him far as I can see.'

'You could have at least given him a change of clothes.'

'This isn't bloody K-Mart.'

He opened up, stood in the doorway; I stepped in.

Dirty blue beams of streetlight came splintering in through the bars on the window. Crickets rasped. Distant machinery rattled and buzzed.

'Danny?' I whispered.

No response. I came closer, saw he was shivering. Not from

cold, surely; the cell was stifling, reeked of warm piss and cold puke.

'Danny?'

I touched his shoulder; he spun round, bewilderment and fear in his eyes. Did he recognise me? Impossible to say, so deep was his trauma.

I followed his gaze: he was staring at Griffo as he loomed in the doorframe, spears of light streaming around the contours of his body.

'Griffo, couldn't leave us alone, could you?'

'You know I can't do that Emily.'

I put my cheek up close to the boy, spoke tenderly. 'Danny, this is Emily. Emily Tempest...'

'Em'ly?' A whisper from the bottom of the well, but a response. I found his hand, squeezed it: his fingers were like twigs shivering in the wind. 'You came...?'

'Course I came. Said I would.'

'Can we go now?'

'It's not that simple, Danny.'

Fear flashed through his eyes; his cheeks were gravel stained, streaked with dust and blood.

'Oh Em'ly, they catch you. Take you by surprise an drag you down.'

'Who does?'

'The yungkunu.' The dangerous spirits that haunt the night. 'Or their shadowmen.' He pulled at my sleeve. 'They killed my father.'

'Your dad's fine, Danny. Got cut up in the fight, but he'll be okay.'

He sighed softly, a breath of relief. 'But it's me they're after.'

'Who are they?'

'The white ghosts—Windringers—miners, drivers, muscle men. You never know who they are, where they come from.' He drew me in close, put his mouth to my hair. 'Emily?'

'Yes, Danny?'

A tortured whisper. 'They waitin out there for me now.'

'There's no one out there, Danny.'

'No, no, there is. You can hear their voices—them terrible voices. Sound like a bird, like a hawk. Make me shiver.' He gazed up at the window, his eyes convex mirrors, full of stars and bars. I followed his eyeline, saw nothing out of the ordinary, heard less: somewhere a drunk yelled, a truck changed gears.

'Please, Em'ly.' He was sweating now, his fingers pressing against his temples, his lips taut. 'Please, can you shut the window.'

Griffo's heavy voice cut in from behind me.

'Time's up, Emily.'

'Hang on a minute, Griffo. Can't you see he's upset?'

'I'd be upset if I'd just killed someone.'

I rounded on him. 'We don't know what happened back there!'

He shrugged. 'I didn't see it, half a dozen others did. Super'll be back soon. You can take it up with him.'

Cockburn. Perish the thought: more sympathy for his car than his prisoners.

As I rose to leave, Danny clutched my hand. 'Emily!'

I leaned back down. 'Danny?'

'Please, I need to get out of this place.'

'I'll do my best.'

'They'll kill me,' he whispered. The whites of his eyes glimmered.

It just about finished me to leave him there, a poor, frightened kid, half out of his mind. Seeing demons wherever he looked, his ears full of terrifying noise, his fingernails scratching air.

I followed Griffo back down the corridor, my mind working, my resolve hardening.

Since the Retention Dams...

Say the name, Emily. Since Paisley—all sorts of things were hardening inside me.

I watched carefully as he put away the keys then joined the others in reception.

I looked Jojo in the eye. 'We need to talk.'

Paper wasps

WE WENT OUTSIDE, GATHERED by the cars.

'Stonehouse,' I said to Meg. 'Anybody out there?'

'Yuwayi. Kitty. Japanangka. Mister Watson. Them Crankshaft boys, Benny and Bernie.'

'Might be best if you went and waited out there yourselves.'

'But Danny...'

'I'll contact Legal Aid first thing in the morning. Try to get him out.' Jojo raised an inquisitive brow and I explained, 'It'd help if he knew you were out there, waiting.'

'Them kurlupartu let him go free?'

'Sure they will. You mob go home now, get some sleep. I'll look out for him.'

It took some persuading, but Magpie and Meg eventually climbed aboard their low-slung motor and drove away.

'Was that wise?' asked Jojo.

'For them it was. I want them out of the way.'

'This isn't some minor infringement—they're saying he killed someone. No way is he going to get bail.'

'Who said anything about bail?' He tilted his head, narrowed his gaze. 'Jojo, I need a huge favour.'

He groaned to himself. 'You're not...?'

'Distract Griffo.'

'You are.' He looked to the heavens and rubbed madly at his beard. 'I bloody knew it. Soon as I saw you coming out of the cell, I knew you were up to something.'

'Just for a minute.'

'Emily, do you have any idea what you're suggesting? How many laws you're about to break?' He raised his arms in despair, managed to look like a turkey taking off. 'Ah, for god's sake, why do I even...? Course you...'

I put up a hand. 'Wireless.'

He stopped dead. Looked back wearily at the station.

He knew its history as well as I did. The ghosts that had seeped into its woodwork, the improvised nooses, the slipped-while-resisting-arrests. He was a whitefeller, but still. He'd spent a lot of his life running round with our mob.

And he was a good man. Somewhere inside, he would have been asking the same question I was, the question Danny's father had asked: how long would the boy last in that black hole? Before he went the same way as Wireless?

For me of course there was no choice. I'd made a promise.

'Christ,' sighed Jojo, shaking his head.

'Park round the back lane.'

'Nothing's ever simple when you're around.'

'I don't make these things happen.'

He looked like he was about to argue the point. Then changed tack. 'I'm coming with you.'

'No you're not.'

302

'Yes I…'

'Listen, Jojo. Darling. I'd love you to come along, but there's absolutely nothing to be gained by both of us getting in the shit. And frankly—black chick raped in the line of duty, just out of hospital, off balance—what sort of a slap on the wrist am I gonna get?' I saw the questions forming in his eyes. 'But you, you're a public servant; you'll lose your job. All your work will go to the dogs—and to the fucking foxes, more to the point: think of all your bilbies. Plus I need you here; you can contact Legal Aid, deal with the police. I'll bring him in, but only if it's to hospital. I'll be in touch.'

'How?' he asked. I knew I'd won.

'Radio? Pigeon? Smoke signals? I dunno—I'll work something out.'

'Where'll you go?'

'Out to Stonehouse, if we get that far. And if this does go pear-shaped…'

'Pear? It's already gone the full bloody watermelon!'

'…I'll need somebody *not* in the slammer to keep my spirits and tobacco up. Now what have you got lined up for Griffo?'

He put a finger under his chin, sniffed the air, scanned the dim silhouette of the trees that lined the dry creek bed, thinking hard.

'Gimme fifteen minutes.'

It took fourteen.

I walked around to the alleyway, found a spot that afforded an excellent view of the station, waited among the shadows.

'Come on, Jojo, pull your finger out,' I muttered, fearful of Cockburn and crew returning before he did.

I sighed with relief when the Hilux rounded the corner and came schlepping down the alleyway.

I stepped out of the shadows. 'All okay?'

'No worries. Chucked in a bit of food, filled your water bottle.'

I peered at the station. All quiet.

'How long will it take?'

'They don't put out a timetable.' He must have spotted my frown in the dark. 'Not very, I don't think.'

'You better bugger off then. Wander up to the BP, grab a bite to eat.'

'I'm so not thinking about food right now.'

'Me neither. Thinking alibis and CCTV.'

I gave him the kiss he had coming, sent him on his way. 'See you soon, Jojo.'

'Bloody hope so.'

'Give my love to Hazel.'

'Will do.'

'What did you use?' I called out as he sauntered off down the alleyway.

'*Ropalidia romandi*.'

'What?'

'Paper wasps.'

He was barely out of sight when a strangulated oath came from deep within the bowels of the station, closely followed by another.

And another: 'Aaaow fuckin Jesus fuck fuck *owww* Christ...'

I heard the front door slam. A burly figure came stampeding out onto the lawn with a surprising grace—more grace than it ever showed on the basketball court—whipped off a shirt, lowered a pair of pants, began slapping and swatting its considerable length and breadth.

I nipped over the fence, disabled the alarm on the back entrance—they'd trusted me with that one—slipped into the building, punched in the pin number I'd noted Griffo using earlier, withdrew the key.

Danny inhaled sharply when I opened the door, exhaled with relief when he saw it was me.

'You still want out of here, Danny?'

'Oh, I have to.'

'Stonehouse?'

He clutched my hand. 'Anywhere but here...'

I locked the door behind us, replaced the key—the longer we concealed our flight, the better.

We were in the car in one minute, on the road in two.

A moving target

SHE WAS SMALL, THAT Hilux of mine, and she didn't have turbocharged diesels, but she could zip along when you wanted her to. I wanted her to now.

We raced down the moonlit highway, uncertain how long we had or where the pursuit would come from. That there would be a pursuit, I was in no doubt whatsoever. A furious one, given Cockburn's inevitable state of mind when he found out what I'd done.

Cockburn's mind: now there was an enigma for you. I wasn't sure the bastard even had one. From what I'd seen so far, if you lifted the hat and peeled back the crisp haircut, all you'd find would be a post-it saying *Standard Operating Procedures*.

How would he react to a jail break on his watch? He'd be ropeable, of course, but would he think clearly? I pictured him studying the map, weighing up the options. There were four or five roads at the disposal of your Bluebush escapee: the north, the south and an array of bush tracks of varying navigability.

Then there were the fringe camps, the blackfeller houses in town, the nearby hills and scrub. Plenty of places to lie low. And Cockburn's manpower was limited, in every sense.

He was the closest thing to sharp in that particular toolshed, but how sharp was that? Would he anticipate my moves?

It was with a vague sense of shame that I realised I didn't know. I'd been so busy making critical assessments of him over the past few weeks that I'd failed to notice whether he was responding in kind.

Some instinctive caution told me to give him the benefit of the doubt. I turned off the bitumen at Teapot Creek, rattled down the backroads, rejoined the Gunshot just before the roadhouse. Slower that way, with more gates and dirt, but less chance of being intercepted or overhauled.

Bats and birds dipped into the headlights' arc. The odd ghostly bullock loomed. An old bull camel, looking surprised but phlegmatic.

I was anxious to reach the turn-off to Stonehouse; when we were on the track, we'd be half way home. Half way to Danny's home, anyway, and I was willing to take my chances. Once there? Plenty of places to hide, plenty of people to cover our tracks and smuggle us grub. We could hang out for months if we had to, certainly for long enough to negotiate with the authorities and ensure the boy was given appropriate care.

Danny curled up in the corner of the cab, not talking, the rhythm of the corrugations, his nervous exhaustion, rocking him into semi-consciousness.

The Green Swamp Well Roadhouse loomed in the distance, lights everywhere, generator pounding into the still night air; I might have spotted one or two figures moving about as we sailed past, but I wasn't hanging round to renew acquaintances.

I noticed Danny had surfaced. He was staring anxiously at the wreckage of Doc's cabin.

'Meg told me you spoke to Jet.'

'China girl? Yuwayi.'

'She showed you Doc's sculpture.'

He swallowed hard. 'Oh, it's a dark thing, them stones—trackin the devil. He was clever, that old man—kartiya, but he know the country.'

'He'd studied it all his life, whitefeller way. He was a geologist—an earth doctor.'

'Earth needs a doctor, things the kartiya do to it.'

Geologists and blackfellers, I reflected. They've got a lot in common: they both inhabit an invisible landscape. A lot of things they don't have in common, though.

'I imagine Doc looked at it a different way from old Windmill.'

'Maybe, but he ended up with the same thing, that's why they finish im. When the devils attack, all you can do is lie low, or get away: movin target harder to hit.'

His eyes flickered nervously, then he put his hands to his head. 'Can you shut the window please, Emily—they talkin too loudly in my ears.'

'Who's talking in your ears?'

'Windringers,' he rasped.

'No such thing, Danny.'

He ignored that. 'They chase after you, cut you open.'

'No one chasin after us.'

A glance in the rear-view mirror made a liar of me. Headlights, bobbing about in the distance, a wildcat's eyes.

I put the foot down. Our pursuer did the same, but he had more foot to put: the distance between us diminished steadily. A random leadfoot, a home-bound drunk or somebody with more ominous intentions?

Danny looked over his shoulder, hyperventilating. Clenched his knees, closed his eyes. 'Oh Jesus!'

'Keep cool.' I gave him a reassuring squeeze of the shoulder. Waited for the flashing blue light to appear, but it never did.

We came rushing up to the wrecked truck that marked the Stonehouse turn-off. Now we'd see who was following what: I flipped off the headlights and sailed into the turn. Drove a hundred yards down the track, then slammed on the brakes and cursed.

Directly ahead of us was a police road block.

Roadblock, Territory style

A RATHER CASUAL, TERRITORY-STYLE roadblock, I had to admit—one cop stirring from a bedroll by the fire and the unmistakable figure of Jerker Jenkins shaking himself down and buttoning up in the bushes. A whisky bottle glimmered among the cups and lanterns. I'd caught them unawares. They'd been told we might be on our way, they didn't know for sure.

I sat there for a moment, wondering what the hell to do.

Whoever was on our tail wasn't worried about soft options like wondering—or indeed, taking his foot off the throttle. He came racing up, roared past in a storm of lights and rattling steel.

Jerker stood there stunned as the car, a leprous HT Holden, went into a slathering spin and slammed into his own vehicle, careening it onto its side.

Two figures had rolled out of the Holden just before impact: one leapt to his feet, began flapping about like an emu on an electric fence: 'Eh! What for you parkin middle of the fuckin road!' The familiar, stringy figure of Bernie Crankshaft. 'Somebody gonna get hurt, you bloody idiot! I might call the cops!'

Did my eyes deceive me, or did he cast a subtle glance in my direction?

Jerker was glowing in the dark. 'I don't believe you jungle bunnies!' I heard him bellow. 'We *are* the fuckin cops! This is an authorised roadblock. Are you blind as well as stupid?'

Benny, the younger brother, rolled over and clutched his face. 'I can't see! I gone blind!'

The second officer—Jake Trail, from the look of him—picked himself out of the bushes into which he'd dived to avoid the oncoming vehicle, regarded Benny with alarm.

'Blind?'

'I can't look.'

He put an arm on Benny's shoulders. 'Take it easy, mate.'

'Emily.' I startled at the voice whispering in my ear: Jet, standing at my window.

'Come. We have seconds.'

'What's going on?'

She squeezed herself into the cabin. 'My car is back along the road.'

I swung round, high-tailed it out of there.

She glanced at Danny, saw the state he was in. 'Boy, you are in good hands. If anybody can set you free...'

His response was a barely audible whimper.

I dropped her at her van, then we drove a mile down the road, pulled over for a hasty, torch-lit conference.

'How the hell did you know we were coming, Jet?'

'The police come looking for you. They make the song and dance! My friend, Constable Blad...'

'Who?'

An impatient gesture. 'The policeman.'

'Jerker? He's your *friend*?'

'When I have a use for him,' she shrugged. 'And I use him now. He tells me you take Danny back to the Stonehouse; that you escape him from the jail.'

'Did he say why he was in there?'

'He did not say, nor do I care. I begin to know your people—the world is their jail. The only puzzle is you.'

'Me?'

'Never mind; now is not the time. Whatever he did—whatever you have done—I know that it is not...bad.'

Not bad? About the closest thing to a compliment you were ever likely to get from Jet.

'We try to warn,' she continued, 'but you go racing past. That is the Emily Tempest, I say to my Crankshafts—always in hurry. And the police, they are in...wait! The brothers were forced to—how do you say, think upon their toes? Improvise?'

'Hell of an improvisation.'

She shrugged. 'Their lives are improvisation.'

'Are there any more road blocks?'

'I do not know, but one, maybe two police drive by in the night. To the west.'

'Shit.' That meant they were probably blocking off the Gunshot Road as well. We might have bypassed a roadblock or two by taking to the back roads, but Cockburn had sussed me out. He'd guessed we were making a run for Danny's country.

He'd covered the track to Stonehouse; what were the odds that he'd done the same for the north track, the route we'd taken in from Dingo Springs? This was a game of chess, with each of us trying to anticipate the other's moves. Was the radio in the overturned vehicle still working? Would Jerker have rumbled the Crankshafts and called for back-up?

What in Christ's name were we going to do now?

I ran a torch over the map, considered our options.

The solution leapt out at me: Galena Creek. Jojo's camp. We could lie low for a day or two, make a run for Stonehouse when the heat was off and the hunt died down. There'd be food there, and water. Maybe a bilby pining for Jojo.

But even getting to Galena Creek would be difficult; there could be roadblocks anywhere along the way. It wouldn't take Cockburn long to figure out what had happened back at the turn-off.

Jet indicated a winged marker north-west of the roadhouse. 'What is this?'

'Airstrip. Must be for the Green Saturn mine.'

I glanced at it casually, then took a closer look: the Green Saturn might not be contributing much to the local economy, but maybe it could make a contribution to our escape.

Out back of the mine was a track that wound down to the south-west, rejoining the road near the old Gunshot Goldfields. It was a roundabout way of getting anywhere, but at the moment it looked like a pretty good way to avoid discovery.

There were risks. The Green Saturn itself, for one. We'd have to circle it in the dark, pick up the track on the far side. What security the mine had in place—and what they'd think of strangers blundering about their perimeter—I'd no idea.

Then there was the Gunshot Field. We'd have to drive right through it, and there'd be people about who knew me: the Rabble.

And then there was my passenger. Since Andulka's death, the Kantulyu had been rigorous in avoiding the area around Green Saturn. Danny was rattled enough as it was; how would he react to the breaking of a taboo?

Badly, I suspected. But we didn't seem to have much choice. The mine was just up the road, and Danny was barely conscious. With a bit of luck, we'd be in and out before he even knew it.

We made our farewells. Or I made my farewells—Jet just

stood on the side of the road in her skinny singlet and big boots, shaking her head and muttering, 'Aiee…This Emily Tempest.'

You can talk, I thought. Jet was taking to the relentless chaos of the borderlands—and there were all manner of borders out here: between black and white, the organic and the mechanical, the random and the damned—like a cockroach to a grease trap.

We left her in a cloud of dust.

Green Saturn

WE REACHED THE GREEN Saturn turn-off without further incident. Turned north. Danny sat squirming in his seatbelt, biting his lips and keeping a sharp eye on the rear-view mirror.

Maybe it was the gravel road. Maybe anxiety drove my foot a little harder into the throttle. Whatever the reason, the mine appeared much quicker than I expected.

We'd been driving for barely twenty minutes when a fluorescent smudge loomed in the distance, an array of lights, reflectors and silver metal throwing a ghostly coruscation onto the surrounding hills.

I pulled over, switched off and stared at the mine.

Ribbons and filaments of fire radiated into the night. A circuit of floodlights illuminated the mine works: headframe and smelter, engine room, workshops, a row of pre-fab huts. On a flat stretch off to the east, a long corridor of lights. The air strip? Bigger than

I'd have expected. There'd be some sort of security. Had they spotted us already?

I doubted it. I'd been hanging around mines for much of my life. Out here in the middle of nowhere, security would consist of some fat drunk a year or two past retirement who'd be flat out warding off sleep, much less intruders.

Not that I had any intention of intruding: my aim was to slip around the mine as unobtrusively as possible, push on down to Galena Creek.

I crept down the road, lights off, motor low. The country this side of the mine was bare and flat, levelled. All the better: less chance of a puncture or of having to make a racket revving out of some ditch. Two or three hundred yards before the guardhouse, I slipped off-road; there'd be a perimeter fence somewhere in there, a maintenance track alongside it.

All went according to plan. I found the boundary, freshly graded, followed it round. The mine was strangely quiet; given the hype, I'd have expected it to be working twenty-four seven, but apart from the odd electronic ping and the generator hum, all was silence.

Until we crossed a grid on the western boundary.

A bank of spotlights exploded in my face and a Humvee came roaring out of nowhere and penned us against the fence before I knew what hit us.

A door flew open, a figure emerged, a voice boomed out of the lightblast: 'Step out of the car!'

I pushed Danny down into the shadows and climbed out, stood against the door. Prepared to bullshit my way out of whatever I'd stumbled into.

'Keep your hands where I can see them.'

Have to think up some pretty convincing bullshit, from the sound of that. I peered at the car: there were two of them. Big men. Hard. A sudden dryness of the mouth, a quickening of the pulse. One stayed in the cabin, the other advanced, raked me with a heavy Maglite and a set of wary eyes. He was decked out in a crisp uniform, gun on one hip, baton on the other, walkie-talkie on his collar.

Security appeared to have been upgraded in my absence.

'Who the hell are you?' he barked.

An unfamiliar surge of panic. I forced myself to think beyond it. Wondered whether the police alert had stretched as far as mine security companies. Maybe not: beneath the strident tone there was suspicion, for sure, the sound of a professional hard-arse. But not the sound of somebody who'd been warned to watch for a black woman and a boy on the run.

Best to play it safe.

'My name Jenny Temple, sir.'

'What you doing driving round, middle of the night?'

I put a hand to my mouth, tried to look uncomfortable: not a difficult thing to do. 'I bin out huntin, got separated from our mob, lost my way.'

'This is a restricted area. You savvy, girl? You not allowed in here! You're trespassing on private property.' He leaned in close. 'I know you people, always sniffin round, lookin for something to steal.'

'Wouldn' be doin that, sir.' I lowered my eyes, fidgeted.

'We'd be well within our rights, locking you up. Hand you over to the Bluebush police. What we normally do with trespassers.'

Fuck, don't do that. 'Just tryin to find the road back 'ome, sir.'

'Home?' He stepped back. 'Where's that?'

'Dixon Creek, sir.'

'Dixon's Creek,' he snorted. 'You're miles off track.'

He lowered the torch. In its reflected light, I caught a calculated narrowing of the eyes, a callous hook on the corner of his mouth. He looked me up and down.

'You on your own out here then?'

'Yuwayi,' I whispered. No need to role-play the leap of fear in the gut.

He swept the Hilux with his flashlight, making sure I didn't have a load of stolen gear. The beam was almost on Danny when the walkie-talkie crackled into life: 'Base to roaming. Everything okay there, Kubal? Over.'

'Trespasser. Over.'

'What have you got? Over.'

'Some little gin sniffing round the boundary. Over.'

'Better bring her in, mate. Brock's down—wants to be notified of anything unusual. I'll put a message through to the cops, come pick her up. Over.'

There was a long, painful silence, broken only by the pounding of my heart. I kept my eyes down, hands clenched. Finally he checked his watch, spoke back to the mic with a dismissive twitch of the lips.

'Bugger it Mark, too much bloody trouble. Let her off with a warning? Over.'

'Your call. Over.'

'Finish me rounds, back in twenty. Over and out.'

He turned to me.

'You understand I just did you a favour then, girlie?'

He paused. I could hear his heavy breath; smell it. It wasn't even that unpleasant. A hint of recently drunk coffee, a twist of spearmint.

My throat worked and I swallowed bile.

Another heartbeat. Then he grunted and moved his mouth in the same dismissive tic. Too much bloody trouble.

'Okay shove off—don't let us catch you running round these parts again.'

'Thank you, sir.' I climbed up behind the wheel, drove until we were out of sight then pulled over. Leaned against the tailgate and vomited, long and hard.

When I straightened I saw Danny staring back at me, aghast. 'You right there, Em?'

Good question.

I was not the same woman I'd been a week ago.

Would never be.

I studied the boy, his anxiety a reflection of my own. Get a grip, I told myself. You have responsibilities.

I ran a hand across my face, tried to still the shaking.

'I'm right, Danny.' As I made my way back to the driver's seat I noticed the first burrs of colour nuzzling the horizon. I rummaged through the bag Jojo had left us. Found water bottles, threw one at the boy, took a swig myself.

'Let's get out of here.'

I stepped hard on the throttle and we roared up into the foothills of the Ricketswood Ranges.

Black hole

AS I DROVE I felt something nagging away at my consciousness. A warning light came on inside my head. Something significant had just happened back there, but I was buggered if I could figure out what it was. Something I'd seen? Whatever it was, it refused to come out of hiding. I shrugged it off.

By the time we reached the old Gunshot Diggings it was light. I slowed down. This was where the Rabble scratched out their miserable existence. There were maybe fifty people, prospectors, drifters and other desperadoes, living out here. Many of them would recognise me. No point in drawing attention to ourselves.

I did spot a couple of blokes up among the cluster of caravans and demountable hovels the Rabble called home: a thin man stretching and staring into the gaping hole of the day, a fat one trying to kick an excavator to death. Neither of them paid me any attention.

The riskiest spot would be at the bore, where we rejoined the Gunshot Road. A lot of the gougers came down to top up their water and chew the fat—what little there was to be chewed in a world where the main activities were swinging a pick and staring at a mountain of rocks for specks of gold.

I approached the stand-pipe cautiously: sure enough, there was an old Mack parked there. I knew that truck. Like a lot of other vehicles round here, it had slowly decomposed into an image of its owner: it was rusted and dusty, worn around the edges, with bits hanging off or welded on, stripped down to the bare essentials. As was the bloke on top of the tray.

He looked up and gave me a wave.

Damn! Geordie Formwood: eye like a hawk, mouth like a front-end loader. We'd be all over the goldfields in minutes if I didn't shut him up.

I pulled over, backed up.

'Geordie.'

'Emily Tempest! Up at first crow call!' The chirpy Aberdonian burr, not what I wanted to hear right now. 'What brings you out the Gunshot, this time of the day?'

'Slight—er—complication in town, Geordie.'

'Complication?' He squinted at me.

'Haven't seen anything resembling a cop round here, have you?'

The squint grew squintier. 'Only you.'

'I seem to have gone across to the other side.'

'Oh. That sort of complication...'

He nodded sympathetically: this was something he could relate to. Most of these characters have spent their lives skating along the outer limits of the law: claims were made to be jumped, unwatched fuel siphoned, miscellaneous objects liberated from owners careless enough to leave them unattended for a split second.

He climbed down from the tray, scratched his baggy britches

321

and his baggier behind, looked up and down the track. He lit up a ciggie and gave vent to the Formwood dawn chorus: a horrible array of snorts, hacks and general crepitation. Christ, if the smokes didn't kill him, I might have to.

'No, Em, haven't seen a soul.'

'Good on you, Geordie—and you haven't seen me either, have you?'

He shook his head, grinned: he knew the routine. 'Hide nor hair.' He peered in the window, saw Danny.

'Hell*ooo*.'

The boy said nothing, but the way he curled into the corner was answer enough for Geordie. He turned back to me. 'Who's your friend?'

'Danny.'

'What's his story?'

'You heard what happened to Wireless?'

The blisters on his lips bristled. 'Aye—fuckin jacks. No offence intended.'

'None taken Geordie—like I said, I'm not with em any more.'

'What's he done?'

'Nothing—but then neither had Wireless.'

His mouth grew granite-edged. 'Never was convinced it was him who done Doc.'

'Me neither.'

I put the car into gear.

'Where you taking him, Em?'

'If I told you, I'd have to kill you, mate.'

He recoiled. 'We wouldn't want that.' He slid a hand down the greasy shorts, gave a farewell rattle of the cavities. 'Good luck, Em. Danny.'

The boy said nothing.

*

I pushed on, out to where the corrugations were enough to rattle your wheel nuts off. Twenty minutes of that and we were on the western extremities of the original fields, where the road crawled round the foot of the abandoned Gunshot Mine. I pulled over, took a look around. Couldn't see much past the encroaching hills and the turpentine scrub. Felt uneasy. I needed a vantage point.

'Why we stopping?' asked Danny.

'Gonna drive up to the summit; check out the lie of the land.'

I worked the truck up to the top of the rise, climbed onto the tray and examined the Gunshot Road: no sign of pursuit, no tell-tale clouds of dust, no movement other than a kestrel floating on distant thermals.

I looked over at the pit, shuddered. I'd never liked this place. I'd come here once as a kid, heard the story from my father. It started as a conventional underground mine, and was dramatically converted into open cut when the shaft caved in on top of the dozen poor bastards working it at the time.

The operation had closed down years ago, but a massive crater remained—along with a bullet-riddled sign saying the company was engaging in 'world-class rehabilitation' of the site.

The only rehab visible thus far was the sign itself, a drooping fence and a clutch of tough little samphire shrubs that clung to the slopes.

On impulse, I clambered onto the roof, peered into the pit. An intimidating chasm stared back at me: stern-faced ironstone walls, deeply incised, gullied and tunnelled. A dizzying, crumbling maw, eighty metres deep, five hundred across. It reminded me of the Drunks' Camp back in Bluebush: dark, scarred. An abandoned mess we'd all rather not think about.

I thought about Andulka's warning that all this blasting and digging was stirring up old ghosts. Had a sense of what he was getting at.

Way down on the mine floor, a murder of crows picked at

something, maybe a wallaby that had gone too close to the edge.

I turned around, studied the plains ahead. There was a handful of abandoned buildings up there: the old Gunshot headworks, a dilapidated office, a workshop, the rock-crushing battery, silent these thirty years now.

Beyond that, scrubby desert.

Once again, all seemed clear.

I made to jump back down, then paused. Was that a flash of light from a mulga copse beyond the buildings? I squinted, shielded my eyes. Wished I'd brought the binoculars. There it was again: a glimmer among the green-grey leaves.

A windscreen, reflecting the morning sun? Somebody with their own binoculars waiting in ambush? Maybe just a bit of scrap metal from the old days, some long-abandoned dolly pot or donkey, a collapsed headframe, a broken bottle.

No option. I had to go and check it out; west was the only road open to us. They'd be coming from the east, and sooner rather than later. I climbed down and spoke to Danny.

'I'm going to scout up ahead.'

'What's there?'

'Probably nothing, but I want to be sure. Best if you wait here.'

He wasn't happy with that, but I didn't give him a choice. I'd lose any chance of stealth if I went out there with the boy stumbling along beside me, jumping at shadows.

There was a honeysuckle grevillea alongside the car. I dragged off a long orange bloom, handed it over to him.

'Try this.'

He put it to his mouth, seemed to find a fleeting relief in the trickle of nectar that ran across his lower lip and onto his chin.

'You be careful,' he whispered, raking my heart with a long, silent plea.

I ruffled his hair and set off.

Crouching low, using whatever cover was available, I worked my way around to the south side of the track. I moved through thick scrub, tall grass, past the abandoned mine works I'd seen from the rise.

The tallest of the buildings was the ore-crushing battery, a corrugated iron tower stretching eighty feet into the air. Even from a hundred yards away, I could hear a patter of eerie creaking sounds emanating from its upper reaches, metal sheets and beams expanding in the morning sun.

I paused. The battery looked bloody dangerous, like it was ready to collapse. Somebody ought to demolish it.

South of the mulga was a rocky rise which offered the prospect of both vantage and concealment. I cut across, climbed its southern slope, wormed my way between two sandstone boulders at the summit, looked down onto the copse.

'Oh Christ,' I muttered to myself. There was a car in there, all right—a cop car.

They'd given up on roadblocks in favour of a more subtle approach.

'Morning Emily.' The voice was smug, familiar—and right in my ear. I whirled round, dropped my face into the dirt, cursing myself for an incompetent idiot.

He was leaning against the boulder to my right, his arms crossed, his blue eyes coldly triumphant.

Bruce Cockburn.

Banging heads and brick walls

I NODDED AT THE pistol on his belt. Snarled, 'You prepared to use that?'

'Prepared to do whatever the circumstances call for.'

'They'll call for that if you expect me to hand Danny over.'

'He's absconded from lawful custody.'

'He oughter be in hospital, not jail.' I climbed to my feet, shook off dust, tried to shake off some of the anger I could feel rising inside. 'How the hell'd you find me, anyway?'

'Getting used to you and your mysterious ways, Emily.'

'I'm supposed to be impressed?'

'Wouldn't expect anything short of the Second Coming to impress you, but I'd be grateful if you'd listen to me.'

'Listen!' I fixed him with a glistening stare. 'I've been listening to you for the past month. Listened while you ponced around the country I grew up in like you owned it. Listened while you sent

Wireless to his death. Listened while you threw Danny into the same hole. I think I'm done listening to you. Sir.'

'You were right.'

I don't know if my jaw actually dropped, but I damn near checked next to my feet. 'What?'

'I spoke to my boy.'

'That's an improvement.'

He hesitated. Removed his shades.

'The incident at the sports ground wasn't as...straightforward as we'd been led to believe.'

'Nothing is. What'd he tell you?'

'He says your young friend—Danny—yes, he did stab the white bloke. But apparently the feller attacked him first. No apparent provocation. Jarrod says the boy was just walking past, feller came out of the shadow of the grandstand. The father was coming along behind, tried to help—it was only when he'd been wounded that the boy retaliated. Seems it was with the attacker's own knife.'

I kicked at the ground with a boot, trying to work this latest piece into the jigsaw.

'Then it was self-defence?'

'Looks like it. Doesn't quite tally with some other accounts we've been given, but it sure as hell complicates things.'

'How's Bandy?'

'The father? Still holding his own I think.'

'Well that's something.'

He adjusted his belt, cast a calculating eye on me. 'So where does that leave us, Emily?'

'Depends.'

'On what?'

'On what's going to happen to Danny.'

'On the evidence so far, nothing will happen to him. There'll be an inquest, but unless something else comes along he'll go free.

327

Mind you,' the sardonic smile, 'you'll be a different matter.'

I'd been wondering about that. Aiding and abetting an escape from custody: what was the going rate for that? Anybody's guess. Making Cockburn look like a fool? Probably worse. And they still hadn't told me what sort of shit I was in over killing Paisley.

Right now, though, that was the least of my concerns. If Danny wasn't bound for the slammer I could take him back, get him some professional help.

There were other things I needed to know.

'Did you find out who the dead feller was?'

'We were working on that when I heard that our prisoner had escaped. Seems he worked for the mines.'

'A miner?'

'Security.'

I felt the discomfort ripple across my skin. 'What was his name?'

'Wellman.'

'Great name for a dead bloke.'

'Couple of the constables have had dealings with him—safety reviews, theft reduction strategies, weapon storage inspection, that sort of thing.'

'Wonder what he was…'

'Suspect we'll find he was related to one of the boys in the fight…'

'*You're* related to one of the boys in the fight.'

'…or just some poor bloody resident who'd had enough.'

I regarded him suspiciously. 'Enough what?'

He shrugged. 'Enough of Bluebush.'

'Enough of the blacks, you mean?'

'I didn't say that.'

Talk about banging heads and brick walls.

'Cockburn, you really don't get it, do you?'

'Get what?'

I raised my hand to brush away a fly, wished I could brush away this knuckle-head as easily.

'These aren't isolated events.'

'I told you we'd investigate.'

'Great investigation it's going to be if you start with the assumption that a security man trying to kill Danny was just some good old boy taking the law into his own hands. Or that Doc was a silly old coot who got himself hammered in a drunken brawl.'

Cockburn gave a reasonable impression of a budgie straining to pass an emu egg. 'Not your conspiracy theories again?'

'There's too many unexplained things going on: too many deaths, too much mystery.'

'Deaths? Mystery? Course there are—that's what this job's all about. People die all the time. They're all mysteries until we figure out what happened. And what's usually happened is that somebody's said the wrong thing to a feller who's had a skinful, or caught one of his mates doing the missus.

'Godsakes Emily,' he was almost pleading, 'look at it rationally: you've got a couple of people killed in drunken fights a hundred miles apart. Nothing at all to say they're connected.'

'That's a connection in itself, whoever's behind it's using the same technique.'

'Technique?'

'Trying to disguise their actions; they've got something to hide. There's a pattern here.'

'You keep saying that.' He folded his arms and sighed deeply. 'But you never give me any proof.'

Down on the sand a meat ant was struggling to lug a butterfly ten times its weight. I knew how it felt.

'It's not the sort of thing you can prove—not by whitefeller standards, anyway, not yet. But sometimes you just have to trust your gut instincts. Even an instinct's got a basis in fact; it's just more subtle.'

'Subtle! First day I arrived in this damn place, one of your fellow countrymen bashed a mate to death because he'd flogged his roast chicken. That subtle enough for you?'

'Probably is, in the long run. Reasons for everything...'

He snorted, pushed back his cap. 'My god, you're an exasperating woman! You make everything so complicated.'

'That's because everything *is* so complicated!'

Somewhere a bird called. The minatory purr of a peaceful dove. I looked around, suspicious. Nothing to be seen, but my discomfort increased. I turned back to Cockburn.

'You can't see the change in something if you don't know what it looked like in the first place, but if you stay out here long enough you'll understand. I'm only a beginner myself, but I've been round long enough to know that things interconnect— deaths and dreams, watercourses, tracks and plants. Everything. And if something's out of place...'

'Emily,' he interrupted. He'd been shifting restlessly while I spoke, scratching his head. Ignorant bastard might as well have looked at his watch. 'I honestly regret what happened to you, and I'm sure the prosecutor will take it into account when they're deciding whether to charge you. But if you blunder about the place seeing conspiracies wherever you look, you're going to go out of your frigging mind. I've been in the force twenty years and believe me: if it's a choice between cock-up or conspiracy? Go for the cock-up every time.'

What was the point? 'All right Cockburn, I give up.' I stepped away, clutched my elbows in frustration. 'Let's just quit while we're behind.'

'So you'll come back?'

'Do I have a choice?'

'No, but I'd like to keep the trouble to a minimum. You're up to your neck in it already. Where's our young friend?'

I pursed my lips, pointed with them. 'Back at the open cut.'

'We'll drive.'

'Rather walk.'

He shaded his eyes, looked out over the plains, through the shimmering scrub. The cicada scream rose and fell away, the rocks radiated heat. The sand was like burning snow. Cockburn had—unusually—a sheen of perspiration across his brow.

'Scorchin out there, Emily.'

'Don't worry, boss—I'm not going to bugger off again.'

'We need to get back—half the station's out looking for you.'

I shrugged. 'Okay, but drop me off early. I want to tell Danny what's going on; he'll jump out of his skin, sees you coming at him in a cop car.'

We walked down to his vehicle in a hot sweat and a cold silence, climbed aboard, drove back towards the mine. I stared at the floor, brooding heavily, wondering whether I'd done the right thing.

Danny was traumatised, but at least he wasn't about to be thrown back into the slammer. That much I could believe; Cockburn might have the imagination of a termite mound but he was, I sensed, a man of his word.

With a bit of peace and some treatment the boy would be okay. Then once we got things cleared up in town, Danny could make a more easy-going trip back to Stonehouse. Chances were I'd be otherwise engaged. Ultimately, I knew, that would be the best medicine: give the country and its healers—Windmill, Meg, even the wandering ghost of Andulka—time to weave their magic.

'Somebody up ahead,' I heard him comment.

I glanced up, made out a figure pottering around the tailings midden near the battery.

'Gougers up and about by now,' I suggested. 'Price of gold the way it is, make a few bucks picking over the old rubbish.'

The man up ahead heard us coming; he paused, rested on his machinery—a jackhammer?—turned his head in our direction.

We were a hundred yards away when something, a shiver of apprehension, flashed through my mind.

'Hang on a tick, sir.'

'What's the problem?'

'Dunno.'

'Well why do you...?'

'Just be careful. Something wrong.'

He clucked his tongue. 'Heard that before, Emily.'

'And I was right then too.'

As if to emphasise his point, he accelerated. The bloke at the battery watched us draw near. He was tanned and taut, muscular. A bag slung over his shoulder, a lock of orange hair bristling out from his hard hat. Vaguely familiar. No surprises there—I'd come across a lot of the men on the goldfields at one time or another— but something here had set the radar pinging.

I couldn't take my eyes off him. He put the jackhammer down, picked up another implement: some sort of axe?

Cockburn sailed on, oblivious.

Where had I seen this bloke before? We were driving into the shadow of the battery when it hit me: outside Danny's place, yesterday morning, operating a jackhammer. Come to think of it, what had he been doing working on his own? And on a Sunday morning?

'Pull up—it's a trap.'

'For god's sake, Emily.'

The fellow on the mullock heap put a foot forward, raised the axe and swung a powerful blow at the rocks by his feet.

A muffled explosion sounded somewhere and the severed ends of a length of wire sprang into the air.

I instinctively followed the line of the longer length, saw that it reached to a point half way up the battery. Heard a peculiar, terrifying sound, a metallic screech, like parrots fighting overhead. The building began to shudder on its foundations.

'Turn away!' I threw a hand onto the wheel, trying to force it round.

'What are you...?'

He shut up when he realised there was a hundred tons of solid steel toppling onto us.

Snowball

IT WAS ALMOST A thing of beauty: sheets of iron broke off and floated away, their drift and spin deceptive, distracting the eye from the terrible energy concentrated in the body of the building.

The parrot calls escalated into a brutal clangour of girders, trusses and tortured steel. The structure fell onto us, into us, its buckling brute strength crushing the car and casting us into a cauldron of chemical stench, of twisted metal and blades of glass.

Maybe I saw it coming earlier, maybe my reactions were a fraction quicker, maybe he was impeded by the wheel; whatever the reason, I made it under the dash and Cockburn didn't.

I glanced at him as a length of steel drove through the windscreen. It speared him under the ribs, pinned him to the seat. His body rocked and folded, his face twisted in shock.

We locked eyes, and the things I saw there are with me still. An understanding, in his last moments, that he didn't understand.

That he'd moved into a world beyond his ken. A place full of paradox and puzzle that could turn on you in the blink of an eye. Coupled with that insight, despair, remorse. A suggestion, even, of apology.

One of his hands moved towards me, didn't make it.

He struggled to speak; was overwhelmed by a crimson gloop that sluiced from his mouth, blobbed and splattered onto his chest. He stared at it in horror, then his head fell forward.

A crunch of boots on rough gravel.

I looked out through the shattered windscreen. Orange Hair was cascading over the rocks, splitting axe in hand, boots a blur.

I tried the door: hopeless, crushed under an avalanche of metal.

Trapped.

Our attacker dragged a sheet of iron aside, clambered onto the bonnet, assessed the situation in a glance.

He tore a length of metal from the wreckage, raised it like a spear and rammed it into the place I would have been if I hadn't hurled myself to one side.

He bared his teeth, lifted the weapon again, determined not to miss a second time. Not much chance of that: we were looking at big fish and small barrels here.

The improvised spear came crashing down—then jerked and fell away as an explosion rocked the cabin and his face fell in on itself, fine red fracture lines shooting out from a hole that bloomed at the bridge of his nose.

He stayed on his feet for a moment, strung out on the rack of his own disbelief, then toppled backwards.

I twisted my head, bewildered.

Cockburn, pistol in hand, the cabin a fug of dust and cordite.

He looked at me, gasping. Puzzled, wondering—as if he were seeing something miraculous. Struggled at words which might have been, 'The boy...'

Dropped the gun, flopped forward.

I tried to stanch the blood, knowing it was hopeless. 'Oh, Cockburn,' I groaned.

I took his hand and held it as he died.

Then I grabbed the gun. Crawled through the shattered windscreen, weapon poised; inscribed an arc through the air.

Orange Hair lay face down in the gravel. His hat blown off, the back of his head ditto. Otherwise nothing.

Nobody else in sight. Operating on his own?

Who the hell was he, apart from a bogus road worker, and how did he fit into this bloody turn of events?

I heaved him over. Ugh. Nice to meet you. Rummaged through his pockets: keys, bullets, a box of detonators, a wallet. The bag he'd been carrying was a leather satchel, vaguely familiar.

I looked inside. A blue folder; scribbled across the top, the words *Snowball Earth.*

I felt like a starving man sitting down to a meal: were the questions that had turned me inside out these last few weeks about to be answered?

In the folder, a canvas-covered notebook, identical to the ones in Doc's cabinet.

The old geologist's frenetic script.

I skimmed through the early pages: field notes from a trip out west. It seemed to be the first of several he'd made with Ted Jupurulla. Their objective: Dingo Springs. He'd come across it years before, doing exploratory work for Copperhead. The place had intrigued him, even then—now he wanted to reassess it in the light of recent advances in geological theory.

I read his response to the peculiar conglomeration of rocks at Dingo Springs, his puzzlement over the proximity of the ice rocks and the volcanics. A dozen pages in, a significant sentence:

Rhyolite flow interbedded in the glacials and the carbonates? And the weathering? Should be low, because of the CO_2 levels. But *not. How can such a thing occur? Unless...ice?*

The first hint that the rocks were talking to him, saying something about Snowball Earth.

I pushed on:

How old? Proterozoic? Need to test the radiometric ages for synchronicity—Namibia, south China—

635 Ma?

The first half of the book was in a similar vein, scribbled observations marked by a growing suspicion that the site might shed light on the Snowball Earth theory. He was old school, hadn't wanted to believe the radical theory, was struggling to reconcile long-held beliefs with the evidence before him.

But further into the journal, other things began to slip into the narrative, the first of them a note on his companion's behaviour:

Jupurulla still troubled—spends all night singing—trying to ward off—ward off what? Damned foolish superstition. Poison? Plants shrivelled—animals—wallabies? 'The songs and the water,' he says, over and over. What the hell's he talking about? Tempted to dismiss it out of hand, but how often have I seen his ramblings prefigure the science?

Several pages later, a set of mathematical calculations:

$K = 10\text{-}3 + 8.6 \, m/d$

$I = 500/50 \, km$

$Vol = 4.9 \, mt$

$Vel = 8.6 \times 0.01$

$P - 086 \, m/d = 31.4 \, m/y$

What on earth did volume and velocity have to do with the rocks? Nothing, surely. He was talking about water, moving water. Something connected to a Proterozoic ocean? Presumably m/y meant miles per year. Not a glacier then. Far too fast. He must have been calculating the flow rate of a present day aquifer, not something from hundreds of millions of years ago.

I recalled what Windmill had said about the rock formation

behind Doc's shack: that it was a map of a water dreaming.

Doc was trying to decipher the flow pattern of the water that lay beneath the del Fuego desert, using a lifetime's accumulated geological knowledge to trace the path of the spring that emerged at Dingo Springs.

The next few pages consisted mainly of annotated illustrations, sketches and maps.

The first was a geological map radiating out from Dingo Springs, from Handbrake Bore in the west to the Ricketswood Ranges in the east. He'd outlined rock patterns, describing alternating layers of shale and sandstone over a granite bedrock, assessed their cleavage patterns and porousness.

The notes here were a puzzle: *fractures exacerbated by the blasting process?—possible—depends upon the shape of the grain— rounded, angular—rapid flow?*

Blasting. Who was blasting? The gougers? Roadworks?— Wishy Ozolins said something about a quarry out this way. Maybe he or his men had been working with explosives.

Another page revealed a wobbly cross-section of the area to the east of Dingo, as far in as the Ricketswood Ranges. Doc had taken particular care to list any other water sources—Wild Dog Creek, the Burning Angel Bore, Water-the-Horse Rockhole, Ricochet Springs, the Billy Cans—and their relationship with the underlying geology, their links to Dingo Springs. Alongside several of the waterholes were dates. What did that mean? That he'd visited them, taken samples?

He was mapping the spread of something. Some contaminant in the water, but he never said what.

The handwriting gradually deteriorated, the notes became more confused, petering out altogether as his health disintegrated. The last entry, a forlorn cry:

Where the hell is it coming from?

Where was what coming from?

I went to put the book back, a last frustrated riffle through the pages. Wait. There was something taped into the back. A series of computer printouts: Kells Laboratories, the University of Adelaide. The lab analyses had come back. The first page:

Water Sample 689: 7Q: Dingo Spring.
Parts per billion: Cs: 127 bql
I : 75 bql
U: 963

The symbol *U* hit me like a stockwhip.
Uranium.
Cs? Cesium. And *I* was iodine, another indicator of radioactivity.

All at levels higher than normal. The water at Dingo Springs— the water that Doc, Jupurulla and just about every other living thing in the region had been drinking—was radioactive.

Those wallabies covered in quicklime. Somebody trying to hide the evidence. What else had I missed? God only knew, but there must have been a multitude of signs: even a blind man had sensed them.

I flicked through the remaining lab results:

Water Sample: 689: 7R: Bolt's Rockhole
Parts per billion: Cs: 67 bql
I : 32 bql
U: 107

Water Sample: 710: 7A. Ricochet Springs.
Parts per billion: Cs: 67 bql
I : 17 bql
U: 68

Scribbled onto the last page of the report, a note in Doc's trembling hand: *Christ—how can a spring in the middle of nowhere be poisoned by RADIO. WASTE?*

Radio: Doc's shorthand for radioactive.

The question that had been tormenting Doc reared inside my own head: how the hell had a waterhole in the middle of nowhere become contaminated with uranium?

Doc had used up the last of his energy and sanity trying to solve the question. I thought of him in his last weeks, a dog-tired old man struggling in the heat to lug those heavy stones into position. Desperate to solve this last mystery.

He had to be sure before making accusations. What had he said to Jojo? He wanted it set in stone. Everybody thought he was mad already: an allegation like this, they'd have ignored him at best; possibly locked him away.

Or killed him.

I put the folder aside, then took another look at it, lying on the ground: the ruffled blue top, the tattered yellow pages. I'd seen it before. I racked my brain, my thoughts hurling through the jumble of associations thrown up by the chaotic events of the last few weeks.

Somewhere in the distance, I heard a bird carol: a magpie. And the pictures spinning through my mind coalesced around a single image.

Magpie! He'd had it. This was the bag he'd been carrying at Stonehouse Creek. I conjured up the memory. Yep, there was a blue folder in the bag. But how the hell had Magpie gotten hold of Doc's papers? I couldn't imagine him killing anybody.

The mental snapshot changed: the accident out on the highway, my first morning on the job. There was Magpie, poking round the scene of the car crash, picking things up. Trying to be of use, sure, but still a magpie—curious, acquisitive.

There had been a bag of some sort among the wreckage he'd collected. I could well imagine Magpie rummaging through it, finding the file. He wouldn't have been able to read it, but the maps and diagrams of his country would have fascinated him.

But there was another image pressing for my attention. I'd seen it since then, I was sure.

Danny, the day I took him home from church. The bag was sitting on the kitchen table. I'd assumed it belonged to Bandy, but I was wrong. It was Danny's. And the blue folder was still in there, jumbled up in the contents.

Danny had found it at the Stonehouse camp, must have suspected it was significant, particularly after Windmill told him what Doc's rock formation meant. Magpie might not have been able to read it, but Danny would have been able to get a vague sense of what was going on.

It was what had tipped him over the edge: the realisation that they—whoever 'they' were—were doing terrible things to his country.

He hadn't understood the details, wouldn't have made much sense of the bulk of the report. But that final sentence—*Christ— how can a spring in the middle of nowhere be poisoned by RADIO. WASTE?*—would have been enough to trigger his deepest fears, even if he had misread the last words as 'radio waves'.

He hadn't known where the toxins were coming from, what they were. All he knew was that they were creeping through his country, and that they were lethal.

He'd carried the secret in his head, not knowing what to do with it, worried who to tell. He'd seen, in the deaths of Doc and Jupurulla, in the attack on himself and his father, what they did to those who knew about them.

The pressure might have been enough to drive him half out of his mind. Enough to merge these dark, whitefeller forces with the dangerous spirits and pale ghosts of the Kantulyu dreaming. What was it he'd called them? His Windringers.

I thought about his whispered warnings:

There's a fire out there, Em, running underground, through the air, like knives flashin. Green fire, burns your blood, kills you slow and hard...They killin our country.

'They'. Who the fuck *were* they?

They'd tried to kill Danny before he was arrested, would have succeeded if Bandy hadn't intervened. But how had they known that Danny, in his own befuddled way, was onto them?

Somebody had seen or heard something: enough to know they had to nip this spreading secret in the bud.

I supposed the man on the ground before me, if he'd still been extant, would have had some light to shed on the matter. Presumably that was why he'd been posing as a workman and watching Danny's house. Looking for a chance to lift the bag.

Who was he working with?

I flipped through his wallet, came across a licence that ID'd him as Desmond Harvey, 27 Korps Road, Bluebush.

Korps Road. He'd be right at home there now.

I dug deeper, found a photo: a quick snap, taken through a car window. A concrete house, a candelabra wattle, three people struggling through the gate. In the middle, a skinny boy in a red and blue footy guernsey glancing back, the whites of his eyes glazed with fear. Bandy Mabulu holding onto one arm. On the other a short woman in a red dress with a mess of black hair. Me.

Who'd taken the photo?

The answer, not just to that question, but to the whole maddening conundrum, hit me like an explosion.

Worse: it hit me at exactly the same time as an explosion—the crashing echo and thump of metal on rock, roaring out from the hill where I'd left Danny and the car.

I looked up, silent sirens screaming in my head.

Danny.

It was him they'd been after all along, and I'd left him alone back there.

Into the abyss

I TOOK OFF AT full tilt, ignoring the heat, absorbing it almost, feeling it burn inside me like a rocket's blast, giving strength to my legs. I raced up the ridge, saw from a hundred yards away that the Hilux was gone. It wasn't hard to follow: the scars in the sand, the broken grass.

The tracks ploughed down the slope to the beetling precipice of the Gunshot Mine. I spotted a broken pole, dragged wire, the remnants of a fence: the car had smashed through, gone straight over the edge.

I sprinted towards the mine, stopped short on the lip of the abyss. Eighty feet below: a shattered wreck, wheels spinning in the air. Red dust drifting.

I reeled away, despairing: how could anybody have survived that?

Oh Christ—what sort of an idiot had I been, leaving him alone?

Then I noticed a skinny black foot poking through a patch of long grass to the left. He must have abandoned ship as the vehicle rolled forward.

I rushed to his side. He was lying on his back, his thin body motionless in its blood-stained guernsey. A brutal wound on the side of his head: a fractured skull? His mouth was open, his eyes were closed.

Most poignant of all, for some reason, the grevillea blossom, still in his hand.

'Danny!' No response. No breath, no pulse that I could find. 'Oh Danny, Jesus, what have they done?'

I ripped into a frantic mouth-to-mouth, my mind racked by a terrible image of what his last moments must have been like, the terror of seeing his wildest nightmares—his Windringers, the yungkunu—rise up from the earth and strike him down.

Bastards! The silent scream rang through my skull. This is what they do: they scarify country, they shred its people and its dreams to satisfy their own appetites. To feed their avarice. They've been doing it for a hundred years, and it's just like Jet said: they change their faces and colours, they rearrange the disguise. But underneath they're all the same, and they never change.

So distracted and distraught was I that I didn't hear the motor's purr, the big wheels pushing through the gravel until they were almost on top of me. Two doors opened, two sets of boots came crunching forward.

They'd been waiting. I raised my head, half-knowing what I would see: a metal-blue Range Rover and two men I'd met before. Both armed.

One was white-faced, athletic, wearing black jeans and T-shirt, carrying a bolt-action .308 like he was born with it in his hands. What the hell was his name? Flint. The last time I saw him he didn't look so cocky. Lying on the side of the highway, his accomplice crushed beneath a wrecked car.

The second man wasn't quite so comfortable with his weapon, as fine a piece of technology as it was. Like his car, the finest money could buy. I already knew he didn't like to get dirt—or blood—under his fingernails. But he was infinitely more dangerous: he was the organiser, the risk assessor. The one who thought on his feet and gave the orders.

I'd only met him once, for a few minutes, but in that time he'd seen a boy break down in church, assessed him as a threat, got close enough to identify him—and set in train a plan to have him eliminated.

There'd been one or two hiccups along the way, to be sure: it was hard to get decent help out here. So Kevin Brock had obviously decided it was time to roll up the sleeves and make sure the job was done properly.

What line of work had he said he was in? Strategic management. Not a word of a lie there; and now I was getting a better idea of the strategies he was managing.

Too late, I understood that they involved all manner of things. Life and death, illusions, dreams, deceits—and a mine that was no longer really a mine at all, but a radioactive waste dump. I'd even heard one of the security team mention his name when we were at Green Saturn:

Brock's down—wants to be notified of anything unusual.

I remembered Jojo saying that he'd left Doc in the care of some men from the Green Saturn mine. The old feller must have let something slip. Signed his own death warrant.

A nod from Brock. The pale-faced Flint sharpened his gaze and raised the .308.

A single mind

FLINT PAUSED, TOOK A look around, suspicious; he'd heard something.

So had I.

'Wait,' snapped Brock.

The source of the noise appeared: another vehicle, rumbling towards us, working its way up to the rim of the mine.

For the first time in my life, the sight of a police Cruiser filled me with joy.

Cockburn had said he had half the force out looking for me. He must have radioed in while he was waiting; either that or he'd arranged to meet one of his men out here. Whatever the reason, I was bloody happy they'd found me.

Flint shifted his body to one side, concealed the weapon.

I tensed, weighing up my options. Brock glanced at me, his voice metal-edged: 'One word and you die now.'

They stood there silently as the car rolled in towards us.

I studied the vehicle. Damn. Only a single occupant. I'd been hoping there'd be an army of them in there. I weighed up the situation. They'd already killed a cop—one more wouldn't make much difference. On the other hand if they shot this one they wouldn't be able to pass it off as an accident...

The rifle moved, ever so slightly, ready for action.

Brock motioned impatiently at his off-sider: 'Put it down.'

The flicker of a lapse in Flint's attention was enough. I threw myself up and into his ribs, knocked him off balance, scrambled up the slope, arms waving.

'Look out!'

The car slammed to a halt and a door flew open. Darren Harley jumped out, his feeble brain struggling to comprehend the scene before him.

'Back off!' I ran up to him. 'They've...'

He let fly with a sudden roundhouse blow to the upper body that would have knocked me to the ground if he hadn't caught me mid-air and begun dragging me back down the slope.

'Harley, you fucking idiot!' I was tangled in boots and arms and torn spinifex 'It's not me it's these prickts! They've already...'

He threw me at their feet. 'Mr Brock.'

I gaped at him, bewildered at first, my short-lived elation dying in the arse as the final pieces of the puzzle flew together.

An insider: there had to have been one.

It was how they'd seen me coming, how they'd kept a step ahead. Harley had been there that first morning, at the road accident. He'd known I was out west with the Stonehouse mob—that was what had prompted them to bury the evidence at Dingo Springs. They'd known Danny had escaped, guessed our destination.

And one more thing. The knowledge rose in my throat.

I climbed to my knees, stared at the senior constable, cold fury sharpening the blades of my gaze.

'You fed me to him.'

'What?'

'Paisley.'

He glanced at Brock.

No. You didn't, did you, you shithead?

Harley wouldn't have had the brains; he was just one of the small-pond bottom feeders Brock was forced to use to achieve his goal. As was Brent Paisley. Doubtless there were a host of others: bureaucrats major and minor, politicians, business figures in Sydney and China, or wherever the filthy bloody stuff came from.

I turned my gaze onto Brock. He gave me the stone stare, his eyes unblinking behind the spectacles.

It had been him, all along. Brock. He was the one who'd organised the whole thing, from framing Wireless to unleashing Paisley. I'd suspected a single mind at work: there it was, laid bare before me. The good samaritan face held its shape, but something hard and hungry had risen to move across the surface. He glanced at Flint—his profile sharp as a cross-cut saw, his nose bent, his lips taut. A figure from the Apocalypse.

He gave the curtest of nods to Flint. 'Finish it.'

Make your mark

BROCK TURNED AWAY, LEAVING the messy end of the business to the hired hands.

Oh Christ, I'd buggered up.

A slew of images raced across my brain. I was facing west, Kantulyn country. In my mind I saw the people who belong to it, who give it meaning. The determined old ladies I'd been travelling with so recently, they at an age when most women have been reduced to gossip and scones: in their slowness they gave me speed. I saw old Windmill, mapping the country with his memory: in his blindness he gave me perfect vision. I saw my poor dead Danny: in his drink and drug-addled bewilderment he gave me clarity.

Stage One: I called to Brock, 'You think I did all this without taking precautions?'

'What?' He turned sharply.

'I know what you're doing. I've known all along. I've left

details—documents.'

He studied me. 'If you want to spend your last moments on earth spinning bullshit...'

'Water reports, Doc's research. I know you're storing radioactive waste in the Green Saturn mine, I know it escaped into the aquifer. The earthquakes, I presume—when was that?—three, four years ago? Come on, Brock, I'm not one of your dumb-fuck local hacks. I figured it out weeks ago. I've made sure other people know.'

Only the sliver-eyes moved. 'Who?'

A snort of contempt. 'You think I'm stupid enough to tell you? Suffice to say they're smart and hard, and they'll nail your balls to the wall if anything happens to me.' Brock didn't move. I shrugged. 'Doesn't have to go this way, Kev. I'm pissed off that you're poisoning the country, but not so pissed off that I want to die for it. I'm willing to make a deal.'

Brock showed the closest thing to an emotion he'd shown thus far, though whether the emotion was frustration or amusement was hard to tell: 'Oh? Nice!' He glanced at his crew. 'She's willing to make a deal.'

'What's she saying?' Flint. Edgy as an architect's glasses. His tongue flickered, his trigger finger twitched.

'What she's saying is that Harvey fucked up. Yet again; and frankly Craig, I'm beginning to wonder about you and your crew of so-called "professionals".'

'Been a shot-firer all his life, Harvs. What he doesn't know about explosives isn't worth knowing.'

'Well I suspect it's blown up in his face.'

Flint stared in the direction of the collapsed battery, cast a look of cold malevolence in my direction. 'It's this one. She's not... normal.'

A look of exasperation spread across Brock's face. 'For the unexpected contingency, you have a fallback position; you take extra precautions. I said you should have stayed with Harvey. He clearly didn't have a clue, bumbling round the desert with the file on him. Now you'll have to go back and pick up the pieces. In the meantime, cut the crap and get this…'

Stage Two: 'What's with the church then?'

Brock paused, off balance. 'What?'

'Sunday morning among the holy rollers. I could understand it if you were buttering up the big boys, but I saw you in there first. You were fair dinkum. And I don't get that—how can someone sit there saying their prayers and then go out and do this?'

Brock stiffened, took off his glasses. The eyes were small and hard, as piercing as lasers. He spoke precisely.

'If you want to make a mark in this world, Ms Tempest, you need to focus your energies.'

Make your mark? Christ, was it as simple as that? How much of the grief in my life—in all our bloody lives—was caused by these cases of arrested development trying to make their mark? Pissing out their turf like a pack of besuited dingoes.

Stage Three: 'For god's sake,' I begged, 'You can't…Please don't do this.'

I could sense their reactions. Harley: surprised, suspicious, but lumbering. No immediate threat, gun still in its holster, clipped. Flint: relieved that a messy operation was about to get a lot cleaner. Brock, the twitch of a lip: he was almost disappointed he'd expected more of me. His eyes quivered with something I recognised in my gut: he wouldn't want to kill me himself, but he was going to get a kick out of watching somebody else do it.

Collectively, I felt them ease off on the throttle.

'Please…' I grabbed Brock's feet.

He gave me the disdainful kick I'd been waiting for.

I rolled with the blow, came up with a fistful of dirt in one hand, Cockburn's Glock in the other.

'Watch it!' screamed Flint. 'She's got…'

Brock was in front: I threw the dirt into his face and put a bullet into his chest. Had the fleeting satisfaction of seeing the shock rip his features apart as he stared down and saw his dreams collapse, his own life begin to spurt from his body.

I whipped the gun at Flint, but he moved more fluently than me: clubbed me with the rifle and spun to deliver a kick in the ribs that lifted me off the ground. Ripped the pistol from my hand, put the other boot into my face for good measure, the heel this time.

Smashed me into oblivion.

Fire's own

THE HARSH SOUND OF a cockatoo screaming.

Was I conscious? Hard to tell. I was lying on my side, head split, body battered. Just about ready to give it up   existence, the world—as a cruel joke. A mockery made of us all by a malicious god with a razor-blade mind.

I'd had enough. This revolving nightmare they called life had just got too much for me. The flip side looked like bliss from where I lay. Tempting to just relax, ease off, float away.

Almost of their own accord—certainly against my better judgment—the eyes prised themselves open. A dark blue blur appeared on the other side of my bloodied lashes.

Oh Christ. Danny, his limbs motionless. They'd dumped me beside his body.

Somewhere behind me, male voices, one of them cursing roundly. 'Clean up! What do you mean "clean up" for fuck's sake?'

Harley, close to panic.

'Just that.' Flint, the efficient NCO. In command now. 'Take Brock back with us.'

'*Back* with us? What, we gunna strap him to the roof rack? What if...'

'Find out what happened to Des—he was supposed to knock this one.' Flint's voice rang with sufficient malevolent energy to silence dissent. 'Get out of here. Been a fuck-up go to whoa, this. Drop the fuck-up on Demsky's lap.'

'And these two?' Louder: he'd turned to face Danny and me.

'Dump em with the car. Nothing to pin any of it on us. Should be able to get out of it with our...'

'What's that?' Harley, puzzled.

'What?'

'On the horizon.'

'Jesus Darren, this isn't a fucking sightseeing...'

A long pause.

'What the...what *is* that?'

'Some sort of—*fire*ball? Bushfire over that way?'

'But look at the way it's floating. And where's the smoke?'

'There's another one. They're...moving. Are they?'

'Hard to...Debris, maybe. Tumbleweed burning maybe.'

'Tumbleweed? Look at the *size* of it. And it is moving— getting closer. You ever see the Min Min lights?'

'They're at night, dickhead.'

My body felt like it was weighed down with anvils, but I dragged myself onto an elbow, struggled to counter the deep draughts of pain I drew with every breath. Turned over.

Harley and Flint were standing near the open cut, gazing at the eastern horizon, spellbound.

I followed their gaze, saw nothing unusual. Blue sky, the risen sun, the purple folds of the distant Ricketswood Ranges. No movement: if anything, the air was preternaturally still.

354

'Getting brighter,' said Harley.

'Some trick of the light? Sun reflecting off something?'

Harley shielded his eyes. 'Whatever it is, it's spinning like a wheel.'

'Come on, let's get out of here.'

But neither of them moved.

I wondered if I was still dreaming. Were these two hallucinating in the heat? Was I?

And then I did see something—but not where they were looking.

Harley's Cruiser, up on the rise behind us, wobbled. A barely discernible movement, a shudder of rubber on stone.

I focused on it, unsure of what I'd seen. It shook once more, ever so gently. A creak that might have been a handbrake. Somebody in the car? Not that I could see, but the windscreen was a swirling, impenetrable reflection of the morning sky. Was that a wisp of smoke out the back of it?

The Cruiser moved again; no doubt about it this time. It rocked on its frame, and then slipped forward. Began to roll down the slope, silent at first but gathering speed as it descended. In seconds it was bouncing over the rocky ground like a rubber ball.

I looked at Harley and Flint: were they deaf? They were still standing there, staring out into the eastern sky, mesmerised.

Mesmerised. Maybe...

The rushing vehicle almost seemed to be burning. Then it *was* burning, smoke pluming from its base and bonnet, lightning flashing from its wheels and windows. The two men were aware of nothing until the fuel went up and the vehicle flew at them like a firebomb. Flint spun round, saw it coming, tried—years, aeons too late—to get out of the way.

The car tore into them both, engulfed them, carried on in its unstoppable fury until it plunged over the edge and into the open cut.

The explosion rocked the earth, sent a plume of smoke spiralling skywards.

One of the men had survived. Kind of: a horrible object wearing what might have been a uniform writhed on the ground, just short of the open cut. His torment agonising to the eye and ear.

Then another figure appeared at the periphery of my vision. A black man, tall and thin, picking himself out of the dust, padding down the slope. He spared a glance for the twisted thing on the ground, then helped it on its way with a toey kick.

Whichever poor bastard it was—Harley, from the look of him—he disappeared over the edge.

'Look like you getting there'

THE INTERLOPER TURNED AROUND, considered us.

I hadn't seen him since I was a child. Couldn't quite believe I was seeing him now, but I recognised him straightaway: the clear brow, the piercing eyes, the thick beard. He was wearing a pair of khaki shorts and a leather strap, an array of tools and weapons on his waist.

He seemed in pretty good shape for a feller who'd been dead for years.

'Andulka.'

He walked back over to where we lay.

He knelt beside Danny, took hold of his wrist, leaned closer, listened to his chest. Looked across at me, a brooding power in his glance.

'This the Jangala boy?'

Was, I thought miserably, nodding. Pity you came too late.

From his belt he pulled out a little paperbark roll. As he opened it I caught a glimpse of its contents: bones, rosin, quartz crystals the size of duck eggs, a pearl-handled dagger, a hair-string ball.

I sat and watched.

He plucked a pair of feathers from somewhere—the air?—placed them on Danny's lifeless eyes. His hands touched together lightly, then parted to reveal a thin flame flickering on his upturned palms. He blew on the flame, then lowered it onto the boy's chest, where it seemed to settle for a moment, then vanish.

Suddenly he got active. He began to pummel Danny's body—shoulders, legs, arms. He rubbed the abdomen and thighs, his elbows working vigorously. Like he was channeling an amateur physio in a bush footy league.

A swelling appeared under the boy's ribs. I frowned, puzzled. The lump became the focus of Andulka's attention. He pressed it, squeezed it, lowered his mouth to it and sucked noisily. He closed his eyes, chanted, and then—or so it seemed to my dazzled eyes—reached into the tumescence and drew out a crystal.

Took a few steps away from Danny, hurled the crystal away to the west.

He turned back to the boy and squatted, eyes closed, humming lightly. Finally he stood up and turned to me. 'He want water, he cured proper.'

Cured? Christ, he was hopeful.

Danny was dead. Like everything and everybody else connected to this disaster.

I let my eyes and mind drift out over the eastern plains, lose themselves in the smoke still billowing up from the wreck below. I wondered whether I should climb down and see if any sign of life remained down there. Thought of all the things they'd done; decided not to bother.

I should be getting back though, I supposed. Alerting the

authorities, those of them who were still alive.

Then I heard a soft groan.

Looked across at Danny. His mouth moved, ever so fleetingly. My heart skipped. His eyelids fluttered, then opened. He put a hand to his face, rubbed his eyes and blinked, shook his head. I crawled across to him on my knees.

'Emily?' he whispered.

'My god.'

'Wha's happening?'

My tongue was frozen.

'Anything to drink round here?' The words resonated with a clarity and focus I hadn't heard from him in a long time. 'I'm perishin.'

Half an hour later Danny and I were sitting in the front seat of the blue Rover. His head was swathed in the bandages I'd found in a first-aid kit in the glove box, but he was breathing with relative ease. He moved to one side, touched the window, groaned with pain. I fired up the motor, glanced back at Andulka.

'Gotta get the boy to hospital. You won't come back with us?'

He shook his head. 'Not my place.'

'Mob of whitefellers sniffin round here in an hour or two—you want your privacy, you better bugger off.'

As we moved away, Andulka put a hand on the sill, leaned into the cab.

'What I bin say to you one day? Take time, listen to country?' His voice was loud, like that of a man who'd spent too much time on his own. He inclined his head. 'Look like you getting there.'

He tapped the vehicle. I put it into gear, moved off.

I thought about old Gypsy's lament for the songs of her country. Maybe they were being broken, those songs. Maybe the forces

359

bearing down on them were irresistible.

But which of us could say?

Maybe the music was more subtle, more durable, than we gave it credit for. Andulka sure as hell hadn't given up.

And as long as that remained so, there was hope for us all.

I touched the brake. Called back at him, 'Not doing too bad yourself, old man!'

He might have grinned, but I couldn't be sure. He turned away and began methodically working his way back down the hill, the open plains ahead of him.

Rowing to Eden

I CAUGHT UP WITH Wishy at the airport. He was nervously pacing the observation deck, the ubiquitous flowers and chocolates in hand.

'Come to join the welcoming party?' he asked. He seemed pleased to see me.

'No. Like to, but it's a family affair.'

'Puh! She'd love to see you. They all would.'

'Still...'

'How bout dropping round for dinner tonight?'

'Maybe.'

He stared off into the distance. A sliver of wind riffled the hairs on his throat. 'You know that little book you sent Simmie?'

A leather-bound Emily Dickinson, the complete works.

'She told me last week there's a poem in there that's you.'

'Let me guess: *I started early, took my dog...?*'

'Nope: went something like *Wild nights, wild nights...*'

I had to laugh. 'Stand her in good stead, that book—probably helped her more than the surgery.'

'She likes those poems—and she likes you.'

'Maybe I will come round. What's on the menu?'

'I was thinking of knocking up a chilli beef hotpot.'

I frowned. 'Knocking up or heating up?'

'Well...'

'That's one of mine, Mister Master Chef.'

'Oh—is it? So many meals in the freezer, I'm getting confused.'

'Everybody wants to welcome her home.'

'Suppose they do.'

'Whole town's been following her progress.'

'That's bloody Mardi—mouth as big as her backside. Anyway Em, always a place for you at our table.'

I'd been spending a lot of time at the Ozolins table over the past couple of months, looking after the twins when Wishy and Loreena were in the States, tending animals and garden when they all went across to join Simone in her recuperation.

I pointed my chin at the sky. 'Looks like we're gonna get some relief at last.' It had been a terrible summer, dry as a chip, hot as hell. But up in the north-west, fat black clouds were gathering. Lightning flickered in the distance.

Wishy screwed up his face, gave the sky a cursory glance.

'Nah, it'll miss us. Too far north. Beginning to wonder if it's ever gonna rain on Bluebush. There's a curse on the place—or a rain shadow.' He returned his attention to me. 'What's the latest with Copperhead?'

'Demsky's lawyers have got him greased up like a pig in a side-show. He's slithering out of anything criminal as fast as he can. McGillivray's a dog at a bone, Feds are pulling the place apart, but the company's sticking to the script: Brock was a rogue operator, mother company knew nothing about any nuclear waste...'

'Christ—if you'd believe that...'

'Believing and proving's two different things, Wishy.'

'They worked out where the stuff came from?'

'It's tricky—not much paperwork, but seems they've been slipping it in for years: Taiwan, South Korea, the Philippines.'

'How was it getting here?'

'Some by plane, some by sea. Brock had worked in the uranium industry most of his career; contacts all over the world.'

'I've heard the war-cry: cradle to grave responsibility. Mine it in the Top End, bury it in the Centre. And Copperhead's crying innocent of all that?'

'Trying to; they're being hit with a shitload of civil charges, though, and the clean-up's probably going to send them broke. At least there'll *be* a clean-up—bastards might have gone on forever if Doc and Jupurulla hadn't sprung em.'

'Paid a price. Both of em.' His face grew dark, then lightened. 'How's old Jet going?'

The runaway nun had helped out with the house-sitting. Wishy had met her, seemed intrigued, amused.

'Surprisingly well. She's linked up with my friend Hazel...'

'The artist?'

'Yep—they're getting on like a house on fire. Talking about a joint exhibition. God knows what they'll call it: Blackfeller Yellowfeller fusion?'

I reached into my saddle bag. 'Wanted to show you something, Wishy.'

I handed over the heavy envelope. He examined it, looked at the sender's name. 'Who's Jim Boehme?'

'Professor of Geology at the University of Adelaide. Old classmate of Doc's as a matter of fact, but that's by the by.'

'Why's he writing to you?'

'Read it.'

'*Dear Emily,*' he read. '*Please find attached a copy of the article, as promised. The lab results are better than I could have dared hope. Haven't had formal acceptance from* Nature *yet, but I'm assured it's on the way; our peer reviewers are as excited about it as we are. Albie's suggestion of a link between the volcanics and the glacials—and the evidence he discovered—is the Holy Grail of geologists the world over right now.*

'*You may wish to run this by the family, but I've taken the liberty of calling it the Ozolins Hypothesis—it was his field work that brought about the discovery, and his brilliant intuition that showed us its importance. I only wish he was here to see it—but then, who knows? Maybe he is.*

'*Thanks again for bringing this to my attention—and for your hospitality—tell Magpie there's a new pair of boots in the mail and that we're looking forward to the trip to Yankirri.*

'*Warm regards, Jim.*'

He looked up, bewildered.

'Boots?'

'Jim noticed he didn't have any when we were out bush.'

'What's this trip to Yankirri?'

'Magpie's getting as good as Doc at roping in the chauffeurs. They're aiming to unlock more country.'

He blinked, put the letter aside.

'What's going on here, Em?'

'It was something you said at Albie's funeral: that his crazy ideas were never going to change the face of outback geology. Well, he's just changed the face of world geology. That's crazy for you—one of the few things that *can* change the world.'

'But I don't...' he scratched a temple.

'When I got back from the Gunshot Road, I contacted Professor Boehme, showed him Albie's notes. Explained his theory, what he'd found. He was up here in a flash, made the trip out west with me and Magpie. The rocks at Dingo Springs pretty well settle the argument: the Snowball Theory's good: it stands. If only half of what Albie was hypothesising turns out to be correct, it immeasurably deepens our knowledge of how climate changes. Of life itself, really.'

Wishy stood there, his eyebrows raised, his mouth open.

Behind him I caught the metallic flash of an incoming aircraft levelling in the cauldron of clouds.

'They're here.'

He wasn't moving.

'I'll see you later,' I said.

I turned to go, took a step towards the door.

'Emily!'

He drew me into a powerful embrace.

'Dunno what I've done,' he said in a gruff whisper, 'to be surrounded by the people I...I'm surrounded by.'

'Nice of you to say so, Wishy.' I turned around. 'While we're all up close and personal, can I ask you a question?'

He eased off.

'It's been playing on my mind ever since I found out about Simone.'

'Yes?'

I looked him in the eye, determined not to miss a thing.

'Where'd the money come from?'

'Money?'

'All this—Simone being treated at the Fred Hutchinson Cancer Research Center, in Seattle...'

'They're the only ones who do it.'

'Yeah, and they charge an arm and a leg. I checked em out-private hospital, transplanting umbilical cord stem cells and associated procedures, whole thing wouldn't have left you any change from a half a million. Then there's the trips back and forth, the

365

stopover in Hawaii. All seems a bit up-market for a run-of-the-mill bush surveyor.'

He looked offended. 'Run-of-the-mill? I'm the boss.'

'Even so.'

He folded his arms. 'That was why I took on the job—needed the money. Pay for her treatment, maybe gain a few inches on the pipe dream that we'd ever be able to afford the operation.'

'You're the regional manager of a government works department, Wishy, not the CEO of BHP. What did you do—hock the office? Auditor'll love that.'

He went and stood over near the observation window. He'd spotted the plane, watched it make its approach.

'Emily, you must be the most relentless creature I ever met.'

'Something half done's a disturbing itch to me.'

He sighed, spoke to the glass.

'The money came from Albie.'

'You said he didn't have any money.'

'And from you.'

'I *know* I haven't.'

'That first day you came round to our place—you told me to get Doc's mineral collection valued. Even gave me the name of a dealer: Cockayne?'

'Yes…'

'Tracked him down. He came up, took one look at the collection, offered us more money than I'd ever had in my life. It was a treasure trove—all manner of stuff in those boxes, names I never heard of: native copper, Gympie gold. I wasn't hanging round to bargain—we knew what Simone's treatment was going to cost.'

It all made sense. Cockayne was as straight as they came; I could follow up with him, but I knew I was hearing the truth.

Wishy cleared his throat.

'Remember that day I came to see you in hospital…?'

'Not likely to forget.'

He swallowed hard. 'Never told you how bad I felt about what happened to you. How it hurt, seein a good woman like you suffering when my own wildest dreams had just come true. And mostly thanks to your help. It's shame, Em. That's what keeps us from...'

His voice caught. 'Even wondered if I wasn't responsible in some way—obsessing about my own troubles, not looking after my brother. Letting you push on, do the right thing and cop the consequences.'

I took a moment to absorb what he said. I linked my arm in his, dragged him out onto the deck.

'Don't need anyone to be responsible for me, Wishy. Usually manage to make a balls-up on my own. Come on, they're touching down.'

We watched the plane complete a mirror-smooth landing, taxi to the ramp. The door opened. A flight attendant was moving into position, but before she could get there, a little blonde figure draped in leis came bouncing out, leapt up onto the railing, slid down the ramp.

A thinner, darker one appeared at the top. Looked around. Folded her arms and breathed deep.

I smiled, turned to the exit. Paused.

'Wishy!' I called back at him.

'Em?'

I blew him a kiss. 'Dunno what I've done either.'

I climbed into the new Moonlight Downs Police Cruiser, drove slowly back to town along the road that curved past the dam. On an impulse I turned the car's nose in, pulled up at the water's edge.

I got out and leaned against the bull-bar, looking at the leaden water. Wiped a little of the sweat off my face. Purple clouds swivelled round the hills. They'd done that a lot this summer, but, like Wishy said, the rain had a knack of falling somewhere else.

I thought about the last time I'd been here. Brutally violated, trying to wash my soul clean.

I'd resolved never to come back; but damn it, you let the past imprison you, you'll die in that jail.

A dark wind rippled the water. The air was electric.

I took a look around. Not many other cars out here today, despite the heat and the humidity. Was that the Christian Fellowship vehicle over there, a spindly figure at the back tinkering with a dinghy and glancing anxiously at the sky?

I wondered what he or any of the other drivers would think of the newly appointed Moonlight Downs ACPO skinny dipping?

Who gives...?

I ripped off my uniform, ran at the water and dived.

By the time I came up for air, visibility was reduced to about fifty feet: the surface was boiling and the clouds were unleashing a torrent of fat black globules, sheets and walls, a world of water.

I'd never seen anything like it: it hammered into my mouth, my eyes, into the dam, onto the crookback hills, the parched plains. It swung with a joyous, musical energy that threatened to dance or damn and make new beings of us all.

Acknowledgments

As always, my greatest debt is to my Indigenous friends from Central Australia who opened their hearts to me and shared their stories.

I've been pestering people all over the country to make sure the details in this book are correct. My thanks to:
   Marion Anderson
   Galen Halverson
   Gavin Mudd
   Maree Corkeron
   Brian Davey
   Phil Hyland
   Simon Maddin
   John Dunster
   Daniel Franks
   Daniel McIntyre

David Nash
John Bell
Joy Bell
Patricia Rich
Gerard Roche
Riva Bohm
Jim Green
Nat Wasley
Wojciech Dabrowka
Graham Brown
Herb Evans
Roger Woods

Apologies to anyone I've left off. It's due more to my chaotic record-keeping than to any lack of appreciation for your efforts.

Of the many books consulted during the writing of *Gunshot Road*, two deserve special mention: *Snowball Earth* by Gabrielle Walker, Bloomsbury Publishing, London, 2003; and *Rock Star* by Kristin Weidenbach, East Street Publications, Adelaide, 2008.

Five friends have looked at this work in its various guises:
Bruce Schaeffer, Steve Manteit, Danielle Clode, Will Owen, Jane Simpson. Thank you all.
Mandy Brett, editor extraordinaire.
Mary Cunnane, agent extraordinaire.
The Literature Board of the Australia Council for the Arts.
Susan Bradley-Smith and my other colleagues at La Trobe University.
To the mob at the St Andrews pub, Helen and Stan, Kerry, Linda, Jo and Drew—thanks for keeping the coffee hot and the office quiet.
Finally, most importantly, to my beautiful girls, Kristin, Sally and Siena: you inhabit every word. Well, the nice ones anyway.